"A riveting, irresistible locked-room mystery reminiscent of Agatha Christie, *Last One Alive* is endlessly entertaining and fiendishly clever. So jam-packed with tension and suffused with dread, you won't be able to put it down!"

CHRISTINA McDONALD, *USA Today* bestselling author
of *The Night Olivia Fell*

"A haunting, claustrophobic, unpredictable thriller for fans of Agatha Christie, *Last One Alive* showcases Amber Cowie's extraordinary talent. As a violent storm rages outside a remote lodge, a group of strangers are stranded in a terrifying cat-and-mouse hunt for the murderer among them. Cowie writes with such skillful description that I could feel the cold and rain seep into my bones, and my pulse spike as the exhilarating story reached a breakneck pace. A bewitching read jam-packed with fascinating characters, this book is an absolute standout."

SAMANTHA M. BAILEY, *USA Today* and
#1 nationally bestselling author of *Woman on the Edge*

"An abandoned lodge. A group of suspect people. An old mystery to solve. And then the guests begin disappearing one by one. Can they figure out what is going on before it's too late? Fans of Agatha Christie and Ruth Ware will want to pick this book up immediately!"

CATHERINE McKENZIE, bestselling author of
Six Weeks to Live and *I'll Never Tell*

"Cowie has done Agatha Christie proud in this stay-up-all-night, keep-all-the-lights-on mystery. With a setting that's remote, creepy, and possibly cursed—and a story both haunting and harrowing—*Last One Alive* will entertain you from the first disappearance to the final dead body."

MEGAN COLLINS, author of *The Family Plot*

LAST ONE ALIVE

A NOVEL

AMBER COWIE

PUBLISHED BY SIMON & SCHUSTER
NEW YORK   LONDON   TORONTO   SYDNEY   NEW DELHI

SIMON &
SCHUSTER
CANADA

Simon & Schuster Canada
A Division of Simon & Schuster, Inc.
166 King Street East, Suite 300
Toronto, Ontario M5A 1J3

This Simon & Schuster Canada edition May 2022

SIMON & SCHUSTER CANADA and colophon are trademarks of Simon & Schuster, Inc.

For information about special discounts for bulk purchases, please contact Simon & Schuster Special Sales at 1-800-268-3216 or CustomerService@simonandschuster.ca.

Interior design by Carly Loman

Manufactured in the United States of America

10 9 8 7 6 5 4 3 2 1

Library and Archives Canada Cataloguing in Publication
Title: Last one alive / Amber Cowie.
Names: Cowie, Amber, author.
Description: Simon & Schuster Canada edition.
Identifiers: Canadiana (print) 20210310596 | Canadiana (ebook) 20210310707 |
    ISBN 9781982183042 (softcover) | ISBN 9781982183059 (ebook)
Classification: LCC PS8605.O9256 L37 2022 | DDC C813/.6—dc23

ISBN 978-1-9821-8304-2
ISBN 978-1-9821-8305-9 (ebook)

To Eve and Thompson:
You are everything to me and that will always be more than enough

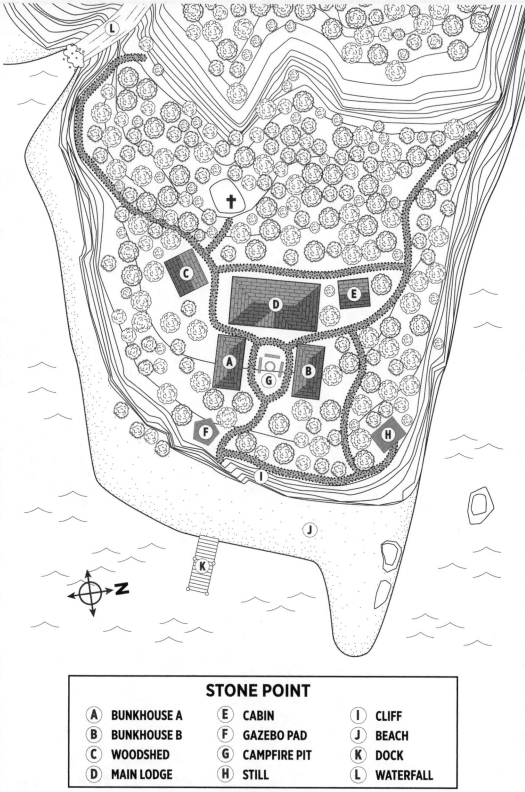

STONE POINT

(A)	**BUNKHOUSE A**	(E)	**CABIN**	(I)	**CLIFF**
(B)	**BUNKHOUSE B**	(F)	**GAZEBO PAD**	(J)	**BEACH**
(C)	**WOODSHED**	(G)	**CAMPFIRE PIT**	(K)	**DOCK**
(D)	**MAIN LODGE**	(H)	**STILL**	(L)	**WATERFALL**

THIS MAP IS NOT TO SCALE

© Ben Greenberg

LAST ONE ALIVE

BEFORE

Penelope stopped outside the door to Marianne's apartment. She pinched the key so tightly that it bit into the pad of her thumb. Now that she was here, she couldn't bear the idea of sliding it into the lock and seeing what was inside. The scene that had been repeating in her head since she heard the news began again as her hand hovered at waist-height. This fixation on a single moment was senseless, yet she couldn't shake the idea that understanding the precise mechanics of her closest friend's last breath would allow her to accept the unbearable truth. Marianne was dead.

In her mind, Penelope heard the thump of her friend's body hitting the floor, heavy and thick as the final beat of a heart. According to several witnesses who had seen Marianne drop dead at the front of her classroom, it had happened fast. The thirty-two-year-old had collapsed while delivering a lecture to her college history class. A brain aneurysm, according to the lawyer. One of the students had described it as surreal. Penelope agreed. Since she'd heard of Marianne's death, the whole world had seemed like a terrible simulation. If someone like her could die in a way like that, how could Penelope trust anything ever again?

When the playback loop ended, Penelope forced the tumblers apart with the key and pushed the door open. She didn't enter immediately. It still felt as though she should wait for an invitation. She counted to four as she breathed in deeply. When no call of welcome came, she stepped over the threshold.

Penelope's chest grew tight at the sight of the sun-filled one-bedroom apartment where she had spent so many afternoons and evenings. She smelled lemons and a faint hint of strong coffee as she looked around at her friend's belongings: paintings, a vase, throw pillows, books. Before Marianne's death, the objects had seemed like the legend of her life— signifiers and set pieces for all the things her friend hadn't had time to tell her in the two years they'd known each other. Now all those stories would remain untold.

A flare of unexpected anger sharpened Penelope's thoughts. It was ridiculous that Marianne had not lived longer than this. It was ludicrous that two years after the end of the pandemic, Penelope's best friend had died from a hidden flaw in her own body. It was horrifying and insane that Penelope was the one who had to clean out her apartment. She had treated it as a joke when Marianne had asked her to become the executor of her estate. What woman in her early thirties needed a will? But that was Marianne. Morbidly practical—the polar opposite of Penelope, with her unflagging optimism and slightly disheveled life.

Marianne planned her vacations to the last detail months, sometimes even years, in advance, while Penelope had once gone camping for a weekend with nothing more than a pack of veggie dogs and a sleeping bag. Marianne bought her groceries using a regimented weekly meal plan. Penelope ate peanut butter crackers for dinner most nights of the week. Marianne filed an online itinerary whenever she went for a hike. Penelope was proud when she remembered to bring a rain jacket to work on over- cast days. Her inability to organize herself had been a sore point all her life, but Marianne had loved her spontaneity. When they were together, Penelope had finally felt like she was good enough. She had even become confident enough to tease Marianne about not worrying until things ac- tually happened. Now it turned out her friend had been right all along. Penelope couldn't help but think that if only she were more like Mari- anne, she might have been prepared for this.

An hour before, in a wood-paneled office downtown, Marianne's estate lawyer had instructed Penelope to empty her friend's home as soon as possible. It would need to be rented again to avoid any extra expense to the estate. *The fridge*, the lawyer had said grimly. *People forget about the fridge*. Penelope had nodded as she closed her hand over the jagged teeth of the key the lawyer placed on the desk. Her collar had become unpleasantly damp after the tears slid down her cheeks.

Now, her throat thickened again when she spotted the red notebook sitting politely closed on the otherwise empty desk by the floor-to-ceiling window at the far end of the apartment. Though its dull leather surface was deceptively innocuous, Penelope knew that it was the most valuable thing in the entire apartment. The small book was the reason she had met Marianne. It had been the subject of so many of their conversations. Including their last.

Penelope had seen Marianne's handwritten poster on the bulletin board of her usual coffee shop. The neatly lettered sign had stood out among the scrawls from dog-walkers, babysitters, and reiki healers advertising their services.

SEEKING WRITING PARTNER WHO IS NOT A JERK, it read. Penelope laughed, and then texted the listed number to set up a time to meet. Being an author was all she'd ever wanted to be. She longed to write the story she'd been telling everyone was coming since she'd graduated high school more than a decade before, but she found it difficult to sit down and get words on a page. A writing partner was exactly what she needed.

She and Marianne had hit it off immediately. After their first meeting, they had planned a standing lunch date every two weeks at the coffee shop for writing and critique sessions. Their relationship had quickly expanded to after-work cocktails, weekend hikes, and home-cooked meals at Marianne's apartment. They had grown close, sharing details of their lives and their interests, though Marianne offered little more than broad strokes about her past. Penelope learned quickly not to ask any probing questions. She only knew that Marianne had a brother whom she rarely saw, her father had died when she was in her early twenties, and she was estranged from her mother.

Penelope had loved the way her coffee dates with Marianne had stolen her away from the sweaty humidity that dripped from the windows of the community center where she managed the recreation programs. (Wednesdays were aerobics.) Six days before the call from the lawyer, Marianne had sat down across from her in their usual spot. The milky, cinnamon scent from her chai wafted across the table. Penelope had spoken right away.

"Have you sent it yet?"

Her eagerness sounded almost greedy, but she didn't care. Marianne was so close to achieving the dream they both shared. An editor had asked to read the completed manuscript of Marianne's novel after seeing the first chapter.

"God, no. I haven't even started typing the rest of it," Marianne said with a groan. She wrote in longhand and needed to transcribe everything before sending.

Penelope bit her lip.

"So do it already. The second chapter is incredible," Penelope said.

So is the rest of it, she wanted to add, but her jealousy choked away the praise. She tamped it down by thinking about the role she had played in crafting Marianne's beautiful novel. For two years she had read and commented on the pages that appeared magically each session like an unexpected snowfall on a winter morning. The next time they met, Penelope's suggestions would be incorporated with the invisible perfection of new flakes landing on the pile. Penelope had been grateful to develop her editing talents, as she was beginning to doubt she had much to offer as a writer.

While Marianne danced through her story, Penelope's ideas for her own remained stiff and unmoving. Though her friend arrived regularly with fresh pages, new ideas, and unexpected characters, Penelope was stuck rewriting her first ten chapters over and over, trying to coax a book into existence. The sample of work she had sent Marianne after spotting her sign was the same thing she was working on now. But more than once, Marianne had told her that she could never have finished the novel without her, and Penelope took pride in that. She knew the work so well it almost felt like her own. Penelope owed it to Marianne—to both of them, really—to compel her to publish it.

"I'm having second thoughts, Penny. It's just so . . . dark," Marianne said.

Despite her friend's concerns, Penelope warmed at her words. The nickname that only Marianne used for her always felt like an adult version of a secret handshake.

"No one has to know it's you. That's what pseudonyms are for," Penelope said. "You submitted the chapter using a blind email account, right?"

She knew Marianne didn't want her administration to discover that their untenured junior professor of comparative history was trying to sell a horror novel on the side. She had created an anonymous email account to ensure the submission wouldn't be traced back to her, but despite these measures, her hesitation had only increased since she'd submitted the chapter. Penelope sensed that the risk to Marianne's academic career wasn't the real issue. There was something within the manuscript that scared Marianne. Something that she wasn't willing to talk about.

"What if someone does find out? I could lose my job."

Penelope smiled reassuringly, though her molars gritted against each other. She could only dream of being poised to prove her family wrong and escape her dull, low-paying job as a recreation manager, but even the possibility of never coming home with hands smelling of old basketballs again hadn't been enough to put words on the page. She looked at Marianne closely as she took a sip of coffee, trying to figure out how to persuade her.

"You'll be selling the movie rights soon, and neither of us will ever have to work again," she said.

Marianne chuckled, which Penelope took as a good sign. But then her friend hedged again.

"Maybe it's not the right time to put something so bleak out into the world."

"That's why it works. Art reflects life, and the world's brutal at the moment. It doesn't matter that it's dark. What matters is that it's great."

Marianne's eyes softened at the praise.

"Thank you. I guess I just worry about creating something that's so creepy. I keep thinking of that phrase, 'you reap what you sow.' Or as my mother used to say: 'cruelty should be reserved for the cruel.'"

Penelope eyed her carefully. Whenever Marianne spoke of her mother, her voice became sharp enough to cut paper. Not that it happened often. She preferred not to think about the past, she told Penelope. Penelope wondered if Marianne was finally going to reveal the truth about her family. Instead, her lips—painted a flattering shade of dark rose—turned up in a small smile.

"But this morning is for writing, not relatives," said Marianne. "How is your work going?"

"Don't worry about what I'm doing," Penelope said, refusing to let Marianne change the subject. "I'm here to light a fire under you. Whatever happened in your life, it gave you the seeds of something beautiful and haunting. It's in the work, Marianne."

Her friend's eyes sparkled with mischief.

"That's true. And at least it has a happy ending."

Penelope paused before answering. "But everyone dies."

Marianne raised a perfectly shaped eyebrow.

"Exactly."

They both laughed. Penelope couldn't stop herself from reaching across the table to lay her hand on top of Marianne's. Her ragged nails looked awful in comparison to Marianne's flawless manicure. Marianne looked down and, for a stomach-churning second, Penelope was terrified that she'd made her feel uncomfortable with the physical contact. But instead of drawing away, Marianne flipped her palm up to give Penelope's hand a squeeze that she felt throughout her entire body. It had been so long since anyone had touched her. The cuff of Marianne's sleeve fell back to reveal the rippled flesh on her wrist. Penelope kept her eyes on Marianne's face rather than her scarred arm, as its origin was another story Marianne didn't want to tell.

"I'm so grateful that you believe in me," Marianne said.

Penelope tried to speak but was taken aback by the catch in her throat. Marianne meant so much to her. She gathered herself, then responded.

"Of course I do, but it's not just about me. The editor is going to love it. The world is going to love it. The entire book is objectively good. Really good. Trust yourself. You need to let someone else see it. Someone who can actually do something about it."

"Okay, okay. I'll do it!" Marianne said with a grin that shifted almost immediately to a mock frown. "Even if it does take me months to type it all out. In the meantime, however, I have to teach a class."

They said goodbye. Penelope left the coffee shop feeling buoyant, as if something wonderful was about to happen. Marianne's novel was done. It was perfect. It was ready.

But Marianne hadn't had a chance to follow through with the editor. Less than a week after their conversation, Marianne was dead and Penelope was standing in her apartment, alone, trying to figure out how she was going to make it through the funeral the next day.

The notebook that contained the final draft of Marianne's work sat on the glass surface of her desk. Penelope approached it gingerly. Her hand prickled as she reached out, like it was a sleeping dog about to snap. When she picked it up, it opened easily to a page toward the back that contained a meticulous outline. At first, Penelope thought it was the framework for a new story Marianne was writing, before she examined it more closely. It was a plan for a research trip. Her eye was drawn to the bottom of the page where a dark mark had bled through from the back side, partially obscuring Marianne's elegant handwriting. Penelope flipped the page to read two words that had been inked over repeatedly.

CALL PHILIP.

Ten numbers were scratched under the message. Unlike Marianne's usual precise hand, the lines wobbled with haste—or was it emotion? Penelope reached into her pocket for her phone. Her shoulders tightened as she imagined Marianne's abandoned belongings creeping up behind her. She dialed the number and was so startled when a subdued voice answered after the first ring that she didn't respond immediately. She had been expecting voice mail. She didn't know anyone who picked up their phone anymore.

"Hello?" the man repeated.

"Hello," Penelope said. The back of her throat seemed to swell. "I've been asked—um, appointed, I guess is more like—"

"I'm sorry, who is this?"

The man's tone had become noticeably guarded.

He's been through so much already, she thought, as she fumbled for better words, the ones that could make Marianne not dead, and take away the strangling responsibility she felt as the executor of an estate she didn't know what to do with.

"My name is Penelope," she said. "I was a friend of your sister's."

THE FIRST DAY

CHAPTER **ONE**

EIGHTEEN MONTHS AFTER
7:15 A.M.

Penelope sipped her coffee as she stood at the window of Marianne's former apartment. She had taken over the lease in the strange days following her friend's death. Later she realized that her grief had prompted her to secure any connection to her old life that was possible. Marianne's death had changed her, and there were times when she hated who she had become. It was difficult now to summon the confidence Marianne's affection had given her, and she often found herself doubting every decision she made. She had hoped that moving into the apartment would help her find herself again, and some days it did. But on mornings like this, when her anxiety was high, she felt like an impostor living in a place that did not belong to her.

Through the window, the fog rolled into the valley like smoke seeping under a bedroom door. It didn't take long for the fat gray fingers to obscure the pink sunrise. *Red sky at night, sailor's delight*, Penelope thought. *Red sky in the morning, sailors take warning*. She swallowed down the dry dread in the back of her throat with a swig of coffee. The hot drink tasted acidic, not comforting. She was too tired to enjoy it. Her insomnia had trapped her in bed the night before, sleepless and sweating. She wasn't sure what had kept her awake: the idea of frigid early spring waves breaking against the small boat and tossing her into icy cold water or the apprehension that going forward with the research trip Marianne had planned before her death was insensitive and foolish. Or both.

In her trip plan, Marianne had listed the nine people who would soon be traveling with Penelope to Stone Point, a treacherous outcropping of land on the west side of Howe Sound. Apart from Marianne's brother, Philip, Penelope didn't know any of them well, and there were several in the group she would be meeting for the first time that morning. It had been more than a year since Marianne's death, yet Penelope still found herself wishing that her beautiful friend could be on the boat with them, gleaning whatever it was she had wanted to get out of the trip.

Her panic rose. She braced herself, then inhaled and exhaled slowly. After the fifth cycle of breath, the feeling dissipated. It was getting harder to control these waves of emotion. She had considered finding a therapist to help, but it was difficult to know where to begin. It worried her to think about telling someone all her secrets. She stepped back from the window, wondering if she should let Philip know that the wind was kicking up. Her apartment was on the seventh floor of a building at the top of Burnaby Mountain. She could see the weather sooner than he could from his place in North Van.

She had also hoped that by taking over Marianne's lease, she would always know what was coming. But it hadn't worked out that way at all.

* * *

One month ago, she had become nervous when Vivian Taylor's name flashed on the display of her phone. Her editor rarely communicated through any other means than email, but Penelope had ignored the last half dozen messages from her.

"Penelope, are you all right? I've been trying to reach you for days," Vivian asked, when Penelope reluctantly answered the call.

Her words were gentle, but her meaning was clear.

"I'm so sorry. It's been a crazy month. I've been so swamped with . . ." Penelope scanned the apartment and stopped on her laptop. "Um . . . social media."

Immediately, she realized it was idiotic to blame something so demonstrably untrue. None of her feeds had been updated in months. Luckily, Vivian ignored her excuse.

"I'm calling to try to get a handle on when we can expect your second manuscript. I penciled in a loose deadline of six weeks ago. Are you ready to send me something? I'm happy to read early pages if it's not quite finished."

Penelope paused before deciding not to lie again.

"I don't have anything to send you."

The ensuing silence was weighted with the familiar heaviness of failure. When Vivian spoke again, her voice was less reassuring.

"Okay. Listen, I don't want to scare you. *The Myth of Vultures* has been out for five weeks and it's still going strong. Penelope, we're so happy with it. We've got some time. But readers don't like to wait. Especially for a second book. Your best shot at having a long career is to send me something new as soon as you can."

Penelope took a breath. "When do you need it?"

"Soon."

Penelope hesitated again before asking a question she didn't want answered.

"How soon?"

"Can you get something together in a month?" Vivian's voice was strained with the tension of barely concealed impatience.

No, Penelope thought. Then the trip plan in Marianne's notebook appeared in her mind. The title, written in Marianne's perfect penmanship, had been *Research for Book Two*.

"How about three?" she answered.

In the weeks immediately following Marianne's death, Penelope had surprised herself by working as if possessed, driven by a mysterious and unrelenting force. Her feverish pace had led to a book deal. She had been offered a huge advance for both her first book and a second with a similar theme of family betrayal. Her debut novel had been rushed to publication and released to rave reviews and astonishingly high sales.

But then whatever had been driving Penelope disappeared. She had been left with no ideas and no pages for a second book, as empty as she had been during her writing sessions with Marianne. Without Vivian's urging, she might have carried on aimlessly for years instead of deciding to lead the trip that Marianne had planned down to the very last detail in the months before her death. Once again, Marianne was saving her. Now Penelope was off to Squamish for a three-night stay with Marianne's brother and a group of near strangers. She could only hope she'd return with what she needed.

The ticking clock on the wall reminded her that she had run out of time. She couldn't afford to be late—it was a tight schedule even if everything went exactly according to plan. She winced as though she were swallowing medicine after she gulped the last of her cold coffee and then hurried to the bathroom. It took ten minutes for her to shower and dress. The night before, she had laid her clothes out on the small bench at the foot of her bed at the same time that she packed for the trip, channeling Marianne's efficiency. She pulled on a lacy bra and matching set of panties, thermal underwear, wool sweater, and jeans. She smiled at the way her serious mid layers hid what was underneath. Though she knew that the trip's purpose was hardly romantic, the thought of Philip looking admiringly at her body as they readied for bed made the slight scratch of the lace edges worthwhile. He liked it when she dressed up for him, and she liked the way he made her feel when she did. He was the first man she'd dated who didn't avoid the sight of the rounded flesh hanging at her waist when she undressed before him. Instead, his eyes slowly traced every curve of her body.

She hadn't meant to begin dating Marianne's mourning brother. The day after their phone conversation, she had walked up the steps of the funeral home, painfully aware of being alone in a crowd. Marianne was her closest friend, but they'd only spent time together one-on-one. She knew no one else in Marianne's life, which only seemed odd after her death.

Two tall men in suits were greeting mourners outside large wooden doors at the top of a set of stairs. Penelope nodded briefly, then dropped her eyes as she made to pass through.

"Penelope?" the blond man asked.

"Yes?"

"I'm Philip," he said. "We spoke on the phone. I've been asked to escort you to your seat with the other speakers."

"Oh, of course," she replied, fighting a blush as an older couple glanced in her direction with interest. Along with the keys, the lawyer had passed on Marianne's request that Penelope read a poem by e.e. cummings at the end of the service. Apprehension about the task had resulted in her filling the previous night with dread, bad television, and worse wine. Close to midnight, she'd forced herself into bed only to toss sleeplessly until dawn.

She followed Philip into the carpeted entryway decorated in muted gray. The room deodorizer was thick and cloying.

"Through here," he said over his shoulder as he entered a small coatroom to the right. "Would you like to take off your coat?"

She slipped it off and onto the offered hanger.

"So you knew Marianne well," he asked. "I hear you're going to read her favorite poem."

He looked directly at her as he spoke. His eyes were the same blue as Marianne's, but while hers had always been soft, his were as guarded as a wounded animal. The coatroom was small and windowless. He smelled like soap. She could see a nick of red on his neck where he'd cut himself shaving. She wasn't sure if it was a question, but she answered it anyway.

"I did know her well," Penelope said. Her voice broke. "I miss her so much."

His face creased with despair.

"Me too," he said.

To her surprise, he began roughly wiping tears from his eyes with the back of his hand. He took a step back and was nearly out of the coatroom before she could speak.

"Wait," she cried, and reached for his arm. "I'm so sorry. I know how you feel. I loved her too."

He looked down at her hand, then back up into her eyes. He grabbed her forearm and pulled her toward him into an embrace. The wool of his suit scratched against her cheek. Her tears made the fabric wet. Their shared sorrow made the embrace feel natural, almost necessary. After a moment, she choked back her final sob, then took a step back, suddenly aware that Philip was a stranger, no matter how much they understood each other's grief.

"Should I—"

Before she could finish, he closed the distance between them again, dipped his head and kissed her on the cheek.

They parted slowly. She stared up at him in surprise.

"I can take you to your seat now," he said. His eyes glinted with something like Marianne's mischief. "Unless you'd prefer to stay here."

She hesitated. The strange circumstances allowed her to be bold.

"I should go. Can we continue this later?"

He smiled. "I'd love that."

He had waited for her near the coatroom after the funeral home had emptied out of Marianne's mourners. Penelope's head swam with new names and faces. Philip's seemed familiar by contrast. In any other circumstance, the idea of him waiting for her would have thrilled her, but the service had made her numb.

"You spoke well," he said. He looked as tired and glassy-eyed as she felt. "Is there any chance you're free for dinner?"

"Yes, I am," she said.

They retrieved their coats and left the funeral home together. It was raining, which was both miserable and appropriate. Philip opened a large umbrella and held it over their heads as they walked to her car. The glistening curtain of water falling off its edge made her feel like she was in a movie. That night, she realized that neither of them had to die alongside Marianne. Because of Philip, she was alive again.

The more she got to know him, the stronger their relationship grew. She liked the way he stuck up for the underdog, slipping a twenty-dollar bill into a tip jar after witnessing the behavior of a rude customer or plugging coins into a parking meter when he spied an attendant heading toward a car with a ticket in hand. Though he owned and operated a successful general medical practice on the north shore of Vancouver, he volunteered once a month in the Downtown Eastside, the city's most drug-involved community, to pay back the privilege he'd been afforded. He had never questioned Penelope's desire to live in Marianne's apartment. During probate, he had petitioned to buy Marianne's old Volvo from the estate for what she assumed were the same reasons as her own. Both of them were moving on, but neither of them was ready to fully let go.

Penelope shook her head to clear it, then wheeled her suitcase out the door of her bedroom. This trip was important for more than one reason. Today was her thirtieth birthday, though Philip had no idea. She had not brought up the date the year before since the last thing she'd wanted to do after Marianne's death was celebrate her own life. Normally, she hated birthdays, but this one felt worth noting, albeit quietly. Not only had she found love, but she was also a successful author—the thing she'd dreamed of defining herself by since she was a teenager. Still, the fact that none of it would have happened without Marianne's death made the day bittersweet. She hoped the surprise of the lingerie in the evening would be a gift to them both.

She headed to the bathroom and cleaned her teeth, then tucked her damp toothbrush into her toiletries bag. She fastened her watch to her wrist, then dusted blush on her cheekbones and darkened her light eyelashes with waterproof mascara. It seemed foolish to apply makeup before a boat trip, but without it, her light eyes became lost in the scattering of freckles on her cheekbones. As she pulled her thick, copper-colored hair into a no-nonsense ponytail, the elastic sprang from her fingers like a flailing frog. She knelt on the cold tiles and patted the underside of the vanity where she thought it had landed. Instead of a coiled band, she felt a cold cylinder. She knew what it was before she saw it.

Marianne's lipstick.

Without thinking, she uncapped the rose-gold tube and traced her lips with Marianne's signature color. It smelled faintly sweet. As she turned away from the mirror, she slid the lipstick into her pocket. *For good luck,* she thought, uncertain if she believed it to be true. She couldn't quite toss off her earlier dread about the red streaks in the sky, but she pulled her small suitcase to the front door, stopping to grab her purse and car keys before leaving. Once the door was secured, she tested the lock to ensure everything would stay safe while she was gone. She was halfway down the hall when she realized she'd forgotten to pack the bear mace she'd purchased the week before in a state of nervous apprehension about the trip. It was probably for the best, since she wasn't completely certain how to work the complicated aerosol spray, she thought.

The elevator chimed softly as the doors opened and she stepped in, averting her eyes from the mirrors on three sides of the compartment as she pressed *P* for parking. She didn't want to be reminded of the way the ice cream and bread from her grief eating had settled around her midsection and backside. She could only imagine what her weight-conscious mother would have to say about the changes to her body. Luckily, she lived too far away to be able to see it. Besides, there was only one person Penelope wanted to impress now, and he liked her just the way she was. The fact that she didn't have to be skinny to be loved didn't completely mute her mother's critical voice in her head, but it helped. Anyway, there were plenty of hiking trails on Stone Point, and she planned to take advantage of them. Philip was right. It was time for them both to move forward, and there was no better way to begin than by shedding the things that were dragging her down.

The underground garage was empty, and Penelope's steps echoed hollowly in the chilled cement surroundings. She approached her small SUV with her key fob in hand, willing herself not to be startled by its unlocking yip. The gloom down here always made her shiver. She hated the feeling of being encased by concrete with floors and floors of heavy stone and wood above her, so she started the car and pulled forward fast enough to make her tires shriek. As the automated exit turnstile opened, she exhaled the irrational panic that she would be trapped in the darkness belowground forever.

Once she was in the open air, she told herself it was natural to be unnerved. The journey ahead was daunting, not just because of the weather and the lingering presence of Marianne. It wasn't every day that she set out to hunt a witch.

CHAPTER **TWO**

8:30 A.M.

According to Marianne's detailed notes, Ruth Stone was a young woman said to be responsible for the deaths of three full-grown men in 1922. She had been sixteen years old the last time she was seen alive at Stone Point. In the years following, rumors of her supernatural evil had proliferated rapidly, ensuring the property Ruth had shared with her husband, William Stone, remained empty until eight years before Marianne had begun researching her. An enterprising couple, Simone and Ethan Redding, had purchased the abandoned outcropping from the Stone estate only to disappear without a trace a few months after their arrival. The mystery of what happened to them had only added to the legend of the Stone Witch.

From her own research, Penelope knew that Ruth Stone hadn't always been known as a witch. Penelope had unearthed her birth certificate, a marriage license, and several local history books from the Vancouver Public Library. According to the sources, the young woman had been born Ruth Flanders in the Britannia mining camp located roughly fifty kilometers away from Vancouver, a growing city to the south. At the time, there was no road to the camp. Traveling there from the city required a long boat ride on the rough water of Howe Sound, a deep fjord filled by the northern Pacific Ocean. Much of the sound was a haunting landscape with kilometers of steeply banked shoreline reachable only by boat. Winter storms often rendered the passage impossible, cutting off the site completely from the city for much of the year.

It was clear that life was bleak and treacherous for mining families like that of Ruth Flanders. Not only was the boat trip to the site unreliable, but their camp was built far up the side of the mountain to make it easier for miners to get to and from work. Once visitors disembarked from the boat, they had to be hauled up by hand in a wooden tram car suspended from steel cables. When Ruth was an infant, the mining camp had consisted of a ramshackle collection of tents and a company store made of plywood. In the oldest photos, the site appeared rugged and harsh—a flat expanse made by excavation and blasts of dynamite. It jutted out of the cliff face, raw and exposed to the wind. Higher mountains loomed around it like angry guardians. In later shots, many of the tents had been replaced with small shacks, a one-room schoolhouse, and a community center.

The area around the mine was home to a sparse population composed primarily of members of two Indigenous nations and a handful of settlers, but the mining camp itself was populated exclusively by miners and their families who had traveled from all parts of the world to find their fortune. Ruth's father had chased gold for most of his life, going as far south as Brazil on a cargo ship to try to make it rich in Minas Gerais. He had come back to Canada with empty pockets, but richer nonetheless with a Brazilian wife who would become Ruth's mother.

At the Britannia Mine, Ruth's father had been a mucker—a man sent into the mines for endless hours of backbreaking work shoveling rocks dislodged by blasts of dynamite. His long shifts meant Ruth had spent most of her childhood alone, as her mother had died in childbirth along with Ruth's infant brother when Ruth was ten years old. Other than that tragedy, Ruth's early life had been relatively uneventful, as she mostly attended the small school and kept house for her father. In 1920, when she was fourteen years old, the town registry showed a marriage between her and a man named William Stone, age fifty. Penelope shuddered at the idea of the match. Her distaste was made worse by what she learned of the family Ruth had married into.

The Stone family was noted in all three of the history books Penelope read. None of the accounts were positive. The Stones were early settlers of a large property in the isolated wilderness located across the choppy waters of Howe Sound on the rugged western shore opposite the mine. The area was still unceded by the Squamish and Lil'wat Nation as it had been part of their traditional territory, which made Penelope wonder exactly how the Stones had secured it. Since only those skilled in trades useful to the mining community or the Indigenous population could eke out a living away from the confines of the camp, the Stone family had resorted to questionable practices to survive.

William's father had begun as an opportunistic salvager due to the geography of their land, which had a hidden shallow sandbank stretching out into the deep waters of the sound. It had been a prime spot to collect debris from ships and other wreckage. Later, William convinced his father and brothers to establish a moonshine-making operation, the product of which they supplied to the miners on a regular basis. Unfortunately, the route between the still and the buyers wasn't without its perils. In 1919, William's two brothers and his father were killed in a boating accident, leaving William alone to run what had become a successful business. Penelope assumed that was around the time he had decided to try to find a wife. Given the ratio of men to women in the area, it was likely common for an older man to take a much younger wife, but the thought of it still gave Penelope the creeps.

In March of 1922, William failed to make his monthly delivery of alcohol to the camp. A small group of miners braved the waters to replenish their supplies. When they arrived at Stone Point, it appeared abandoned. Upon further investigation, the group stumbled upon what was left of William Stone. He was placed in a macabre position, his body frozen upright inside the woodshed. William's young wife was nowhere to be found.

Fearing the murderer was still on the loose, the miners raced back to the settlement of Squamish to notify the Vancouver constable through telegram. Two detectives from an agency of privately employed mercenaries were sent within the week. Exactly what those two men found at Stone Point was never revealed. Their failure to report back triggered another search party that discovered their two crumpled bodies on the hard sand of the beach at the bottom of a rocky cliff.

Despite an extensive search of the property, Ruth Stone had never been found. People were eager to discover a reason for the killings, to find a rational explanation that could assuage their fear. Almost immediately, Ruth became the primary suspect in all three murders. But no normal young girl was strong enough to kill three adult men. The absence of her body and lack of explanation for the killings resulted in rumors of something supernatural on Stone Point.

First, the talk about Ruth being a witch was quietly whispered.

Eventually, the accusations became louder.

Finally, they were repeated enough that they became something like the truth.

CHAPTER **THREE**

As Penelope pulled into Philip's driveway, she was reassured by the sight of his tall frame on the steps of the cedar-shingled house she had visited many times in the last year. She stepped out of her car as Philip, clad in a lime-green coat, walked toward her with a large backpack slung over his shoulder. At the funeral, she had found it disconcerting to see that his eyes were the same light blue shade his sister's had been. It hadn't taken long to shake the similarity, however. His expression was often guarded, where Marianne's had been open as a door.

"Ready for a witch hunt?" he asked, placing a soft kiss on her lips.

"Let's say that I'm ready for the story of my life," she said with a smile to assure him of the excitement he wanted to see. "As is my editor."

The mention of Vivian made her smile fade as she walked around to the other side of the car. Philip preferred to drive, and she was happy to let him take control of the rest of the trip. Once they were both safely buckled in, he slipped the vehicle into gear and backed onto the street.

Being the passenger gave Penelope a chance to focus. The tale of the Stone Witch was fascinating, morbid, and intense. The legend contained similar themes to Penelope's first novel, which had hinged on the tragedies embedded in a dysfunctional family. She knew Ruth was the perfect inspiration for her next story, and once again she thanked Marianne for the idea. And Philip, of course. Without his thoughtful encouragement, she might never have been able to overcome her reticence at gathering a group of strangers for a weekend getaway. Having a man like him by her side helped her force away the concern that she didn't have a second book in her. The evening following the call with Vivian, she had numbly relayed the new deadline to him over a large slice of tiramisu. She had been surprised and flattered by the way he had made her problems his own, almost as if their lives were intertwined already. Almost as if he planned to marry her.

When she'd brought up the Stone Witch, shame about her lack of creativity had prevented her from mentioning Marianne had come up with it first. Fortunately, Philip's excitement had superseded her half-truth.

"The Stone Witch? I haven't thought about her since I was a kid," Philip had said with a grin. "God, we used to scare the hell out of each other with that story on our camping trips."

Penelope's curiosity was piqued by the mention of the camping trips. She wanted him to give her the history that his sister never had—like how Marianne's wrist had been so badly scarred. But like Marianne, Philip didn't speak much of their childhood. So instead of prying into the past, she had concentrated on the witch.

"You know the story?" Penelope asked.

"Know it? She's basically the Bloody Mary of the Pacific Northwest."

"What, so you say her name in the mirror three times and she appears?"

Philip laughed. "Not quite. We used to tell each other that she was scared of the fire. She could only get you in the dark. It made going to the bathroom at night terrifying."

"So lots of people around here know the story of Ruth Stone?"

"Anyone with a knowledge of local history, yeah," he said. "I could probably find a few people who would talk to you."

"Oh, Philip, that would be wonderful," she said as she thought of Marianne's detailed notes. "I have a few people in mind as well. But really the best way to do this kind of research would be to go to Stone Point itself. It just feels like such a weird thing to ask."

"No! It's an amazing idea," Philip said after a moment. "Let's get a list together of people we want to include. If you work out how to invite them, I can figure out the rest. It's a bit of a journey to get to Stone Point, but I'll sort out the planning part. You start writing."

His enthusiasm had convinced her. Again, he reminded her of his sister. Marianne had always encouraged Penelope to make space for her work. Once, she had arranged to have meals delivered to Penelope's door on a weekend that Penelope had promised to devote to her manuscript. Penelope had never admitted that she'd spent much of the two days binging reality television while devouring the food. She'd squandered Philip's generosity in a similar way. Despite all the time he had given her, she had little more to show for it than a double-spaced page with vague notes to herself like: *Explore relationship between Ruth and her father?*

"I hope you packed rain gear. It's going to get wetter as we go, I think," Philip said, interrupting her thoughts.

Penelope nodded, letting her gaze drop past his close-cropped dark blond hair and sharp jaw to his slim fitting Arc'teryx jacket. Everything about Philip seemed acclimatized to the rain like a sea otter effortlessly gliding through cold water. She still wasn't used to the endless wetness of the West Coast. On days like this, the suffocating dampness made her long for the four seasons of her youth in the center of the country, far from the ocean, but she would never admit it to Philip. This was his home. He had spent years building up his medical practice and had recently hired two new general practitioners, meaning he could now set his own hours.

This was where he wanted to stay, especially now that memories were all he had left of his family. When he and Marianne were in their early twenties, their father had been killed in a car accident, and since then they had taken care of each other. Now he was all alone.

"I have two raincoats and a pair of waterproof pants in my suitcase. I hope that's enough."

He looked over at her with one eyebrow raised. "Probably not. But I've been assured the lodge has an excellent gear room for drying our stuff if need be. I've also got an extra set if you need it."

She sighed inwardly but smiled outwardly for Philip's benefit. "I guess that's the first requirement for a West Coast eco-lodge."

She knew they were lucky to be visiting the property now and not during the nearly hundred-year period after Ruth's disappearance when it had been left to rot. She shivered. Of all the information she had unearthed about Stone Point, the unexplained disappearance of the former property owners, the Reddings, was the story that unsettled her the most. A century-old witch tale was easier to accept than a recent inexplicable tragedy.

The last vestiges of the city sped past them. Philip navigated the SUV around a sharp bend in the road, anticipating the curve even though Penelope could scarcely see a foot beyond the hood. She had never traveled north of the city before, and the dense fog and twisting road made it seem as though they were entering another world. Philip placed one hand on her leg, keeping the other confidently on the steering wheel. He didn't seem bothered at all by the thick mist that now encased them.

"Star and Neil called me on the satellite phone last night. They arrived safe and sound and should have lunch waiting for us shortly after we get there," he said.

"Great."

She was comforted that the caretaking couple—former students of Marianne's—were already on-site. They had needed someone to arrive before the rest of the group to make sure everything was in order. Since neither Star nor Neil had much to offer in terms of academic expertise or practical experience, they had seemed a perfect fit to perform the menial duties required over the course of the trip. Philip had arranged for them to get things organized and prepare meals and take care of kitchen details so the rest of the group could focus on research. Confirmation that the remote communication system was working was also heartening. Everything was going perfectly as planned.

The thought of food reminded her that she had forgotten to eat breakfast. She opened the glove compartment and fished out two items from her emergency stash. She had something to confess to Philip and didn't want to do it on an empty stomach.

"Granola bar?"

"Thanks."

She unwrapped one and handed it to Philip before doing the same for herself. They chewed their first bites in silence. She swallowed hard. Her throat had dried out again. She could feel the scrape of it going down.

"Your mother called me last night," she said.

Penelope wasn't surprised to see Philip's mouth turn down at the mention of Estelle Walsh. She had been a terrible mother to her children. She had left her family when both of her kids were very young to pursue her career. When Penelope had shown him the list of people she wanted to invite, he'd been shocked to see Estelle named as the group photographer.

"I'm happy to get someone else," she had said, seeing his reaction.

After a moment or so, he had looked at her again. "I don't know anyone else with her talent and knowledge of this area," he grudgingly admitted.

Though he and Estelle had managed to have a few civil conversations immediately following Marianne's death, Penelope knew they'd spoken very little over the last year, and Philip showed no desire to initiate deeper intimacy. Penelope was dreading the moment when the two of them came face-to-face again. Especially after the conversation she'd had the night before.

"How is Estelle doing? I haven't spoken to her since . . ."

He trailed off as he always did when Estelle came up.

"She's fine," Penelope said.

After a few tense moments, Philip spoke again. His voice was tight, as if he was forcing out the words.

"So why did she call?"

"She had questions about a shuttle to Squamish from the airport," Penelope said. "I gave her the information she needed."

"So what's the problem?"

His assumption that there was an issue might have seemed overly harsh if he wasn't right. Penelope cringed at the memory.

"Well, I was looking at the list of names while I spoke with her. I got distracted wondering if anyone else needed transportation from Vancouver. And then . . . I called her Fran."

Philip looked at her with a trace of a smile.

"Fran Brant?"

It was the name of another woman on their team. She was the president of the naturalists club and something of a local historian. During the telephone calls they'd had prior to the trip, Penelope had enjoyed Fran's conversation, and she was looking forward to meeting her in person. Unlike Estelle.

Penelope's voice was miserable when she answered. "Yes. Your mother was obviously offended. She corrected me, then asked me to spell her name out carefully so she could be sure I knew it."

It had been humiliating to recite the letters over the phone.

Philip shook his head. "Don't let her bother you. She doesn't like many people."

"Yeah, I got that vibe."

In the hope of avoiding one of his distant moods, she steered the conversation to the lighter subject of a movie they had seen several nights before. The kilometers clicked by until Philip tapped the left-turn indicator as he braked gently at a traffic light buffered by a fast-food restaurant on one side and a glass-fronted tourist center on the other.

"Is this it?" she asked, trying to keep her voice airy and devoid of the uneasiness rippling through her body.

"This is the place."

Their car rolled down what looked like the main street of the small city. Penelope looked longingly at signs for art galleries, clothing stores, and tea shops, wishing that she and Philip were here for a romantic get-away instead of a research trip. The vibrant commercial district gave way to a more industrial area. Philip turned left again at the end of the road. Penelope could barely make out the indistinct forms of docked ships in a small channel of water directly in front of them. A weather-beaten sign announced their arrival at Squamish Harbour. Philip maneuvered the car into a tight space in a parking lot.

Penelope thought she could discern the shapes of a small group of people standing on the dock about six meters away. The fog made them as vague as apparitions. Several large, anchored boats were tethered to lines closer to them. They bobbed aimlessly as small waves broke against their hulls. Philip turned to her, and she smiled brightly in an attempt to regain the optimism that had defined her before Marianne had passed away. She wanted to reassure him that this trip was exactly what they needed to leave their sadness and grief behind and to take her career to the next level. He seemed to receive her message and he nodded before speaking.

"Here we are. Next stop, Stone Point."

CHAPTER **FOUR**

9:32 A.M.

When she stepped out of the car, Penelope tasted salt on her lips as if she had been crying. Her shoulder muscles stiffened involuntarily at the frigid wind rolling off the water. Philip was already at the back of the SUV, unloading her rolling suitcase and his backpack. He gave her an encouraging smile as he toted them past her to lead the way down the slippery stairs to the dock. The mist wavered and the small gathering of people grew slightly clearer. She waved, but no one responded in kind. As she followed Philip, the white clouds swarmed in again, making it hard to see anything beyond her own feet.

   She continued to the place where she'd seen the throng of people, trying to channel Marianne's effortless ability to inspire confidence. It was so important for them to like and respect her. It had been so strange to call each member of the group to invite them on the trip, but it was a duty that she didn't want to pass off to Philip. He had already been so apprehensive about his mother. Unfortunately, their complex relationship was only one of the reasons everything was awkward. Penelope wasn't like Marianne. She had to work hard to gain trust.

Being an author still felt like a pretend job, and she had found herself stuttering as though she was on a job interview when she tried to explain who she was and what she hoped to accomplish. She again omitted all mention that she was carrying out the plans of her deceased friend, as she suspected that would have made the conversations even more challenging. Each person had been surprised enough to receive her invitation. Hector Anderson, a history professor, had seemed downright suspicious. In the face of their discomfort, she found herself offering to pay for their time and lodging. One thousand dollars per person plus a free trip to a beautiful West Coast lodge for a weekend on Penelope's dime. If this trip didn't yield a manuscript, she would be out five figures and no closer to keeping her promise to Vivian.

Once down on the dock, Penelope became more disoriented by the lack of visibility. There was almost no differentiating the ocean waves from the milky air that loomed around them. She had to pause for a moment before placing one foot in front of the other. The narrow dock suddenly felt like the road to oblivion.

Stop being silly, she told herself as she attempted to follow Philip's confident strides. It was difficult to keep up with him at the best of times. Now his body transformed into a gray shadow as the distance increased between them. She picked up her pace and joined him as he greeted Danny Mason and Nina Withers, who would serve as their wilderness guides.

She had met the astonishingly fit couple the summer before at a barbecue. They and Philip were members of the same bike club. Penelope had felt like a frumpy housewife clad in a frilly summer dress, while the three of them were in muddy bike jerseys and shorts after a long ride.

"Philip. We were wondering if you had slept in, mate," Danny said.

His faint Australian accent gave the words a light inflection, though neither he nor Nina smiled at their arrival. Penelope was taken aback. She hadn't realized they were late. Danny stretched out his hand to Philip, then nodded toward Penelope. Like Philip, he wore his hair cropped short, but his was black instead of blond. Philip had told her that Danny had grown up in the outback before moving to the northern hemisphere. His dark brown skin had the weathered look of a person who'd spent most of his life outside.

"Hello," Penelope said. "So glad you could make it. Both of you."

Nina met Penelope's eyes without changing her expression, then looked away. Penelope sighed inwardly. She had found the woman stand-offish during their first meeting, and it seemed that no headway had been gained since then. Nina's long blond hair was pulled back under a wool toque and her athletic frame was clad in a blue puffer jacket and waterproof pants. Too late, Penelope realized she also should have worn something to keep the water off her legs. Her jeans already felt damp. She could hear the waves slurping at the side of the boat. A bang from inside the aluminum cabin made her jump.

"Is this our boat?" Philip asked.

"You tell me," Danny said.

She looked over and her heart sank. A man wearing red flannel was standing near the steering wheel with his back to her, a hammer in hand. On the website Philip had showed her, the boat had been described as "a cuddy cabin designed to weather rough waters." Penelope had assumed it would be sturdier. The narrow aluminum vessel was visibly dented in places and much smaller than she'd expected. The seating area barely looked large enough to shield six people from the weather, and the tattered canvas roof stretching over the two metal benches offered little reassurance of cover. There were additional seats at the back, but they were exposed to whatever wind and water might come their way. Squeezing eight people, the captain, and their gear onto the ship meant that some would be riding with no protection.

Danny let out a small snort. "You know, you could have saved yourself a few dollars and hired me to get us across instead."

"Oh," said Penelope. "I didn't realize you . . . did that."

It seemed worse to add that it was Philip, not her, who had hired the boat captain, and she waited for him to jump in. Danny and Nina both looked at her as Philip eyed the horizon, seemingly oblivious to the tension. Her cheeks grew warm.

"Did you send your bikes over early as well?" she asked, counting on her casual question to cover her discomfort. Philip had arranged for his bike to be shipped on the boat along with the caretakers.

"Of course they did," Philip said. "We'll be slipping in a ride or two this weekend."

"Too right," said Danny.

"With Liam too?" Penelope asked.

She hadn't seen Marianne's ex-boyfriend since the funeral, though she knew Philip still met with him regularly. She wondered if his name made him think of his sister, but his expression remained relaxed.

"I don't think he'll want to miss out. He's definitely the kind of guy who likes to be at the center of the action," Philip answered.

"Well, feel free to take as many rides as you want," she said, hoping he'd take the space he needed if things with his mother became tense.

Danny cheered. "All right. The boss is letting us play hooky already."

Philip laughed. "I'm going to hold you to that, Penny."

Despite her success at getting on Danny's good side, she flinched at the nickname. Only Marianne had called her that. Philip noticed her reaction.

"I'm sorry. I forgot," he said in a low tone.

"It's okay," she said, even though it wasn't.

Despite her constant criticism of her own daughter, her mother had taught Penelope that if she didn't have anything nice to say, she shouldn't say anything at all. The last thing Penelope wanted to do was make Philip feel guilty, but the unexpected memory of his sister fazed her.

Nina eyed her closely before breaking the silence.

"We're stowing the bags by the captain's seat. It's going to be tight."

The small of Penelope's back grew clammy at the woman's warning. Luckily, the man in red flannel on the boat called out to them before she had to come up with an answer.

"Let me take care of those bags for you, miss."

Up close, his cheeks were wind-beaten and his nose looked red and tippled. Penelope sensed the damage might be more from whiskey than the elements, which added to her unease.

"Captain Rodney Tedders—you can call me Captain Rod. I'm here to get you across the sound in one piece, though I can't guarantee you'll be dry when you get there. You must be Penelope? These two were trying to convince me you weren't coming, but I knew you'd never miss a chance to catch a spooky witch."

Something in his chest rattled as he laughed. Danny gave him a thin smile as Philip reached over and shook the man's hand with a friendly greeting.

"Danny, do you want to take a look at the charted course?" Philip asked. He and Danny stepped onto the deck of the boat before the captain could invite them. "That okay, Captain?"

"Be my guest. I've got the map laid out there. It's a pretty straight shot from here, once we pull up anchor and get out of the blind channel."

Before Penelope could ask what a blind channel was, Captain Rod took the backpack and suitcase from Philip's hands, struggling briefly with the collapsible handle of Penelope's case. She should have brought a backpack instead, she realized in dismay once she saw the small storage area for their gear. Two expensive-looking but well-used backpacks were already there—presumably belonging to Danny and Nina. Philip's fit right in beside them, but her suitcase was too large and unyielding to be wedged inside. The captain eyed it dolefully. It looked like the kid at the playground that no one wanted to play with.

"Don't worry about getting it in there," she called from the dock. "I can put it under my feet."

"No need, no need, I'll find a place to stow it," the captain said. "It's rough water between here and there. Don't want this kind of thing rolling around the deck."

She watched his repeated attempts to push the solid frame of the suitcase into the narrow space between his chair and the metal bench with embarrassment. When he finally managed it, he turned back to her, panting slightly. Penelope gave him a grateful smile.

"Thanks for doing that."

"At your service. Listen, I'd like to push off as soon as possible. Looks like there's rain coming."

"We're still waiting for—" She did a quick head count. "Four more."

Nina pointed toward the end of the dock. The fog had thinned a little over the course of their conversation. Penelope could make out two figures as well as the looming shape of a mountain directly in front of them. One person seemed to be kneeling.

"Those two were here before us. Their gear is already on board," Nina said before following Danny and Philip onto the boat. Penelope's insides dipped when she saw the boat sink low into the water.

"Just two more, then," Penelope said.

The captain nodded. "All the same to me if we get caught in the rough water, but I don't think you're going to like it much if we start bouncing around like a bingo ball."

Her insides rolled again, but she ignored it as best she could. While the captain busied himself on the deck with a coil of rope, she walked tentatively to the end of the dock. When she got closer, she realized that the crouching figure was a woman in her fifties who appeared to be poking barnacles. A small man she thought was in his seventies was watching her with a bemused expression.

"Hello. I'm Penelope Berkowitz. Are you here for the trip to Stone Point?"

The woman stood up, brushed off her men's work pants, and straightened a neon windbreaker over her narrow chest. Its garish pink-and-orange color blocking was dated enough to look fashionable again, but combined with the woman's salt-and-pepper no-nonsense, do-it-yourself haircut, it was clear that the piece hadn't been purchased recently. Overall, she gave the impression that she didn't care what other people thought of her personal style. Penelope was immediately drawn to her.

"Fran Brant," the woman said. She shook Penelope's hand, and her touch was as warm and soft as her large brown eyes behind thick glasses. "I'm so pleased you've decided to write about Ruth Stone. She's been misunderstood for far too long."

The man harrumphed as he offered his hand to Penelope.

"That's an interesting point of discussion, Fran. I'm Dr. Hector Anderson, Professor Emeritus, History Chair, University of British Columbia."

His skin was as dry as his credentials, and his uncovered bald head combined with his short neck reminded Penelope of a beetle. She smiled to shoo away her first impression. Hector was a critical part of the team. Not only could he offer much in the way of local history, but his academic expertise lent the expedition integrity.

"Nice to meet you. Thank you both for joining us. I'm looking forward to hearing your perspectives."

Hector sucked in a breath as if she had just invited him to deliver a lecture. "Don't be guilty of misreading history. Fran and I have had many a discussion about this very topic. Ruth Flanders was no babe in the woods when she married William—"

A loud motor vibrated through the air and Hector was forced to stop speaking. His pained expression at the noise suggested the owner of the vehicle had already fallen into his bad graces. Penelope swallowed hard. There was only one person still to join the group with the courage to ride a motorcycle up the winding highway to Squamish in bad conditions, and it certainly wasn't Philip's mother. The revving stopped abruptly and the three of them stayed silent as footsteps thumped solidly down the narrow wooden plank to the dock. The fog served as an echo chamber for the heavy boots, while shrouding the man in mystery.

"Liam?"

Penelope's voice faltered unexpectedly when his face became clear. Marianne used to call him "soap opera handsome," and Penelope knew why. He was taller than Philip and his dark brown skin glowed with exertion from the ride. His jaw was strong, shadowed by stubble, and his short hair was thick and tightly curled. She could see raindrops sparkling within the strands.

"The one and only. Hello, Penelope. Nice to see you again."

Liam surprised her by stretching out his arms before pulling her into an embrace. They had only met once before, at Marianne's funeral. She'd been expecting a handshake. When he moved away, their faces were close enough to make her feel a frisson in the air between them. His eyes were a darker gradient of his skin. He smelled like a mix of leather and peppery aftershave. Suddenly she remembered that Marianne had said he was the best kisser she had ever known. Her cheeks grew warm again. She could sense Fran's and Hector's presence behind her.

"Thanks for coming," she murmured.

"Happy to," he said with a smile.

Though she knew Liam's experience as the owner of a vineyard might come in handy to determine the location and mechanics of leftover stills from the Stone moonshine operation as Marianne had suggested in her notes, Penelope was now certain that Marianne had included his name on the list for more personal reasons. All Penelope knew of their breakup was that it had been sudden and intense. Marianne had never wanted to talk about the details, but Penelope had guessed that there was unfinished business between them. She wondered how he grappled with the fact that it could never be resolved.

Hector cleared his throat.

"This is Dr. Hector Anderson." Penelope stepped aside to let the two men shake hands, noticing that the professor's head barely reached the top of Liam's shoulders. "And Fran Brant."

Liam smiled as he greeted the older woman, then looked closely at her face after they shook hands. He flashed a perfect white smile in her direction. "Fran Brant. You look familiar to me. Have we met?"

"I have that kind of face," she said. "I believe the captain is waiting for us on the boat."

Liam looked at his watch, a flicker of sheepishness in his eyes as he glanced back at Penelope. "Sorry. Got a bit of a late start this morning."

She hurried to reassure him. "No problem. We're still waiting for one more."

Philip stepped off the boat and approached the group. "Liam! Nice of you to show up."

"I knew you wouldn't leave without the wine, man."

"Good of you to make sure it was properly aged."

"Least I could do," he said with another grin, shrugging his shoulders at the dig. "Want to give me a hand?"

The two men walked together back to the parking lot to collect the case of wine strapped to Liam's bike. Penelope wondered if Liam had ridden his motorcycle the entire five hundred kilometers between his vineyard and Squamish. She found the idea both foolish and slightly sexy. When she and Liam had met, it had been little more than a quick introduction. Still, she couldn't help but be intrigued by him, and she forced her attention back to the other guests.

Penelope, Fran, and Hector made their way to the boat. Penelope stepped on first, then held out a hand for the others. Fran got on confidently, seeming not to notice Penelope's gesture, but Hector leaned heavily on her as he gingerly stepped off the dock. The boat rocked under their feet while they moved to the covered area. Penelope braced herself to avoid stumbling. *It's only a forty-five-minute ride*, she thought, as she settled onto a metal bench beside Fran and opposite Hector. The captain was now at the front of the vessel. Danny and Nina were seated close to him in the spaces nearest the bow. All three were looking fixedly at a map spread out across the steering wheel.

"Well, this should be an interesting weekend," Fran said.

"It's a great group," Penelope replied, relieved when Fran nodded in agreement.

Sweat from navigating the different personalities had dampened her underarms. The boat rocked again with new weight as Philip and Liam returned with their final group member. Penelope mentally kicked herself for not waiting on the dock to greet Estelle. Philip's face was harsh, and he didn't look in Penelope's direction as his mother stepped onto the boat. Estelle sat down beside Hector, directly opposite Penelope. Elegant lapis lazuli studs provided a pop of color that offset her dark clothes. They were nearly the same shade as her eyes, a richer, deeper version of her son's. And her daughter's.

"Hello, Estelle. Welcome aboard," she said.

Estelle looked at her blankly.

"Penelope Berkowitz," she said to jog the woman's memory, and smiled.

Estelle blinked.

"We spoke on the phone."

"Oh, of course." Estelle's lips lifted, though her eyes remained expressionless. "Penelope. Glad to see you have your names straight now. It's so nice to meet you. I am looking forward to hearing all about your work once I get myself organized."

She leaned forward. Her silver hair was cut in a long bob. Her navy-blue down jacket was subtle but beautifully tailored. The brand wasn't one Penelope recognized. It looked European.

"Your lipstick is lovely," Estelle said.

Penelope hoped that her surprise wasn't readily apparent. She had forgotten about applying it that morning.

"My daughter used to wear that shade," Estelle continued. "I found it so flattering on her since it's not a color everyone can wear."

Estelle turned to Philip, who was still standing at the stern, before Penelope could be certain she had been insulted.

"Would you mind gathering my bags, Philip?"

Without a word, Philip stepped back onto the dock and collected the items she had left behind. Once back on the boat, he knelt down to stow the large camera bag and sleek backpack. Penelope noticed they fit nicely in the small space. Estelle thanked him in an offhand way, and Philip met Penelope's eyes with a steely expression.

"All set, Captain," he called to the front of the ship.

"Aye-aye."

Liam and Philip eyed the tightly huddled group inside the covered area. The only seats remaining were at the back of the boat.

"I guess we'll be riding rough," Liam said.

"You seem like you've got a strong constitution, just like my son," Estelle said, leaning back and looking up as she appraised him. "I'm sure a little rain is the least of your worries."

Liam nodded but without his usual grin. Penelope wondered what Marianne had shared with him about her mother. Before she could consider it further, Captain Rod let out a cry.

"Here we go," he shouted.

The rumble of the motor halted any further exchange. The boat jolted to a sudden start the moment Philip and Liam had settled in the back. Penelope's body temperature seemed to drop immediately. The wind whistled in her ears. She watched the fuzzy outline of the boats in the harbor fade away as if they had never existed at all. Despite the fierce conditions, she felt better than she had in days. Though she hadn't played the primary role, assisting Philip with coordinating the boat trip had been incredibly challenging. It was a relief to know the hardest part of the trip was over.

CHAPTER **FIVE**

10:17 A.M.

As she had guessed, the protection offered by the canvas roof was scant. The wind off the water was cold enough to burn Penelope's cheeks and ears. Frigid drops flecked her face like spittle from an overenthusiastic conversation partner. Her jeans—now soaked—sucked at her legs as she looked around at the others. Beside her, Fran was silently sipping from the plastic cup of a thermos she had packed for herself, while Danny and Nina leaned across the gap between the benches in quiet conversation. Across from her, she could hear Hector outlining his academic background to Estelle, who looked unimpressed. Marianne had been so good at making people feel comfortable immediately. The first time they'd met, she'd admired Penelope's earrings as if she could sense that they were pieces of jewelry that defined who Penelope wanted to be. They'd been the first item Penelope had purchased when she'd arrived on the West Coast.

Penelope twisted her cold hands together in her lap, knowing she should say something to welcome and unite them now that they were all together, but the throttle of the engine made it difficult. She decided she would wait until they got to their destination to make a few remarks. It would be easier if Philip was beside her. Estelle made her nervous.

Like his sister, Philip always knew how to make her feel better. In retrospect, there was a devastating logic to their relationship. Marianne had left a hole in both their lives so deep the only solution was to fill it with each other.

Penelope had never dated someone like Philip before. Her last boy-friend had been a coworker from the gym. After their breakup, he had forgotten to pack his birth certificate but remembered to collect his bong. Bong Man was just one of a string of half-hearted failed relationships. When he left, she had mostly given up hope of ever marrying someone. Vancouver was a difficult city in which to meet people. During their weekly phone calls, her mother had begun to suggest that she should come home to find someone. Penelope demurred.

Marianne's friendship had given her a reason to stay, though she still longed for a partner who would surprise her with an impromptu trip to Mexico like her sister's husband had done in their second year of marriage. So the first time she mentioned Philip to her mother, she had casually noted that he was a handsome doctor, a pillar of his community. She had felt like a witch dropping a trail of candy for an eager child, but it was good to think about her family knowing someone like him was by her side. She couldn't help but anticipate the way her mother's eyes would light up when she saw him standing next to her sister's dumpy tow truck–driving husband whose initial romantic gestures had devolved into slaps on her sister's backside when she delivered beer to his man cave in the basement.

Penelope looked toward the back of the boat where Philip and Liam were engaged in conversation. The fog had begun to lift. They hurtled along toward the clearing horizon in a choppy flow over the waves. High above the trees on the shoreline to the right, she spotted a group of turkey vultures circling a tall tree. Their wide black wings—edged with long feathers that looked like fingers in silhouette—swooped and dipped ominously. She squinted, trying to make out if any might be impostors.

It was Marianne who had taught her about the hawks that had learned how to fly with the vultures, blending in until they were ready to feed. Biologists called it aggressive mimicry, but Penelope always thought of it in layman's terms: a wolf in sheep's clothing. The behavior was the central theme of *The Myth of Vultures*—an analogy for the false and hurtful relationships in the book, which had been praised by critics as being "insightful" and "unflinching." Apparently, deception from those closest to them was an idea that many people understood.

As the boat chugged onward, Penelope gasped in awe when the mist lifted completely. The mysterious dark blue velvet expanse of Howe Sound stretched to the south, seemingly limitless and unbounded, though she knew the body of water joined Burrard Inlet at a point only a few dozen kilometers away. The sound was a geological wonder, a crevasse in the earth which had been fed by the ocean for centuries. Its depths plunged down past the point where the light could reach, stretching as far below the surface as the peaks on either side of it rose to the sky. The steep mountains surrounding them humbled her. She marveled at the sights while taking a deep breath of the salty, crisp air. Buoyed by the clear path now before them, she felt brave enough to welcome her guests. She straightened her shoulders before she began, but Fran spoke first.

"What a nice surprise! I was worried that we'd be stuck in the fog all day," she said in a voice that would have been a yell were it not for the background noise of the boat. As if on cue, the captain throttled down, changing the loud thrum of the boat to a low rumble.

"The view is amazing," Penelope agreed.

"I never get tired of Howe Sound," Fran said. "Do you know it well?"

"No. This is my first time on the water. I'm more of a landlubber myself." She frowned slightly at her dorky choice of language, but Fran's expression didn't change, so she continued.

"You live in Squamish, right?"

"Yes. I grew up in Vancouver, but my family owns a cabin just outside town. When I took early retirement, I moved here formally. It's been about three years now."

"It seems like a great place."

Fran nodded then raised her voice so it would be heard from the opposite bench. "Where are you from, Estelle?"

Penelope knew that Fran was at least a decade younger than Philip's mother, but Estelle's polished demeanor contrasted starkly with Fran's tanned face, which was well-worn by the elements and the effects of time. In the harsh light bouncing off the gray ocean, Fran seemed like the older of the two.

"Pardon me?" Estelle said, turning her head from the back of the boat. "I'm so sorry. I was distracted by the landscape."

"I was just wondering where you live?"

Estelle smiled faintly at Fran as if charmed by the antiquated question. "Oh, here and there. I don't really have a fixed address."

"Have you spent much time on the West Coast?"

Estelle's eyes flicked toward her son in the stern. "Not recently."

Fran followed Estelle's gaze, then looked curiously at the other woman but didn't continue with her questions. Hector seemed eager for the break in conversation and jumped in, speaking loudly in Penelope's direction.

"How much do you know about Stone Point, Miss Berkowitz?"

"Penelope, please," she said with a smile. "I've done some reading."

"Who have you read?" Hector asked.

Penelope's mind went blank, but luckily Hector didn't seem to want an answer.

"I only ask because so many historians have taken such a . . . strangely sympathetic view of Ruth Stone in recent years," he said with pursed lips. "For example, I've had many conversations with Fran during meetings with the local naturalists about this area and I was wondering how much of that kind of opinion has colored your own."

Penelope was taken aback by the question. It was hard to understand exactly what Hector was getting at, so she responded as indirectly as possible.

"I've made quite a few visits to the Vancouver Public Library archives for primary sources," Penelope said, smiling again to ease her discomfort. "It's been relatively easy to trace Ruth Stone's early days at the mines. Her mother and her only sibling died during childbirth when Ruth was only ten years old. It seems as though Ruth was taken in by the community, in a sense, so her father could keep working."

"Yes. That wasn't so unusual in those days. Due to high mortality rates, many children were left without mothers," Fran said with a nod.

As Fran continued, Penelope dared a quick glance toward Estelle, whose expression seemed to have darkened.

"The mining camp was small, and families looked out for each other. Her mother was the mining community's only midwife for many years. She likely developed a lot of—"

"Midwife," Hector interrupted dubiously. "Diana Flanders was a lot more than that."

Penelope was confused by the stern look Fran threw in his direction. "Careful, Hector."

"I'm sorry, I feel as though I'm missing something already. Please humor me," Penelope said. "Was Ruth's mother a . . . healer?"

"Her mother was from Brazil, where traditional plant medicine was common," Fran answered. "Diana wasn't the name she was born with— she took it when she came to Canada, to try to integrate into the culture. She was an herbalist and was documented as being a source of remedies and salves to many people in Britannia."

Hector shifted in his seat.

"It must have been so strange for her to live in a mining camp in Canada after growing up in South America," Penelope said.

"Absolutely. But there were people from all over the world at the mining camp, which might have lessened the ostracism slightly," Fran said.

"Unfortunately, not by a lot," Hector said. "I found a church notice from the camp condemning the use of unprescribed medicine by describing it as 'beyond the pale.' It seemed like a veiled reference to Diana's practices, which may not have been medically sound."

Fran snorted. "That's an apt description of the way a brown-skinned woman was regarded at the time."

Penelope glanced toward Liam. He was the only person of color on the boat and would likely be able to provide further insight into their speculation about racial discrimination. Before she could call out to him to ask, Hector jumped in again.

"Let's not get too anachronistic, Fran. That expression has nothing to do with race. A *pale* is a fence post, for Pete's sake," Hector said. "Though I agree that Ruth's less-than-stellar reputation might have been fostered by her mother's unconventional behavior and background."

Penelope was struggling to catch up. In all her research, she had never found a photograph of Ruth Stone. She had no idea the young woman had been of mixed race, though it should have occurred to her given the diverse demographics in Brazil. It went a long way to explain the vitriol that had been directed toward her after the death of William Stone.

"I suppose Ruth's background being considered unsavory was all the more reason her father married her off as a child bride," Estelle said.

Penelope was surprised but pleased that Philip's mother had done some research of her own, though her tone was faintly bitter. She made a note to ask Philip about it later. Had Estelle also been married young? Perhaps that was the reason she had left her family behind. Marianne had always been adamant that she would never have children of her own. Penelope had been sad that her friend's abandonment had made her so certain at such a young age.

Hector interrupted her thoughts.

"*Child bride* is a modern term. Penelope, I hope the intent of this trip is not to write some kind of revisionist history. I get more than enough of that in my department. I make it my duty to discipline careless historians as soon as I see them making those mistakes and I won't stand for it here, either."

"Regardless of the historical period, an unhappy marriage is a prison of its own," Estelle said.

Hector frowned at her. Estelle returned the look with a neutral gaze that Penelope couldn't help but respect. There was a quiet defiance in the placid facial expression that reminded her of Marianne. During one of their weekly writing sessions, Marianne had begun clapping her hands when an older man had snapped his fingers at a server. When the older man had turned to her in surprise, she had calmly told him that she thought he was trying to start a song and she didn't want him to play all alone.

Hector continued.

"In 1920, Ruth Stone was nearly fifteen years old. She would have been considered a grown woman. If anything, she had more privilege than most girls her age. She attended school up until her marriage. She knew how to read and write. It wasn't as if she was a matchstick girl when she arrived at Stone Point. If anything, it would have been more difficult for her to remain unmarried. Being a spinster was no joke in the interwar period."

Penelope was beginning to doubt Marianne's choice in academics. Hector seemed to have a decidedly rigid point of view about women, which might not bode well for the group. Fran straightened her frame like a boxer setting up a combination.

"Surely there were more suitable husbands for her than a man more than three times her age with a history of violence?" Fran said.

"What kind of violence?" Estelle asked.

There was an edge to her voice that Hector didn't seem to notice. His face purpled slightly as he began to speak, but his response was cut off by the gruff words of the boat captain.

"Ruth Stone might have been considered a woman, but I doubt she was ready for the difference between her life up in the mining camp and being the wife of a moonshiner across the sound. The winters are long here, and that one was real bad. It was hard even for the First Nation folks to get across the sound that year, and their boats were built for rough water. She would have been alone for months, with no one but her husband to keep her company."

"Sounds like a nightmare," Nina muttered.

They were the first words she had spoken to the group since they'd left the dock. Penelope looked over at Danny, who was absorbed in a map and appeared not to have heard his wife indirectly disparage the institution of marriage.

"The worst kind," Estelle said quietly.

The captain kept going. Out of the corner of her eye, Penelope saw Fran was looking back and forth between Nina and Estelle with a concerned expression.

"Maybe so. The way they tell it around here is that it was miners who found him once the winter storms passed. Walked up those rock steps, calling William's name, just like normal. They probably thought he was down in a still, maybe out of earshot, so they let themselves into the house. Just a cabin back then, not like what that young couple did to the place later. It's real nice there now. God knows what those two fellas thought when they came upon William Stone's half-frozen body in the woodshed, staring back at them as soon as they opened up that door. They say she kept him out there all season, you know."

Penelope felt another wave of nausea, but this one had nothing to do with the jumping of the boat.

"Because the ground was too hard to bury him?" Nina asked.

"Well. Probably that and the lack of supplies. She ran out of food."

Nina paled and the captain laughed.

Danny chuckled along with Captain Rod. "She ate him?"

"They say she'd only gotten at the leg, but who knows what would have happened if those guys hadn't dragged his body right into their boat and called in the detectives."

Hector spluttered. "I've never seen any documentation about that lurid detail."

The captain laughed again.

"They didn't print that part in the city papers. Hard to keep something like that under wraps in a small town though."

"I suspect the truth has been embellished in the retelling—" Hector began.

The captain turned serious as he interrupted. "I'll tell you this, sir. I get a real bad feeling when I boat out there, and it took some convincing to get me to take this trip. What happened to that Redding couple a few years ago was no joke."

Penelope shivered. Philip had told her that the Squamish property management company that handled the lodge had been thrilled to take their booking. Apparently, there were few tourists who were eager to make the long, cold boat ride across the sound to the site, and she could hardly blame them. The unexplained disappearance of the Reddings was bad enough, but the physical discomfort wasn't helping. Her jeans were now stiff and cold enough to chafe against the soft skin of her thighs every time she moved.

Fran spoke. "It was an awful tragedy. Nobody knows for sure what happened to them, but I've heard some talk. People around here guessed murder–suicide. He could have killed her, then thrown himself right off the bluff where the bodies of the two hired agents were found. It's a thirty-meter drop."

"But what about their . . . remains?" Penelope asked.

"Plenty of bears and cougars around here that could have dragged them off," the captain answered.

Penelope immediately regretted not going back for her bear mace.

"Or maybe the ghost of Ruth Stone got hungry again," Danny noted with an inappropriate smile that the captain didn't return.

"Well, I'll tell you one thing. It's an awful blow to a fella like me to drive a couple to a place like this then never see them again. One day they were here just like you. Then they were gone."

His words wiped the smile off Danny's face. The rest of the group shifted uneasily. The captain pulled the wheel hard to the right and the boat jerked, jostling Penelope's ribs into an unpleasant encounter with Fran's elbow. The sound of the motor increased to the same decibel level as a scream. A crag of orange and brown granite appeared on the western shore to their right.

"There it is," the captain shouted. "Right on schedule."

The wind picked up and the boat heaved over the waves, seeming as reluctant to arrive as Penelope. The motor roared as the rocky cliff loomed beside them. Penelope wondered if it would seem more welcoming if she didn't know how many people had been killed by being pushed off it.

CHAPTER **SIX**

11:07 A.M.

The captain steered the ship in a wide loop toward the long dock that stretched out from the shore like a finger beckoning them closer.

"The wind whips this sandbank like cream over the winter," the captain said. "Looks different every spring. Strange that way. Gotta be careful coming in here. They don't call this Stone Point just for the family name. There's some real jagged rocks down there that can catch a boat by surprise."

The captain gestured to the depths beside the boat. Penelope looked down. Though the water was churning, she caught a glimpse of dark sharp shapes below the surface. That must have been the place where William Stone's father had collected the pieces of wrecks that had sailed unknowingly onto the dangerous hidden shoal.

Penelope braced as they bumped the wooden pier. Philip and Liam hopped out, each carrying a coil of rope to secure the boat to the metal hooks of the dock. Penelope noticed that the captain had not cut the engine. Instead, he cycled the throttle down to a low, slow gear.

"Keep it loose, boys," said Captain Rod. "I'm not staying long."

The waves banged the boat against the dock like a hand pushing it toward the bluff. As Fran, Estelle, and Hector disembarked, Penelope's apprehension grew. Despite her unease, she said a quick thank-you to the captain, then followed the others. She was the leader. She didn't have a choice.

The weathered planks of the dock were slick with moisture, and her heel slid alarmingly on the first step. She focused on keeping her footing as Danny and Nina began to pass the group their bags from the storage area. No one said a word. Penelope wondered if they were all fighting the same dread she was. She took a long, slow breath to try to ease the tension tightening her chest.

"All set?" Captain Rod called as Nina and Danny joined the others.

"Should be," Philip replied, hoisting his backpack over his shoulder and pointing to a figure approaching them from the other end of the dock. "Look! Here comes Neil."

"Okay, I'll be on my way, then." The captain pointed toward the accumulating mass of dark gray clouds in the sky. "That storm's coming and I'd rather not get caught in it. If you need me, your fella's got my number and so does that good man right there." He gave a big wave to the young man closing in on the group. "Otherwise, I'll see you on Monday."

"Thank you," Penelope said. She hoped the others couldn't hear the strain in her voice.

He grinned, revealing teeth yellowed by what she assumed was coffee, tobacco, and time.

"Take care of yourself. And give Ruth Stone my regards."

The captain touched the brim of his worn baseball cap with a wink. Penelope stared at him, unable to respond. The motor revved back to full capacity. Danny tossed the thick rope onto the boat deck as Philip called out a farewell.

The boat sped away fast enough to make Penelope's heart begin to pound again. She turned to Philip, hoping her question seemed more efficient than panicked. "What time is he coming on Monday?"

"Nine a.m.," Philip answered as he lifted a hard-sided case from its place on the dock.

"Better make sure that sat phone is charged up to the gills," Danny said, pointing toward the item in Philip's hand.

Penelope nodded distractedly. Nina gave her a glare, and Penelope realized her silence could be interpreted as a lack of regard for their safety.

"Of course I will," she said before waving at the young man who was now less than a meter away from them.

In response, he pushed his dirty blond hair out of his eyes with a sweeping, contrived gesture that reminded Penelope of the beach scene in *Top Gun*, though it was unlikely Neil had ever seen the movie. Based on Marianne's notes, she knew he was in his early twenties, but his fresh face and wide smile made him look more like a teenager. His hair was shaved close on the sides and his strong thighs pressed against the denim of his jeans. *Another mountain biker*, she thought as Philip placed a hand on the young man's shoulders.

"Everything okay here so far?"

"Yes, sir. We await your every command," Neil said.

The slight twist to his mouth undermined his sincerity. Danny and Liam laughed at Neil's faux deferral to Philip, and the younger man's eyes shone at the positive reception.

"Neil and his girlfriend, Star, will be our staff here," Philip explained to the others. "They've got us covered with all the comforts of home."

His easy demeanor reassured Penelope that her nerves were natural but unfounded. Between Marianne's guidance and Philip's coordination, this trip was well planned. All she had to do was shake her fear and find her story.

"Before we go up, I'm supposed to ask the group to gather for a photograph," Neil said.

"Why?" Fran asked.

Penelope flashed her a grateful look. As far as she knew, the idea had not been part of the itinerary.

"I found some stuff in the lodge to do it, and instructions. It was supposed to be a tradition for new arrivals, before the owners . . . you know."

Neil pulled his finger across his neck, then closed his eyes and stuck his tongue out. The moment he opened them again, he looked eagerly toward Liam and Danny. They both awarded him with another small laugh, though the expressions of most of the rest of the group—particularly Nina—became sterner. Hector was too distracted to notice the hubbub. The older man was staring at the enormous rock behind Neil. Penelope followed his gaze.

The huge granite feature stood over thirty meters high. Penelope knew massive boulders were common in the area, but it was still astonishing to be faced with such enormity. The largest of the rocks—called the Stawamus Chief—was honored by the Squamish and Lil'wat Nations. Climbers came from across the world to ascend routes up its granite walls. But this one was different. At its base was the site where the two hired agents had met their death, and, if the captain's and Fran's theories were correct, it was also the place where Ethan and Simone Redding had perished. Water gathered and dripped off the mottled brown, gray, and orange crag like sweat.

As she stared, she realized that the notches in the rock face were not random.

"What is that?" she asked Hector.

"It's the way up. These stairs were made by William Stone's father. They started as little more than footholds and grips, but year after year he chiseled them into what lies before you. They're a real piece of history," Hector said with reverence.

Penelope and Fran murmured their appreciation, before Estelle addressed Neil.

"Taking a group portrait is an excellent way to start the trip. We can use my camera," Estelle said. "Unless you brought one."

She looked at Neil's empty hands pointedly.

"I was just going to use my phone," he said. "It takes awesome pictures."

"Mine is probably a bit more awesome," Estelle said.

Penelope couldn't tell if the woman was mocking Neil, who seemed oblivious to her sardonic tone. Estelle's face remained neutral and professional as she called out to her son.

"Philip, can you bring my equipment to the end of the dock? Can everyone else gather at the last step? I'll need to set up a tripod, but it won't take long."

Philip nodded without looking in his mother's direction, then skirted around Neil and headed toward the base of the stairs, bags in hand. Fran and Estelle followed. Penelope could hear Fran asking about Estelle's career before they left earshot.

"Will you be carrying our luggage up?" Hector said to Neil.

Penelope looked down at the black wheeled suitcase beside him. It was nearly identical to hers. She cringed inwardly. Neil nodded and grabbed the handles of both suitcases.

"Sure," he said.

"I'll take that one," Penelope said, reaching for her own case.

"It's no problem, ma'am," said Neil.

Penelope sighed at the dubious honorific before relenting. "Thank you."

"You can carry mine, too," Liam said, throwing his heavy backpack at Neil, who dodged it and let it thump onto the dock. Liam laughed as if Neil had passed some kind of test of testosterone.

"I'll come back for that one," Neil said. "If the Stone Witch doesn't get to it first."

Before he finished speaking, their attention was caught by a scuffling sound near the cliff. Fran tensed and reached for the binoculars around her neck. A loose rock rolled down the side of the cliff face and landed on the beach to the left of the group. Penelope tried not to let her trepidation show. Part of her had anticipated something far worse than a fist-sized rock. Neil raised his eyebrows.

"See? She's here, man."

"Well, I don't want to insult her with my underpants. Might as well carry it myself," Liam said with a grin before walking to the pack. He slid the straps over his shoulders, then headed down the dock.

"Good idea," Neil called to his back.

Penelope fell in step with Neil, trying not to flinch at the sound of the small wheels rattling against the slats of the dock.

"How was the first day here, Neil?" Penelope asked. "Everything running smoothly?"

"Yeah, sure," Neil said before pausing and turning toward her. His eyebrows crumpled together, making him look like a little boy. "I mean, it's a bit spooky at night. Kind of glad to have you all here."

"What kind of spooky?"

She pitched her voice to be heard over the waves and the clatter of the suitcases. Neil scanned her face as if trying to gauge her trustworthiness. He seemed to find what he was looking for because he continued in a rush of words so hurried it made his sentences sound like questions.

"Okay, um, I was kind of low-key messing around with stuff because I was bored? I moved a photograph onto the wall, from the shelf above the fireplace, you know? I thought it looked better there. Less, like, creepy. It was an old one, of her and her husband? But then, the next morning, I came into the main lodge and it was above the fireplace again. Right where it had been before."

Penelope rolled her shoulders to release the crawling sensation his story had given her. Stay positive, she told herself. A photograph of Ruth was a real find. There had to be an explanation for the strange incident Neil was describing.

"Could Star have moved it?"

Neil began to answer but was distracted by the sight of a young woman with bright pink hair who had joined the others gathered at the base of the stairs. Estelle was adjusting her tripod about two meters away from the rock.

"Welcome to Stone Point!" the young woman cried as she beamed at the group. "Are we taking the photograph now?"

"Yes, you're just in time. You must be Star," Penelope said.

"I am!" she said happily, before leaping toward Neil and planting a loud kiss on his mouth.

And I'm Penelope, she thought, trying not to take an active dislike to Star. She had always felt uncomfortable around people like her, whose beauty awarded them with an unearned share of confidence. It didn't seem fair to have so much of both when Penelope struggled to maintain an average score in both categories.

"Okay, everyone. Please stand together," said Estelle.

The group moved into position as Estelle directed them to the left and right while gazing through the viewfinder of her camera. Penelope, Star, Fran, and Hector were in the front row and knelt in front of the taller members of the group. Nina, Danny, Philip, Liam, and Neil were excitedly discussing bikes behind them. It was the first time she had heard any enthusiasm in Nina's voice since the couple had greeted her at the dock. Estelle stepped away from the camera with a remote shutter in her hands.

"All set," Estelle said. "I'll count down from three."

"Say cheese," said Philip when his mother joined them.

Penelope pasted a smile on her face as the camera flashed white in her eyes. Estelle took two more shots, then returned to the tripod to check the images.

Hector and Fran immediately turned to the rock behind them and began running their hands over the surface in a way that suggested they were searching for something.

"What are you looking for?" Penelope asked curiously.

Fran's face lit up with excitement.

"There should be an inscription here on the rock."

"Made by the Reddings?" Penelope asked.

Hector's face pinched as if she had given him a lemon to suck on. "No, no, no. I thought you said you had read up on Ruth Stone."

His scolding was interrupted by Fran.

"Now, now, Hector. You have a body of knowledge greater than most books," she said.

Hector gave her a small, pleased smile before continuing his search.

"What kind of message are you looking for?" Penelope whispered to Fran.

"Apparently, there's a carving on the rock that was discovered along with the bodies of the agents. No one knew how long it had been there. It could have been decades old. But the prevailing theory was that it was Ruth herself who carved the words."

"Why would she do that?"

Fran's face became solemn. "As a warning."

"Here it is!" Hector cried.

She moved forward to see what he had found. Others in the group joined them. The riser of the bottom step was decorated with a pattern of lines and symbols. No, not symbols, she realized as her vision sharpened. Words. Hector moved his hand aside to allow them to read the inscription. Danny spoke above the constant crash of the waves on the beach as he read aloud. With each word, his voice deepened with disbelief.

"'Turn back now. This isn't your home. Any who stay will be left all alone,'" he said.

"Friendly place," Liam said after a beat.

"Just wait until you climb those stairs," Neil replied with another grin, though this one looked decidedly shakier.

The call of a seagull cut through the air as the group began to move. It was as hoarse as a scream. Penelope fought the urge to join in.

CHAPTER **SEVEN**

12:11 P.M.

Penelope wasn't sure which part of her hurt more by the time she reached the top step: her lungs or her thighs. She was embarrassed to mention either, though she feared her lack of physical fitness was readily apparent. She had considered herself in relatively good shape back when she took advantage of the free classes offered to recreation center employees. But months of inertia and stress-eating coupled with a new job that consisted mainly of staring at a computer had eroded any gains she'd made. Climbing ten stories of uneven stairs was a humbling experience.

The only people who were behind her were Hector, who had said repeatedly as he walked that no seventy-five-year-old man should be expected to make the climb, and Star, who had stopped every fifteen stairs or so to place a palm on the rock with a mystical expression on her face.

Predictably, Neil, Nina, Danny, Philip, and Liam had bounded up like mountain goats, while Fran and Estelle had gone at a steady pace about a dozen steps ahead of her, involved in quiet conversation for most of the way. She was curious about what common ground Fran had found with Philip's aloof mother and had wanted to join in but was too winded to form a complete sentence. To add insult to injury, she noticed Fran was limping slightly, which made Penelope even less proud about her slow, uninjured pace.

Thankfully, at the top of the stairs the ground was level, and Penelope could pause to catch her breath. In front of her, the trail continued through the varied green, black, and brown of the Douglas fir and cedar forest. The branches were blurred from the drops of rain that clung to them from an earlier storm, making the scene look like one of Emily Carr's watercolor paintings. On her immediate left, an odd, flat concrete pad about four meters across had been poured. It looked recent—certainly not old enough to have been part of the original Stone settlement. Penelope walked over to it. She guessed that the Reddings had laid it, but its purpose—and pentagon shape—was elusive. The view from the pad was stunning: a vista of gray ocean and dark blue mountains, but its unfinished state gave it an ominous air. Sharp rebar rods had been carefully placed upright in all five corners but were only half-buried. The result suggested spikes laid out for a barbaric ritual.

"Cool, right?"

Penelope jumped at the unexpected sound of Star's voice behind her but recovered quickly.

"What's it for?"

"No idea," the young woman said with a shrug. "I've been using it for yoga. I light a small fire before I begin, to bring in all five elements."

Penelope looked at the young woman skeptically.

"You mean four elements?"

Star smiled. "In the Chinese tradition, we count five. Fire, wood, water, earth, and metal. They're all here. My grandfather used to say that places like this have power. Can you feel it?"

Penelope shook her head, wondering if she should apologize for her cultural insensitivity.

"You will," said the young woman as she moved on.

Penelope took another look at the strange site. One edge of the flat pad stood close enough to the cliff to concern her. Had the Reddings factored erosion into their construction plans? She gave the concrete one last glance before continuing up the path. The only thing more unsettling than the jagged spikes sticking out of the ground was being left alone in a place as strange as this.

The dense, dark forest that surrounded the trail made the air seem cooler and damper than it had on the boat. After about five minutes of walking, the forest opened up into a cleared field. Penelope could see three large buildings sitting in a horseshoe shape around a bonfire pit circled by rough wooden benches. The long sides of the two rectangular cedar-shingled buildings closest to her flanked the firepit. Large windows winked at her from the narrow ends of each of the buildings and faced the trees she had just passed through. She knew from the rudimentary site plan sent by the property manager that these were the new bunkhouses built by the Reddings to house anticipated guests. Penelope's mouth dried as she wondered if anyone had stayed here besides the ill-fated couple.

An enormous lodge with windows stretching across most of its front façade loomed in the center of the horseshoe. In the low light, the glass became a wobbly mirror, reflecting the gray sky and standing trees back to the group, while revealing nothing of what was inside. The site plan had shown that the bulk of the building was a new addition to the small cabin Ruth and William Stone had called home. The property manager had seemed to consider the fact that the original structure was kept intact a selling point, but Penelope had found the idea distasteful in theory and even more upsetting now that she stood before it. She wondered why the Reddings had decided to restore and then actively use a building that had, by most accounts, been the site of an unhappy marriage that ended in the death of William Stone. She scanned the structure. Sure enough, at the far-left side, she saw older logs that had faded to gray, likely hewn by William's father from trees cleared from the ground on which she was standing. Unlike the warm orange cedar of the new build, the century-old wood was nearly colorless, and its bark was peeling like a nasty sunburn.

The rest of the group seemed to have scattered to the wind and Penelope kicked herself for not working harder to keep up so she could organize them properly. It was lunchtime and they hadn't given anyone a clear meal plan. Marianne would never have let them go hungry. Her own stomach growled. Already, the trip seemed to be falling apart. She saw Philip seated on the steps located on the long side of the bunkhouse on her left with a smile on his face.

"Hey, beautiful. Sorry to rush off. It felt so good to be out of the city that I got ahead of myself."

"No problem. I think it's time for me to consider getting a little more cardio."

Penelope hoped her face didn't look as blotchy and sweaty as she felt. "Are the others going on a bike ride?"

"Nina, Liam, and Danny wanted to get a ride in. I told the rest of the group to get settled in their rooms and join us in the main lodge when they were ready."

"How did they know which rooms were theirs?"

Philip's smile broadened.

"I told them."

Penelope sighed in relief at the way he had taken charge in the areas where she'd fallen short. They were a good team.

"You didn't want to ride?"

"I would rather be with you. I'll ride tomorrow."

Penelope hugged the compliment to her chest like a security blanket.

"It's nice to see Liam getting along so well with Neil," Penelope said. She liked the idea of the group beginning to gel.

"Yeah. Liam lost a brother when he was younger. Car accident. I wonder if Neil reminds him a bit of that."

Penelope tilted her head, wondering if Philip, too, was thinking of Marianne. He continued speaking.

"I knew that Simone and Ethan Redding built the bunkhouses and upgraded the well system during the renovation, but I've only seen them online. They're even better in real life. There's a generator outside the main lodge that provides power to all the buildings, though the original structures are still heated with wood fireplaces. Each of the bunkhouses has a double suite and three singles. There's a little cabin on the far side of the lodge"—he pointed in the direction of the largest building—"where Star and Neil have settled in. We'll take one of the suites. Nina and Danny have opted to share the other one so they can keep each other updated on any logistical issues that come up."

Penelope was surprised by his phrasing. It made her recall Nina's strange comment on the boat. Were the two of them having marital issues?

"Why wouldn't they want to stay together? Is their marriage not going well?"

Philip looked startled.

"Marriage?"

"Are they not . . . ?"

Philip laughed. "Those two are no more married than Fran and Hector. They're just business partners. Honestly, if they had tied the knot, their marriage would be troubled as hell. Nina's gay."

Penelope's face flushed in embarrassment, which she was certain would not help the sweat blotches subside.

"I guess I just assumed—"

Philip cut her off. "It's okay. But don't make a habit of it. Assumptions can be so dangerous."

His jaw twitched slightly before his smile returned. Penelope was embarrassed. He was right. Assumptions were dangerous, especially for a doctor. It was his duty to get the facts first before forming an opinion.

"Do you want to freshen up? We're on this side." He gestured toward the building behind them. "Bunkhouse A."

"That sounds perfect," she said, noticing that Neil had left her suitcase right outside the door.

"And where will I be sleeping tonight?"

Hector's voice came from behind her, once again making her jump. She needed to eat something. Between the stress of planning and the strenuous activity of the morning, she was on edge. Luckily, Philip's smooth instructions made up for her skittish response.

"You are right across the way in Bunkhouse B, Hector. Choose any single room you want. Might as well get the jump on Liam. Neil left your case by the door."

Hector nodded and started walking across the clearing just as Star came running down the path from the lodge in fitted yoga gear.

"There are sandwiches inside if you want lunch! Dinner is at seven!" she called breathlessly as she flew past them. "I'll be leading a group yoga session on the cliff in twenty minutes."

"Okay, thanks," Penelope replied to her back, amazed that the young woman was able to sprint after climbing the stairs, let alone teach a yoga class.

Philip lowered his voice. "Be glad you're not in the cabin with Star and Neil. The Reddings dug septic systems for the bunkhouses, but the cabin remained as is. Definitely a bit more . . . rustic. No indoor plumbing, just an outhouse."

Penelope stifled an uncharitable giggle at the thought of Star having to squat over a hole in the ground. She reached out a hand to pull Philip to his feet. "Shall we?"

"Thought you'd never ask."

He opened the bunkhouse door, and they entered a white-walled hallway. Directly in front of them was a door with the number two on it.

"Fran is in there," he said quietly, before pointing down the hall to the right. "And my mother is at the end in number four."

Philip turned left toward a door at the end of the hall. "The room between them is empty. I suppose Nina can always move in if Danny snores too loudly."

As he opened the door labeled one, Penelope gasped. The floor-to-ceiling windows she had seen from the outside made the room seem like part of the forest. Green cedar branches framed the edges of the window and dappled the gray light streaming into the room. A rough oatmeal-colored woven carpet covered most of the floor, except for the far right, which was tiled to accommodate a deep claw-foot tub that faced the lush forest. A pocket door to the right of the tub presumably led to an en suite bathroom. Four plush navy pinstriped armchairs were placed in a conversational setting to the left of the tub in front of the window. The elegant arrangement of the furniture made the placement of the king-sized bed seem strange. It was left of the door and had been wedged into the corner so two sides of it were pinned against the walls, though there was more than enough space in the room to pull it out and leave both sides accessible. She decided not to mention it to Philip. The room was gorgeous enough to forgive a small oddity.

"It's beautiful. I may never leave the room. Do you think I could write my next book about breakfast in bed and long baths?"

She sank down onto the soft surface. The thick blanket hugged her in welcome.

But Philip was frowning.

"We'll have to rearrange a little. I don't want to be jammed in a corner when there's all this space."

She was pleased he'd noticed it too.

"It almost seems like someone pushed it aside while cleaning and forgot to move it back," Penelope agreed. She sat up and smiled as Philip walked toward her. "Are you hungry?"

"In a way."

As soon as his lips touched hers, Penelope forgot about the placement of the bed, the stiffness at the front of her thighs, and the niggling worry that she should be entertaining the group. *Happy birthday to me*, she thought. It had been a good idea to go with the sexy underwear. His body was warm and strong. They fit together perfectly just as they always had. Afterward, they lay together. He reached for her hand and for a moment, she forgot why they were there. Slowly, she came back to reality.

"I suppose we should check on the rest of our guests," she said. "How are you feeling about being around your mother, by the way?"

When he didn't respond, she propped herself up on an elbow to look at his face. His even breathing and relaxed expression made her smile. He was asleep. She, on the other hand, felt more awake than she had all day. She slipped off the bed and gathered her clothes before using the toilet and sink. It was probably a good idea to do another head count of her guests. The last thing she wanted to do was lose one of them on the first day of the trip.

CHAPTER **EIGHT**

When Penelope stepped back outside, the whisper of wind had increased to a colder kind of conversation. The clouds looked darker and thicker than they had on the dock, but so far the rain had held off. She slipped her cell phone from her back pocket to check the time, only to realize that she didn't have a signal. *Hopefully the lodge has its own Wi-Fi,* she thought. It was nearly half past one in the afternoon.

"Hello, Penelope," a voice called from a wicker chair at the end of the deck.

Her body didn't tense as it had when Star and Hector had surprised her earlier. She supposed she had Philip to thank for that.

"Hello, Fran," she said. "Would you like some company?"

"I would like nothing more," Fran replied. "I wasn't sure what to do with myself until dinner. How about taking a little stroll with me instead of hunkering down on the porch? My hip starts to ache when I sit for too long."

"That sounds lovely," Penelope said, ignoring the pleas from her aching thighs and empty belly as she followed the older woman off the porch and onto the trail that led up past the right-hand side of the main lodge. Penelope noticed she was still limping slightly.

"Do you have a problem with your hips?"

"Just the one," Fran said. "Combination of old age and a botched surgery. But my father always said that if you can move, you should. Plenty of time for staying still later."

"Sounds like good advice," said Penelope.

As they neared the lodge, she saw a shabby outbuilding to the left of it constructed of the same faded logs as the original section of the main lodge. Gaps of light peeked through the cracks between the wood, making it seem less like a residence and more like a shack. Penelope guessed this was the infamous woodshed. Her skin crawled and she was grateful when Fran took the trail that veered to the right rather than the one leading left, which hugged the shed.

As they continued along, she felt happy for the chance to get to know the older woman better. Fran was an important part of the research she was doing—as both a Squamish local and a celebrated botanist, she had been the most intriguing expert on Marianne's list. Besides, it would be nice to explore the forest. Since moving to the West Coast, she hadn't seen much of anything but the streets of Vancouver.

Penelope had been raised in a medium-sized city surrounded by other medium-sized cities. The closest thing to wilderness that she and her sister had experienced was late summer evenings in a neighborhood park, catching fireflies and slapping mosquitos. Her parents and older sister still lived there in small bungalows on top of what used to be farmland. She knew they would never leave their codependent life of weekly dinners and gossip. When she went home to visit, she felt like even more of an outsider than she had when she was growing up as the second-rate sibling, deeply invested in Harry Potter and the Twilight series. Her quiet love of books had never been able to match her older sister's cheerleading, quarterback boyfriend, and promise rings. But the publishing of her novel had proven—at least to herself—that peaking in high school wasn't so great after all, and books really were cooler than warm beer and being felt up in the back of a Honda Civic.

She realized she was lost in her own thoughts and forced herself to return to the task at hand.

"Have you seen anyone else around?" she asked.

"Estelle went out for a walk earlier, but she didn't seem to want company," Fran said. "The mountain bikers are still out on the trails, I think. Hector and I had lunch together, and he's in the main lodge doing some reading. I'm sure he'll regale us with his insights at dinner." She smiled as Penelope chuckled. "Don't mind Hector. He means well, but men like him are used to having the floor. Not a lot of space for different opinions or approaches, especially when it comes to controversial women."

"Yes, I noticed that," Penelope said wryly.

As they came around the far right of the main building, she saw a squat log cabin with a plume of smoke coming from the chimney in a thin imitation of the billowing clouds pouring from the lodge. It too was made of gray and peeling logs. This must be the cabin where Star and Neil were staying. They began to walk up the right side of the bluff.

"The bikers took the path that goes up past the woodshed on the south side. I figured this one would be best for a walk," said Fran.

"Perfect." Penelope was grateful for the older woman's gentle pace. She caught the clean scent of cedar on a rising gust of wind.

"Storm is coming," Fran said.

"Let's hope it passes us by."

Fran paused and looked up at the bruised sky. "Hope's not going to do much good at this point. It's coming, whether we like it or not."

Penelope's shoulders tightened, but despite that, she nodded amiably, and the two women carried on in companionable silence. Like the trail she'd taken from the concrete pad to the bunkhouses, this path was also shrouded by thick tree branches. Red soil from the decomposition of stumps and fallen trees softened their steps. Fran stopped and knelt down to stare at the ground.

"Is everything okay?" Penelope asked.

"This track . . . it looks like it might have come from a cougar," Fran said.

She brushed debris from a slight depression in the mud. Penelope's heart thudded as the other woman stood up.

"Those animals are dangerous as heck but notoriously shy. Keep talking and it will likely keep its distance."

How likely? Penelope wanted to ask, but the other woman had moved on as if predator cats were nothing to worry about. Penelope tried to adopt a similar approach, but her eyes darted up to the trees around them to ensure something wasn't about to pounce. Once again, she cursed herself for not retrieving that stupid can of mace. Fran pointed out a large crumbling log with several small saplings sprouting from the top.

"That's called a nurse log," she said. "When one tree dies, it gives life to so many others."

"That's quite beautiful," Penelope said. It was nice to celebrate a part of the forest that wasn't trying to kill them.

Fran nodded before beginning up the trail again. The forest was unusually silent of bird calls and scurrying rodents, which Penelope chalked up to the coming storm. The mist in the air, the immensity of the trees, and the lushness of moss and undergrowth made everything feel as damp and dense as the tropical rain forest she had visited during a vacation to Costa Rica many years before. Unlike the warm southern forest, however, there was a chill in the air that seeped through Penelope's jacket, fleece, and long underwear. The lace of her panties dug into the crease of her hip. She wished she had thought to change into a more comfortable pair after these ones had served their purpose.

The path grew steeper, and Penelope's muscles complained. Just as she was about to ask Fran for a break, the trees thinned and the two women found themselves on a windswept ridge overlooking gray crashing waves more than sixty meters below. Penelope was awed by their power and her fragility. If this was where the Reddings had met their end, it made sense that their bodies were never recovered.

"I shouldn't be too hard on Hector," Fran said, distracting Penelope from her morbid thoughts. "He and I have known each other for a long time, and we agree on a lot of things about Ruth Stone. It's true what he said about Ruth's age. It wouldn't have been unusual to be married so young at that time. Especially in a mining community like Britannia."

"I'm certainly glad those days are past," Penelope said.

"The troubling thing for me is that the man she married was fifty years old, which must have been difficult for her. I've often thought about how isolated she was out here. It would have been hard for someone so used to the hustle and bustle of the mining camp. By the time she was a teenager, it had grown to a small village. Many of the remaining photos of Britannia show festivals and parties and dances—there was a real sense of celebration and cohesion in the community, probably because they were so isolated from other places. They even had a beauty pageant; Ruth was crowned the Copper Queen the year before she came to Stone Point. It was quite the honor, and I'm guessing it would have been hard to leave behind all the people she grew up with. She must have been lonely. Maybe that's why she wrote those words on the steps."

Penelope cringed at the memory of the harsh inscription. Loneliness was one thing, but what kind of girl wrote something like that?

"How often would she have been able to visit the camp?"

Fran sighed. "It's only a guess, but I would assume once or twice a year. A lot would have depended on how often her husband let her in the boat when he went to town to deliver his moonshine and pick up supplies. And . . . I don't get the impression that William Stone was the type of man to do his wife or anyone else a lot of favors."

"What do you mean?"

"Well, I'm only telling you this because I know you're writing a novel. This is my version of history, keep in mind, supported by some verifiable facts and some of my own lived experience. It's fairly well documented in the police ledger that the Stones were a rough bunch."

Penelope nodded. So far, Fran was confirming what she already knew.

"In the early days of his marriage, William Stone spent a lot of time in the saloon on Saturday nights, drinking whiskey and going wild. Fist-fighting, mostly, but there was one report of him stabbing a man over a pair of boots."

"Wow."

"The man died and, apparently, William kept a lower profile after that, leaving the bluff alone to make his monthly moonshine deliveries. I have to wonder, if a man is that used to drinking and violence, what happens when there's no one else around but his wife when he gets into his own supply?"

"You think he was violent toward Ruth?"

Penelope's mind started racing as she thought back to her outline and how much more depth she could give it.

"It's just a theory, but why else would a teenager kill a full-grown man? Especially since she probably wasn't able to boat out of here on her own during the winter storms. Sadly, violence against women wasn't uncommon in those days, which is not to say it's vanished in our time. It was just more open and accepted when Ruth was alive. A lot of people held the belief that a man owned his wife and could treat her in whatever way he thought best, and the law supported it. The rule of thumb and all that."

Penelope stared at Fran blankly. In response, the other woman pulled down a thick branch from a cedar tree on the side of the trail.

"The expression used to be a legal precedent. It was permissible to beat your wife with a switch, so long as its width was less than this." She held out her thumb alongside the branch, which was slightly thinner in diameter. "This one would have been fine."

"Good grief."

"Yes, it's excruciating to think about. It's still horrendous for women trying to escape abusive situations these days, but at least the law doesn't actively condone their assault. Not explicitly anyway."

The two women walked in silence for a moment. Ruth's position in life had been worse than Penelope had guessed, but Fran's repeated parallels between the past and the present made Penelope wonder about the woman's own history with men. There were still so many inequities in the world. Another thought prompted by the conversation on the boat came back to her.

"Do you think her race made her more vulnerable?"

Fran nodded. "Absolutely. There wasn't much for law out here—the mine was forced to hire private mercenaries when they needed enforcement, just like the ones who were sent to investigate William's death. The records show that those agents didn't look too kindly toward people of color. Given the fact that she was mixed race, Ruth might have been perceived as Indigenous outside the mining community where she grew up, which would have been anathema at the time."

"So she didn't have many options for a fair trial if she had been responsible for William's death? Even if it was self-defense?"

Fran shook her head. Her eyes were sad.

"No. I doubt that would have been a defense the court would have even considered. Anyway, that's just one theory. Another part of me wonders if people would have viewed William's death differently if Ruth hadn't already been seen as something of an oddity because of the knowledge she could have picked up from her mother, young as she was. It wasn't uncommon for women with the ability to procure plants that could, say, terminate a pregnancy to be deemed a witch by men who wanted their wives to keep popping out babies until their bodies stopped working."

"How could Ruth help other women when she lived all the way out here?"

"Well, I read one diary of a Squamish woman who spoke of paddling to Stone Point in the summer to visit Ruth for a 'treatment.' I'm not sure what condition besides an unwanted pregnancy would be urgent enough to prompt a woman to cross the sound alone. Ruth might have been taught things by her mother that most other women didn't know.

Or maybe she learned it from medicinal healers in the Indigenous bands nearby who dropped by for a taste of William's shine."

Fran stopped and tugged at a tree with scrubby needles and shriveled blueberries.

"Western juniper. This could have been something that Ruth knew about. It's not safe by any stretch of the imagination, but women throughout the centuries have used it to get rid of unwanted pregnancies."

Penelope looked at the plant. She had been careful all her life. Like Marianne, she'd never been driven to have children, though, unlike her friend, she hadn't entirely ruled out the idea. Still, the thought of being at the mercy of her ovulation cycle or—worse yet—her husband's desire was abhorrent.

"Did Ruth and William have any children of their own?"

Fran shook her head.

"No children in the two years they were married. Could be a coincidence, or it could indicate that Ruth knew what she was doing. When I was invited on this trip, I started thinking of how the men in town might view a woman living so far away, using plants as medicine and maybe even birth control. I suspect there would be plenty of men who would be eager to think the worst of Ruth when William was found dead, even if it had nothing to do with her at all. History is written by the victors and all that."

"But what else could have happened to him?"

"Making moonshine is a dangerous business, especially in those days. What if William drank from a poisoned still and the only thing Ruth was guilty of was trying to survive a long winter without enough rations to get by? It's not pretty to think about, but I might do the same thing in her situation."

Penelope shuddered at the idea while nodding in agreement. Fran stopped on the path and turned around, leaning down the slope toward Penelope, obviously excited to share her defense of the young woman.

"And what if the men who found William jumped to the same conclusions as Hector right off the bat? Maybe they were yelling and screaming about Ruth being a murderer while she hid out of sight, trying to determine if they would condemn her right away. When she saw that there was no way she would be judged impartially, maybe she made a plan to kill anyone who came to the bluff looking for her. It's no small feat for a girl to kill two police detectives, but this was her home. She knew it inch by inch. She would have had the advantage at every turn."

The trail narrowed and the two women stopped. The soft ground beneath their feet had turned into hard granite. The path before them was narrower than the span of Penelope's hand. A few meters ahead, it disappeared into nothing more than a rocky ledge.

"I'm not sure it's passable beyond this point," Fran said.

"So there's no way to walk in or out of here on this side?"

"Not as far as I know. From what I could see on the topographical maps, it's just wilderness north of here. If you could find a way down to follow the shoreline, you'd end up at a mill site called Woodfibre, but it would be treacherous to navigate the tide. There are a whole lot of choke points between here and there."

"What about the trail the bikers took?"

"It looked like it dead-ends at a waterfall. I'm hoping to take a walk up there tomorrow if you'd like to join me."

"Yes, that sounds wonderful. I'm so glad we had a chance to talk. You're the first person I've spoken with who didn't arrive here convinced that Ruth Stone was a witch."

Fran smiled. "I'm glad too. Of course, I'm still keeping my bed pushed against two walls tonight."

Penelope was astonished.

"Yours is like that too? I thought that Star or Neil had forgotten to put things back after cleaning the rooms."

Fran laughed softly. "No, it was done on purpose. It's a protective measure, like garlic for vampires."

"For warding off witches?" Penelope couldn't keep the note of incredulity out of her voice.

"Yes," Fran said. "That way, the witch can't walk around your bed when you're sleeping. Three times around, and you're dead by morning. Or so they say."

Penelope rubbed her arms briskly as the comfort Fran had provided during their conversation dissipated. "Do you believe that?"

"I always think that in a place like this, it's better not to take chances."

Penelope bit back her response. The only way they could have truly avoided risk was by not coming at all.

CHAPTER **NINE**

Penelope was happy to feel the ground begin to level beneath her feet as they reached the bottom of the path. The back of the caretakers' cabin came into view. Despite the hardscrabble walk down the slope, she hadn't managed to shake the chill from the misty air. She glanced at her watch. It was nearly six o'clock.

"I'll meet you in the lodge, Fran. I'm going to grab a jacket before I go for dinner."

The older woman nodded agreeably.

"I'll head in now. It'd be best for me to sit down for a spell. Might have overdone it a little," Fran said.

She looked fatigued and her hand was laid protectively on her right hip, which concerned Penelope. The two parted at the front steps of Neil and

Star's cabin. Fran headed to the larger lodge where the windows glowed with a faint light, while Penelope continued down the hill, finding her bearings upon her second view of the bunkhouses. The lodge faced east, which promised a lovely view of the sunrise but would considerably shorten their daylight hours. In the time they had been out on the trail, the sun had slipped behind the bluff she and Fran had climbed. The overcast sky had deepened to charcoal. The evening was quickly creeping toward them.

As she rounded the corner of Bunkhouse B, she saw a dark figure come out the front door with an arm cradled around something. It was difficult to be certain who it was, but the slow, shuffling gait made her nervous.

"Hello?" she called.

The figure jumped, and Penelope heard the sound of breaking glass alongside a cry of alarm that she immediately recognized.

"Oh no!"

She took the steps two at a time to stand beside Hector. A small light by the door of Bunkhouse B cut through the gloaming of sundown. He had a jar nestled in the crook of his elbow, but another lay in pieces at his feet. Sweetness hung in the air.

"Are you all right?"

Hector nodded, looking down with a morose expression at what seemed to be sticky liquid.

"I'm fine, though I can't say the same for my honey. I was bringing it over to you and Philip," he said. "I wanted to say thank you for the invitation. I don't get out much these days."

Penelope was touched and heartbroken as Hector extended the surviving gift toward her. The mason jar looked like it could have come from her grandmother's pantry. In shaky writing on the jar's label were two words: Hector's Nectar.

"It comes from my bees. I keep them. It's a hobby."

She smiled at him gratefully. "Philip and I will share this one. Hector, this is lovely. Thank you so much."

He bobbed his head. "My pleasure."

"And please, head up to the lodge. I'll take care of this."

Hector nodded again. "Thank you. My knees are not what they used to be!"

He walked up the path while she found cleaning supplies in a closet just inside the front door of the bunkhouse. She swept the broken glass as best she could, using the edge of her foot to slide the remaining honey between the slats in the deck boards. Once done, she hurried across the space between the two buildings to grab her coat.

Bunkhouse A felt empty as she opened the front door and moved down the hallway. It was only when she reached for the handle of their room that she realized she had forgotten to ask Philip for a key. She tried the doorknob half-heartedly, certain that Philip would have locked it, and was pleasantly surprised to feel it give way in her hand. She grabbed her fleece off the back of the chair and left the room in hungry anticipation. She wasn't used to skipping meals. As she closed the exterior door, she heard an echoing thud from the other side of the clearing and looked up to see Danny exiting Bunkhouse B. His bright red puffy coat stood out in the gathering gloom.

"Hello, Penelope. Coming to dinner?" Danny called.

Even in the growing dusk, she could see his hair was wet from the shower.

"Yes. I completely forgot to have lunch today. Did you get something to eat?"

"Nina packed us some granola bars for the ride, but a good solid feed would be much appreciated."

They fell into step together, walking past the firepit and up the short path to the lodge. Penelope was pleased to see Danny's demeanor had grown friendlier. Given his occupation as a backcountry ski and hiking guide, she guessed that he probably got cranky when he was forced to sit in the car for long stretches. She wondered if he was always more amenable after he exercised—or when he was separated from his surly wife. Business partner, she corrected herself. It was difficult to dislodge the belief she had held since meeting the two of them. First impressions were always hard for her to shake.

"How was the biking?" she asked.

"Great. We got up to the first ridge and did a few lines before exploring the rest of the grounds. These trails are sweet as. Do you ride?"

"A little," Penelope said, choosing not to admit that the one time she'd gone out with Philip the past summer had terrified her enough to make excuses for the rest of the season.

"You should come up with us tomorrow."

"We'll see. Most of the morning will be filled with our tour around the property. We're hoping you can take us to William's old still and some of the other historical sites. Maybe in the afternoon?"

"Right-o," said Danny. "We got a pretty clear sense of the lay of the land now so it should be fun."

He paused when they were about a meter from the steps to the main building. The music coming from inside the log building was enticing. Between that and the promise of food, she felt as if she was being beckoned inside, but Danny seemed to have something else on his mind. She shifted from foot to foot to ward off the increasing bite in the early spring air as Danny continued.

"Look, Penelope. I just wanted to say thank you. I haven't had time to tell you how much I appreciate you giving Nina another chance after what happened."

Penelope tried not to let her confusion show. The last thing she wanted to do was offend Danny just when he seemed to be warming up to her.

"Of course," she said, playing along as she tried to figure out what he was talking about.

Danny nodded twice then took a deep breath.

"What happened was an accident. Anyone who has any experience with the mountains knows that it could have happened to anyone. But there's always going to be some people who don't trust me because I'm not Canadian. There's a real locals-only mentality in the guiding community. Rumors spread fast in our industry and people were already yapping on about my inexperience. What happened just added fuel to the fire."

Danny's bitter words got Penelope's mind racing. She racked her mind trying to figure out what he was talking about. Had Marianne mentioned something about the guides to her? She didn't recall anything from her friend's notes or past conversations. She knew that the three of them had been on a skiing trip the winter before she and Marianne had met, but she couldn't remember hearing any details about the trip. Now, the thought of her forgetting something important about her friend—or worse yet failing to learn something that had mattered—made Penelope feel as if she was losing her all over again.

The darkness was blurring the edges of Danny's strong features, but his expression was expectant. She had to say something, but she had always struggled during times of heavy emotions. Her mother's voice echoed in her head: Play nice, Penelope.

"Accidents happen," she responded, hoping the firmness in her voice overcame the cliché. "I'm just happy to have you here."

Danny's shoulders slumped as if he'd been holding his breath.

"That means the world to me. It's been a real battle trying to get back in good standing after this whole business. There's always somebody waiting to tear you down, right? This trip is going to help us heaps with our credibility. I know Marianne would never have wanted us to fail. Nina was one of her closest friends, after all."

Penelope was taken back again. This time, she was too surprised to hide it.

"She was?"

Danny nodded absently. "Yeah, they all went to school together. Since they were little."

Penelope nodded, though her mouth was dry. She hadn't realized the two women had been close. Marianne had never mentioned Nina to her at all. Danny kept talking.

"Thanks, mate. Look, don't mention this to Nina, okay? She doesn't like to talk about it. I just wanted to say I appreciate you giving us a second chance."

He turned and walked up the steps. Penelope hurried behind. He opened the large wooden door and held it for her. Something seemed to have been settled between them, though Penelope wasn't exactly sure what it was.

CHAPTER **TEN**

6:13 P.M.

There were so many bright-colored waterproof jackets hung on hooks in the large entry room that for a fleeting moment, Penelope felt as if she was walking into a field of flowers. Danny hung his red coat up and Penelope hooked her black one beside the lime-green soft shell she knew belonged to Philip. They walked across the tiled floor toward a set of large French doors paneled in polished golden wood. Two brooms were placed upside down on either side of the entrance, like knights guarding a gate, but she didn't have time to give them much thought. The moment Danny swung the doors open, she gasped in amazement at the stunning sight. Someone—likely the Reddings—had constructed a wall of smooth stone that stretched from floor to ceiling around an in-set cast-iron fireplace, where a fire crackled comfortingly in the grate. The mottled gray, white, and orange slabs looked like the hulking rock wall that had greeted them upon arrival. Thankfully, as far as she could tell, no ominous messages had been carved into these.

Her eye was drawn immediately to the framed image on the mantel above the fire. She approached it with excitement, guessing this was the photograph that Neil had mentioned earlier. Judging by the clothing worn, it looked to be a grainy reproduction of an image from the 1920s. Ruth and William Stone were seated on the same rock steps that the group had climbed that afternoon. Ruth was a frail-looking, dark-haired, dark-eyed girl in a simple shift dress. William's heavy arm hung around her thin shoulders possessively. His features were somewhat obscured by a crumpled newsboy cap, but his mouth had a cruel downturn. Penelope gave him little more than a quick glance, as it was the girl's face that commanded attention. Though her small frame had been positioned to emphasize a connection between the couple, the young girl's expression was fierce, nearly angry. When Penelope met Ruth's gaze, the girl's eyes burned. Clearly, the Reddings had decided to honor history by placing the photo prominently in the room, but Ruth's raw stare was a haunting addition to an otherwise beautiful and welcoming space.

Penelope blinked and looked around the room to shake the unsettled feeling the photo had given her. The exposed blond wood of the rafters had been polished and oiled so they shone in the warm firelight, and the white walls and open layout gave the room an expansive feeling. Hector was seated on one of the four tan armchairs grouped to the left of the fireplace with his head in a book and didn't notice her looking over at him. Two sets of high shelves flanked a large window behind him. A grandfather clock stood beside the fireplace; its second hand ticking reverently. There was a door on the wall to Penelope's left, presumably leading to the original sections of Ruth and William's cabin. She wondered how those rooms compared to the stunning work that the Reddings had done in the new build.

Danny strode to a wooden table where Nina was standing over what looked like an unfolded map. More maps hung on the back wall beside another set of shelves that contained two phones that reminded her of a slightly larger version of the portable handheld telephone she'd had as a kid—Penelope assumed they must be the satellite phones. There was another framed photo on the wall, but Penelope was too far away to be able to tell who was in it. She made her way toward the large seating arrangement where the others had gathered.

Fran and Liam occupied two cream-colored armchairs on either side of the fireplace, while Philip was seated on a matching couch facing the flickering flames. At the far right of the room, Estelle was working at a desk beside Neil. Both were staring at a computer monitor that looked to be about ten years old. An enormous photo printer hummed beside them.

Penelope returned Philip's smile as she settled onto the seat beside him. The high ceilings provided the perfect acoustics for the powerful piano keystrokes of Glenn Gould, which reminded her fondly of the first time Philip had introduced her to his favorite pianist after an exquisite home-cooked meal at his place. It had been their first real date and had lasted the entire weekend. Behind her, tucked into a small alcove at the farthest back corner of the room was an old-fashioned pinball machine, a blond wooden bar, and a pool table. The Reddings had clearly intended the space as a lounge for all their guests to gather and entertain themselves.

"Fran was telling us about your walk in the woods before Liam regaled us with his wild adventures," Philip said as he took Penelope's hand in his. "Sounds like there are fantastic trails all over the bluff. She said you went back to the bunkhouse to grab a jacket. I'm sorry that you couldn't get in."

"I got in no problem. The door was open."

Confusion scored lines across Philip's forehead. "That's odd. I swear I locked it."

Fran spoke to Liam before Penelope could respond.

"How far did you make it up the trail?" Fran asked. "We just did a short up and down. It gets dark early here and neither of us wanted to miss dinner. The trail became pretty faint up by the ravine."

She smiled at Penelope as Liam answered.

"Yeah, same. We got to just above the first ridge," Liam said. "There's an awesome view from up there. You can see nearly the whole sound. We got in two downhill lines before it got dark."

His cheeks had the same glow of exertion she'd seen after his motorcycle trip and his dark eyes gleamed in the reflecting light of the fire. He looked so handsome that Penelope squeezed Philip's hand a little tighter. Nina and then Danny pulled two armchairs over from the arrangement near Hector and settled down beside the group.

"I was looking for a detailed map of the entire bluff, but no luck," Nina said. "We tried to track one down before we left the mainland, but the development was so new that all we could get our hands on was a rudimentary site plan. I was hoping that the Reddings had put something together for guests, but I can't seem to find anything."

"Guess we'll have to draw it out ourselves," Philip said, and Danny chuckled. Nina frowned.

"It seems odd that there's nothing around," Nina began before being interrupted by Star entering the room from the door Penelope had noticed earlier.

A slow smile spread across Liam's face as Star approached. The young woman stopped beside Fran's armrest with a pad of paper in hand. "Dinner will be served in thirty minutes," she said. "Can I offer you all a pre-meal cocktail?" She raised the pad theatrically as if taking orders at a truck stop, giggling at the last word like it was funny for her to be asking. A long row of beaded bracelets slid down her slender arm, and her silky pink hair danced along with her laughter.

Penelope was once again glad it was Star who had to use the outhouse of all the people on the trip. And she was grateful that Philip wasn't gazing at Star's pretty face with the same rapture as Liam. The sparkle Penelope saw in Liam's eyes made her wonder if another woman had something to do with him leaving Marianne.

Liam responded to Star first. "I brought a case of my limited release cabernet if there are any wine drinkers in the house."

"I would love to try a glass," said Fran.

Danny and Nina nodded as well.

"Why not?" Penelope said, not wanting to interfere with the growing cohesion of the group.

"So, everyone is having wine," Star said brightly. "That makes it easy."

"I would prefer tea, if there is an option to dissent. I don't care much for New World wines," said Estelle dryly.

Liam looked away from Star for the first time since she'd arrived, to face Estelle. "That's because you haven't tried mine yet."

Estelle ignored him. "Tea, please."

Luckily the awkward exchange was interrupted by Neil coming up behind Estelle, holding a piece of thick cardstock in his hand. Penelope could see that whatever it was, it was sturdy enough to stand on its own. Liam looked at Estelle sideways, then back toward Star.

"I'll have her portion," he winked.

"Of course," Star said, dutifully making a note on her pad.

Penelope couldn't help but wonder what it said. Extra wine for the hot guy?

"Perhaps you could check with Hector as well?" Philip said softly, gesturing toward the corner where the older man still sat with a book in his hand.

Star giggled again. "Oh, sure. I didn't even see him there."

The group quieted as she asked him the same question.

"Star is an unusual name," Hector responded. "Where does it come from?"

"I'm an unusual woman," she said with a toss of her head. "So, wine then?"

Hector sighed at the rebuff. "That would be fine, dear."

Philip looked at Penelope with pain in his eyes. She knew he hated seeing Star being so dismissive to Hector. Before she could redirect the conversation, Liam rose.

"Why don't I help you, Star?"

"That would be awesome." She turned toward Liam with an expression that was one blink away from eyelash batting. Her tone couldn't have been more different from the one she'd just used with Hector. "I don't, like, know where anything is."

"Me neither. We're a great match," Liam said as they walked toward the kitchen. "Are you from around here?"

It was a shame that the acoustics in the room were so good. Liam's brazen flirting with a woman at least ten years younger than him was disrespectful at best, Penelope thought. She was glad Neil didn't seem to be paying attention. A quarrel between her caretakers would make the evening more complicated.

"I grew up in West Van," Star said just before the two of them slipped through the side door.

That fit, Penelope thought. West Van was the wealthiest part of Vancouver. So not only was Star pretty and young, she was also rich. She wondered why Star accepted the offer of such a menial role on the trip if she didn't need the money. Before Penelope could puzzle further, Neil flipped the piece of paper he was holding over to show a newly printed photograph of the group to everyone.

"Come on, guys, this has got to be displayed, right? Maybe if we show Ruth how happy we are to be here, she'll let us stay," Neil said.

His irreverence revealed no trace of the worry he'd shared with her earlier, though Penelope suspected that was its source. She looked at the photograph in his hand starting with her own face. Luckily, the picture had been taken before her hair had become plastered to her head with sweat, and her kneeling position didn't accentuate her extra pounds. She scanned the rest of the group, amazed at how Estelle had captured the essence of each person. Danny and Nina looked determined, while Liam's radiant smile was almost exuberant. Fran gave off a pleasant enthusiasm that provided balance to Hector's stern expression. Star's and Neil's raised peace fingers and cockeyed grins were playful and lighthearted. In the center, Philip's calm smile seemed to hold the group together.

"What a great shot!" she said.

"You're very talented," Fran echoed.

Estelle smiled at them both in turn and Penelope felt a rush of warmth at being able to crack the woman's cold demeanor. No matter how terrible a mother Estelle had been, Fran seemed to be growing fond of her, which made Penelope want to get to know her better as well. Like Danny had said, maybe everyone deserved a second chance.

"Pretty cool, right?" Neil said, grinning. "This printer is the shit."

Philip shook his head slightly as Estelle rolled her eyes. So much for changing the woman's mood.

"I'm not sure I'd put it quite like that. It's decent equipment, though dreadfully out of date. We did manage to coax a relatively acceptable print out of it," Estelle said.

Neil didn't seem bothered by Estelle's correction as he gaped at the photo.

"I'm surprised it wasn't liquidated after the property was sold," said Danny.

"As far as I know, everything was left as is," Philip said. "The property managers are still hoping to sell this place as a turnkey operation to new owners. Is that correct, Hector?"

Penelope was touched by his attempt to include the older man after Star's rude treatment of him.

"That is absolutely correct, Philip. It's been on the market since a year or so after the Reddings disappeared, however. They're not exactly lining up for it."

Philip chuckled and Hector responded with a small laugh of his own.

"I can see the listing now," Neil said. "Fully functioning West Coast eco-lodge. Comes with your very own private witch."

This time, nobody laughed. Philip pointed in the direction of the fireplace.

"Should we place the photo on the mantel beside the Stones?"

"Definitely," said Neil, not waiting for the group's assent before crossing the room to the crackling fire.

He positioned the photograph on the narrow ledge using the rock wall as a support. Penelope found the juxtaposition between Ruth's penetrating stare and the goofy expressions on some of the faces in their group jarring.

"Neil was right earlier. It was supposed to be a tradition," said Nina in a low voice that suggested Penelope was not the only one who was unnerved.

"What do you mean?" Danny asked.

"Look at this," Nina said as she walked over to the corner and took down the framed photograph Penelope hadn't been able to see clearly earlier. She came back to the group and showed them the image. "The Reddings posed in the same way, on the steps. They must have wanted all their groups to go home with a picture of their own to remember their stay."

Penelope stared at the attractive couple in their early thirties. Their eyes gleamed with hope, and both looked healthy and strong. It was hard to imagine how people like that could just disappear.

"Would anyone mind if I put this alongside the others?" Nina spoke tentatively, and Penelope suddenly wondered if the woman's standoffishness came from shyness rather than snobbery.

"I think that would be a wonderful way to honor them," she said. The sight of the Reddings brought Marianne to her mind. Just like them, Marianne had been lost to those who loved her well before her time.

Nina propped the third photo on the mantel. As Penelope stared at the missing couple, the fire caught on a knot in the wood and sent sparks flying.

Ruth's eyes lit up as the reflection danced across the glass.

CHAPTER **ELEVEN**

Star's call from the kitchen interrupted the somber mood in the room. Penelope was grateful for the reprieve. Before she'd arrived here, the myth of the Stone Witch and the mystery of the Reddings had seemed remote and fascinating. Now it was bordering on eerie. Of course, it didn't help that she was nearly weak-kneed from hunger.

"Oops. Guess I'm supposed to be working," Neil said.

He ducked out the door through which Liam and Star had left. As he passed, Hector looked up from his book and cleared his throat. The group turned in his direction and he didn't hesitate before seizing the floor.

"Did anyone else notice the brooms placed on either side of the door of the entryway?"

Penelope nodded. His question stirred up her earlier curiosity about the strange choice in decoration.

"I did. It seemed like an odd way to store them," she said.

"Oh, storage was most certainly not the intention. Those brooms were placed there to serve a purpose," Hector said.

He paused and smiled before continuing to speak.

"As soon as I saw them, I remembered a Slavic tradition that was likely the root of our own Western superstition of witches riding helter-skelter through the air on broomsticks. In Eastern Europe, witches took the form of household spirits, not necessarily malicious, unless the household contained chaos. If it did, the witch would start whistling. If discord continued, she would begin breaking dishes. If anger in the home increased and she felt she was being treated badly, she could gain enough power to threaten bodily harm, even kill. One sure way to mark her presence in the house was the sight of wet footprints on the floor."

Penelope shivered.

"So people had to hit her with a broom?" Danny asked.

He looked like he was having a hard time keeping a straight face.

Hector frowned. "Upside-down brooms placed by the door were a way of making her leave: it was said to help families sweep her out of the house."

"Wet marks on the floor seem like a pretty vague way to track a witch in these parts," Danny said with a laugh he could no longer contain. "We live in a coastal climate, mate. Aren't there wet footprints in everyone's house?" ·

Hector looked offended at Danny's glibness as he responded.

"My guess is that most people don't wear their footwear into the bedroom. Most of the time, the prints led directly toward a bed. If she was provoked enough . . ." He paused again to give Danny a reprimanding gaze. "The witch was said to enter the rooms of people sleeping and sit on their chests, either cutting off their breath with her weight, or in some cases, actively trying to strangle them."

Danny's smile faded. No one spoke until Fran's quiet voice cut in.

"That sounds a lot like sleep paralysis," she said. "I've heard people describe it as waking up from a nightmare only to find an old woman perched on top of them."

Hector beamed as if she had passed an oral exam. Penelope looked closely at the older woman. Something in her voice suggested she was describing her own experience. She wondered if Fran had difficulty sleeping, like she did.

"Exactly. Many historians have attributed the Slavic myths as a way to describe precisely that phenomenon."

Once again, the group fell silent. After a moment, Hector continued to address them as he would a group of students.

"On the note of witch lore, does anyone have anything specific to contribute regarding the myths that surround the Stone Witch?"

Danny raised his eyebrows in Nina's direction, but her face remained blank.

"Don't worry, Hector," Philip answered. "I've filled Penelope in on all the old ghost stories I heard growing up. At least three people we knew said they got violently ill paddling past Stone Point on kayaking trips. We used to tell each other that the Stone Witch was everywhere, especially at Halloween. Penelope is well prepared for this mission. We'll be lighting the sacrificial bonfire at midnight."

"History is nothing to make light of," Hector said, his mouth pursed.

Philip backtracked immediately. "I'm sorry. Forgive my stupid sense of humor. I'm letting my childhood memories get in the way of our research." He put his arm around Penelope's shoulder to apologize to her as well. The weight of it felt good.

"Did you bring that book with you?" Nina asked, pointing to the hardcover that Hector still held in his hand. "*The History of the Occult?*"

"No," Hector said. "Perhaps unsurprisingly, whoever stocked this library had a fascination with witchcraft and legend."

"I suppose we aren't the first people to try to track down the truth about Ruth Stone," said Fran lightly as the door to the dining room opened once again and Liam came out brandishing a tray.

"But hopefully we'll be the ones who succeed and put the falsehoods surrounding her existence to bed," Hector said.

"Who wants wine?" Liam interrupted as he set down the tray and waved the glass he'd already filled for himself.

Despite Hector's perturbed expression, Penelope accepted a drink gratefully. Previously, she had questioned Marianne's logic in including Liam on the guest list, uncertain that a winemaker would add much to the trip. As she held the glass stem in her hand, she realized how foolish she had been.

"To our success," she said, as she raised her glass in Hector's direction.

The old man appeared slightly mollified and did the same in return. She clinked glasses with Philip and the others before taking a long drink.

After the toast was made, Philip excused himself to check on dinner, while the rest of the group settled comfortably in smaller conversational clusters around the well-appointed room. Penelope took another large swallow of wine. She was still slightly unsettled by Hector's creepy myths and Danny's confusing gratitude. Hopefully the drink's effects would help her enjoy getting to know the group. Well, most of them anyway. She was happy Star was tucked safely away in the kitchen.

Liam drifted over to her. "What do you think of the wine?"

"It's delicious," she said, fervently hoping he wouldn't ask her for more detail.

The truth was, she couldn't tell a five-dollar bottle from what Liam had poured. Though she had welcomed the first sips, she now felt envious of Estelle's steaming mug of tea as the wine began to slosh around her empty stomach. Alcohol often gave her a headache and trouble sleeping. She couldn't afford a restless night when they had so much to do the following day. Liam, on the other hand, didn't appear to have the same reluctance toward booze. The flush on his cheeks had deepened from its earlier post-exercise glow. In comparison to his nearly empty glass, hers looked almost untouched.

"You're a writer, right? Have you checked the shelves to see if your book is here?"

Liam grinned mischievously, and despite her earlier irritation at the man's flirtatious behavior, Penelope couldn't help but respond with a smile of her own.

"I haven't."

"What? That's the first thing I would have done. You're a big deal."

Despite the glassy sheen that was developing in his eyes, Liam was easily one of the most handsome men she had ever met, with his broad shoulders and perfect smile. Those thoughts made her feel disloyal to Philip, who had yet to reappear, as well as to her memory of Marianne. She started to make an excuse to exit the conversation when Neil stepped out of the dining room doorway, bowing dramatically.

"Dinner is served," Neil said, rising with a flourish of his hand.

A whiff of acrid smoke reached her nose. Penelope hoped that Star hadn't burned their first meal together. Breaking bread at the beginning of a trip was so important to set the mood for the days to follow. She wanted everything to be perfect tonight.

Penelope was surprised to hear Fran laugh at his dramatic affectation. Neil grinned in her direction. The boy definitely liked an audience.

As she began to move toward the door, indicating with a tilt of her head for Liam to join her, she saw the tall man hesitate. Instead of following, he made his way to the shelves where Hector had been sitting. The older man was walking toward the dining room with the rest of the group.

"Let's find your book," Liam said.

Penelope reluctantly moved to his side as Hector disappeared through the door with Neil close behind, leaving the two of them alone. Though the smell of dinner wasn't promising, she was so hungry, and she hoped indulging Liam wouldn't take too long.

Liam traced the spines of the books with his finger. "What's it called?"

"*The Myth of Vultures*," Nina said from behind her.

Penelope jumped. She hadn't realized the woman was still there. Liam's expression became quizzical. Penelope wasn't sure if it was because of Nina's unexpected presence or the name of her book. Before she could explain that it was named for the central metaphor of the novel, rather than an esoteric biology textbook, Nina joined them, staring Penelope full in the face.

"That is the title, right?"

There was an edge to the woman's voice that made Penelope nervous.

"That's right. Have you read it?"

Nina nodded. "I couldn't put it down. That last scene was—"

Before Nina could finish her assessment of the most brutal part of the entire plot, Liam cried out triumphantly.

"Ah-ha!"

He held the book high. Penelope felt a flush of pride. Two and a half months after publication, she still wasn't used to her name being on the cover of anything, and she was surprised to find it on any bookshelf, let alone one in such a remote location.

"It's always nice to see it out in the world," she said softly.

"I can only imagine how much it means to you to have your words published," Nina said.

"It is an amazing feeling." The wine in Penelope's system made her bold enough to bring up Marianne. "Writing is how I met Marianne. We regularly shared our work."

Nina blinked slowly. "Is that right?"

Her question seemed odd, but Penelope pressed on.

"I didn't know the two of you knew each other so well," Penelope said, her blood racing. Was she imagining it or had Nina paled slightly?

"That's how Marianne was," said Nina. "She liked to keep her friends separate. There was nothing she hated more than people playing favorites. She didn't like giving anyone anything but her full attention."

Penelope had never thought of Marianne in that way, but it rang true. There was a deep intimacy in Nina's insight, although she seemed cooler than ever. Before Penelope could pursue the idea, Liam spoke again.

"Marianne, Schmarianne," he said. "We're talking about your book!"

Penelope couldn't help but look at him with distaste at his dismissal of someone who had been so important to all three of them. He didn't seem to notice.

"Can't wait to read it. I'll start tonight," he said brightly.

She swallowed her annoyance at the man's callousness toward her closest friend and his former partner. As an author and the trip's host, she owed it to him to show graciousness.

"I am excited to hear your thoughts," she said. "Shall we?"

Once again she motioned toward the dining room. This time, Liam nodded and strode ahead, holding the door open for her. As she walked into the room, she heard a bloodcurdling scream.

CHAPTER **TWELVE**

7:26 P.M.

"SURPRISE!"

The group stared at her expectantly. She fought the urge to run out of the room. Her heart was pounding hard enough to make it feel like something was gulping inside her chest. Instead of fleeing, she smiled weakly while surreptitiously taking a long slow breath to calm herself. As she exhaled, she looked from one shining face to another before landing on Philip. His expression was joyful, and she couldn't help but smile back. The breathing had worked. She was now relaxed enough to take in the efforts he had made for her.

The large dining room was filled with silver and red helium balloons. A banner wishing her a happy birthday had been strung across the wall facing the door. A dozen more balloons had been grouped together and tied onto a chair at the head of the table, which was clearly reserved for her. There was a huge centerpiece of flowers full of her late winter favorites: blood-red lilies and golden roses. Philip motioned for her to sit.

"He told me to stall you," Liam said with glee. "I knew a writer would never be able to resist talking about her books."

Penelope hoped that Liam's mischaracterization wouldn't make the others think badly of her. In truth, she rarely spoke about her own work.

"I can't believe you knew it was my birthday," she said to Philip as he pulled the guest of honor chair out for her.

"I know a lot of things," he said playfully. He brushed her lips with a kiss before she seated herself. "Happy birthday, Penny."

His wishes were echoed by the others. She thanked them profusely, letting their warm words ease the chill left behind by the nickname. Between that and Liam's insistence on reading her book, Marianne was taking over her thoughts at a moment when she should be focused on the present.

The conversation swelled around her as Neil circled with another full bottle of Liam's wine. She took a moment to further inspect the room. The huge farmhouse table was big enough to seat at least twelve people and filled most of the space. To her right sat Philip, and beside him Danny, Nina, and Estelle. Liam slid into the seat directly on her left, beside Hector. Fran smiled at her from her position on the far side of the older man. The beauty of the decorations couldn't completely distract from the shabbiness of the dining room. The interior of the log walls was in the same dismal condition she had noticed earlier on the exterior. The peeling, gray bark made the room seem abandoned. She wondered if the Reddings had intended the original structure to remain so dreary to underline its history or if they had disappeared before they could complete their plans to restore it.

A cold draft blew across her arm, leaving a ripple of gooseflesh behind. She wondered what purpose this room had served for Ruth and William. The original structure had been much too small to have a space reserved exclusively for dining. Could this have been their bedroom? The idea of eating in the same room where Ruth and William Stone had slept made her blood tingle.

Neil deposited a small plate in front of her on which a charred piece of toast languished beneath a watery tomato mixture glopped on top of tough-looking greens. One small nibble at the edge of the toast confirmed that it had been the source of the burning smell from before. She set her fork back down and opted to pick up her newly filled glass of red wine rather than try to eat any more. Better a headache than a stomachache. She noticed many of the others had pushed their plates aside as well. The emptiness in her body caused by hunger seemed to expand into her chest cavity. Had her unerring trust in the plans laid by Philip been a mistake? Star and Neil seemed hopeless at the jobs he had assigned them. Had he been right to ask them to serve as caretakers?

At least Danny, Liam, and Philip were munching away on the dreary appetizer, though that was probably more a testament to the amount of wine the three of them had consumed than proof of the dish's edibility. Their conversation about craft breweries in Vancouver had become loud and boisterous. Each of them could barely finish a sentence before another jumped in with a new recommendation. She knew the group wasn't likely to get quieter so, after another sip to give her courage, she stood up at the head of the table. Maybe they hadn't secured the perfect caretakers, but she could still save the evening. Philip raised his glass as the others quieted down, and then looked up at her in expectant silence.

"Thank you for joining me on Stone Point," she said. "Tonight is a special night but it's just the beginning of our adventure."

The bright smiles of Fran, Philip, and Liam buoyed her spirits. Even Nina and Estelle looked a little pleased. Danny threw a wink in her direction. She focused on the positivity rather than the one negative note. Hector's expression had soured after he tried a bite of his bruschetta.

"As you now know, this trip happened to coincide with my birthday and I'm so grateful to Philip for this lovely celebration."

She smiled at her boyfriend, and her heart swelled with something close to love.

"Let's drink to more happy coincidences as we work together to un-cover the history of a fascinating woman. To Ruth Stone!"

As the rest of the group extended their glasses toward her, a loud bang made her jump before she could raise her own. She fought to catch her breath as an empty string with the rubbery remnants of a popped balloon snaked down to the floor from the bunch in the corner. The tense moment that followed was broken by Liam.

"Philip! Told you not to buy the cheap balloons," he teased.

Fran laughed, and the taut atmosphere in the room eased as Danny and Philip joined in. Though Estelle still looked pained, for a moment, the celebratory mood seemed intact.

Then, one by one, it began again. This time, it was everywhere. Penelope flinched and recoiled as the balloons exploded in rapid succession all around. Estelle whimpered. It was impossible to anticipate where the next sharp crack would come from as the balloons popped in an erratic way, first in one corner and then the next. Penelope's eyes darted from one place to the next. The seconds of silence between the reports were almost worse than the noise itself, lulling her into thinking that no more balloons would fail. The moment she convinced herself that it was over, another balloon burst. The awful clamor seemed to go on and on. Then it was over as suddenly as it had begun. She glanced around the room. There was not a single intact balloon left. Instead of the floating joyful colors she had seen when she came in, the chairs, walls, and floor were now draped with broken skins and useless string.

Danny drained the glass in front of him before speaking.

"Jesus," he muttered. "That's a first."

Philip reached for Penelope's hand.

"No kidding," he said. His words were nonchalant, but his skin was clammy.

"Guess Neil was right after all," said Liam. "The witch is coming, ladies and gentlemen."

He followed the dire pronouncement with a grin, downed the last of his wine, and motioned to Neil for a refill. Philip did the same, though with noticeably less bravado. In the silence, the ticktock of an unnoticed clock to her right became audible. She looked over and saw a duplicate of the five-foot-tall, wooden grandfather clock from the main room. She cleared her throat, struggling to find a way to reassure the group, when Hector spoke.

"You can't honestly believe that a set of weak balloons and a change in air pressure can somehow be attributed to a young girl who has been dead for presumably nearly one hundred years, can you?" he asked.

"Isn't that what we're here to find out?" Danny replied. "I mean, I'm pretty agnostic with this kind of stuff, but so far, the Stone Witch hasn't failed to disappoint. Besides, you're the one who pointed out the witchy broom décor."

"It was likely embedded in the Reddings' marketing plan to try and revive some latent superstitions. Surely it was to their advantage to have visitors buying into the myth of the property," replied Hector.

"Maybe they didn't put those brooms up for effect," said Liam in a mock spooky tone. "Maybe they used them to fly around at night looking for Ruth!"

Hector frowned.

"Well, one of the Reddings must have been worried about something. The bookshelf is full of information about witches. Maybe what happened to them wasn't an accident," said Estelle. She hugged herself tightly as she looked quickly toward Philip, then back down at her plate.

No one responded. Penelope wondered if, like her, they were all wondering about the young couple and whether their ending had been more ghastly than any of them had previously considered. Star entered the room from the swinging door to the kitchen. Her enthusiastic expression contrasted starkly with the others.

"How was the bruschetta?"

She beamed, seeming not to notice that most of it remained untouched. She pronounced it with a hard k sound, which Penelope tried not to let get under her skin. She knew it was correct, but it still seemed overly pretentious.

"Delicious," Liam said, turning a smile to her.

The rest of the group shifted uncomfortably as Star gazed at them, clearly hoping for additional affirmation. Nobody volunteered.

"Perhaps we can move on to the next course?" Penelope said.

"Of course!" said Star.

She and Neil began clearing the plates.

Philip looked at her gratefully. "Hopefully we can salvage at least one part of your birthday celebration with a decent main course."

Penelope was heartened by his words. The underlying sentiment was so similar to her own thoughts after the bruschetta disaster. No matter what happened, she was grateful to have him by her side. Hector interrupted her thoughts.

"And I'm assuming we'll have a large breakfast first thing tomorrow morning. We must have full bellies before we head down to William's old still. I'd like to have the group up and at 'em by seven a.m. sharp," he said in a pedantic tone.

Penelope rushed to speak before anyone else could respond with derision.

"Hector, that's a great point, though I'm not sure we need to leave quite so early."

She turned to Danny with a quick smile of encouragement before addressing the rest of the group.

"After breakfast tomorrow morning, I hope that each of you will join us for a guided tour of the site's features with Danny and Nina. Hector and Fran will be generously providing the historical and ecological context. Danny or Nina, is there anything we need to know in terms of clothing or preparations?"

Danny stepped in smoothly and the rest of the group looked at him. They needed something to focus on, Penelope realized. It was going to be critical to keep this group on a tight leash if she wanted to stay on track. She willed herself to channel Marianne's leadership skills as Danny began his instructions.

"Righto. I'd like everyone to gather at the firepit between the two bunkhouses at eight a.m."

Hector huffed slightly, but Penelope tried to ignore it. Danny continued.

"Nina and I did a tour of the property at the end of our bike ride, and we've pinned down the location of the original structures that remain on the bluff: this room being one of them, as well as the woodshed, the kitchen, the cabin, the rock steps, and William's still."

"Estelle has graciously offered to take photographs along the way," Penelope added. "So don't forget to wear your best fleece jackets."

Fran smiled and Estelle acknowledged the statement with a nod. Her face still looked drawn, and Penelope wondered if the strange incident with the balloons had taken more out of the older woman than she'd assumed.

"And Liam will give a brief talk on how the still functioned," Philip said.

"Eight a.m.?" Liam groaned. "Not sure how intelligently I'll be speaking at that time of day."

Estelle eyed his empty wineglass pointedly. "Well, there's one way to—"

Penelope interrupted. "I'm looking forward to a great discussion about Ruth and William. Fran has already shared some early intriguing thoughts with me."

"Do tell," Hector said, as Fran caught Penelope's eye with a knowing look that said she grasped how hard Penelope was working to redirect the group.

Fran began to explain. "Like many of you, I've been doing a lot of research into Ruth Stone. We are so lucky to be living in a time when women's stories can be rediscovered and retold—"

This time, it was Hector who interrupted.

"I'm going to stop you there, Fran, before you make the mistake I fear you are heading toward. We must be so careful, as historians, to not let our present reality blur our understanding of the past. Too many of my colleagues have been guilty of this kind of anachronism, dredging up recent history and trying to look at it with our current values and social norms. It's not useful or productive."

He paused as the kitchen door opened again and both Star and Neil entered with steaming bowls of chili.

"And now, the main course," Neil said.

"It's vegetarian," Star said eagerly, evidently missing Hector and Danny's disapproving expressions as they stared at the collection of steaming beans and veggies in front of them.

Penelope waited until the rest of the group was served before dipping her spoon into her own bowl. She was relieved to find the chili bland but edible. Her appetite returned and she dug in. The room filled with the sound of clinking silverware. Neil and Star returned to the kitchen, likely to enjoy a quick bowl of the same meal themselves.

Philip looked over at her and whispered, "Thank god she got one thing right."

Penelope nodded as she saw Danny lean toward Nina, presumably to mention something along the same lines. She hoped that full bellies would help dissipate any lingering unease in the room. After several moments, Hector pushed his empty bowl aside and began to speak as if there had been no interruption. Penelope sighed inwardly.

"As I was saying, Ruth Stone was no feminist hero, at least, not one I'd want to lay any claim to. She managed to kill two men who were hired almost exclusively for their ability to act as mercenaries, which is no small feat. In fact, her ability to do so perplexes me and many others to this day. Autopsies were rudimentary back then, so no clear cause of death was determined, but it looked as though both had somehow fallen from the top of the cliff to the beach."

"Couldn't she have taken them by surprise and . . . whoosh?" Danny asked.

His boisterous spirits seemed to have returned.

"Perhaps," Hector acknowledged. "But there's another macabre detail to share. Further to the discussion we had on the boat, it bears mentioning exactly where William Stone's body was found. It was placed directly inside the door of the woodshed, propped against the wall. Now, I don't know if you noticed the shoddy construction of the shed, but the wood is not tightly notched together. There are large gaps between the logs, making the interior of the shed quite visible. The first men on the scene— William's potential customers—spotted William's body from the exterior of the building. They said it seemed as if his eyes were staring at them as they approached. They were so taken aback by the fact that the dead man had been put in a place where Ruth would have seen him many times a day while collecting wood during all the long months of the winter that both wrote it down separately in their journals and reported it in their interviews with the police. Can you imagine? Having a dead man staring at you as you do your daily chores? Perhaps tomorrow morning we should start at the woodshed so we can get a true sense of Ruth Stone."

No one answered as they contemplated the gruesome information. Estelle seemed to have grown paler. Nina stared at her half-finished bowl before laying her spoon down. Fran also placed her fork gently beside her plate before she spoke.

"Perhaps he wasn't moved there," she said. "Perhaps he died there. You've noted that no coroner could determine exact cause of death in those days. It could have been a heart attack. In the photograph, he looks so much larger than her. It begs belief that she could move him anywhere. In fact, that seems to me to be the fatal flaw in the argument that she was responsible for his death. If anything, his location was all the more tragic in my mind if it forced Ruth to perform the basic needs of survival with her dead husband watching her."

Hector rushed to respond.

"Oh, but Fran, those journals I alluded to contained more than just a description of William's location. Both men also noted two sets of tracks leading to the shed. One set was small and the prints were precise. Running behind them was a long row of parallel lines, as if the dead man had been dragged nearly half a mile up a hill so the corpse could be placed in the most gruesome way possible. The men said it seemed as if it had been done for their benefit: a warning of what they could expect."

Fran looked at him skeptically.

"How on earth could those marks have been preserved in the ground over an entire winter season? And if it was performative placement, why would she have tucked him inside the shed? Why not down at the point where anyone boating by would see him?"

Before Hector could answer, a loud cry and clatter came from the kitchen. Philip jumped up with Liam, Danny, and Nina close behind. The moment before they reached the door, Neil emerged through it, nearly smashing Philip square in the face. Neil's wide eyes made him look younger than his years.

"It's Star," he said urgently. "She's hurt."

CHAPTER **THIRTEEN**

8:37 P.M.

Penelope rushed to join the others in the small kitchen, taking in the room with a whirling glance as she tried to determine how badly Star was injured. It too was built with the rough wooden logs that made up the walls of the dining room. Star was mewing sadly on the left side of the room, beside a huge cistern and a large washing basin full of sudsy water. An ancient potbellied stove with a flat top for cooking sat directly in front of her.

Penelope felt her knees weaken at the sight of the young woman's right hand, which she was clutching palm side up. Across the tender flesh, Penelope could see a wide patch of unnerving pink bordered by tendrils of curling skin retreating from what looked like a nasty burn. She darted her eyes to the exterior door on the right where the woodshed was situated. It was stupid, but she half expected William Stone to be staring lifelessly at her through the kitchen's dark, uncovered window and was relieved to see nothing but the distorted contents of the room reflecting at her. As she looked back toward Star, she noticed a black cast-iron pan on the particle board floor beside the young woman, along with shards of a broken plate.

Philip calmly asked Star to lay her hand in his before turning to Nina.

"There's a first aid kit beside the satellite phones. Can you grab it?"

She nodded and ran out of the room as Philip focused on Star.

"What happened?"

Star's face had whitened so much that the soft skin under her eyes looked slightly purple. She spoke rapidly.

"I was putting a plate away and I wanted to put the pan back too. It was clean, no one had used it, it was just sitting on the table. When I grabbed the handle, it was so hot I couldn't hold on to it, like it had been on the stove for hours. It hurts so much—oh god, am I going to have a scar?"

Penelope watched Philip. Though his demeanor remained professional, she could see the tension tightening his jaw. Was he thinking of Marianne's scar as well? She'd always assumed he was there when Marianne had got it. Penelope quickly dismissed the thought, and glanced at Neil, who was shaking his head as he stared at Star. He immediately noticed her gaze.

"Don't look at me. I didn't touch the pan!" He addressed the next words directly to his girlfriend. "I was scraping the plates, Star. I swear."

Star looked at him wordlessly. She seemed paler than before. Liam spoke up.

"Listen, I know I'm not the only one who could use another drink, right? Neil? You in?"

Neil looked down despondently. No one else answered.

"Okay, I'll go check on the others," Liam said before grabbing a half-empty bottle from the dented stainless-steel table in the center of the room and exiting the kitchen. Half-full, Penelope corrected herself. She needed to stay optimistic.

"Can someone find Star a chair?" Philip asked before turning back to the young woman. "I'm going to need to examine your hand. Is that okay?"

Star nodded.

"See what I mean? It's just like the photo thing," Neil said. His misery seemed to have made him frantic. "Crazy things keep happening here. But now it's getting dangerous."

"Okay, okay, how it happened is not important right now," Danny said as he pulled an old wooden chair from a corner to a spot beside the worktable. He guided Star into it, being careful to avoid touching her burned hand.

Penelope was struck by the measured approach he was taking to the situation. He appeared to be a man who was accustomed to being self-possessed in a time of crisis. She remembered the accident he'd mentioned earlier and wondered how much practice he'd had with injuries. Or worse yet, fatalities.

Danny's competent kindness continued. "Star, take a deep breath. This is a solvable problem, nothing that Philip hasn't seen before. He may look a bit goofy, but he knows what he's doing."

Star smiled wanly as Philip rolled his eyes at her in exaggerated good humor. Nina reentered the room with a small white case in hand. A bright red cross was painted on the front. She set it down on the worktable. The tarnished surface was covered in vegetable peelings and cans with sharp lids peeled partially back. The young couple were sorely lacking in kitchen skills. She should have insisted on checking their credentials. Why on earth had Marianne wanted them on the trip?

"I'm going to clean this up for you now, Star," Philip said. "Is that okay?"

His voice was gentle as he helped the shaken woman lay her hand on a section of the table that Nina had quickly cleared. The burn was deepening from pale pink to an angry fuchsia. It ran diagonally over the length of her palm, the edges of skin around it whitening unnaturally. Despite Penelope's intentions to be a stalwart nurse, she recoiled at the sight. Philip looked over at her, seeming to clock her squeamishness.

"Penelope, can you go and tell the others she's okay? She needs a covering on this but it's no big deal."

"Definitely," she said, perhaps a touch too quickly. She tried to recover by returning Danny's nod with a curt one of her own as she walked toward the door.

"Neil, do you want a glass of water?" Penelope heard Nina's unexpectedly warm voice as she left the room. "Sometimes it helps with shock."

She sounded as calm as Philip and Danny, as if she too had learned how to process panic in difficult situations. Philip had once told her that part of his medical training was focused on helping students become emotionally detached during emergencies. He noted, however, that it wasn't until he experienced real-life encounters with tragedy and death on the job that he'd learned to deal with it. His insight made her wonder what the two guides had seen in their lives.

When she returned to the dining room, Fran, Estelle, and Hector looked at her expectantly.

"Everything's okay. Star burned her hand. Philip is helping her," Penelope said. She was pleased that her voice sounded steady despite the way the chili was bouncing around in her stomach.

"A burn? Good lord," Estelle said. Her voice seemed fainter than usual as she continued. "That sounds serious. Is it serious?"

Fran laid a hand on the other woman's forearm, which was resting on the table, and Estelle looked at her with what seemed to be a grateful expression. Penelope was amazed that Fran had managed to gain the guarded woman's trust in such a short time. She would never have dared to comfort Estelle in such a way. Then again, Fran didn't have to worry about the complex woman potentially becoming her mother-in-law. Fran's voice stopped Penelope from getting too far ahead of herself. She and Philip had only been together for a short time. They hadn't begun speaking of marriage, though the idea was a sweet possibility for Penelope. She hoped Philip felt the same.

"Should we call the captain back to pick her up early?" Fran asked.

Penelope shook her head. "It's not an emergency. With a little rest, she should be fine, though I'm not sure how much cooking she'll be able to do."

Estelle and Hector both raised their eyebrows as if relieved by the possibility.

"Perhaps we can take turns making meals for the rest of the weekend," Fran said.

"I'm not much of a cook," Estelle said.

"Neither is Star," Hector replied.

Estelle laughed, though she had the grace to try to disguise it as a cough. Penelope looked down so no one would see the agreement in her eyes. *Star's injury is a blessing in disguise*, she thought, as she noticed how many bowls on the table had been left unfinished.

"You're sure it's not something we need to deal with right away?" Estelle asked.

Her eyes had clouded again and her expression was hard to read. Was it fatigue? Or regret? Marianne's old injury returned to Penelope's mind. Had Estelle been present when her daughter was hurt? Was there something she could have done to help her? Penelope realized she was taking too long to respond.

"No, Philip has it under control," she said.

Fran patted Estelle's arm. "We are lucky to have your son on-site."

Penelope was surprised again that Fran had worked out the relationship between Philip and Estelle so quickly, but she supposed it was natural for the two women to have shared basic information as they got to know each other. Estelle nodded and straightened her shoulders. The vulnerability that had softened her features disappeared.

"You're right, Fran. We are lucky indeed."

Penelope made a mental note to relay Estelle's vote of confidence to Philip later. Though their initial encounters had been strained, the trip might still provide a chance for the two to heal the rift between them before it was too late. The door to the kitchen swung open. Danny, Nina, and Neil entered the room, each carrying an unopened bottle of champagne and wearing decidedly more positive expressions than they had in the kitchen. The sight of the alcohol made her realize that Liam was nowhere to be seen.

"Star is saved and more importantly, so is the party. The doctor sent us in with a prescription for everyone!" Danny said, brandishing a bottle.

As if on cue, Liam bounded through the door from the main room and cheered as Philip and Star entered from the kitchen. Star raised her hand, which was wrapped in a loose white bandage. She smiled fuzzily at the group.

"How are you doing, Star?" Fran asked.

"Well, I've never been burned like that before. It was a bit . . . gross, but luckily, Philip bandaged me up. He had some pain medication too."

"Which you will not be mixing with alcohol," Philip said with a smile. He turned to the group. "The others, however, are free to try and rescue our evening from its various mishaps. Shall we have a final birthday toast to Penelope in the main room?"

Fran, Estelle, and Hector rose, and the group walked into the large space. Penelope felt better once they returned to the beautiful room. Without discussion, everyone headed straight to the seating arrangement near the maps where they had begun the night and began chatting quietly as Danny and Liam popped the bottles and filled the flutes that Neil had collected from the kitchen. Philip leaned toward Penelope. The tightness in his jaw had disappeared and he looked relaxed again.

"I'm sorry that this evening didn't go as planned. I was hoping to make your birthday a little more special and a little less disastrous."

He touched the pad of his thumb to her lower lip affectionately. She treasured the sensation for a moment before moving her lips close to his ear.

"I had a wonderful day," she whispered. "Besides, my birthday doesn't officially end until midnight."

He chuckled low in his throat. "Very true."

He kissed her and she smiled after he pulled away. She liked knowing that the best was yet to come.

The fire crackled soothingly. Penelope leaned back against the soft fabric of the couch, casually eavesdropping on the conversation between

Philip, Danny, Liam, and Nina about plans for an afternoon ride the following day. Liam's wine must be good, she realized. Instead of a headache, the two glasses she had consumed had left her feeling pleasantly blurry. The adrenaline from Star's accident began to wear off and in its place was a deep but not unpleasant exhaustion. She took the last sip from her glass and set it on the side table, about to signal to Philip that it was time to say good night, when Danny coughed.

At first she thought nothing of it. Then he coughed again, louder this time. The sound was forced and dry. The others around him also seemed to sense that something was wrong. They paused their conversation to let him catch his breath. He held up a hand as the cough returned. This time, Penelope could see that it shook his entire body. His breath sounded labored as he tried to pull air in. He stood up. Philip rose to his feet at the same time.

"Danny, are you okay?"

He clutched the base of his neck, seemingly unable to answer.

"He's allergic to peanuts!" Nina cried before rounding on Star. "Did you put peanuts in the food?"

Star shook her head vigorously, her pink hair shivering behind her. Danny's face began to redden and his eyes bulged.

"Does he have an EpiPen?" Philip asked urgently.

"It's in his coat!" Nina cried.

Philip tore out of the room. Veins threaded across Danny's forehead as his coughs continued, racking his body. His breathing became more labored. Spittle flew from his mouth. He began to claw at his throat. A desperate whistle replaced the violent coughing spasms. Penelope stood alongside Nina and Liam, watching in horror as Danny's face turned from red to blue. Now, she couldn't hear any breaths at all.

"He's running out of air!!" Nina yelled.

Penelope rushed toward the kitchen, hoping there was something in the first aid kit that could help. She sped through both sets of doors and grabbed the case, returning to the group in seconds. She ripped open the kit with such haste that packages of gauze and alcohol wipes flew over the floor. Fran and Estelle hurried to pick them up, as if tidying the supplies could help Danny. Philip returned brandishing a needle. He jabbed it into Danny's thigh right through his jeans. Danny's arms flailed wildly, knocking Nina down. Penelope couldn't take her eyes off the two men as Philip pressed the plunger.

Fran had tears running down her cheeks as Danny slumped to the floor. Liam grabbed his feet, helping Philip lay him down. Danny's head lolled. Philip and Liam pushed him onto his side, and Philip positioned Danny's arm straight out from his shoulder to brace him in place. Penelope could see that Danny's back was not rising and falling with breath. The room was deadly silent, save the occasional snap of the fire consuming a log, and Philip's hurried gasps.

Suddenly Danny jerked upright, sucking in air like he'd been drowning. His eyes were still closed, but he was breathing. Penelope's thoughts had been replaced by a single repeating phrase. *He's alive. He's alive. He's alive.* His swollen face began to deflate before their eyes.

Philip spoke in a gruff voice. "We're not out of the woods yet. If there are undigested allergens in his system, he might have another reaction. He's going to need to get out of here tonight."

"So it was an allergic reaction?" Neil asked frantically.

Philip nodded.

"That's my best guess," he said.

Fran sniffled beside Penelope. Star burst into tears.

"Philip told me not to add peanuts. I swear to god, I checked the labels. I made sure," Star sobbed. "Please, you have to believe me."

Fran put her arms around Star as her weeping rendered the rest of her speech indecipherable.

"It's okay. We all make mistakes. It will be okay," Fran said.

She led Star to the sitting area by the dining room door. Penelope met Philip's eyes and saw fear in them. How could a boat get to them tonight? It was pitch-black outside and she could hear the rattling tree branches as the wind gathered force. Philip left the group without a word and walked to the radio in the corner. He picked up the handset and began speaking.

"Mayday, mayday. We need emergency services to Stone Point. Immediately. Mayday."

In the silence that followed his plea, Penelope realized someone was missing. She turned to the grandfather clock to see Nina's crumpled body at its base. There was a red pool around her head matched by a crimson stain on the sharp corner.

"Nina!" she cried. "We have to help Nina!"

CHAPTER **FOURTEEN**

9:47 P.M.

Fran distracted her from the new ugly words playing over and over in her mind—*she's dead, she's dead, she's dead*—by handing her a mug of something warm. Penelope looked up at Fran's kind face and nodded in thanks before the older woman settled down on the couch opposite her between Estelle and Hector. In the wake of Danny's collapse and Nina's death, most of the group had drifted back to the large seating arrangement, but it no longer felt cozy and safe despite Philip's arm around her shoulder. The dead woman on the floor cast a chill in the air.

The shadows in the corners seemed deeper and darker than they had before. She dared a glance at the stained base of the grandfather clock where Nina's body still lay but averted her gaze almost immediately to its face, only to see that the hands were no longer moving. In horror,

Penelope realized that they had stopped at 9:23 p.m., what must have been the precise moment of Nina's death.

Shock blanketed her senses. Hours before, the flickering light of the fire had seemed so reassuring. Now it reminded her of the sacrificial bonfire Philip had joked about earlier. She struggled to concentrate. Heavy fatigue pulled at her as if she was a child who had stayed up too late and was drifting in and out of the waking world as the grown-ups spoke. When she lifted the warm earthenware mug to her nose, the clean scent of peppermint helped her focus on the conversation rising and falling around her. She sipped the steaming liquid, keeping her eyes fixed on Hector, Estelle, and Fran rather than Nina's lifeless body stretched out on the floor behind them.

"We can't just keep her there," Estelle said sharply.

An awful thought darted into Penelope's mind. *There's always the woodshed.* She almost choked on her second sip of tea. Philip mistook the sound for a sob and rubbed her back. He looked like he had aged ten years since he'd checked Nina's pulse to confirm that the blow to her head had stopped her heart.

"We're sending out regular calls on the sat phone. All we can do is keep trying," he said.

In the corner, Neil repeated their mayday call into the radio.

"What about Bunkhouse B? There's a spare room in there. Liam and Hector, you okay with that?" Philip suggested.

"We can't keep a dead body in a bed intended for people to sleep in," Estelle said. "Philip, this is unacceptable. May I have a word with you alone?"

Her eyes were fierce, no longer vulnerable as they had been during his rescue of Star. Penelope dully remembered thinking that the young woman's burn would be the worst thing they would have to endure over the weekend. Philip's expression grew stormy in response to his mother. He met her gaze. For a moment, his eyes burned with the same intensity as Ruth Stone's in the portrait above the fireplace. Then the anger seemed to be replaced by hopelessness as he shrugged.

"Whatever you want to say to me, you can say to the group," he answered.

Though his voice was calm, Estelle shrank back from him as if he had yelled. None of the others seemed to notice.

"Should we consult Danny?" Fran asked. "They were business partners."

Estelle, Fran, and Hector all turned to look at the corner by the pinball machine where they had laid Danny down with pillows and a blanket. His eyelids flickered with restless sleep. For the moment, he was incapable of making the decision about what to do with Nina's body.

Star's sobbing increased from the reading corner closest to the dining room, where Liam had repositioned an armchair to nestle beside hers. Penelope did her best to ignore her plaintive cry of *I didn't*. At some point, she would have to start checking the labels of the food items Star had used. She was reluctant to confirm the group's suspicion that the young woman had been careless, but there was no other possible explanation. Danny's reaction and Nina's subsequent accidental death were likely on Star's hands. Once Penelope proved it, the young woman would have to live with it for the rest of her life. Penelope felt sorry for her, even as she ached to get far away from Star and Stone Point as soon as possible, but she knew there was little chance that a boat could be sent before tomorrow morning. The wind was blowing harder against the windows than it had been an hour before.

She set down her tea and readied herself to rise, when Hector cleared his throat.

"What about the woodshed?" he proposed.

Penelope was deeply grateful that she had not been the one to suggest it when she saw the disgust flicker across Estelle's face.

Philip rushed in to support the older man. "It seems like the best possible place," he agreed.

"We could take out a stack of wood so no one has to go back inside until the rescue boat arrives," Penelope said in a muted tone.

Fran sighed, seeming to feel as conflicted as Penelope. "I agree, though something about it is so awful."

Estelle spoke again. Her bitterness seemed to have increased.

"This whole evening has been horrific. I'm going to leave you to carry out whatever plan you see fit. Hopefully the boat will be here first thing." She stood without making eye contact, smoothing down the front of her pants, which were now as wrinkled as Hector's face.

"Take care of yourself," Fran said with compassion.

Hector stood as well. Exhaustion made him sway in place.

"Hector, you should get some rest too," said Philip.

His body quivered in relief. "Are you certain I can't assist you?"

"Absolutely. We can handle it," Penelope said. "Good night."

"I suppose it is best for me to accompany Estelle down the path," he said.

Estelle acknowledged Hector's attempt at chivalry with a curt nod, though she probably knew just as well as Penelope did that he needed assistance more than her.

"Is there anything I can do to help?" Fran said, rising as the others began walking across the room.

"No, Fran. We appreciate it. But Neil, Liam, and I can get it done," Philip said.

Penelope swallowed hard at the idea of the three men carrying Nina's body.

Fran blinked slowly, then nodded. "I'll see you in the morning, then. Good luck to you."

"Thank you, Fran," Penelope said, standing to embrace the woman. "Tomorrow will be a better day."

Fran looked into her eyes. "I hope so."

As Fran left, Philip and Penelope walked to the small desk in the corner of the room where Neil was sending a repeater signal over the sat phone.

"Anything you can tell us?" Philip asked.

"It seems different from last night. It's not picking up a signal," Neil answered dully.

"A tower could be down," Philip replied.

"What do you mean?" Penelope asked.

Philip tried to reassure her. "It happens sometimes in remote locations. A tree falling can knock out the whole system. I'm sure that's why the Reddings provided a backup phone. They'll work better out in the open—we might be able to bounce a signal off a different satellite tower. Neil, do you mind taking them down to the beach? You should be able to get through to someone down there. Bring both just in case one is faulty."

Neil agreed, then rose from the chair with the two bulky phones in hand and began moving to the door. Their size was almost comical compared to modern cell phones. Penelope was reminded of the shoe phone from a detective show she had watched in reruns as a young child, and then felt troubled by the inanity of her thoughts. She wondered if inappropriate humor was a sign of shock.

"I'll go with you," Penelope said, even though the idea of traipsing through the dark forest made her head swim. "You don't have to do this alone."

"That's not necessary. I've got this dialed," Neil said with a bravado he seemed to have learned from action-hero movies.

Neil walked out of the room without a glance toward his girlfriend. Another sob from the corner caught Penelope's attention. She and Philip looked over at Star and Liam.

"I'll talk to her while you take Nina . . . out of here."

She grabbed a small notepad and pen from the desk in front of her.

"Thank you," he said. "I can't believe this has all gone so wrong so quickly."

"It's not your fault, Philip. Please try not to listen to Estelle. I know the woodshed isn't an ideal location, but we're doing the best we can. If she can't understand that, I don't know how we can convince her otherwise."

"My mother has always liked to blame others when problems arise. She was the same at Marianne's funeral, don't you remember? She screamed at the florist because he showed up with pale yellow lilies instead of white ones."

Her memory was muddy. She hadn't noticed Estelle's outburst at the funeral, but that wasn't worth mentioning. Her behavior tonight had been horrendous enough.

"She's difficult for sure," Penelope agreed. "Unresolved issues."

Philip's face darkened. "Well, if anyone deserves those, it's her."

"What do you mean?"

He looked away. "Listen, you invited her on this trip and I let it happen because I know she's talented. But my mother has a temper when provoked. She didn't . . . she didn't always treat us well when we were kids. She always told us cruelty is for the cruel when she punished us."

That was what Marianne used to say. Penelope swallowed hard. Marianne's scar and Estelle's shaken reaction to Star's injury came to her mind. Had Estelle caused the injury to her child? Is that why Marianne had never told her what happened?

"Was she . . . abusive to you?" Penelope asked.

Philip winced before answering. "Yes."

"Oh, Philip. I'm so sorry."

He rubbed his jaw hard enough to redden the skin beneath the stubble beginning to form. His eyes were still dark and his face was so rigid with pain that it looked close to fury. But as quickly as it had come, the emotion faded and he met her eyes with gratitude.

"Thanks. I don't know why I'm talking about this now. It's a story for another time."

She gave his hand a squeeze, wishing there was more she could do—and more she could ask—but he was right. This was not the time.

"Let's get this over with, so we can both try to get some sleep tonight," she said.

She kept her fingers locked in his and her eyes straight ahead as they walked across the large room to Star and Liam. Star's face was in her hands and the man was now kneeling before her. Penelope was struck by how inappropriate, almost sexual his positioning was. Liam must be drunker than she'd realized.

"Star?" Penelope said as gently as she could. "How are you doing?"

When she pulled her hands from her face, Star was nearly unrecognizable as the pretty young woman they'd met earlier. Red blotches covered her swollen eyelids and cheeks, and her nostrils were unpleasantly damp.

"I just . . . can't believe it." Her voice hitched around another sob as she covered her eyes again.

"Liam, can I have a word?" Philip said, taking a step backward and indicating the other man should join him.

Liam rose unsteadily.

"Sure thing," he said with a slight slur before the two of them took a few steps away.

Penelope slid into the seat beside Star.

"Star? I know this is really hard, but I need you to make a list of everything you used when you cooked lunch and dinner. Even mayonnaise, mustard, spices. We have to get to the bottom of this."

Star nodded morosely as she took the offered pen and paper. Behind her, Penelope saw the two men lifting Nina. As the men shuffled through the main room with Philip holding Nina's upper body and Liam holding her legs, Star whimpered.

"Focus on the ingredients, Star," said Penelope. "It's going to be okay."

A tear dropped onto the paper as the young woman looked down once again. Penelope wished she had a box of tissues. Instead she patted Star on the shoulder as she wrote. After a few more words, Star handed her back the notepad.

"That's all I can remember. Maybe I should go back and look to make sure I didn't forget anything?"

The woodshed could be seen from the kitchen. Penelope didn't see a need to make the young woman witness what was happening there.

"Let's start with these things. If we need to go into more detail, we can do it tomorrow, okay?" Star nodded. "Can I walk you to the cabin? Neil should be back there soon."

Star stood and followed Penelope as they walked back to the gear room. Danny was still lying prone on the floor in the corner. Penelope was sure that Philip would check on him before heading to bed. As Star shrugged into a fleece jacket, Penelope looked sadly at Danny's red coat hanging beside her own. She knew it had only been a few hours since she and Danny had come to dinner, but it felt like a lifetime had passed since they'd arrived on Stone Point. She supposed that for Nina, it had. The fact that they had saved Danny and lost Nina was too horrible to hold in her head for long. She hurried out of the lodge with Star by her side and turned left toward the small cabin.

The air rippled with the deceptive calm of an oncoming storm. Penelope could smell the pending rain as she looked up at the blank black sky, the stars hidden by the gathering clouds.

Star walked slowly down the path, holding up her cell phone as a flashlight to guide the way.

"At least it's good for something here," she said. "I can't get a signal to save my life. They said there would be Wi-Fi here."

There was little point in responding to the petty complaint. Despite her earlier impression of the young woman, Penelope felt nothing but compassion for her now. When they reached the door to the cabin, she gave the young woman a quick hug.

"This won't seem so bad in the morning, I promise."

Star gulped to contain another sob. "Thank you. I really was trying to be so careful. This is the first job I've ever had. I wanted to show my dad that I could do it."

Better luck next time, thought Penelope, but she pushed the snideness aside and held on to her empathy for the young woman's situation. The night's events were starting to wear on her badly.

"It's all right. We'll figure it out. Get some sleep, okay?" She smiled reassuringly, hoping Star could see her expression in the dim light of the phone.

"Okay."

After Star was safely inside the cabin, Penelope returned to the lodge where Liam and Philip were standing inside the gear room. Liam left with a hurried good night. He seemed shell-shocked. Penelope couldn't blame him.

"I'm going to check on Danny one last time," Philip said with a kiss on the top of her head. "I'll see you in a moment."

Penelope murmured assent, then stepped lightly down the wooden steps. At the bunkhouse, she eased the door open and closed slowly to make sure not to disturb Fran and Estelle, though she doubted the two had managed to fall asleep already after the chaos of the evening. As she turned the doorknob to her room, she felt a catch in her throat as it resisted the rotation. She released it, and then tried it again, certain that she had left it unlocked when she'd grabbed her coat after her walk with Fran. This time, it moved smoothly in her hand, and she entered the room. She closed it then checked to make sure that the latch hadn't accidentally slipped to a locked position for Philip. Once inside, she felt a powerful release of tension. The pretty room was glowing softly from the light of the bedside lamp she'd left on. It was almost enough to make her believe that nothing horrendous had just happened.

She slipped out of her sweater and jeans and let them drop on the floor at the foot of the bed, too exhausted to bother folding them and placing them back in her suitcase. She pulled her socks and bra off as well and added them to the pile before walking to the side of the bed not pushed against the wall. Her bare foot touched something unpleasantly damp, and she scrambled backward, grabbing the phone out of the back pocket of her jeans for an additional light source. She touched the carpet where her foot had been, only to find a wet spot. She must have left it earlier when she came in to grab her jacket. At least, she hoped that was the source. Hector's lecture about house witches came into her mind.

The moment she formed the thought, she heard the door to the bunkhouse swing open and hit the wall with a crack as loud as thunder. Footsteps hammered down the hallway in time with her heartbeat before the door of the bedroom burst open. Philip entered and stopped abruptly in the shadows the lamp couldn't touch. His voice was tight with fear.

"Danny is gone. Danny is gone!"

CHAPTER **FIFTEEN**

The wind rattled the panes of glass in the windows as Penelope struggled to comprehend what Philip had said.

"What do you mean, gone?" she asked.

"Danny isn't where we left him. He's gone," Philip repeated.

Penelope half sat and half fell onto the bed.

"Where could he have gone? Did you look in his room?"

Philip nodded, exhaling loudly.

"He wasn't there either. He's going to be disoriented now, probably wandering around trying to find his way back to the bunkhouse. God, maybe he's looking for Nina. We've got to track him down."

Penelope was already pulling her clothes back on. "Let's go."

The two of them rushed from the bunkhouse back into the cold, dark night. She could hear something scrabbling away from them into the underbrush. At least she hoped it was moving away from them. Fran's discovery of the cougar print came to her mind, and the muscles in her shoulders clenched.

"Let's start on the trail close to the woodshed. Maybe he headed up the hill instead of down," Philip said.

She placed a hand in his and they hurried side by side toward the lodge. An owl hooted, loud and low. Was it her imagination or was something behind them? Her legs tightened in fear, and she forced her knees to bend.

"Where is Neil?"

"Still down at the beach, I think. I haven't seen him."

The thought of the young man wandering through the dark landscape scared her almost as much as the possibility of not finding Danny. Her panic made her mind race back to her questions from earlier in the evening.

"Philip, Danny thanked me for letting him and Nina guide this trip. He said people had been spreading rumors about him since he'd been part of an accident. What was he talking about?"

Philip's voice was as rushed as their footsteps.

"Nina lost someone a few years ago during a ski guiding trip. Her client fell into a tree well and broke their leg."

"What's a tree well?" Penelope interrupted.

"The branches of an evergreen tree are wider at the bottom than the top, right? In the winter, those lower branches stop snow from falling directly against the trunk. In places where the snow gets really deep, the base of the tree ends up surrounded by a big hole, only you can't see it because the wind pushes the top of the snowbank up against the tree, making it seem solid until you ski over it and the soft top layer disappears beneath your feet. They can be deep too, like twenty feet."

"Their client fell into that?" Penelope asked in horror.

"Yeah. Danny and Nina scoured the mountain for hours, using headlamps after it got dark. Somehow, they managed to follow the tracks and rescue their client, though she was close to hypothermia by the time they dug her out. Her leg was badly broken."

"Why didn't you tell me this earlier?"

"Danny swore me to secrecy. They somehow convinced the client not to report it. Guess they were lucky she was a friend of theirs."

Penelope could hear something odd in his voice. "So it was their fault?"

"Well, they'd taken her to an area that was prone to avalanches and deep wells, and Nina had left her alone to ski a line by herself while Danny stayed up top to fix a problem with the snowmobile. Even in-bounds, ditching a client like that is a direct violation of guiding regulations. Nina could have easily lost her license."

Something still wasn't adding up.

"Why did he tell you all this?" Penelope asked.

"Danny got drunk with me a few weeks after and told me the whole story. He was devastated by what happened and needed to get it off his chest."

"Oh my god."

"They told the hospital that it had been an accident and Nina had been there the whole time, but the extent of the client's hypothermia caused some members of the guiding community to question the story. If Nina had been doing her job properly, the client wouldn't have been trapped down there for that long. The story didn't make sense. They lost some business after that, and they were worried about their ongoing operations. I should have told you all this when you wanted to hire them. I thought I was helping a friend. I made a mistake. Do you think what happened to them had something to do with that?"

She squeezed his hand, unsure what she thought. "This is not your fault. I was the one who told you to hire Star, too, despite her lack of experience. If this really was an allergic reaction and Danny's out there all alone, who else is to blame but me?"

Philip swore. "It's all just a big mess. Look, I don't see him up here. Let's take another look at the lodge and see if he's found his way back."

The two of them returned to the building. Her throat contracted in apprehension as Philip pushed open the door into the gear room. Penelope's eyes darted to the hook where Danny's jacket had been. It was empty. Once inside the main room, Penelope rushed to the crumple of blankets that had covered Danny. The fire spat out an ember. Penelope flinched.

"He's not here," she said stupidly.

Philip nodded.

"We have to search the bluff. He could be anywhere by now."

The prospect of heading back out into the black night made her want to throw up.

"Okay," she said.

She made a move for the door but Philip remained still, so she stopped too.

"There's one other thing, Penelope. I swore to Danny that I wouldn't tell anyone, but you have to know the whole story." He paused. "The client I was talking about? The one who nearly died?"

"Yes?"

"It was Marianne."

THE SECOND DAY

CHAPTER **SIXTEEN**

4:21 A.M.

Footsteps woke her from a deep sleep. She struggled to place herself.
The bed was soft but unfamiliar. The pillow smelled of detergent and
trees. The room was darker than it should be; a streetlight usually shone
in her window like an urban nightlight, but here she couldn't see her
hand in front of her face. As her mind cleared, she remembered the
boat ride, the group dinner, Nina's death, and Danny's subsequent disappearance.

She and Philip had searched outside for hours but had been forced to
accept their failure when their flashlight began to dim alarmingly. There
had been no sign of Danny anywhere. Penelope felt sick at the thought of
the man still wandering around the forest in an incapacitated state. *At least
he had the wherewithal to take his coat*, she thought. It showed that despite

his compromised physical state, he was still capable of protecting himself. He was an experienced wilderness guide, after all. He would be okay.

She turned to Philip's side of the bed, closed her eyes, and laid her arm across his warm body. He stirred and gave a low grunt. She had woken once in the night when he rose to use the bathroom but had returned to a luxuriously sound sleep. The comfort of his presence was short-lived. The footsteps began again. They were getting closer. Bone-chilling cold crept across her body as a high-pitched whistling began. The noise was so similar to Danny's labored inhalations from the night before that she almost called out his name, but something stopped her. The whistle rang in her ears like a scream. The steps got closer still. Then, they halted. In their place was nothing but a ragged, rattling breath.

She willed herself to open her eyes. Before her was a version of Ruth Stone's face from the photograph above the mantel, but this one was twisted with hate and rotting with decay. Ruth's fierce eyes had become deep, empty sockets that stared lifelessly into Penelope's own, like a reaper coming to collect what was due. This is how it felt for Danny, Penelope thought, as the fingers reached for her neck.

Penelope shot up in bed, grabbing at her throat to fight off the imagined hands. The room was quiet. Philip's gentle snores were as light and regular as the lapping ocean waves coming faintly from the beach. She dared to stretch a hand into the dark, empty space beside the bed, half expecting to be seized by the monstrous nightmare creature. Instead, she was met with no resistance. There was nothing there. She was safe from everything except the horrors produced by her mind.

She breathed in through her nose then out through her mouth, making sure her inhale was the same length as her exhale as the internet had suggested when she'd searched for tips on managing anxiety. *One, two, three,* she counted. After several rounds of breath, her mind finally let go of the image of Ruth Stone's ruined face. She grabbed the battery-operated clock from the nightstand and looked at the time. Four twenty-three a.m. Her heart sank. Based on her many sleepless nights over the last year and a half, she knew she wouldn't be able to fall back to sleep now. Something became activated inside her body when she woke after four a.m., as if the merest hint of dawn was enough to make her ignore the reality of the darkness. Philip stirred again as the weight of the bed shifted under her restless movements. So far, she had managed to shield him from the worst of her early-morning insomnia, but the longer she tossed and turned beside him, the greater the chance she had of waking him up. Besides, there were things to do.

She still had the list that Star had written for her the night before in the pocket of her jeans. It would be wonderful to reassure the group with a simple solution to the first awful problem before they revealed that Danny was missing. Hopefully they could also share that Neil had been able to call the boat last night. The sooner they could all get home, the better.

She folded the blankets back gingerly and rolled off the bed, careful to move slowly enough that the weight redistribution wouldn't jar Philip. She found the crumpled pile of clothing she'd discarded for the second time the night before and dressed herself in the dark. With cell phone in hand, she opened and closed the door soundlessly, and then made her way down the hall with the screen's glow to guide her. She paused as she reached the main door. The bunkhouse was still enough to trigger an illogical wave of fear that she was the last one alive on Stone Point. Just her . . . and Ruth. She shook her head at the silly thought and gently pushed the door open.

Penelope retraced her steps from the night before up the sloping path past the firepit to the lodge. She averted her eyes from the left side of the large building. Even in the darkness, she could sense the presence of the rickety woodshed, which now housed Nina's remains. She could only hope that the chill in the air would slow the decomposition of the body. The idea was horrific and she pushed it aside quickly but it was too late. Her lingering unease about the tree-well story Philip had told her surfaced again. Last night had hardly been the right moment for analysis, but in the dark morning, the fact that Danny had covered up the negligence of his partner by swearing Philip to secrecy seemed harder to swallow. Sure, she had often covered for her coworkers at the rec center, but their slipups had been sleeping in or leaving early, not leaving someone to suffocate in snow. She couldn't understand why Marianne had kept their secret as well. Why had she agreed to hide the facts of an accident that had left her injured, nearly dead? Was it possible that Marianne's loyalty ran that deep? She was still hurt about learning about how close Nina and Marianne had been. She had considered herself to be Marianne's best friend. Now it seemed that she had only been one of many.

A snap in the bushes behind her brought her focus back to the pitch-black path. A cougar? Her hands flooded with a pulse of blood that made her fingertips feel fuzzy. The cold, dark velvet air around her was nothing like the city-tinted nights she knew. This darkness was thick enough to feel. Her tiny, shuffling steps made the walk seem endless, but she didn't dare move faster for fear of coming face-to-face with a wild predator. She felt a rush of gratitude for the small window of light coming from her screen, reminding herself to charge her phone when she got to the lodge. Or better yet, to find another proper flashlight in case—Penelope swallowed hard—Neil hadn't found a stronger signal for the satellite phone and they were forced to stay here another night. She tried to shake off the thought, but it persisted.

Stone Point was surrounded by kilometers of forest on three sides with nothing but the deep, tumultuous ocean on the fourth. There were no neighbors to run to if the boat didn't come. Before they left, Philip had told her how remote this location was. She had marveled at his comfort with the wilderness, vowing that she wouldn't let her nerves be evident to her rugged West Coast boyfriend. But now as the forest creaked and waves hissed, she finally realized what it meant to be this far away from everything. She had never felt so alone, and she hated it.

She sent out a silent, undirected prayer to any listening god that the group—including the missing Danny—would be taken safely off the bluff before the sun set again. The idea of having a glass of wine with Philip at a mainland hotel far from here, away from the rest of the group, and the horror they had witnessed made her ache with longing.

The waves crashed against the rocky beach below, pulling small rocks toward the deep with each retreat. Their relentlessness made her shudder. The wind picked up and blew hard against her face, tugging the breath from her lungs. The high branches of the trees chattered to each other fiercely as she reached the steps of the lodge. A sharp call pierced through the rustle of branches and breaking waves. She jumped. *It's an owl*, she said to herself. *Just an owl.* But her hand was shaking so hard she lost her grip on the door latch. On her second attempt, she clutched it tight enough to hurt and pushed inside as quickly as possible.

In the still air of the gear room, she breathed in to try to calm her racing heart. They would find Danny as soon as the sun came up, she told herself, grasping for the endless optimism that Marianne had loved in her. Neil had likely spoken with the mainland last night. For all she knew, Captain Rod was heading to the harbor at this very moment to prepare for an early-morning journey across the sound. What had happened to Danny and Nina was an accident.

With a start, she realized that as the trip coordinators, she and Philip were now in the same position that Danny and Nina had been during the aftermath of Marianne's injury. She had to take responsibility, not dodge it as the two of them had done. It was up to Penelope to find the cause of Danny's allergic reaction and put any possible suspicion about foul play or negligence to bed.

It was cold in the lodge. The fire had gone out. The darkness allowed her to avoid looking at the bloodstain at the base of the grandfather clock where Nina had hit her head. She knew she would have to clean it before the others woke up, but she couldn't face the gruesome task without coffee.

She guided herself through the dining room. As she was about to push open the kitchen door, she realized the room was silent. The ticktock of the grandfather clock, identical to the one by the fireplace, had stopped. She walked toward it, holding her phone up for light. The glass face of the clock reflected a warped view of the beam of light with her ghostly shape behind it. Her mouth dried, and her lips caught unpleasantly on her teeth. The hands of the clock were set in an identical position to the one in the main room—frozen at nine twenty-three. The moment Nina had died. Goose bumps prickled against her shirt sleeves. It doesn't have anything to do with witches, she told herself. Or Nina. Hector had said barometric pressure had caused the balloons in this room to pop. Could that have stopped a clock as well? She hurried away, still trying to make the argument convincing enough to get rid of the prickles on the back of her neck. *Stay positive*, she thought.

As she entered the kitchen, she was pleasantly surprised by the warmth of the room. A sharp pop from the cast-iron stove in the corner told her that the fire was still burning inside it. She found and filled an old-fashioned espresso pot and placed it on the top of the stove before adding another log to the fire. The action brought the woodshed and Nina to the front of her mind again, but she pushed the thought away.

As the coffeepot heated, she pulled the notepad from her back pocket and began gathering the ingredients Star had listed, placing them one by one onto the stainless-steel table, which was still cluttered with the detritus of meal preparation from the night before. Once she had gathered everything on the list, she examined the ingredients of each, setting them down once she determined them to be peanut-free. The espresso pot whistled, jerking her out of her concentration, and she looked around the room, finally locating a thick porcelain mug in a cupboard to the left of the sink. The warm smell of coffee reminded her of the afternoons she had spent with Marianne, huddled over a table in the small café where they'd met. Penelope wished she knew how her friend would have handled the insane events of the past twelve hours.

Back at the table, she picked up a small bottle. *This is it*, she thought as she turned the container of sesame oil in her hand. Or rather, blended sesame oil. Though the front of the bottle declared it to be pure, the ingredient list confirmed that the contents had actually been mixed with peanut oil, likely in a cost-saving measure for the company. Penelope wondered if Danny had grounds for legal action given the lack of clarity on the label. She sipped her coffee, pleased that she could ease the group's concerns as soon as they awoke. There was nothing nefarious afoot. Danny had gone into anaphylactic shock due to a simple mistake. Nina had been killed in a tragic accident. It was illogical to think that what had happened to the woman was deliberate. No one would intentionally try to kill someone like that—there was no guarantee her fall would have been fatal.

Pinning down these facts made it easier to be optimistic about the rest of the trip. Though her mother and Marianne both loved the sunshine-y spin Penelope worked hard to put on everything, hoping for the best didn't always come naturally to her. It was good to be able to rely on the facts to shore up the positive sentiments she would soon be expressing to the group.

Her relief let her absorb the world around her. The small sounds of the kitchen crept into her awareness: the scratching of a rodent in the old walls, the ticking of the cooling espresso pot, the persistent tap-tap-tap of a branch at the window behind her. She willed herself away from thinking that it was the ghost of William Stone trying to make his way into the home he shared with his child bride. Still, the kitchen felt less cozy after the thought crossed her mind. She left the sesame oil where it was, then carefully placed the other ingredients back into the spots they'd occupied on the shelves before clearing the worktable and gathering cleaning supplies. Though she wasn't looking forward to it, she needed to relight the fire in the main room and get rid of the bloodstain before the others woke up.

Once through the dining room, Penelope flicked on the overhead light. The tepid glow wasn't enough to stop the darkness from the windows outside from pressing inward. She looked curiously at two empty tumbler glasses on the table in the reading nook. Someone must have come into the room for a nightcap while she and Philip were searching for Danny. She moved toward the fireplace. As promised, the men had left a neat pile of wood beside it, as well as a small stack of newspapers and a box of matches.

She stacked a few small logs loosely on top of each other in a teepee formation like she had seen Philip do during a marshmallow roast after their one and only bike ride last summer, crumpling dry paper into the slots between the kindling. The match caught instantly and within seconds, she felt a burst of triumph as the fire began to dance with the paper, licking at the dry wood surrounding it. She hurriedly wet and mopped up the dried blood from the base of the clock as warmth and light filled the dark room. After a quick trip to the kitchen to empty the reddened water, she returned to the main room with a fresh cup of coffee.

Penelope's eyes drifted toward the photo of the group that had been taken less than twenty-four hours ago, when Nina was still alive. At first, the discoloration on the image appeared to be a trick of the flickering light, but it was too precise and too fixed to be dismissed. She leaned forward then jerked back. Nina's face in the photo had been scratched by something sharp. There were two empty, yellowed holes where her eyes had been. Penelope turned her head in horror toward the shot of Simone and Ethan Redding, only to see their faces had been disfigured as well. Though Penelope wanted to scream, no sound passed her lips. There was no point. No matter how loud she cried, the only people who would hear were just as trapped as she was.

Worse yet, one of them had done something unthinkable.

CHAPTER **SEVENTEEN**

5:48 A.M.

Forty-five minutes and two cups of coffee later, Penelope had nearly convinced herself that the marring of the photographs had been a printing problem. Estelle had made a point of noting the low-grade equipment—perhaps the same issue that had affected the original print made by the Reddings had created the awful effect on Nina's face as well. Maybe Penelope hadn't noticed the flaws the night before because the light had been dimmer than it was this morning. But as much as she hated to consider the worst-case scenario, she had to do that as well. The scratching might have been a drunken gesture, an ill-conceived expression of grief or anger after the chaos of the previous evening.

She knew someone had been drinking in the main room last night after she, Star, and Philip had left. Could Liam and Neil have decided to perversely honor the dead after a few too many drinks? It seemed like something Neil might do, especially if a drunken Liam was egging him on. Penelope was well aware that the combination of testosterone and alcohol rarely led to sound decision-making. Still, as she removed the photos from the mantel to save anyone else from bearing witness to them, she couldn't tolerate looking directly at Ruth Stone's face in the portrait she left in its original position. It was an illogical effort to avoid summoning something untoward, but a tiny part of her suggested that she hadn't considered every possibility. Though she wasn't willing to entertain a supernatural explanation for the damage to the photographs—at least not yet—she also wasn't willing to tempt fate. She placed the other two altered shots facedown on the bookshelf beside the fireplace and tried to relax.

The sound of the front door opening startled her into spilling the last few drops of cold coffee on her hand. When Hector walked in from the gear room a moment later, Penelope could see the darkness trying to creep in behind him. He was carrying a battery-operated lantern, and his face glowed in the wide circle of light it cast.

"Good morning, Penelope," he said, setting the lantern on the coffee table and easing into the armchair closest to the fire, which he seemed to have claimed as his own.

"Good morning, Hector. You're up early. Did you sleep well?"

"Well, new beds and old bones don't always agree with each other. I don't sleep much these days at the best of times, and given the troubling events of last night, it was difficult to fully rest. Any news about the boat?"

Before she could reply, the door opened again and Fran entered, rubbing her hands together.

"So nice of you to light a fire this early," Fran said. "The wind is cold this morning."

Penelope smiled in greeting before throwing on another log. She hoped that soon she would be able to tend to the fire without thinking of Nina in the woodshed.

"Morning, Fran. I was just about to start breakfast," she said. "But before I do, I need to tell you both something. The good news is that Danny seems to have recovered."

Both Fran and Hector immediately looked over to the place on the floor where Danny had been the night before.

"Did he stay in the bunkhouse last night, then?" Hector asked.

"Have you told him about Nina?" Fran said at the same time.

Penelope took a deep breath.

"Well, the bad news is that we're not exactly sure where he is. Unfortunately, at some point last night, he wandered off," she said as both their faces creased with worry. "Philip is certain the aftereffects of the epinephrine disoriented him."

Hector goggled at her as Fran brought a hand to her thin chest in shock. Penelope hurried to reassure them.

"He's an extremely skilled guide who is accustomed to the wilderness. He's bound to turn up again at first light."

"What about the boat?" Hector asked, his voice tremulous.

"I'm not sure. We didn't see Neil again last night after he left to find open ground for the satellite phone. It's difficult to get a signal here because of all the tree cover, but I'm confident we'll sort it out this morning," Penelope said with optimism so forced it sounded artificial. "My guess is that he went to bed after he attempted to contact the mainland. Hopefully he got through."

It was hard to remember the harrowing walk she and Philip had taken along the trail overlooking the empty beach the night before without fanning her own fear. They'd called Danny's name until the back of her throat was raw. The others seemed to sense her internal struggle. Hector raised his eyebrows skeptically in response to her cheery sentiments. A flurry of conflicting feelings danced through Fran's eyes. She seemed to settle on acceptance.

"Well, I suppose we should get everyone some food, then. Let me help you," said Fran. "Danny is sure to be hungry when he gets back."

Penelope agreed, pleased to have company in the kitchen and an ally in keeping the group calm.

"I suppose there's nothing else for it but a good meal at this point," Hector said.

Penelope squashed a wave of frustration as he picked up a book, apparently unaware that he too could help prepare meals. She told herself to be kind. He was from a different generation.

"Hector, do you have enough light?" she asked.

"Yes, I'm fine, dear. It's a simple joy, reading in front of the fire in a room like this."

He was right. The warm light from the fire made the space feel almost cozy again. She had to credit Ethan and Simone Redding for the new build. The beauty they'd created was helping to dissolve her uneasiness at the memory of Nina's blank eyes and Danny's disappearance.

She and Fran walked through the dining room, which was still cluttered with dishes from the night before. Penelope's heart sank as she saw the vase of flowers. The blooms had wilted and shriveled, lolling over the edge like seasick passengers. She had never seen flowers die so fast. *We'll have to deal with that as well*, she thought. When they reached the kitchen, it felt chilled and severe in comparison with the glowing main room.

"Damn," said Penelope. "I think the fire's gone out."

"Let me," Fran said as she knelt in front of the black stove. The cast-iron door shrieked in protest when she opened it. "I'm not sure what you had planned for breakfast, but we'll certainly need a fire. Will Star and Neil be coming in to help us?"

"They should," Penelope answered. "But I can't be sure at this point."

The mention of the caretakers reminded her of what she had discovered that morning.

"Fran, I examined the ingredients of all the items we ate last night. Star used a blended oil that contained peanuts—it was labeled badly."

"That poor girl. I had such a strange feeling last night that something bad was about to happen . . . and then, well, it did."

The fire caught. As Fran stood, her knees popped like the wood in the stove. She winced and laid a hand on her hip. Before Penelope could ask if she was okay, the woman continued.

"Does that ever happen to you? That kind of odd feeling?" Fran asked.

"Not really," said Penelope.

"Hmm," Fran said with a faraway expression. "Once, I had a neighbor come by with a box of my favorite cinnamon rolls from a local bakery. When I asked her why she'd thought to bring them, she told me that sometimes food was the only comfort. A moment after she left, I got a call saying my sister had died. Every time I eat a cinnamon roll, I think of my neighbor. It was as though she knew what I was about to go through."

"I'm not much of a believer in the paranormal," Penelope said, though the words brought Ruth's haunting stare into her thoughts once again.

"I'm not either. Still, there are moments when I get these strange feelings," Fran said. She stared out the window of the kitchen, which was still black with night, and then shook her head as if to clear it before continuing in a more matter-of-fact tone.

"Anyway, let's hope for the best for Danny and the boat. Think this crew will like bacon and eggs?"

"That sounds perfect," Penelope said, grateful that the woman had abandoned the eerie conversation.

As Fran opened the large modern fridge beside the back door, Penelope detected a faint whiff of rot. Hoping that she could leave the problem for whoever cleaned the property after her guests had been safely returned home, she grabbed two large skillets from the shelf under the sink and placed them on top of the stove. The smallest pan of the set, which had burned Star, was in the sink where it had been left the night before. Fran collected the bacon, eggs, and a loaf of bread, which she set down as she spoke.

"I have to tell you that I'm oddly relieved to hear what happened to Danny has been confirmed to be an allergic reaction. I heard Danny and Nina screaming at each other yesterday, and my mind went to dark places last night as a result. Nina was so angry."

Penelope froze.

"What were they fighting about?"

Fran looked at the egg carton, opening the stiff lid slowly before meeting Penelope's eyes.

"Nina was accusing Danny of lying."

"About what?"

"It was something about a radio, but she got interrupted before she could finish. Halfway through a sentence, she stopped talking. Then, I heard Star saying hello. She had been doing yoga in the forest, apparently. I'm not sure how much of the conversation she heard."

"Oh." Penelope's mind was racing.

"I didn't mean to eavesdrop, Penelope. I was just in the wrong place at the wrong time. After you left to get your coat, I realized I also needed another layer of clothing, so I headed down to the bunkhouse as well. It was nearly dark. I don't think they saw me at all, and it seemed so awkward to interrupt their argument."

"Yes, of course," Penelope said, hoping Fran realized she hadn't been judging her.

The other woman sighed with something that sounded like relief.

"I shouldn't be gossiping, but you seem like someone I can trust, and I felt so terrible about it last night that I hardly slept. I'm so happy—well, not happy I suppose—but reassured that what happened was an accident, pure and simple. The argument was just a terrible coincidence. I'm sure you're right, and we'll all be home soon."

It was surprisingly comforting to hear her own words repeated back to her, though after what Fran had told her, Penelope was less certain they were true. What could Nina have been so angry about? Was there something about the skiing accident that she had never revealed? Something that Danny wanted to hide? Penelope couldn't shake the feeling that it all had to do with Marianne. She forced herself to focus on preparing breakfast. If nothing else, she would think better on a full stomach.

"You're right. Food first, then we'll find Neil and the satellite phones."

Fran nodded and began laying slices of bacon in the pan. It began to spit and jump almost immediately. The scent jogged an unpleasant memory of Star's burnt skin. Penelope collected the loaf of bread, then placed several slices on the rack at the bottom of the stove. Behind her came the soothing sound of Fran tapping and cracking eggs into a bowl. The flicking whisk provided an almost musical accompaniment to her next words.

"Will we go through with the tour this morning?" Fran asked.

"We'll make a decision once everyone's here," Penelope said. "If Neil was successful, we may need to pack up right away and head down to the beach. If not, it might be good to give everyone something to do."

She looked in the direction of the woodshed. If they did go on with the tour, there was at least one place they wouldn't be visiting. Outside the window, the darkness was beginning to gray. Instead of energizing her, the sight of the coming dawn made her feel exhausted.

The door swung open and Philip entered. His normally glowing complexion looked worn by stress.

"Morning." He kissed Penelope on the cheek, then nodded at Fran. "Hello, Fran," he said before turning back to Penelope. "Any sign of Danny? Or Neil?"

Penelope shook her head. Philip sighed.

"Okay, what can I do to help? We should eat as fast as we can, then get back out searching. I stopped at Danny's room on the way up, but his bed hadn't been slept in. I knocked on the door of the cabin, but no answer. I assumed Neil and Star were here already."

"We haven't seen any of them yet," Penelope said, emphasizing the last word to convey an outcome she didn't entirely believe would happen. "Our plan is to eat breakfast first, then track them down."

Philip nodded his approval.

"Toast?" Penelope said.

"Coffee?" Fran said at the same time.

In another situation, they might have laughed. Instead, Philip answered without amusement.

"I walked up with Estelle," he said. "I'm sure she could use a warm drink and something to eat."

Despite everything, Penelope was glad to hear Philip's concern for his mother.

"How is your mother doing?" Fran asked.

Penelope turned to flip the bacon, wondering if Philip would be as surprised as she was that Fran knew about the relationship between him and Estelle. He didn't seem to notice.

"She's quiet. I don't think she got much sleep last night. I filled her in on what happened after she went to bed. She's eager to get home as soon as possible," Philip said, crossing to the sink to refill the coffee maker. "Just like the rest of us."

Philip touched the small of Penelope's back as he returned the pot to the stove.

"It's still early. Danny probably made shelter somewhere. His head will be clearer this morning and he'll find his way back. Neil and Star are probably still asleep. As soon as Neil wakes up, we'll get one of the phones from him if he didn't reach the mainland last night. There might be a stronger signal if we get a bit higher."

"Even through the clouds?" Penelope asked around a lump in her throat.

"I don't know," Philip said.

She saw worry in his eyes and realized he had been trying to convince himself along with them that everything was fine.

"Well, let's hope for the best," Fran said again, as she began pouring the beaten eggs into the heated pan on the stove. "Would you two mind finishing the eggs? I can clear the dining room."

"Absolutely," Penelope said, relieved at the older woman's take-charge attitude.

Philip took the offered spatula and began scrambling the eggs. Penelope filled him in on the sesame oil Star had used and the mysterious argument between Nina and Danny. Philip rubbed his jaw as she finished.

"Listen, this is a terrible thing to ask, but did you see Nina fall? Is it possible that Danny pushed her?"

"It happened so fast," Penelope said as she tried to replay the events of the night before. "I was focused on him not her. I didn't even realize he had knocked her down until it was too late. But how could it have been intentional? He didn't fake that allergic reaction. There's no way it could have been planned."

"You're right," he said. "It's a ludicrous idea."

Instead of making her feel better, his words cast doubt on her certainty. There was so much she didn't know about Danny and Nina. Was it possible that the whole thing had been staged?

"We have to make sure they're all safe, Philip. If it wasn't an accident and Danny is still out there . . ."

She trailed off. Articulating the horrible possibility of Danny deliberately killing Nina made her feel as though she was in a bad movie.

Philip understood what she had left unspoken. "This is surreal," he said. "We'll keep the others together as best we can without spooking them. I'll try to track down Danny. I'm sure this is all a misunderstanding. But just in case."

The coffeepot began to hiss. Penelope moved it to the island before turning back to her boyfriend. His eyes were glassy.

"Nina was Marianne's best friend for years. She loved my sister so much. I worried about her when we were younger. It was so apparent to me that it went beyond friendship for her. And now they're both dead."

"I'm so sorry," Penelope said, rubbing his arm.

"This is such a disaster. I know how worried Danny was about losing his guiding permit. It was tied to his visa, so it wouldn't have been just his job if it was revoked. He would have had to go back to Australia and give up everything he had built here."

"What are you saying?"

"I thought he told me all about the accident because I was his friend," Philip said. "But after hearing about the argument between them, it's starting to sound like he was using me as an alibi. What if his version of the story wasn't true? What if it was his negligence, not Nina's, that caused Marianne's accident?"

Penelope blanched. "It all happened years ago. Surely there's a statute of limitations on negligence."

"Yes, yes, you're right," Philip said, seeming eager to agree. "It's crazy to think that this had anything to do with what happened to Marianne."

She nodded as he continued.

"It's just . . ."

"What?"

"When we were kids, Marianne was obsessed with justice. An eye for an eye, you know. It was something my mom taught us."

His expression darkened at the memory.

"Anything I did to Marianne, she'd find a way to pay me back in full. I never understood why she didn't hold Danny and Nina accountable for what had happened to her."

His description of his sister was at odds with the kind woman she had known, and Penelope felt compelled to defend Marianne.

"She was protecting her friends," Penelope said. "She knew they made a mistake."

"If it was a mistake, why was Nina so angry at Danny?" replied Philip. "He must have said something she didn't like."

A memory shot through her confused thoughts.

"The satellite phone," Penelope said.

"What?" Philip looked confused.

"On the dock when we first got here. Danny was talking about the danger of forgetting to charge them. Nina heard it. She looked angry. Maybe that's what actually happened on the day Marianne fell into the tree well. Maybe Nina couldn't get help because her phone wasn't working."

Philip's eyes widened. "We've got to keep this between us, okay? Stay alert today."

"Okay."

Penelope's heart pulsed uneasily but she attempted a weak smile. He kissed her on top of the head before loading the large platters that Fran had thoughtfully left by the stove with bacon strips and toast. Penelope slid the finished eggs onto a second plate and grabbed the fresh pot of coffee. The two of them entered the dining room, where they found Estelle, Hector, and Fran already gathered. Penelope was relieved to see Fran had removed the haggard centerpiece.

"Has Neil woken up yet?" Philip asked.

"No," said Estelle.

"I'm sure he'll be here soon," said Fran.

Estelle regarded her with a weary expression. Penelope could see the night's effects in the deepened shadows under her eyes. The rest of the group filled their plates and ate in silence.

"We'll be taking our tour of the bluff as planned at eight a.m.," Philip said as Hector placed his fork and knife carefully on his empty plate.

"Do you think that's wise?" Estelle asked with a frown. "I thought it would be cancelled. It seems a bit inappropriate. Shouldn't we spend our time trying to get out of here?"

"We've got a plan for that," Philip answered. "Neil will be the point person with the radio for now."

"It's important for us to keep busy," Penelope said, placing her hands under the table so Estelle wouldn't see them shaking. Philip nodded at her support.

"And when will Neil be assuming those duties?" Estelle asked pointedly.

"Soon," Philip said. "No point in abandoning the trip's purpose entirely," he added. "Besides, we might find a better spot to get a call out if we explore the area a bit."

"You sound like your father," Estelle said as she narrowed her eyes. "It seems foolish to walk around here anymore than necessary. I'll be in my room if help arrives."

Fran's eyebrows knit together in response to Estelle's slight. Philip and Penelope exchanged a quick glance while Hector's expression shifted to one of surprise at the revelation of Estelle's relationship to Philip. Penelope wondered if it was better to allow Estelle to go alone or to keep her with them. Should she continue to give the group a possibly false sense of security, knowing what she did about Danny? She opted for calm rather than undue alarm.

"That's fine, but please don't go anywhere but the bunkhouse," Penelope said. "There's no telling when the boat will arrive, and we'll need to load up as soon as possible when it does."

"I'll make sure to pack my bag," Estelle said dryly as she slid back from the table, leaving her unfinished meal in front of her.

Fran closed her eyes for a moment longer than necessary as if trying to work out what had just happened. Penelope was relieved at Estelle's departure. The less she had to deal with her today the better. Regardless of Marianne's trip plan, she should never have invited Philip's mother and she never would again. But for now, she had to make nice.

"Let's meet at the firepit in twenty minutes," Penelope said after a glance at her watch.

"Lovely," Hector said. "I'll go grab my walking sticks. Please ensure the pace is suitable for all ages."

He followed Estelle and left the room.

"I'll clean this up as fast as I can," Penelope said, gesturing at the messy plates and the broken balloons still strewn listlessly around the room.

"I'm happy to help," said Fran.

"I'll head back to Neil and Star's cabin and get one of the satellite phones. I'll pound down the door if I need to and tell Neil he's got to find a signal if he hasn't already," said Philip.

"Good plan," said Penelope.

She gave him a quick kiss before he left, then she and Fran began gathering the plates. When she came to the place where Nina had sat the night before, she felt sick at the reminder of her absence. Fran looked equally disturbed when Penelope joined her in the kitchen. Before she could ask the woman if she was okay, a hulking shape outside the window made her heart leap. She squinted, and then realized that the men had pulled the bikes out of the shed and leaned them against the building after they'd left Nina inside. She was grateful for their morbid practicality.

"Penelope, I have to ask you something," Fran said.

"Go ahead."

"Well, during breakfast, I remembered a guided trip I took to the backcountry a few years ago. It was in terrain similar to this—lots of wild animals and cougars. Before we left, our guide asked us to prepare by learning how to shoot. It was a good suggestion."

"Okay," said Penelope, unsure of Fran's question.

"It made me think. Is there any chance that Danny has a gun?"

CHAPTER **EIGHTEEN**

The moment Philip returned to the kitchen, Penelope asked him about a gun. He couldn't hide his unease as he told her and Fran that he had no idea if Danny had been carrying. Just as agitating was the fact that there was still no response to his knocks on the door of the cabin, which had been dead-bolted closed.

Penelope's nerves jangled as she washed the dishes. Could Danny have stashed a gun in his backpack? Or unloaded a piece of equipment from the boat without them noticing? Their arrival had been so hectic that Penelope couldn't be certain. The three of them made short work of cleaning up before heading down to the firepit. As foolish as it felt to keep going with the research as planned, none of them wanted to cancel the tour and risk unnecessarily alarming Hector. The last thing they needed was to incite a collective panic. They'd just have to hope that Neil had persisted well into the night before successfully reaching the mainland, then collapsed with exhaustion. She knew it was unlikely, particularly given her earlier assumption about him drinking with Liam, but she felt powerless to change the itinerary.

Once outside, Penelope saw that the sky had lightened further. A thick band of clouds gathered on the horizon. The air was damp and cold. She shivered in her fleece jacket as she breathed in the smell of salt and rot from the sea below. Beside her, Fran's limp seemed worse than it had been yesterday. As they made their way down the trail, she saw Hector at the firepit with two wooden walking sticks in hand. When she got closer, she noticed that the handles had been carved into the shape of bees. Penelope had a fleeting thought of asking Hector to lend Fran one of the sticks when the door to Bunkhouse B swung open. The crack of it hitting the outside wall rattled her teeth.

Liam emerged, looking worse for wear. His eyes were sunken and glazed; his skin both pale and ruddy. Penelope realized she had forgotten to check on him that morning. She felt a pang of guilt. How was she going to keep the group safe when she wasn't keeping track of them? His face provided her with all the evidence she needed as to at least one of the people who'd left the tumblers behind on the table the night before. But exactly how many drinks had Liam consumed? And who with? She was becoming queasy just looking at him.

"Good morning," Philip called.

"Is it?"

Liam's voice was froggy, but he smiled at the group despite his clear hangover. He didn't seem fazed that no one returned the expression.

"Are you joining us for the tour?" Hector asked.

"Tour?" Liam rubbed his face blearily, then jumped back from something at the top of the stairs. "Jesus, what's that?"

The group got closer. Penelope's heart sank. A swarming mass of ants were writhing together on a darkened patch of wood. The state of Nina's body came to her mind in a sickening flash.

"My honey!" Hector said in Penelope's direction. "I thought you'd cleaned this up."

Penelope shrugged weakly, trying to shake off the imagined horror. "I swept it as best I could. I must have missed a spot."

"Ugh," said Liam, looking disgusted. "What I need is some coffee and a long ride to clear my head."

Philip glanced at Penelope. Once again, it seemed impossible to keep the group together without explaining their fears about Danny and Nina. The question of who Liam had been with in the lodge the night before strained inside her mind, eager to be asked, but now was not the time.

Philip answered Liam. "I've got you covered," he said, as he pulled a thermos out of the daypack he was carrying. Penelope was struck by his thoughtfulness. At least one of them was paying attention. "Here's some coffee. Your bike's where we left it last night. If you see Neil, ask him to leave the sat phones for us. We'll be back shortly."

Philip turned to the others. "Looks like it's just the four of us. My initial plan was to start with the older buildings: the woodshed and the cabin, but given the circumstances, we'll do a shorter version by going to William's still first and then heading down to the beach. Maybe we'll find Neil down there. Sound okay?"

Penelope could tell he was unsettled, though he was doing his best to contain it. He tended to overexplain things when he was nervous.

"Yes, that sounds wonderful," Penelope said in a tone that she feared was more hollow than hearty. It was difficult to keep up the façade of being cheerful as the idea of Nina as an insect feast lingered in her mind.

She followed Philip and the others as he led them down the sloping trail past Bunkhouse B, scanning the thick forest for a sign of a red jacket among the trees. Though she wanted to locate Danny, her eye twitched with apprehension at the possibility of his presence. The wind picked up and the trees began to moan as their branches swayed. Beneath her feet, the trail was unpleasantly spongey, like a giant earth-covered slug. Her legs still ached from the activity of the day before. She wished for the warmth of Philip's hand in hers, but the path only allowed for two people to walk abreast, and Hector had already hurried forward to match Philip's pace.

She could hear the two of them—mostly Hector—talking, though it was hard to make out the words. Something about the importance of the still in the area's history. Penelope was amazed the man was able to carry on with his lectures in spite of everything. At the edge of the bluff, the trees thinned and the group paused to regard the breathtaking view of the ocean battering the raw edge of the cliff below. Fran's head turned to the right and Penelope followed her gaze. The top of the stairs they had climbed the day before was roughly thirty meters from where they were standing.

"I noticed that strange fixture on the way up. It's certainly not original. Do you know what on earth it was for?" asked Hector, with a point in the direction of the pentagonal pad. The unfinished concrete looked dull in the gray light.

"According to the site plan the property manager gave us, the Reddings intended to build a gazebo there, but they never finished it," Philip said. "I don't much like the look of that rebar. It should be roped off."

Hector murmured assent. The four of them then turned in the opposite direction, heading left on a trail which came perilously close to the cliff edge. The narrow path became steeper as they headed down the scrabbly slope. Penelope continued to keep her eyes peeled for any sign of Danny on the beach below. She saw nothing but large boulders and the unceasing surf. After one hundred meters or so, they came to a low rise in the land, a natural forested bench. Then the trail veered away from the cliff face, back into thick forest, which lessened the light of the sky. Once they'd walked for another five minutes, Philip held up a hand to stop the group, then knelt to examine a patch of moss a slightly different color from that surrounding it.

"This area looks like it's been disturbed. The site plan showed William had a still close to here. This might be it."

Hector leaned forward.

"Do you see a trap door? William distilled underground so he could access the aquifer easily," Hector asked. "It also provided the best possible temperature control at a time when refrigeration was so uncommon."

Philip grunted in response as he ripped away a six-inch layer of earthy moss from the ground. Whatever was under there had been buried for a long time.

"We found it," he said, pulling at the metal ring that had been drilled into the wooden trapdoor hidden below layers of soil.

Penelope was glad to hear the note of triumph in his voice, though her happiness didn't last long. As she, Fran, and Hector bent to look at the aged trapdoor, Penelope grew cold. She had never been a fan of tight spaces.

"Shall we?" Philip asked eagerly, but the door refused to budge.

Penelope felt a wash of relief.

"It's stuck," Philip said.

His effort made veins rope up his arms.

"Maybe we should—"

Before she could finish her suggestion to abandon the pursuit, Philip wrenched the wooden door away from the dirt crowding its edges. A wave of fetid air rushed toward them and Penelope coughed to rid her throat of the musty, acrid particles. All together, they peered into the black hole that had emerged before them. A wooden ladder, with several rungs missing and others that had rotted through, snaked its way down a muddy, earthen wall.

"Hector, can you make it down?" Philip asked, already stepping onto a rung.

"Of course," Hector scoffed, as he laid his walking sticks beside the hole. "I wouldn't miss this for the world. William Stone's moonshine was known to be the best in the Pacific Northwest. The loss of supply after his death led to a dearth of alcohol in the mining camp. Many people resorted to their own homemade operations, but having neither the expertise nor the recipe—"

Penelope took a deep breath and followed Philip down the ladder as Hector continued his monologue to Fran, unabated by the diminishing audience. The wooden rungs were soft, nearly slimy in her hands, and her fingers were instantly chilled by the coldness of the dirt around them. It felt wrong to travel so deeply into the earth. Her legs stiffened in resistance, as her body fought to stay aboveground. Philip flicked on a flashlight once he reached the base of the ladder and shone it up toward her. The light helped a little. She kept her breathing even as she concentrated on moving one foot and one hand at a time, lowering herself into the dark cave that reminded her of a grave.

Long slow breaths, in and out.

Several rungs down, her head brushed against thick cobwebs and her scalp danced at the idea of a fat spider crawling in her hair. Finally, her feet found the ground. The relief at being off the rotting ladder was almost enough to make her ignore the frigid puddle soaking through the boots she'd bought for the trip. So much for the waterproof quality the salesperson had touted so keenly. She stepped to the side of the ladder to let Fran and Hector make their way down. Once they were all in, Philip swept his light around the hole. What she saw made her yearn to return to the daylight above them, bleak though it was.

It was a cramped space, small enough that the four of them were forced to stand unnaturally close together to avoid touching the crumbling walls. Raw roots hung like spindly fingers from the dirt ceiling. Creeping insects darted away from the flashlight's beam, seeming angry at being disturbed. Their many legs skittered into the tunnels they had carved in the walls. Penelope huddled closer to Philip. A trickle of water could be heard but not seen. The wind gusted and howled across the small square of dim light at the top of the ladder. Penelope caught sight of a pile of rubble in front of her as Philip continued to circle the light around the hole.

"Philip, bring it back. I think there's something here," she said.

She peered at the heap of loose earth in front of her while willing nothing to jump out. It looked like the remnants of a small slide, as if part of the cave had collapsed many years before. There was no hope of making their way farther into the underground space, Penelope noted in gratitude.

"I'm not sure it's safe to be in here," she said.

"We won't stay long," said Philip.

Water gurgled as Philip placed a hand on the large green-tinged copper kettle beside him.

"This must be the original equipment," he said in amazement. "Look at the oxidization."

Hector joined him and began a detailed and unrequested explanation of how moonshine was made. Penelope fought to concentrate on Hector's words instead of the clawing panic that was scratching at her throat. She struggled to draw in another slow breath of the dirt-laced air. The walls seemed to advance toward her. The place felt as if it could collapse at any moment. Would the sound of Hector's voice cause the walls to cave in? She leaned forward to keep herself in the small beam of the flashlight, feigning interest in the still to combat her claustrophobia. Her parking garage was heaven compared to this.

"Shhh!" Fran said sharply, as Hector paused to underline a long and complicated point. "What was that?"

Penelope craned her ears in the damp darkness, struggling to hear anything besides the pounding of her heart and the whistle of the wind.

"What?" she asked.

"It sounded like footsteps," Fran said worriedly.

Fran scrambled up the ladder and the others followed, the light jerking alongside Philip's hasty movements. Penelope cleared the dark hole and took a deep, hurried breath. After one gulp of fresh air, she heard it too. Before she could fully process what was happening, Neil came pounding down the trail toward them. She knew even before he spoke that something was horribly wrong.

CHAPTER **NINETEEN**

Neil's eyes were wide enough that Penelope could see the red around the rims. He looked terrified.

"What's going on?" Philip asked.

He placed his hands on Neil's rapidly rising and falling shoulders. The gesture was so similar to the one Philip had made when greeting Neil the day before, yet the context was so different, that Penelope felt a nauseating sense of déjà vu. His face was as white as her frozen fingers. He responded in a rush of words.

"I crawled over Star to go to the outhouse because our stupid bed is pushed against the wall. I didn't want to wake her up, but she didn't even stir. I didn't think it was weird until I came back and saw her face. I was yelling and I ran into the lodge but there was nobody there—oh god, her eyes . . ."

He had to choke back a sob that sounded larger than his throat could handle before he was able to continue.

"They were open—her eyes were open like she was staring at me but . . . oh my god, oh my god."

Fran took Neil in her arms as his emotions overcame him. Philip started running. Penelope followed. They covered the ground between the still and the cabin in a blur of panicked speed and entered the small house with Penelope nearly tripping over Philip's heels. Gray light streamed into the single-room cabin from two wooden-paned windows that rattled in a gust of wind as Penelope's eyes darted to the still body on the brass bed pushed into the corner of the room.

Neil was right. Star's eyes were open, but Penelope could tell immediately that she wasn't seeing anything. The sparkle from the night before was gone. Star's gaze was now flat and lifeless.

"Oh my god," Penelope said.

Philip crossed the room, feeling Star's neck with two fingers.

"No pulse."

He frantically began CPR. Penelope watched as Star's chest compressed under Philip's strong hands. He breathed into her mouth over and over, leaning over to listen at intervals. Penelope scanned the room for something, anything, that would help. The walls were the same faded logs as those of the kitchen and dining room, though the floor was only a rough plywood. The small room felt cold with seeping moisture despite the small potbellied woodstove in the righthand corner closest to the door. Penelope saw two jackets hung on a row of hooks along the wall and a large pile of laundry heaped on the floor beside two backpacks. On the far left was a small table and chairs. Beside her was a counter with a two-burner hot plate and a shelf that contained jars of instant coffee and teabags above it. She joined Philip at the bed, feeling helpless and stupid as he continued CPR. She had learned the procedure at the rec center, but she knew Philip was far more skilled. After what seemed like hours, he raised his hands then let them fall to his sides, shaking his head before he checked Star's pulse again.

Penelope put her hand on his shoulder as he hung his head. They stayed in silence for a moment before he took Star's hands in his own to scan her unnaturally pale forearms. He laid her arms down gently, and then pulled the top corners of the faded patchwork quilt over her face. When Star's eyes were no longer visible, Penelope's chest relaxed enough that she was able to speak.

"How did this happen?" she whispered.

Philip ran his hands through his hair.

"I have a theory, but without blood work and a toxicology report, there's little I can do. There's no visible bruising on her except a slight discoloration on her arm."

The door opened and Neil came into the room before Philip could explain further. The young man sat down heavily beside Star and began to cry.

"She's dead, isn't she?" he asked.

Philip answered gently. "Yes."

"I did it," Neil said.

Penelope's body jolted with adrenaline.

"What are you talking about, Neil?" she demanded.

The young man's head was bowed and his shoulders were shaking. It was difficult to make out his words.

"I did it. I left the frying pan on the stove. I wasn't paying attention. I was the one who burned her hand. I felt terrible. I didn't tell her. I thought, oh shit, it will heal. Now it never will."

Penelope and Philip looked at each other.

"I'm so sorry, Neil. Star would have forgiven you," said Penelope. "She was a lovely girl. You have to forgive yourself too." She was unsure how to ask the next critical question, but they needed to get out of this place as soon as they could. Star's death had just underlined how unsafe they were here.

"Where are the phones?" she asked softly.

Neil looked at her and then to Philip. His eyes were full of watery confusion and pain.

"What do you mean?"

"You had the satellite phones last night, Neil. Did you reach the main-land?" Penelope spoke slowly in case the young man was in shock.

"No, I tried for a while but I couldn't get an answer. When Danny came down to the beach to help, I gave them to him and went to bed."

"Danny came to you?" Philip asked in horror. "What time was that?"

"I don't know. Like an hour after I left? Or less? My phone was dead. I don't know what time it was."

Penelope was too stunned to say anything.

"We'll give you a moment alone, Neil," said Philip.

As they closed the door, she realized that though the bed had been pushed against both walls, it hadn't saved Star from anything. She hoped the superstition would be strong enough to keep the rest of them alive, even as the fear swirling inside her indicated that they would need a whole lot more than that.

CHAPTER **TWENTY**

10:29 A.M.

They raced from the cabin to the lodge. As they rushed into the large room, Penelope saw Hector facing the fireplace all alone. He didn't turn when they approached. Penelope guessed what was capturing his attention even before she saw the group portrait. In the newly altered shot, Star's eyes had been marred the same way as Nina's. The disfigured photograph of Ethan and Simone was mercifully absent. She went to the shelf where she'd left the two photographs she'd removed earlier and saw that neither had been moved. This was a new print, which meant whoever was doing this had multiple copies of the group shot. The realization sent a shiver up her spine.

"Who could have done this?" asked Hector, his voice shaking with trepidation.

Philip swore loudly. Energy seemed to drain out of him as he lowered himself onto a chair by the fire. "What the hell is happening here?"

Penelope sat down beside him on the arm of the chair and laid a hand on his shoulder before answering.

"There was a different version this morning with only Nina's eyes scratched," she said as she passed him the photograph she'd collected from the shelf. "Star hadn't been touched. This is a whole different print from the one Estelle and Neil made. Someone is doing this on purpose."

Fran entered the room. She looked at the small group in fearful disappointment.

"No sign of Danny in the bunkhouse. Is Star okay?"

Penelope shook her head mournfully. "Star passed away last night."

Fran took a step back in shock. "Where's Estelle?"

"Hopefully she's still safe in her room," replied Penelope.

"I'll go check," Fran said, and hurried out.

"Where's Liam?" Penelope asked, knowing Fran was right to account for everyone.

"Presumably he went on a bike ride, as he said," Hector answered.

Before Penelope could respond, the door opened again and Neil stormed over to Philip, who rose to his feet just as Neil grabbed the front of his shirt. Penelope stood to defend him as Neil hissed directly into Philip's face.

"What did you give her?" Neil yelled.

Philip raised his arms as if under arrest.

"What?"

"Last night! After you bandaged her hand, you made her swallow some pills. What did you give her? Danny was your friend, right? Were you trying to get back at her for what happened last night? Did you send him to take the phones from me?"

Penelope hoped everyone could see the flaws in his logic, but his accusation was so vile she had to refute it.

"Neil, Philip treated Star before anything happened to Danny. What you're saying doesn't make any sense."

Neil let go of Philip's shirt, but anger still distorted his features.

Hector jumped in. "The important thing is that we get a boat here as soon as possible. Neil, did you get through—"

"What did Danny say to you when he took the phones?" Philip interrupted.

Hector paled. "Danny has the phones?"

"I don't know." Neil answered Philip without acknowledging Hector. "He was all messed up and acting weird. He said something about high ground. Going to high ground."

"Then that's where we need to go," Philip said. "Hopefully he's found a signal."

Neil's face fell and his shoulders slumped.

"I can't believe she's gone," Neil muttered. "Her family has already been through so much. Last year, Star's younger sister almost overdosed. She's got a wicked gambling problem and got in way over her head. Star wanted to take this job to help her sister out with the massive debts she ran up. Her father cut her off financially after he found out about her casino habit."

"Oh god," said Penelope. "That's heartless."

She had been so wrong about the young woman.

"Maybe it was the witch," Neil said, his words tumbling together again. "Maybe she killed Star."

His erratic thought pattern was worrying.

"Neil, you have to calm down," said Penelope. "Can I make you a cup of tea? You've had such a shock."

The young man stared at her blankly. Before she could move, Liam and Estelle walked into the room. Despite her previous annoyance with them both, Penelope was glad to see them alive and well.

"Nothing like a bike ride to shake off the cobwebs," Liam said cheerfully.

His hair was still damp from a shower, which reminded her of Danny from the night before. The thought was almost enough to unleash the emotions she was trying to keep in check. A low rumble of thunder shook the building, and she looked outside. Though the sky was now smeared the black, purple, and charcoal colors of a deep bruise, no drops fell.

Fran returned, her choppy hair more disheveled than usual.

"Estelle, thank god. How are you feeling?" she asked.

"Well enough to take a walk, thank you. I didn't go far but I ran into Liam partway up the trail. I think I managed to get some shots that capture the oddness of this place," Estelle said, swinging her camera bag off her shoulder. She looked around. "Has Danny turned up yet?"

Neil scowled but stayed silent.

Hector pursed his lips and began to explain.

"We were just—"

Philip cut him off. Penelope thought it was kind of him to rescue the older man from delivering the bad news.

"I'm afraid we haven't reached the mainland to get a boat. What's worse is that Star has had an accident," Philip said.

Estelle's jaw dropped, but she recovered quickly. "What kind of accident?"

Philip shifted uncomfortably after a glance in Neil's direction. The young man looked distraught. "It's too early to tell."

"Is she okay?" Estelle asked.

"Unfortunately, no," Philip answered. "I couldn't revive her."

Estelle's face tightened, and Penelope understood the horror she must be feeling at receiving all this bad news at once. Danny was missing. Nina and Star were dead. No boat was coming. Philip's mother walked toward the mantel where the ugly photograph still rested. When Estelle turned her head back toward the group, Penelope was struck by the hollowness in her eyes. She looked so different from the elegant woman on the dock or the casual guest who had just breezed into the room. She seemed as if a giant void had opened inside her.

"How did this happen?" Estelle asked. "How did Star get hurt?"

" 'How' is the question we're all asking right now. But just wait." Neil's face sharpened in fury. "When Star's father finds out, his team of lawyers will be asking us all a lot more than that."

"What do you mean?" asked Philip.

"Her family is rich. I mean West Van wealthy. Their house is on oceanfront property, and it's huge. Her dad's a big-time lawyer and he's got,

like, a million other lawyers working with him. They destroy people."
His voice became more subdued as he continued. "I've seen it happen to a
woman who didn't deserve it. I can't imagine how they'll act with people
who do. They nearly got one of Star's teachers fired after she accused Star
of, like, using an online essay."

Hector made a surprised noise from the corner before he spoke. "I
knew you looked familiar."

Neil turned to face him. "What do you mean?"

"I was at the academic hearing you are referencing. The hearing for
Marianne Solanger, the professor Star's father tried to get fired."

Penelope felt cold when Marianne's name was mentioned. This was
the first she'd heard of her friend's academic challenges.

Hector continued. "I didn't realize Star was the student in question—
it was handled anonymously. I spoke on Ms. Solanger's behalf. Were you
one of Star's witnesses?"

"I was," Neil said.

His anger seemed to have been replaced with shame.

"Star tried to get Marianne fired?" Philip asked. The incredulity in his
voice matched Penelope's own emotions.

Liam let out a curse word. "I remember when all that happened. She
hated that girl."

Penelope looked at him in disbelief, and Liam seemed to register that
he was speaking ill of the dead.

"Sorry. No disrespect intended. I'm devastated about Star. We had a
drink together last night after everything happened. She was great."

So that's who left the glasses behind, thought Penelope.

Hector puffed up his chest and continued as if he hadn't been interrupted. "Indeed. I was the only reason Ms. Solanger wasn't let go. We
were able to shift responsibility for the mishandling of the matter onto
a teaching assistant who had been bribed by Star to favorably grade her
essay. She was disciplined accordingly."

"Were you able to prove that? Marianne told me she thought the other
woman had been unfairly fired," Liam asked in a shocked tone.

Hector seemed indignant. "I saw a signed confession from the teaching assistant. If Ms. Solanger was not privy to that information that was a failing on the part of the disciplinary committee."

Penelope sank back onto the chair. Her thoughts pounded against each other like the waves breaking outside on the beach. Why would Marianne want Star and Neil on this trip after they had done something so awful to her? She looked at each person in turn as she remembered the way their names had been listed in the precise swoops and curls of Marianne's handwriting. Liam had broken Marianne's heart. Estelle had abandoned her. Star had tried to ruin her career, and Neil had helped. Hector had punished someone Marianne believed to be innocent. Danny and Nina had nearly killed her. Penelope looked back at the photograph resting on the mantel. The pleasant expressions on the untouched faces in the group seemed to mock her. Their smiles looked like masks. But the empty eyes were worse.

Penelope felt sick. Marianne hadn't assembled her allies on this trip. She'd invited her enemies. With a sinking heart, Penelope realized that what she had done to Marianne was the most awful thing of all, though Marianne didn't know about that. Besides, Marianne's own brother was on the list. Surely Marianne didn't want to hurt Philip. She wasn't thinking straight. Fran's voice was a welcome reprieve from her loathsome thoughts.

"Was Star taking any drugs? Prescription or otherwise?" Fran asked. "Or maybe this was a seizure brought on by the stress of what happened to Danny?"

Penelope wanted to hug the woman, but she stayed in her seat to avoid drawing undue attention. Her thoughts were still too disordered. Fran's presence was the biggest flaw in her wild theory. There was little chance of Marianne hating kind-hearted Fran, and no evidence that the two had ever met. Marianne's notes had indicated Fran was selected for her widely known knowledge of plants and local history—not some personal grudge.

"No!" Neil said firmly before his voice quavered. "At least, I don't think Star was taking anything. But I didn't even know she was on the pill until, like, two weeks ago."

Estelle regarded him with a contemptuous expression as Fran went to his side.

"It could have been an unintentional overdose. Sometimes, people take a combination of medications that they don't realize could kill them," Fran said. "If she was on birth control, she might have been taking other things as well."

Philip spoke up. "It's a reasonable working premise, but for now we can't dwell in hypotheticals. I'll get Neil's stuff out of the cabin and bring it to the bunkhouse then I'm going to take a ride up the side of the bluff near the waterfall. Maybe Danny ended up there."

"I'm coming with you," Liam said. "We'll go past the plateau we were on yesterday. Hike it if we have to. There's plenty of high ground up there, and we might even be able to get above the tree line. My bike is outside."

Philip nodded at Penelope, seeming to signal that she was now in charge of keeping the group calm. Penelope didn't know if she was up for the challenge, but she nodded back. The two men moved into the gear room.

"Who's ready for an early lunch?" Fran said. "I can pull something together."

"I'll be right back to help," said Penelope as she followed Philip to the entry room. She found him shrugging on a raincoat over his thick sweater. Liam was nowhere to be seen, presumably already outside.

"Please be careful and do your best to get us out of here."

Philip kissed her lightly.

"I promise. I got us into this mess. I should have planned this trip better. But I'll get us out."

Penelope shook her head, unwilling to let him shoulder the blame when the doubts about Marianne were still so prominent in her mind.

"I gave you the list of people to contact. If anything, I'm the one to blame," she said.

She didn't think now was the time to mention her fears about his dead sister, but something must have shown on her face. Philip embraced her.

"Penelope, this is all a horrible coincidence. Whatever happened between Danny and Nina had nothing to do with Star's death. Look, I didn't want to mention this in front of the others but I'm nearly certain that Star was into drugs. Last night, at dinner, her pupils were the size of pinpoints."

"You think she was high?"

Star had been overly flirtatious with Liam. Penelope had chalked it up to the man's charm, but she was relieved to be wrong.

"I do. If Star's sister was into risky behavior like gambling, Star could have been seeking thrills in a different way. But don't say anything for now. We need to wait for a coroner's report. The group doesn't need additional theories. They need to get home."

It was good advice for her to follow as well. Marianne had been her friend. Her suspicions were just a way of trying to make sense of tragedy.

"Then you need to find our phones," she said.

She stood on her tiptoes for one last kiss. Philip was right. There was a simple explanation for everything. Star had been careless while cooking because she was high. Nina had been knocked down by Danny in the throes of an anaphylactic reaction. Danny had probably already reached the captain for a return boat. She felt better than she had since the moment she'd heard Danny's roughened cough the night before.

She reentered the main room only to find it empty. Voices were coming from the dining room. Before she joined the group, she yanked the foul image of Star from the mantel and slid it into the drawer of the small table beside the reading area, closing it firmly. Her stomach rumbled as she readied herself to eat what she hoped would be her last meal on Stone Point.

CHAPTER **TWENTY-ONE**

11:33 A.M.

Neil was hunched over his plate at the dining room table with the others. He thanked Fran for the peanut butter and jam sandwich in a quiet voice. His behavior had changed drastically from the boisterous young man who had met them on the dock, let alone the ferocious boyfriend who'd just confronted Philip. All emotion seemed to have been drained from him now. His eyes were sunken into dark hollows, and he moved as if detached from his actions.

The group ate in silence. In the place of conversation, Penelope's thoughts hummed in her head like hornets. It was nearly noon, and there was still no sign of a boat. If Philip didn't find Danny soon, they'd be stuck here for another night.

Hector excused himself from the table the moment he had finished the last bite of his sandwich.

"I suspect the safest place to be if a boat does arrive is the main room next door. If anyone needs me, I'll be in the reading nook."

"That sounds wise," Estelle murmured. "I'll join you."

Penelope once again let go of her irritation at their lack of assistance. They were all on edge. Better to have them out of the room than under her skin. Fran stood as well. The fine lines on her skin deepened into a wince when she put weight on her hip. She began to clear the table.

"Please, Fran, I can take care of this," Penelope said.

"Many hands make light work," Fran replied with a smile in her direction.

"I'll help too," Neil said. "I guess it's kind of still my job."

"That would be wonderful, Neil," said Fran with an encouraging look. "Would you mind taking the fixings into the kitchen?"

Neil dutifully followed Fran's direction, while Estelle and Hector walked into the main room without a thank-you or a backward glance. Penelope looked over at the closed door and sighed. Her frustration was harder to shake than she thought.

Fran met her eye. "There's more to Estelle than you think," she said as she twisted the bread bag closed. "She hasn't had it easy."

Penelope wondered what Estelle had revealed to Fran, but there wasn't time to dig deep with Neil waiting for them in the kitchen. She decided to keep the conversation light for now and ask more probing questions later.

"Maybe so," she replied. "But it would be nice to get a little help once in a while."

She nudged the kitchen door open with her toe, then held it for Fran. Neil was already at the sink. Fran walked to the fridge to put away the sandwich materials. When she opened the door, the unmistakable smell of decay wafted into the room, stronger than before.

"What stinks?" Neil asked.

"I'm not sure, but something has definitely gone off in there," Penelope said. "I thought I smelled it this morning, but it's gotten worse. Fran, can you keep the door open? We need to find it."

Fran obliged, shifting her good hip against the door to allow access to the fridge. Penelope poked around the shelves but there was nothing there that seemed like an obvious culprit. Everything was sealed or tightly packaged. Penelope pulled open the crisper door. The smell from inside was powerful enough to make her retch. Among the carrots, apples, and tomatoes, Penelope spotted a mesh bag full of greens that were rapidly decomposing into mush.

"Oh, wow. This must be it," she said, holding the dripping bag at arm's length before depositing it in the sink. Neil made a strange sound when he saw it.

"That was the last thing Star ate," he said. "Yesterday, she foraged for these wild onions to go in her salad. She was a vegetarian. Foraging was like her new thing. She wanted to live off the land, you know?"

Penelope nodded. "That's very honorable."

"Where did she find these?" Fran said with a frown. She opened the drawstring at the top of the bag carefully before extracting a slimy mint-green stalk.

"Not sure. Close to one of the trails, I think. I was out for a bike ride."

"Did Star serve these to the group?" Fran asked sharply. "Did you eat them?"

Both Neil and Penelope turned in surprise at her uncharacteristically harsh tone.

"No. Star used ordinary onions for everyone else. She couldn't find a ton. I had the same thing you did last night," Neil said. "Why?"

"These aren't wild onions. Oh, that silly girl. Foraging is not something that should be taken on by the inexperienced." Fran looked at them with sadness and what seemed to be a touch of relief in her eyes. "This explains everything. Star poisoned herself with these. Its Latin name is *meadow deathcamas*, but most people refer to it as 'the death lily.' Highly toxic and extremely dangerous. We need to get these out of the kitchen. Penelope, can you clean out that vegetable drawer carefully? I'm afraid we'll have to throw out everything that was in there with them. We're lucky no one else was affected."

Neil swore. "What am I going to tell her father?"

"Let's deal with that when we need to," Penelope said.

"You're right. Let me grab my jacket," the older woman said as she slipped out the kitchen door.

Neil turned to her with a look of frustration but she cut him off before he could flare up again.

"Philip is going to bring your stuff down to Bunkhouse B. Just in case."

Neil nodded as Fran returned. She picked up the small bag and the vase of dead flowers that she had left on the worktable.

"All right, this should do it. For now, we need to make sure that no one else gets sick," said Fran.

Penelope offered her thanks as the older woman left through the back door. No matter what Neil was fearing, she knew that an accidental poisoning would be a lot easier to share with Star's parents than a drug overdose. She got the bucket out from under the sink along with rubber gloves and a rag and set to work cleaning the fridge. Despite the memory that surfaced of mopping up Nina's blood, relief nipped at her like an enthusiastic dog. Philip had been right. This was all an awful coincidence. At her direction, Neil tossed the remaining vegetables and fruit into a large garbage bag and set it down by the door while Penelope scrubbed the drawer and shelves of the fridge. When she was finished, she surveyed the results. It was hard not to be concerned about their lack of fresh fruit and vegetables. If a boat didn't come soon, they'd be stuck without roughage for the rest of the trip. Fran returned to the kitchen and Penelope was surprised to see her mouth was now pulled down at the corners. She wondered why. They couldn't bring Star back to life, but at least they now had a definitive answer about how she had died.

"You okay?" she asked as she joined Fran at the sink to rinse her hands of the putrid smell.

"What? Oh yes, I'm fine. It's such a shame about Star. What an awful, avoidable tragedy."

Penelope nodded.

"We all done in here?" Neil asked, running his hand through his hair. "I might as well make sure Philip got everything." He hovered as if seeking reassurance.

"Yes, thank you, Neil. You were a great help," Penelope said.

He nodded dolefully, though Penelope could see a faint blush appear on his cheeks. He was so young. Both women watched him leave the room. As soon as the door was closed, Fran spoke softly.

"Now that it's just us, I can tell you. I found something when I was disposing of the plants. Something I think you'll be interested to see, though I wasn't sure if Neil was up to it. Are you able to absorb a little more history today? I think it could be good for your story, but I don't want to be crass after all that's happened."

Penelope was again warmed by the woman's thoughtfulness, as well as curious about what kind of discovery would affect Fran so deeply. "I would love to come with you."

Fran relaxed. "Great. It would be best to invite Hector and Estelle as well, I think. Hector will be very intrigued by this, and it can't hurt to get a photo."

"You're right," said Penelope.

It would be good for the others to have something to do besides wait for the boat, she thought. Besides, the more she could keep the group focused on something the better. Maybe they'd even run into Danny along the way. The discovery that Star's death had a simple explanation gave her hope that Danny's strange behavior would be accounted for as well.

Hector had settled in the reading area and Estelle was seated on a chair beside him, looking at images on her camera. Penelope was irked to notice that they had let the fire go out—she would have to light it again when they returned—but she was pleased when both Hector and Estelle agreed to the invitation.

Penelope took the rear of the group as they left the lodge. The moment she pulled the kitchen door closed, a force from inside seemed to push it at the same time slamming the door violently against the frame. The noise reverberated like a gunshot in the heightened stillness, reminding her of Liam's exit from the bunkhouse earlier that morning.

"Sorry," she said as the other three turned in shock.

Her own hands were shaking but it wasn't the sound that had scared her. She had never felt a door move as though it had power of its own. She looked inside the window half expecting someone—or something—to be staring back at her from inside the cabin.

CHAPTER **TWENTY-TWO**

12:39 P.M.

Directly in front of the kitchen door was a rising path over a steep slab of granite. Fran, Estelle, and Hector kept their heads trained forward when they passed the woodshed on the left. Penelope held her breath and did the same, unsuccessfully willing herself not to recall the seething ants from earlier.

The air was still full of moisture. She could smell the rain coming, but instead of the usual sweetness, salt stung her nostrils. Charcoal clouds were now piled on top of each other in the sky. The wind gusted in the trees, lower now, making the branches whip and prick her face as she followed Fran and the others up the overgrown path. Penelope doubted she would have been able to find the line without Fran's sure-footed steps at the front of the pack. She nearly tripped over Hector, who was struggling to keep up with Fran's pace.

"Like a fool, I left my walking sticks back at the still," he admitted to her. "We'll have to collect them after this expedition, or I simply won't be able to keep up with all you young people."

Despite everything, Penelope smiled. Estelle and Fran were closer to Hector's age than her own. At the crest of the granite slab, the trees thinned. Below them was thick green forest. Beyond that, she could see the raging ocean. In the face of the coming storm, it was a bleak and beautiful view.

Fran stopped and knelt in front of a mass of stones, and the other three gathered around her. As she looked closer, Penelope's mind organized the rocks into a deliberate pile—it was a cairn. Wide rocks on the bottom served as the foundation for narrower ones laid on top. The triangular tower was about waist-high, approximately the height and shape of a small child. Dark green moss blanketed the base. Penelope got closer. Under the plant cover, she could see the same white, orange, and gray colors as the fireplace stone. The wind kicked up on the exposed point, harsh as a slap from a cold hand.

"I came up here to get rid of the lilies, but found this instead," said Fran. "Look."

She pointed to a spot at the base where a large smooth rock had been placed. Its creamy, dull surface was edged with moss, but Penelope could see letters etched into it like the message that had been scraped into the stairs at the beach, though the meaning couldn't have been more different. The jagged words nearly broke her heart.

You were loved.

Tucked under a stone at the bottom of the cairn Fran pointed out a silk ribbon, so dirtied and faded that it was almost the same color as the earth. Penelope stepped back to let Estelle photograph it.

"Goodness me," said Hector. "This has never been documented before. It looks like a grave."

"But who is buried here?" Penelope asked.

"It seems too small for a grown man," Fran said. "And that inscription. It's so intimate."

Estelle raised her camera then lowered it slowly without taking a shot.
"Could Ruth Stone have had a child?" Estelle asked Fran.

"There was never one who was recorded," Fran said. "But if she did, I'm sorry that this is how it ended for them."

Penelope found the idea terribly sad, and Estelle seemed overcome as well. She swiped at her eye before quickly raising her camera once again.

"Please remind yourself that we cannot be certain what is buried here without digging it up. It could have been a loyal pet, perhaps a dog or a cat," said Hector.

Fran raised her eyebrows in disbelief.

"No one could care for an animal enough to do this. Whoever lays here was cherished."

There was a surprising edge to Fran's voice. The woman was clearly shaken by what they had found as well. She winced again as she stood up and began to speak.

"What this really shows me is that so much of Ruth Stone's story is untold. What if she was pregnant when William died? She would have had to deliver this child all alone."

Penelope's heart grew heavier.

"She was so young. It's so tragic," Penelope said.

As the group regarded the grave again, the wind blew hard enough to needle its way through her clothing down to her bare skin. She shivered as Fran spoke again.

"The worst part is that now Ruth Stone has been reduced to a silly witch, either feared or ridiculed, as women often are. I think she deserves her true story to be told."

Penelope smiled at Fran, whose eyes now shone with tears. Maybe this trip would serve its purpose after all.

Hector cleared his throat. "And whose truth is that? This is all speculation," he said.

Fran looked at him as if he still didn't understand.

"History often is, Hector," she replied.

He shook his head, and Penelope could see he was about to launch into a long-winded response. The wind whipped up again. Her hands began to ache from the cold.

"Can we continue this inside? I'll make us all some tea. Estelle, do you need more time?"

Estelle straightened up, screwing the lens back on her camera. "I think I have some usable shots, though I might need to adjust the exposure." She looked at Fran. "Fran, why on earth were you burying lilies? I don't understand how you came up here in the first place. Was it some kind of ritual?"

"No, no. I had to dispose of an extremely toxic plant," she said, looking at Penelope as if seeking permission to share what they'd learned. Penelope nodded. Estelle and Hector deserved to know the facts. Fran continued.

"While you were in the main room, we discovered that Star was foraging for greens and ended up ingesting poison instead," Fran said. "It's likely what caused her death."

"Oh, how awful," Estelle said. They all paused to acknowledge the loss of Star before Estelle spoke again. "I know it's cold comfort to have a diagnosis for her, but it is better to know. Especially after all the awful business last night. The hardest part of death is often the mystery of it— the uncertainty of how and why it occurred."

Penelope found herself unexpectedly moved by Estelle's words. She decided to trust them with the rest of the information they had gleaned.

"Danny's reaction and Nina's . . . death were accidents too. Through no fault of her own, Star used a bottle of sesame oil for our dinner that was poorly labeled. It actually contained peanuts," Penelope said. "I have no doubt that Danny's disappearance will be easy to explain as well."

Hector and Estelle both looked visibly relieved as they took in the news.

"Thank you for telling us. It's been harrowing to be so unsettled about what's going on. There was part of me that was beginning to think Stone Point really was haunted," Estelle said.

You're not the only one, thought Penelope. She was pleased to have found common ground with Philip's mother. Maybe people really could change.

"Hopefully Philip and Liam have found Danny. But in the meantime, I think we all need something warm to drink," said Penelope.

The others agreed and began back down the trail. Hector continued to struggle. Penelope kept a close eye on him to make sure he didn't stumble.

"I'd like to freshen up before tea," Estelle said when they reached the lodge.

"I'll walk you down to the bunkhouse," said Fran. "I'd also like a moment."

"That's perfect. Would you ladies mind accompanying me a bit farther down the trail so I can collect my walking sticks?" Hector asked.

He blinked heavily as the women agreed. Penelope hoped again that Philip and Liam had found a way out. The events of the past twenty-four hours appeared to have fatigued Hector immensely, and she felt the same way. She considered offering to fetch the walking sticks for him but decided against it. She didn't want to offend him.

Penelope let herself into the kitchen as the others made their way back onto the trail that led to the bunkhouses. The door eased open and closed, as normal, providing further assurance that she had let her imagination get away from her earlier. Penelope had an entirely new perspective now that she'd seen the small grave. The idea of a teenage girl, all alone in her small wooden cabin, snow pressing against the flimsy glass in the windows and ice gathering on the doorknobs, was sad rather than frightening. Poor Ruth. She had gone through so much.

Penelope slowly filled the kettle and placed it on the stove, stoking the fire inside. She took her time. It was nice to be alone for a short period. She wasn't used to spending so much time with a group of people. The wind had gathered enough force that she could hear it whistling through the cracks in the logs as she gathered cups and a teapot. She made her way into the main room to get the fire going, to take the chill out of the air before everyone returned.

This time, the flames were slow to catch and she had to rebuild the fire carefully before they began to lick at the kindling. When she stood up, she began to stretch before the sight in front of her made her stop, horrified. The group shot she had taken down from the mantel earlier had been set in front of the old portrait of the Stones. Instead of Ruth's face, she saw the blank eyes of Nina and Star.

CHAPTER **TWENTY-THREE**

3:11 P.M.

Fury simmered within Penelope when Neil refused an offered cup of tea in a moody tone. As she served Fran and Estelle, she kept her emotions to herself. The last thing she wanted to do was sow additional discord in the group after so many of them had shared a significant moment at the cairn. They settled around the main room, where she had once again removed the photograph. This time, she shoved it behind a bench in the gear room, hoping it would never be found again. The two women let her know that they had accompanied Hector down the path to collect his walking sticks, but the trip had worn him out so much that he'd needed to take a nap. Penelope was uncomfortable leaving anyone alone, but she could hardly begrudge an elderly man his rest after all that had occurred.

The moment Philip returned with Liam, she called him to the kitchen to tell him about the reappearance of the photograph. She grew more enraged as she described the reenactment of the macabre prank. She was oddly grateful for the powerful emotion. Anger was a sharper tool than fear.

"The worst part is that everyone had an opportunity to do this," she said, struggling to keep her voice down. "People have been in and out of the main room all afternoon. I can't rule anyone out except Fran, who's been with me the whole time."

But that wasn't entirely true either, she realized. Fran had left the room earlier to get her jacket and was out of her sight when she went with Estelle and Hector down to the still.

"Actually, scratch that," she said, before realizing the crudeness of the phrase in the current context. "I can't eliminate anyone who was with me. Did you and Liam stay together while you were out?"

"No. We decided to split up when there was no sign of Danny. We wanted to cover as much ground as possible. He rode to the northwest side of the bluff, and I went to the south."

"So basically, it could be anyone," Penelope said with frustration.

"Yes."

The idea of Neil displaying the vile image of Star again made her go cold with anger, but the gesture was so attention-seeking that he was the most likely candidate. Was he acting out his trauma like a small child?

"But why? What is the point of it? It's so cruel," she said.

"I agree. Someone here thinks we need to be punished," said Philip.

Penelope didn't know how to respond. Luckily, she didn't have to as Philip continued.

"Better to nip it in the bud and let whoever it is know that they've been caught and it needs to stop." Philip exhaled heavily as he looked out the window. "See those clouds building? This is going to be a huge storm. Feels like we're stuck in a fish tank during a house fire." Penelope had never seen him look so defeated. "I checked Danny's room on the way up in case he made his way back or at least dropped the phones there, but no dice."

Penelope swore before she remembered that there was some good news she could share.

"Well, at least we've managed to solve one mystery while you were gone."

She filled him in on Star's fatal foraging error. He blinked hard before responding. She could hear the relief in his voice.

"I can't tell you how much better that makes me feel. And it's all the more reason to clear the air about this photo. The storm is going to hit any minute. We'll be stuck inside together until it passes, so we should try to get everyone back in good spirits. Or as good as possible, I guess, given the state of things."

"Wherever he is, I hope Danny has found shelter," said Penelope.

"Me too. Where's Hector? I saw everyone else as I came in. This might be a good chance to distract the group with another discussion on Stone Witch theories, and he's always up for that."

"He's taking a nap. The poor man was beat."

"All right, let's check on him after we talk to the others. I seriously doubt that Hector was responsible for the photos, but we should make sure he's okay."

Penelope agreed, grateful for Philip's willingness to take the lead. Back in the main room, she saw that Estelle had spread a contact sheet of photographs over the coffee table in the reading area and Fran was sitting beside her looking at the shots. Liam and Neil were playing a listless game of pinball. The low level of conversation made the roar of the wind hitting the house more pronounced. Penelope felt a cold draft coming from somewhere.

"Everyone, we need to have a group discussion," Philip said loudly from the center of the room in front of the fireplace.

Penelope kept her eyes on him to avoid seeing the mantel again. As the group looked up from their various activities, the air began to hiss. She searched for the source of the ominous sound—was it a gas leak?—before she realized that the storm had finally broken. Rain streamed down the windows in sheets. It looked like buckets of water were being heaved toward them in quick succession. The trees beyond the glass were little more than dark smudges. Despite the thick double panes, Penelope could hear the whomping of the wind. The temperature dropped. The force of the storm was unsettling.

"Surely Hector's not sleeping through this," said Philip, already halfway across the room. "I don't want to leave anyone unaccounted for right now."

"I'll come with you," said Penelope in agreement. "We'll wake him up if we need to."

The discussion about the photograph would have to wait. She couldn't bear to have another person in their group go missing. Not now, as the storm picked up steam, and not Hector. She was surprised by how fond she'd grown of his impromptu lectures.

Liam called to them before they reached the gear room, and she turned. There was little evidence of the earlier hangover remaining in his clear eyes.

"Where is Hector?'

"In his room," Penelope answered. "He was exhausted."

Liam's expression turned grim. "Neil and I were just in the bunkhouse. His door was wide open. The room was empty."

Philip let out a curse word. "That's exactly what I was afraid of."

"We've got to find him," Penelope said.

"The best way to do this is to get everyone out looking for him. We all in?" Philip asked.

The group agreed quickly, though Estelle's voice was the last to give assent.

"Good. Let's split into two groups. We can cover more ground that way," said Philip. "Be sure to stick with your teams, okay?"

Penelope looked sideways at Philip. She knew staying close together wasn't just about keeping everyone safe. It was also the best way to make sure whoever was messing with the photograph wouldn't have another opportunity.

Estelle stood. "Neil, Fran, and I will check Bunkhouse B again. Hector is likely just in the bathroom. This seems like a lot of fuss when we haven't searched it thoroughly."

The two women moved to stand beside each other, and Neil joined them without a word.

"Great. Liam, Penelope, and I will walk the path to the still, then circle back. We'll meet on the porch of Bunkhouse B in twenty-five minutes. If necessary, we'll begin searching the upper trails after that, but hopefully, we'll have tracked him down by then. Okay?" said Philip.

The group headed to the gear room together. Penelope made a quick stop at the washroom before grabbing her raincoat, which Philip had thoughtfully hung up the night before. As she slipped it on, Liam swung the front door open and Penelope's spirits sunk further at the sight of the torrential rain. It made the world look like a child's drawing: black vertical lines of streaming water obscured the view of anything beyond what was immediately in front of them.

"Coming?" Liam called.

She braced herself then walked down the rain-soaked steps toward Philip, who slid his hand into hers.

"You ready?"

His voice was raised to ensure she heard him over the pounding rain.

Penelope nodded as she cinched her hood tightly. The rain drummed against her head and drowned out other sounds, but at least the jacket was keeping it off her skin. For now anyway. Philip walked alongside her to the path. She raised her hand to wave as Neil, Fran, and Estelle set off. Within seconds, Philip's hand grew almost too slippery to hold, but Penelope gripped it tighter. She didn't want to be alone in this storm. The rain fell from the sky, and then back up again as it bounced off the moss, stones, and trail. The mud sucked at her boots like a hungry creature.

She was amazed at Philip's and Liam's fast pace in the nearly sightless landscape. Without Philip's hand, she would have knocked herself into a tree, or worse, stepped right off the cliff she knew was at the base of the trail before it looped back toward the still. The thought of the sheer drop made her miss a step and she stumbled, her hand slipping out of

Philip's grasp. Her kneecap hit something hard, her hands landing flat in squelching earth as she broke her fall. When she pushed herself up, she saw Philip's face in front of her own.

"Everybody all right back there?" Liam called.

Philip looked at her questioningly. "You okay?"

His concerned expression was slightly obscured by the black hood drooping over his forehead. Despite it, she could see drops of water dripping off his nose. She nodded, embarrassed at her lack of coordination. Behind him, she saw the large outline of the bunkhouse. Her fear of the cliff had been foolish; they weren't even halfway down the path. He put a hand under her elbow to help her stand. She tried to ignore the sharp pain from her knee as her pants pulled at raw skin. She must have been cut by something but there was no time to check.

"Let's keep going," she said, letting him get ahead before she followed, limping slightly. As much as she wanted to hold Philip's hand, the water running down the hill had narrowed the path too much to allow it.

They passed the bunkhouses quickly. Then the forest closed around them, wet fingers of cedar brushing against her cheek as though they were trying to lay claim to her body. The wind pushed the rain into her mouth and eyes. *In and out*, she reminded herself, ducking her head to avoid the onslaught of water from a branch knocked by Philip's shoulder. Then, Philip stopped so abruptly she kicked the back of his heel with the toe of her boot.

"Sorry," she muttered, stepping backward.

She peered out from under her hood. The forest was beginning to thin. They were nearly at the edge of the cliff.

"This way to the still," Liam called over his shoulder as he led them to the left down the waterlogged path.

She and Philip followed. She didn't bother to muffle her panting, knowing the sound would be lost in the rain. Her feet slid frighteningly on the wet roots, which were now as slick as a plastic waterslide. She leaned her body away from the edge of the cliff to her right, and took another deep breath when the trail cut back into the forest. They closed the distance to the still. When they arrived, Liam was peering into the open mouth of the hole in the ground. They'd forgotten to replace the trapdoor when they left. Milky mud was pouring inside so rapidly that the hole nearly blended into the rest of the slick ground.

"Do you see anything?" Philip shouted.

The endless spatter nearly drowned out his words.

"It's too dark. Do you have a flashlight?" Liam yelled back.

Philip shone his light into the dark cavern in response. It didn't help much. The rain was eroding the rough sides of the hole into an ugly waterfall. Beyond the reach of the light, the cave looked black and endless. Penelope had to remind herself that it was only five meters below the surface.

"How did you find the still in the rain?" she asked, pitching her voice loud enough to be heard.

Liam gestured to something on the ground. "I tripped over that. Otherwise, I could have gone in headfirst."

Penelope saw the body of a bee almost obscured by mud.

"That's Hector's!"

Her heart pounded. Fran and Estelle had said they'd helped him retrieve his walking sticks. Why had Hector returned? She moved toward the first rung of the ladder, preparing herself to descend once again. But before she could, Philip began to make his way down.

"If I can get lower, I can shine my light all the way to the bottom," he said.

Six rungs down, he paused and aimed his flashlight toward the base of the still. When she saw what was below, she gagged. There at the bottom of the ladder was a body lying facedown in a coffee-brown pool of mud.

Philip swore as he saw it too. "Hold this steady."

He came up a few rungs, shoved the flashlight into Penelope's hands, and clambered back down the ladder. She was forced to follow him with the flashlight wedged under her armpit so she wouldn't have to climb one-handed. She stopped where Philip had paused and directed the light down. It was difficult to keep the beam from shaking as Philip reached the body. He turned it faceup.

It was Hector.

Liam made a sound like a cross between a cry and a curse. Penelope's tears mixed with rain as Philip cradled Hector's torso. He pressed his fingertips against Hector's throat then ripped his hood back from his own head to lean against the other man's chest to listen for breathing. He worked rapidly as he once again began CPR. Penelope scrambled down and braced herself against his back to keep him from sliding around on the slick ground. Her heart broke as, over the course of several minutes, his movements slowed.

Philip looked up at her and shook his head.

"Hector is dead."

"We forgot to put back the trapdoor," Penelope said dully. "He must have fallen in."

She wasn't sure if she believed her own words.

In the awful yellow glare of the flashlight, Philip shook his head.

"There's an injury on the back of his skull. It looks bad enough to be fatal," said Philip.

Penelope was confused.

"But he fell forward into the hole," Liam said. "How did he hit the back of his head?"

Philip lay Hector gently onto his back, and then Penelope began to climb the ladder. She could hear Philip following behind her. Once above-ground, Penelope shone the light toward him to guide his way. Neither Liam nor Penelope said a word as Philip rose out of the hole.

"I'm not sure this was an accident," Philip said when he was out of the pit.

"What are you saying?" Liam asked, his voice higher than usual.

Penelope could only stare at Philip as he ground the heel of his hand against his jaw, inadvertently smearing mud on his face.

"I think Hector was murdered," Philip replied.

His voice was emotionless, but his eyes were full of terror.

CHAPTER **TWENTY-FOUR**

4:43 P.M.

The three of them trudged back up the slippery path as the rain continued to pour. The frigid water numbed Penelope's hands, making them feel swollen and clumsy. Moisture leaked through the failing seams of her jacket, which invited the wind to follow. Penelope was chilled inside and out as she ran through every possible plan to get them away from Stone Point. They had to escape. But how could they leave without a phone or a boat?

Their party of ten had dwindled to six. Three of them were dead; one was missing. She no longer felt comfort in previous suggestions that this was a dire coincidence. Someone was hunting them and there was no way to know who was next. When they reached the gear room, she peeled off her dripping layers, then slid her phone from her pocket. The battery was almost dead. She needed to find a charger fast. The dim screen showed that it was close to five p.m., just over an hour before the sun went down, but the storm had made visibility so poor it might as well have already set. They were stuck inside until the rain stopped. Hopefully whoever had attacked Hector would be pinned down as well. Unless, of course, that person was already in the lodge with them.

Footsteps clumped toward the front door from outside, and Penelope looked at Philip with a wary expression. The door opened. Soggy versions of Fran and Estelle entered, with Neil following close behind.

"Did you find him?" Fran asked, pulling her hood from her head.

Before they could answer, her face pinched with worry as she scanned the room and saw no sign of Hector. Drops of water spilled from her teal and purple coat onto the floor, joining the puddles that had already gathered at their feet.

"We found Hector," Philip replied.

The look on his face indicated that the discovery had not been what they had hoped.

"But the witch found him first," Neil said bitterly.

"What happened?" Estelle asked, letting her gaze skip past Neil to look straight at Philip. She seemed deeply troubled.

"We're not sure," Philip answered. "We need to talk," he said, holding the door to the main room open to let the others pass through. "Please, everyone gather together."

Neil, Estelle, Fran, and Liam filed past in a subdued march. Penelope hung back to try to get a quick word with Philip, but before she could speak, she heard a stream of expletives coming from Neil. The cursing was followed by upset voices from the others. Penelope and Philip rushed into the room to see what was going on. The photograph was back on the mantel as if Penelope had never taken it down. But this time, Hector's eyes had been gouged in the same way as Star's and Nina's. A gasp caught in her throat. When she was able to force herself to speak, anger and terror pitched her voice louder than intended.

"Who keeps doing this?" Penelope asked.

Her mind raced as she tried to figure out who had been alone in the main room since she'd removed the photograph. Could it have happened when she was in the bathroom? Or had Fran, Neil, or Estelle left their group at some point? No matter what, the culprit was fast. Almost inhumanly so. She swallowed hard.

"Keeps doing it? What do you mean? When did this begin?" Liam's voice was frantic and confused as he looked to her for an explanation.

She remembered that he had slept late and missed the first conversation about the photograph. *Early bird gets the witch*, she thought, and nearly choked on an inappropriate laugh that felt close to a sob. Neil, Estelle, and Fran joined Liam in a circle around her.

Her heightened nerves made it difficult to answer his question. "I found it this morning. Only Nina had been . . . disfigured then. Fran, Philip, and . . . Hector saw a different version when we came back from our walk. Star's eyes . . . someone had done it to her too."

This time, it was Neil who swore. Once again, she could see the red tissue flaring at the corners of his eyes like those of a scared rabbit.

"It's the witch. It's the flipping Stone Witch. We should never have come here."

Liam placed a hand on the young man's shoulder.

"You've got to get it together," he said tightly. "We're going to get out of here. The witch isn't real, okay? You're freaking out."

Neil nodded, though he still looked disturbed. Philip came forward to rest his warm hand on the small of Penelope's back before addressing the group.

"Let's talk about this calmly," he said.

He led Penelope to their now familiar place on the couch and settled beside her. The others followed. Penelope focused on Estelle and Fran as they sat down across from her instead of allowing her eyes to travel to the reading area where Hector had been so often. Her heart felt hollow as she remembered the jar of honey waiting in their room. Neil and Liam took the armchairs. Too late, Penelope realized she should have relit the fire. The lack of light and warmth combined with the watery view out the windows made the room feel dreary and dark.

Philip began. "Hector sustained a fatal injury. It's hard to say defin-itively how or what occurred, but it appears to have been a blow to the back of his head."

Fran put her hand to her mouth. "How on earth did it happen?"

"I can't be certain, but it looks like he was wounded prior to fall-ing into the still. We found his body facedown as if the force was what knocked him into the hole," Philip said.

Estelle leaned forward, seemingly about to say something, but then stopped herself.

Fran spoke instead. "So someone did this to him?"

"It looks that way," Philip answered.

"Then it's three murders," Neil said dully.

"And counting. Jesus. Does anyone else need a drink?" Liam asked.

He didn't wait for an answer but walked past the pinball machine to the bar. He pulled a bottle of whiskey down from a glass shelf and poured himself a generous two fingers. Penelope noticed a small safe that looked like something from an upscale hotel behind the bar that she assumed had been intended to store valuables for guests. The fact that the Reddings had installed more security for things than for people made her want to scream.

"No, not three murders," Fran contradicted. "Penelope and I are certain that what happened to Star was accidental. She unwittingly ate deadly plants that she thought were wild onions. Besides, no one could have planned Danny knocking Nina over and, even if they had, how could they have known it would be fatal? Philip, the ground is slick as anything right now. Isn't it possible that Hector fell?"

Fran's brown eyes darted between Philip and Penelope before she con-tinued speaking.

"This could all be a horrible run of bad luck. Not deliberate acts of violence."

"Thank you for being reasonable, Fran." Philip's face was set in sol-emn lines as he spoke. Penelope wondered if he looked the same way when delivering bad news to his patients. "I've been operating on the same assumptions up until this point—that the deaths of Nina and Star were horrible accidents. But what happened to Hector looks much more deliberate." He paused. "I do not feel comfortable accusing anyone of malice. But Neil has told us that Danny took our satellite phones. He hasn't been seen since and that worries me."

Liam and Estelle looked stricken by the news about Danny. So far only she, Fran, and Philip knew that Danny might have had a motive to get rid of Nina, but the idea that Nina's death had been planned was still so hard to believe. Penelope wondered if it was time to let the rest of the group in on Danny's argument with his business partner. She had dismissed the idea earlier, but bodies were now stacking up.

If—and it was a big if—Danny had staged an allergic reaction to kill Nina and then taken their sat phones, she would have to look at everything else in a different way. Star had overheard Danny arguing with Nina. Slipping the death lilies into Star's foraged food before they gathered for dinner would have been easy—the kitchen had been left unattended nearly the whole day as the group settled on Stone Point. Using the back door for easy access would have been straightforward. Danny could have gone in and out without being noticed. But why kill Hector? Had he known something that incriminated Danny that he hadn't thought to share with the rest of them? Hector had been a small, aged man. Danny could have overpowered him with a quick push. How else could she explain the missing man, the mounting deaths, and the lost satellite phones? An awful thought occurred to her. Danny could be working in collusion with one or more of the people in the room. She moved to the fire for a reprieve from her anxious thoughts, stacking the tinder carefully as the others sat in tense silence, as if preoccupied with their own horrible ideas.

Suddenly, Liam jumped to his feet and approached the mantel. The muscles of his face were tight with stress.

"I can't stop thinking of Marianne. Not after what Estelle told me this morning," Liam said. He wheeled around to face Estelle, whose jaw had dropped. "We all knew her. Every single one of us. Isn't that right?"

He stared directly at Penelope as his question hung in the air. She felt a flash of guilt. Had Liam guessed that she'd stolen Marianne's idea for the trip? Even Philip didn't know that. Besides, Fran had no personal connection to Philip's sister. Liam continued and Penelope was relieved when his gaze shifted to the older woman.

"That energy she had, that way she could tell what you were thinking. I haven't been able to shake the sense of her since I got on the boat. The moment I saw you, Fran."

"Me?" Fran said in disbelief.

Liam spoke fast. "It took me forever to realize who you were but now I know. You were Marianne's neighbor, and you were friendly at first. Marianne used to bring you stuff from that bakery on the corner. But then things got weird because you always lectured her about outdoor cats because of Pete, remember? Marianne's cat?"

Fran stared at Liam with an odd expression on her face. Penelope willed the woman to defend herself, but instead she stayed silent. Liam turned to Philip.

"One day, Pete disappeared. Remember that?"

Philip didn't respond, seemingly as taken aback by Liam's outburst as the rest of them. Though the question hadn't been for her, Penelope nodded at the reminder of the black-and-white cat in a photograph Marianne had hung on her wall. Though he'd gone missing a year before she met Marianne, she knew her friend had been devastated by the loss of her pet.

Liam continued. "Marianne was convinced that Fran had something to do with it. She never spoke to her again."

Fran inhaled sharply, and Penelope couldn't help but rush in to defend the woman.

"But that doesn't prove—" Penelope tried to speak, but Liam wouldn't be interrupted.

"And that stuff that Hector was talking about? Star's academic probation? Marianne didn't like the way Hector had thrown a teaching assistant under the bus to save her job. You know what she was like about people playing favorites. She never forgave him for it."

"That TA really was on the take though," Neil said. "She did give Star the paper."

Again, Liam didn't acknowledge the words.

"And that photograph on the mantel. Marianne looked so goddamn much like Ruth Stone that I started dreaming of her. Neil and Estelle have too. Haven't you?"

Penelope remembered her terrifying dream from the night before. She dismissed the idea immediately. That horrible creature hadn't been Marianne.

"It's true that I haven't been able to sleep properly since we got here," Estelle began. Penelope expected Liam to cut her off as well but instead he looked at her deferentially. "The nightmares . . ." Estelle trailed off before finding words again. "They won't stop. That photograph unnerved me too. That was exactly what Marianne looked like when she was angry. That same hard glare."

Estelle's certainty added to Penelope's bewilderment. She had never noticed a resemblance between Marianne and Ruth. Then again, Marianne had never been angry with her. Her head swam as Liam spoke again.

"Yeah. Marianne looked at me like that when we fought. I couldn't stand it. She used to make me feel like nothing. Worse than that."

Estelle wiped a tear from her eye. Philip frowned, but Penelope wasn't sure if it was Liam's wild accusations about his sister or the way he was distracting the rest of the group. The enormity of Liam's statements seemed to suck the remaining fuel from the fire. Penelope placed another log into the flames, grateful for an excuse to contain her emotions as she struggled to reconcile the memory of her kind, supportive writing partner with the woman Liam was describing. She blew gently at the embers until the wood caught, then turned back to the group. Almost immediately, a resounding thud from behind her made her jump. Penelope turned back to the fire, half convinced that something was about to rush toward her, only to see that the log she had carefully placed had fallen out onto the brick hearth. Orange fingers licked the blond wood. Rivulets of sap rose to its surface like sweat on skin, spitting and popping in her direction, with tendrils of smoke rising from underneath.

"Get it off the floor!" Liam shouted. "It's going to burn the lodge down."

Penelope yanked a set of tongs from the large hook beside the fire; the stiff metal handles screeched in protest as she clamped them tight around the flaming log and shoved it back into the fire. Liam lunged forward to pull the grate across, to contain any other falling pieces. Raw flesh stung her wrists and hands.

"The witch is back," Neil muttered.

"That was my fault," Penelope said with a reassuring glance entirely at odds with how she felt inside. "I got distracted. I should have secured the grate."

"Another accident," Estelle said, in a hard-to-read tone.

"It's still possible that all three deaths were accidents. We can't be certain of anything until help comes," Fran said.

Penelope looked at the pale faces of the rest of the group as she collapsed beside Philip. Was it possible that one of them was a killer? But why?

"Help isn't coming," Neil said. The panic was evident in his voice. "We don't even have a phone."

"Please try to stay calm," Philip said. "There's a boat booked for nine a.m. on Monday morning. Even if worse comes to worst, that's just a day and a half away."

Penelope put her hand on his forearm to show support for his words, even though she knew she couldn't be the only person in the room doing the math. Three accidents—if they were accidents—had occurred in less than a day. One person had gone missing. Six of them were left. The odds were not favorable.

"Look, let's forget all this shit about the past. What we need is a map, a proper one like Nina mentioned last night," Liam said. His demeanor had changed since she'd shoved the log back into the fire—less spooked and more practical. Still, he poured himself a second drink as he kept talking.

"This is a bluff, not an island. There has to be a way to head north on these trails and get up the backside of the bluff. There must be something up there. Philip and I only got to the second ridge this afternoon before we split up. The trail gets rough as hell from there, but once this storm clears, we might have better luck breaking through the trees."

"Then it's settled. As soon as the sun rises, I'm heading out," Estelle said.

"I'm coming with you," Liam said.

"In the meantime, what about a signal fire?" Fran asked. "If we make it large enough, a passing boat could see it. People fish around here. Once the waves are calm, we might be able to flag someone down."

Penelope nodded at Fran's suggestion. Philip seemed lost in thought.

"There must be flares or something around here as well," Liam said. "Did anyone see anything in the woodshed?"

Penelope sucked in her breath at the mention of the building, as Philip shook his head and spoke.

"No, but that doesn't mean they haven't been stashed somewhere else. We'll do a thorough search this evening. At this point, it makes sense for us to stay in groups."

Penelope couldn't stop herself from eyeing the others, trying to see if any objected to being paired off, but she could see no reluctance in their faces.

"Fran and Estelle can partner up—" Philip was forced to stop when Neil jumped in.

"Seriously? Is no one going to talk about the fact that there's a murderer here?" he asked. "What if one of us—or more—doesn't even make it through the night?"

"Neil, we have to focus on the basics. Don't let the other stuff distract you," Liam said, ignoring the fact that he had been the source of much of the confusion. His words were slightly slurred now, and he seemed to have forgotten his eerie theory about Marianne and Ruth. "If we stick together, we'll all be fine. If these accidents were deliberate, we'll make sure that no one goes anywhere alone for the rest of the trip. It's only a day and a half, okay? You can stay in Bunkhouse B with me tonight."

Penelope realized that with Hector, Danny, and Nina gone, the bunkhouse was nearly empty. Neil turned to him as eagerly as a son would to a consoling father.

"I just want to get home as soon as possible. I hated school, but it seems like flipping heaven now," he said.

Liam opened a beer and slid it toward Neil, who settled on a stool before lifting it to his lips. Everyone else seemed to have run out of things to say. Penelope could hear Neil swallowing. As he set the bottle down, he cracked a smile that was wide enough to feel out of place even before he spoke.

"Who knows? Maybe I won't even have to go back to school. If I can escape this horror show, I'll sell my story to a screenwriter and make millions."

His callous humor made Penelope cringe. Estelle's grimace indicated the same distaste. Even Fran, who so often rushed to the young's man defense, seemed disappointed. Penelope looked at Neil carefully. According to him, he had lied on behalf of his girlfriend during her probation hearing. Was it possible he'd also been deceiving them? Could all his anger and panic about Star be a front? She tried to think clearly.

Of all the people gathered before her, Neil had had the greatest means and opportunity to harm Danny, Star, and Hector. He had been one of the first to arrive, and he and Star had access to everything. Not only had he been present in the kitchen throughout the day and night, but he had been in and out of sight throughout the trip. Nina's death could have been a happy accident for him if he'd been planning to kill them all one by one anyway. Penelope's suspicions swirled. The young man had been desperately seeking the attention of others since they first arrived. She'd already considered the scratching of the eyes something Neil might do for the sake of drama. Might he be capable of even more than that? Did Neil realize that he had just suggested a gruesome motive for himself? Was it possible he was staging a horrific tragedy so he could sell the story? Did he covet fame enough to kill?

Estelle's voice broke into her thoughts.

"Neil is right. We must address the enormous elephant in the room."

The other woman's jaw seemed locked in determination. Penelope was struck by the hardness in her face and eyes as she kept speaking.

"Danny's been missing since late last night. We now know he's stolen our communication equipment," she said with a sidelong glance at Penelope. "He is an experienced wilderness guide. He didn't come here to learn more about an imaginary witch. He came here to murder us all."

The room erupted with interrupted sentences.

"Why on earth would he—" Fran asked.

"The witch is not imaginary. You didn't see the—" Neil protested.

"This is not helpful at all—" Philip argued.

As the others fought, the fire popped and sent another shower of sparks into the air. Fran rose and the voices fell silent, providing a welcome halt to the clamor.

"We can't resolve anything by fighting. I know it might seem difficult, but we really must eat something before we continue this discussion," the older woman said.

"I'll help you," Penelope said as she got to her feet. Fran was right. They'd all think better with food in their stomachs.

Philip stood as well with a heavy sigh.

"Fran is right. Food will help."

The three of them headed toward the kitchen, but before they reached the door, a pulverizing noise came from outside, loud enough to shake the floor beneath their feet. Penelope jumped back and stared irrationally at the fireplace, wondering if the stone wall had collapsed. It was intact. The loud crash was followed by a series of smaller creaks and groans that seemed to be coming from the kitchen. Her eardrums wobbled unpleasantly as a repetitive ringing drowned out her ability to think. Luckily, Philip took charge.

"In here," he shouted as he moved toward the door.

She followed him mindlessly into the dining room. Nothing was amiss. Then, to her horror, the overhead light flared and died, leaving the dim room lit only by the dull dusk clouded by the storm.

Philip swore. As he swung open the door to the kitchen, her heart sank like a stone. Half the roof had been caved in by a tree falling onto it. The back corner of the kitchen beside the stove was now a jagged hole exposed to the elements. The trunk of the invading tree was at least twice as large as the span of her waist. Inside the small room, it looked enormous. The floor was thick with mud, rocks, and splintered wood. Debris made up of cedar fronds, splintered wood, and bark covered every surface. Branches thicker than her wrist snaked out, making it hard to move into the room. Rain dripped onto the cast-iron stove, which hissed in response. A sharp gust of wind whistled into the small space. Penelope shivered as Philip turned to her in shock.

"It must have knocked out the generator. We've lost power."

The rain began to fall harder as if in response. No one said a word as the light leached from the room. The sun was setting on Stone Point. Penelope could feel the darkness coming.

THE THIRD DAY

CHAPTER **TWENTY-FIVE**

12:07 A.M.

Penelope was devastated when she returned to the lodge with Philip and Liam later that night. After more than six hours of attempting to restart the generator's dented body, they had been forced to accept that the tree had mangled it beyond hope of repair. They walked through the damaged kitchen to the dining room, where they saw that Fran had prepared a late candlelit meal for them of tuna, bread, and dried fruit. Beside the collection of food was a pile of candles and flashlights. Estelle, Fran, and Neil were sitting at the table looking despondent.

"So that's it? No power?" Estelle asked after Philip let the others know of their failed attempts.

"We might be able to get the generator going again in the daylight, but it's raining too hard right now to see much that can be salvaged," Liam said.

"We gathered all the torches and candles we could find," said Fran. "The Reddings had a few windup flashlights in case the batteries ran low, so that's some consolation."

Penelope was filled with too much gloom to pretend to be optimistic.

"It doesn't look good," she said.

"What about the roof in the kitchen?" Estelle asked. "Is it stable?"

Liam shrugged. "Honestly, your guess is as good as mine. The sooner we get out of this place the better is all I can say."

His words were slurring together more markedly than they had before. He had been sipping from a flask during their repair attempt and now had a glass of wine in front of him from the bottle he'd grabbed on his way through the kitchen. Everyone but Neil had refused his offer of a drink. Once they finished eating, there seemed to be no point to staying in the lodge. All sense of congenial gathering was gone. They were in survival mode.

Penelope and Fran volunteered to clean up while the others headed down to the bunkhouses together. After a moment, Philip and Neil thoughtfully returned with coats for the two women before leaving again, as the kitchen was now cold and damp enough to require rain gear. Penelope's jacket was so soaked there was almost no point in donning it, but she decided that even a wet layer was better than nothing at all. As she slipped it on, she noticed a lump in her pocket. She reached in, hoping she hadn't forgotten her bear mace after all. Instead, Marianne's tube of lipstick shone rose-gold in her hand. It seemed bizarrely out of place in the grubby kitchen. Liam's earlier words about her friend rang in her head. She tucked the lipstick away, reminding herself to deal with it later.

Despite the meager offerings, most of the food Fran had prepared for dinner had been left untouched. Penelope set it back in the fridge, opening and closing the door quickly to try to keep what was left inside as cold as possible. As they worked, the rain drummed into the buckets they had set out.

"Those need emptying," Fran said.

"We'll do it after we put this stuff away," Penelope agreed.

"Hopefully the storm stops soon," Fran said as she placed dried apples into a container. "This rain will have animals out looking for shelter. I'm worried about what could come in here seeking refuge. There are all kinds of creatures that wouldn't be very nice to deal with if they found themselves trapped: fishers, foxes, even raccoons. Worse yet, bears and cougars might catch scent of the easy pickings down here. Particularly the . . . contents of the woodshed."

"I wish we had a dog or cat to keep them away," Penelope said worriedly.

"A dog, maybe," Fran said. "But a cat in these woods would wreak havoc on the native songbird populations. I'd sooner chase a weasel out with a broom."

Penelope looked at Fran, remembering Liam's words about the woman's relationship with Marianne. Fran seemed to know what she was thinking.

"I'm sorry. All that talk from Liam of outdoor cats and Marianne got me rattled. I did like Pete, for what it's worth. I just like songbirds more."

"I understand," said Penelope after a pause she hoped was too brief to register.

Since Liam's outburst, irrational thoughts about Marianne's real reason for wanting to research Ruth Stone had been distracting her too. Was it possible there was a deeper connection between the two women than she had realized? She pushed aside her doubts about the older woman. No matter what, she trusted Fran a whole lot more than she trusted Liam.

"Shall we get to those buckets?" Penelope asked.

"Yes, absolutely," said Fran with a look of relief.

As the two worked, Penelope tried to take the heavier load. Fran's limp had grown more pronounced over the course of their chores. Once she'd tipped out the last bucket and returned it to its former place, she turned to the older woman.

"I'm worn out. Fran, are you ready to head to the bunkhouse?"

"Yes, thank you," she said, patting Penelope's arm gently.

Her touch was tremulous, and Penelope could sense her exhaustion. After grabbing a box of candles each from the cupboard in the reading nook, they headed out into the driving rain with Philip's small flashlight to guide the way. The ground was now completely saturated, and the path looked more like a small creek than a trail in the beam of the torch. They kept to the edge of the rushing water, where the slightly higher ground was slick with mud but not flowing beneath their feet. It was slow and slippery going, and Penelope was relieved when the solidity of the bunkhouse came into view. They entered together, shaking the water from their outerwear.

"Take care of yourself, Fran, and try to get some rest. We're right down the hall if you need anything."

Penelope gave the woman a quick embrace. As she turned to her own room, she saw that Estelle's door was already closed. She resisted the urge to knock on it to ensure Philip's mother was actually in there. Too late, she realized that she should have insisted they all sleep as a group in the lodge rather than disband into separate rooms but there was no helping it now. After letting herself into her bedroom, she closed the door tightly and turned the dead bolt, pulling on the handle to make sure it was secure. The movement was so similar to the one she had made when leaving her safe, warm apartment that she almost broke down in tears. Only the sight of Philip sitting at the end of the bed kept her from falling apart. He yawned as she sat down too. Candle flames quavered from the bedside table.

"It's nearly one a.m.," he said. "I'm so tired I can barely see straight."

"It's been quite a day. I think we could both use some rest, though I'm not sure I'll be able to sleep. What if something else happens?"

"We just have to get through the next thirty-two hours. The boat is coming on Monday morning. The worst thing we could do now is give up."

"You're right," she said, trying to summon a semblance of her characteristic cheer.

The effort wore her out. As she lay her head on his shoulder, she heard him draw in a slow, ragged breath. She wondered if he had been trying to convince himself at the same time he was reassuring her. But when he spoke, his words surprised her.

"I was the one who found Marianne, you know? The first time."

Penelope raised her head. Confusion cut through her weariness. She had no idea what Philip was talking about.

"What first time?"

"After her first seizure. When her AVM started to get worse."

"AVM?"

"Sorry. It's the technical term for her condition. She always accused me of being too jargon-y about it," he said. "Basically, it's a malformed tangle of blood vessels. It was the reason for her aneurysm."

"She knew?"

Penelope wouldn't have guessed that she had the energy to be so stunned.

"We both did. She had it for years—it was diagnosed when we were teenagers. We knew it could rupture at any time. Did she never tell you?"

Philip leaned his body away so he could look at her fully. Darkness bled into the edge of her vision, which was already blurry with fatigue and self-doubt. She hadn't known any of this. Why hadn't Marianne told her?

"No," Penelope said quietly, setting aside the questions she would never be able to answer, in place of the ones she could. "What happened when you found her?"

"It was awful. I thought she was dead. I came home from work early one day to see if she wanted to go to a matinee. When she didn't answer, I opened the door. Pete was in there meowing and trying to wake her up, but she wouldn't budge."

"I was a med student at the time—working crazy hours, barely ever home. I thought I was ready to be a doctor, but I couldn't handle it when the patient was my sister. I had to call 911 and watch like an idiot as they resuscitated her. I never took another day with Marianne for granted. It was excruciating when she decided to move out of our apartment. I knew she needed her space, but I wanted so badly to keep her close. I thought I could protect her."

Philip stopped abruptly. Penelope had never seen him look so broken.

"What am I saying? Today must have shaken something loose inside my head," Philip said. "I need to get some sleep."

Though she wanted badly to know more about Marianne, she placed a hand on his arm. They had plenty of time to get to know each other's history. Like Marianne always said, it was a story for another time.

"I'm so sorry, Philip."

His nod of appreciation was interrupted by another deep yawn before he turned to her with a warmer expression.

"I appreciate that. That's what I've always loved about you. Your loyalty."

She inhaled sharply at his raw expression. He quickly broke eye contact so she changed the subject.

"Should I head down to the beach with Fran and Estelle in the morning to get the fire going?" she said. "Or is there a better plan?"

"I'm not sure. I don't want to leave you alone, but I think joining Liam on the hike out is probably my best option. One of us needs to keep an eye on him. Especially after today."

And Neil, she thought, before realizing the full implication of what Philip was saying.

"I thought Liam was your friend."

"Friend." He frowned. "I guess he was, before he started dating Marianne. We go back a long way, but it hasn't been the same between us since they broke up. After that, I could never call him a friend again. I tried to reconnect when I drove to the vineyard last Christmas, but there was too much baggage."

His expression had darkened again. She knew her next question wasn't going to help, but she needed to know.

"What exactly happened between them?"

"She never told you that either?" Philip looked incredulous. "God, she kept so much inside. I didn't realize how private she had become. When we lived together, she was an open book. She told me everything."

Penelope was hurt by the insinuation that Marianne hadn't trusted her, but she pushed it away so she could focus on Philip's explanation.

"Liam and Marianne were trying for a baby. It was a long shot and dangerous for her, but she wanted it so badly: They were both thrilled beyond belief when she got pregnant. She was about four months along when she miscarried."

"Oh my god," Penelope whispered. "When did this happen?"

"About five years ago."

The year before she and Marianne had met. Back then, Marianne had told her she'd been writing the manuscript for a year. She had talked about the catharsis of the process, how putting a scary story on the page had been the only way to free herself from the burden of carrying the pain around in her head. Penelope had thought she understood in an abstract, creative kind of way. Now she was shocked to realize how little she'd actually known about Marianne's suffering. The realization made her sad—and scared. If Marianne had been able to hide so much from her, was it possible that someone else on the trip was doing the same thing? Penelope's thoughts were interrupted by a flare of anger in Philip's eyes as he kept talking.

"There were complications with the miscarriage. Marianne needed an emergency hysterectomy."

He waited for Penelope to put the pieces together.

"So Liam left her because she couldn't have children anymore?" Penelope said.

"At first, he told her he needed space to mourn, but then he stopped returning her calls. She blamed me for introducing them. She told me that I should have known how awful he was."

"Oh, Philip. That's not true. How could you have known?"

So Liam had fooled her as well. He had seemed selfish not cruel. But a man capable of leaving his grieving, healing girlfriend behind seemed capable of anything. More importantly, he and Philip had been separated when Hector was killed. Liam had also been sidling up to Star before her death. She remembered the two glasses on the table. Was it possible that Liam had poisoned her? They'd all accepted Fran's theory about the death lilies as definitive, but Philip was right. There was no way to be certain without a toxicology report. Worse yet, even if they could determine that the death lilies killed Star, there was no way to know exactly how they'd gotten into her food. Neil had told them that Star had eaten them herself, but she couldn't trust him either. A chill rippled up her spine as Philip continued.

"I wish I had never set those two up," he said with a heavy sigh. "I know now that Liam's definitely not trustworthy, but that doesn't necessarily make him a killer. I'll head up the bluffs with him tomorrow just in case. Maybe Danny collapsed up there with the phones. Maybe there's still a reasonable explanation for all this."

"Maybe," Penelope said.

Doubt made her draw the word out long and slow. Philip noticed.

"And maybe not."

"I can't help thinking that Danny could be trying to kill us all," Penelope blurted.

Though the words were terrible, it felt good to say them out loud instead of letting them bounce around her head any longer. Marianne was right. Getting it out was cathartic.

"I know." Philip's shoulders slumped. "I didn't want to harp on it with the rest of the group, but Danny does seem to be the most likely suspect, doesn't he? He could be an active threat. Let's decide tomorrow what the best thing is for you to do. I can barely string a thought together. Right now, I just need to get some sleep."

Penelope kissed his warm lips, wishing she had the energy to do more. They pulled apart, found their pajamas, and headed to the bathroom to brush their teeth. Even in the unsettling location, it felt nice to perform such mundane duties with him by her side. One thing was for sure. Philip was not the kind of man that Liam or Danny were. She slid over to her side of the bed and Philip joined her. She heard his breath slowly even out while hers did the same. As she drifted off, she decided to accompany him up the bluff in the morning. She didn't want to be away from him for a single second.

With Philip's arm across her middle and the thick covers weighing down her shoulders, she felt safer than she had all day.

Until the screams began.

CHAPTER **TWENTY-SIX**

1:17 A.M.

Philip jerked upright, fumbling for his flashlight in the black room. The light bounced off the wall, then directly into her eyes before he got it in hand. He rushed out of bed, slid back the dead bolt, and twisted the door open with Penelope on his heels.

"Was that Estelle?" she asked.

"I don't know," he said over his shoulder.

They rushed down the now silent corridor. The blackness in the hallway was so thick that it almost seemed as if they weren't moving at all. Had she imagined the shouts? Then a raw cry came again.

"Let me out!"

Estelle's voice was hoarse and emotional. This time, it was accompanied by loud thumps like a body hurling at the door. Philip and Penelope moved as fast as the thin beam would allow. The darkness felt claustro-phobic. With each hurried step, Penelope imagined something lurking beyond the shadows of the beam, waiting to swallow her whole.

Finally, they reached the door.

"Estelle? Estelle? Let us in, Estelle. Are you okay?" Philip called.

He pulled on the door. It didn't budge, so he knocked hard. Down the hall, Fran's door swung wide.

"What's going on?" she asked. Her voice was shaking. "Is everyone okay?"

"It's Estelle," Penelope answered.

"Mom? Are you there? Are you okay?"

Another thud came from inside. Panic pulsed through Penelope. Philip must be terrified as well. This was the first time she'd ever heard him call Estelle anything but her first name.

"I'm trapped! Let me out."

Philip took a step back. "Get away from the door."

He dropped his shoulder and bashed into the wood. The frame buck-led at the force. He backed up again and repeated the effort, again and again. This time, the hinges gave way and the door crashed open.

"Oh thank god," Estelle cried. "There's someone in here. Someone's trying to attack me."

She rushed into the corridor and stood panting between them. Pe-nelope saw the bedroom was lit by a single sputtering candle on Estelle's nightstand. The corners were dark. Penelope was terrified by the thought of someone entering Bunkhouse A. Danny? Neil? Liam? Ruth?

"Are you okay? Are you hurt?" Penelope asked.

Estelle didn't answer. She was wild-eyed and trembling. Adrenaline flooded Penelope's body as she stared at the obviously shaken woman. Fran joined them and reached an arm around Estelle's shaking shoulders, as Philip scanned the light up and down his mother's face searching for wounds, while Penelope patted the woman's head, arms, and legs, looking for blood.

"I think she's okay," Penelope said to Philip.

"I need to check the room," he responded, squaring his body in the doorframe.

Before he entered, he swept the space with his flashlight. Penelope peered in behind him, and then the two of them took a step inside and began the search. The bedroom seemed empty, save for a queen-size bed wedged into the corner. At least it was witch-proofed, Penelope thought stupidly before taking in the rest of the space. A large armchair was placed by a window, and she saw a door on the far right. Philip walked toward the bed, then ducked down to look underneath it. Penelope sucked in her breath, exhaling only when she saw his head pop up again.

"Nothing there," he said.

"Does that lead to the bathroom?" she asked Estelle with a gesture to the door.

Estelle nodded before smoothing both sides of her silver bob.

"I heard something, I swear," Estelle whispered to Fran, who was pinching the edges of her frayed plaid bathrobe together at her chest.

"You did the right thing. It's much better to be safe than sorry," Fran said.

Estelle seemed encouraged by Fran's words. She gave the other woman a small nod of thanks.

"Philip, you check the bathroom. Please check everywhere. Maybe they went in there." Estelle's fear was evident in her voice as Penelope and Philip moved toward the door on the far wall.

"Who was here?" Penelope asked.

"I'm not . . . I'm not sure," the woman said.

Penelope opened the door, and then stepped back. Philip entered with his flashlight held at chest height. For a moment, she felt like she was part of a police duo, and she had to force the nearly hysterical smile off her face. Before Philip had completed a full circle around the tiny bathroom, she could see that the small space was empty too. Estelle was alone. There was nothing in her room to be feared. At least nothing they could see.

"Was there anything in there?" Estelle asked as they came out of the bathroom.

Philip shook his head. He took his mother by the shoulders, speaking clearly and slowly.

"Who came into your room?"

Estelle looked at him. Her glazed eyes seemed to focus, as if his presence had brought her back to reality. When she spoke, her voice was firmer than it had been before.

"I can't be sure now. I heard someone moving around. At least I thought I heard . . ."

"What did you hear?" Philip asked.

"A noise, like a thump. I jumped out of bed to leave, but I couldn't get out of the room. The door was locked. I couldn't even turn the knob; it felt like someone was holding it from the outside, like they were trapping me in."

Penelope remembered her doorknob sticking the night before.

"The doors have been jamming for me too," Penelope said. "Are you sure that no one came into your room?"

Estelle shrugged weakly. "It was a nightmare, I guess." She turned to face her son. "I'm so scared here, Philip. I hate this place. I want to leave."

Philip's jaw tightened. Penelope could see the tension beneath his professional medical demeanor. Luckily, Fran spoke before he could.

"Why don't you come stay in my room?" Fran said. "There's a spare bed in there. I have to admit, I was having a hard time falling asleep on my own."

Penelope was certain that despite her fear, Estelle's natural reserves would cause her to dismiss Fran's kind offer, but the woman's expression was grateful as she answered.

"Are you sure you don't mind? I don't want to be alone either."

"I'm happy to help," Fran said. "We have to stick together."

All four of them headed to Fran's bedroom. Her door had been left open and Penelope was reassured by the warm orange glow coming from inside it. Unlike Philip and Estelle, Fran had lit dozens of candles. Her room looked as bright and friendly as a romantic restaurant.

"I'm going to take a look around, just in case," Philip said, pointing his flashlight into another dark corner.

"Be careful," Penelope said.

She still felt unnerved despite his thorough search. Penelope followed the two women inside Fran's room. One bed was pushed into the corner, while another floated in the center of the room.

"Is there anything I can do to help?" Penelope asked Fran. "Should we rearrange the furniture a little to keep the witches away? It seemed to work in your room, Estelle."

The joke fell flat. Fran looked at her with a determined expression, while Estelle's face remained blank.

"We're fine for now, but I'll call you if that changes. At least we know now we'll be able to hear each other if we need it."

Penelope nodded and wished the women good night before joining Philip in the hallway. Neither she nor Philip said a word until they were back inside their room, dead bolt in place.

"I'm glad she's okay," Penelope whispered as they settled back into bed.

"Physically, yes. Mentally, I'm worried she's starting to fall apart," he said.

"Aren't we all?" she replied.

In response, he cradled her body, pulling her close.

"We just need to make it for two more days," he said. "The boat will be here first thing Monday morning."

Her heartbeat slowed. A powerful wave of weariness washed over her as she nestled into Philip's chest. All the adrenaline that had built up in her system after hearing Estelle's screams began to flush away, leaving her almost incapable of speech. But as she drifted off, something important floated to the surface of her mind.

"Philip?"

"Hmmm?"

"Why does Fran have a gun on her bedside table?"

CHAPTER **TWENTY-SEVEN**

6:28 A.M.

Philip stirred groggily as she slid out from under his heavy arm.

"What time is it?" he asked with eyes still closed.

"Six thirty."

He opened his eyes fully.

"We should pack our bags and get moving as soon as day breaks. The sun will be up in less than an hour."

Though the terror of the night had lessened in the dull morning, Penelope couldn't agree with him more.

"That's exactly what I was thinking," she said. "I hope your mother is feeling better after some sleep."

Philip sat up. He brushed his rumpled hair back and, despite everything, Penelope was struck once again by how attractive he was.

"At this point, I'm not willing to rule her out as the person behind this whole business."

Penelope stared at Philip in shock. "Why on earth do you think that?"

Philip seemed startled at her strong reaction.

"I'm not saying it's absolutely her. But it has to be one of us, and I know she has a temper she can't control. You haven't seen it yet, but I have. I'm not willing to trust anyone, especially her. You're the only one I know is on my side."

Penelope was strangely flattered, though she was worried about the way Philip was letting the past cloud his judgment.

"And I trust you too. Obviously. But we can't assume the worst of everyone else. Danny has been missing since the first night. He's the obvious suspect, just like we talked about. We know he had something to hide and that Nina was arguing with him the night she was killed."

Philip's forehead wrinkled.

"You're right. But after last night, I think it's best for us to stick together today. I don't want to be separated," he said.

She was relieved.

"I agree. We'll let Fran and Estelle handle the signal fire on their own. I'm coming with you up the bluff."

"Yeah, that sounds good," he said.

"There's one more thing. Everyone is on edge now. Seeing that gun last night made me worried. Now that Estelle is staying in her room, it could get in the wrong hands. The thought of Estelle panicking with a loaded gun . . ."

"Agreed." He flashed her a quick smile. "But don't worry. It won't be loaded. I'll take the bullets out this morning when I check Fran's room. I'm going to give the bunkhouse another going-over. Maybe I missed something last night."

"Good idea," Penelope said, marveling at his resourcefulness. She had no idea how to handle a weapon. It was reassuring not to have to rely solely on herself to survive.

The two dressed quickly. When they walked outside, Penelope filled her lungs with air sweetened by the rain from the night before. It was clear now but cold. The sunrise had brought faint light but little warmth. Estelle, Fran, and Liam were already gathered by the wooden benches around the firepit in the colorless morning. The clouds hung low and the ground gave slightly under her feet as they walked toward the others. She sensed the rain could begin again at any time. In the far distance through the gaps between the trees, the ocean was gray and violent, white-capped waves tumbling and breaking over each other. It looked hopelessly rough for a fishing boat. An icy gust swept past them, knocking tree branches and chilling her cheeks.

"No sign of Neil?" she asked.

"That kid is definitely not an early riser," Liam replied.

His eyes were bloodshot. Penelope tried to smile but her feelings toward him had changed after hearing about the way he'd treated Marianne. How could he have left her when she needed him the most? She drew in a breath to help her focus. In and out as slowly as she could. The cold air was like a cup of coffee.

"We have to wake him," she said. "No one should be alone today at any time. It's the only way to keep us all safe."

"Absolutely right." Fran nodded, hugging her arms around her body as the wind circled them again.

"He's in the second-to-last room on the right," Liam said.

She and Philip crossed the divide between the bunkhouses and stepped onto the deck. Her heel crunched on something, and she kicked away a small shard of glass. Her heart sank as she realized it was all that was left of Hector's honey jar. They walked inside Bunkhouse B to see a mirror image of their own. Three doors to smaller bedrooms lined the corridor. At the end of the hall to her right was the door leading to the largest room. They walked to the bedroom as Liam had directed. Philip knocked twice.

"Neil?" he called. "It's time to get up."

No answer. He knocked again, then looked at Penelope with a drawn face.

"Let's try the handle," she said.

Philip reached down and turned it, breathing in sharply when it opened easily. They glanced at each other in surprise.

Philip called out as he walked into the room. Penelope followed. It was identical to Estelle's.

"Neil?"

It was clear that Neil wasn't inside. In the dim light from the window, curtained with only a white sheer fabric, Penelope noticed that the color scheme was the same as their room: gray, oatmeal, and white. It was as if the Reddings had tried to mimic the bleached landscape of driftwood, sand, and gray water. The bedcovers were tossed around messily, sheets twisted and the quilt hanging half off the side. To her left, the bathroom door was open. They searched it quickly. There was no sign of Neil anywhere. She stared at Philip. Unease rose in her throat. She wasn't sure if she was more worried for the young man's safety—or that of the rest of the group.

"We need to find him," she said.

The two of them went from room to empty room in a fruitless search. Neil was nowhere to be found.

"Let's get back," she said, squeezing Philip's hand as they retraced their steps back along the hallway. The bedroom doors they had closed behind them stood like sentries as they passed by again. Though she knew the rooms were empty, she was happy to be back out in the open air once they left the bunkhouse. There were so many places here where someone could hide. There was no way their group of six—five without Neil— could secure the entire area.

Philip shook his head as Estelle, Liam, and Fran looked toward them expectantly.

"He's not in his room. Or anywhere in the bunkhouse," he said.

Fran raised her hand to her thin neck where the sinews were standing out in sharp relief. The sight reminded Penelope of the ghastly figure in her nightmare. She crossed her arms around herself for comfort. Estelle glared in her direction as if Neil's disappearance was Penelope's fault. The other woman seemed back to her old self, a marked difference from the vulnerable side she'd shown the night before. Penelope sighed.

"Good lord," Fran said softly. "That poor boy."

Liam raked at his hair. His skin had an underlying pallor that Penelope was beginning to sense was typical for him in the morning.

"Neil was upset yesterday. When you went to check on the kitchen, he kept talking about the witch and that damn photograph. Maybe he needed time to get himself together this morning."

The absurdity of his statement made the entire group turn to him with a mixture of skepticism and apprehension on their faces. Penelope broke the silence.

"You think he went for a walk alone in a remote location before sunrise in a place where three people have already been killed?"

Liam responded to her doubt with stubborn conviction.

"He's a kid, Penelope. They don't always make the best decisions. He had this crazy idea to start a signal fire in the dark. I told him he would break his neck if he tried going down those stairs in the middle of the storm, but he said the fire would be more visible at night. I thought I had talked him out of it but maybe he stuck to his guns. He's got more guts than brains. It's kind of how guys in their twenties are."

He met Philip's eyes and Philip responded with a tentative nod, though she guessed that Philip had never let his heart rule his head.

"I'm sure he's fine," Liam continued.

Penelope didn't agree but she let it slide. Arguing with Liam wasn't going to save Neil.

"If he was planning to light a signal fire last night, maybe we should check the beach? He could have headed there," Fran said.

"That's a great idea," said Penelope, thankful for a logical suggestion. "Let's walk down there together and see. After that, we'll head up the bluff."

Liam was shaking his head in disagreement.

"The clouds are clearing, Penelope. We have a much better chance of finding a way out today than we did before. Look at the chop out there. No boats are coming in. We've got lots of time to build a fire this afternoon if our hike doesn't get us anywhere. If you want to stick together as a group, let's go up the bluff first, then worry about the beach."

The insistence in his voice notched up the frustration she was working hard to contain. How could he be so sure about Neil's safety?

"What about Neil? We need to track him down first, Liam. That has to take priority over the hike," Penelope said.

She hated unnecessarily risking all their lives if Liam was right and Neil was just being reckless, but it felt like a better plan than following Liam, who was acting selfish at best and suspicious at worst.

"He's fine," Liam said impatiently. "We all make decisions, right? If he chose to go off on his own, I'm sure he'll be able to make it back."

Penelope couldn't take it any longer.

"We have to find him. Use your head. He might be hurt. Or he might be trying to hurt us. I know if I was the killer, I would realize that the easy pickings are over. We're all on guard now. It's going to be harder to get to us since we've realized that we're being hunted. The way you're talking, it's starting to make me wonder if you know more than we do about what happened to him."

The others gaped at Penelope as she hoisted her backpack over her shoulder. Her bleak breakdown of the situation seemed to have shaken them, but she couldn't look on the bright side any longer. Fran, Philip, and Estelle lifted their bags as well. The scream of a seagull pierced the air as Estelle cinched the straps on her heavy-looking bag before she spoke.

"Let's walk down to the beach and look for him. If he's not there, we can get the fire going anyway. There's enough wood in here to start it. Hopefully, we can find some more dry fuel down at the beach to keep it going. Otherwise, we'll bring more down later. Let's go."

She was stronger than she appeared, Penelope realized. Liam blew out a gust of air before relenting.

"Fine, we'll light the fire fast, then."

"Oh damn. I forgot my hat—" Philip said.

"Hurry," Penelope answered.

She played along with his ruse, knowing this was his only chance to disarm Fran's gun. She ignored Liam's glares as the group waited impatiently in tense silence while he dashed into the bunkhouse. Penelope was impressed with the speed of his return. He gave a tight nod in her direction as he fell into step beside her, which eased her panic by a fraction. At least she didn't have to add getting accidentally shot by Estelle to her list of worries.

The dense forest encroached upon the path from both sides as they walked down to the beach. *Neil or Danny could be hiding in there*, she thought. More frightening was that Danny might have a gun that they had no chance of controlling. For all she knew, Neil could also be carrying a weapon. The skin on the back of her neck crawled as she imagined a bullet entering her spine before she could register the sound of a shot. Why had she decided to take this trip? For months, her second book had been all she could think about. Now, she wished she had abandoned the editorial contract altogether. Her need to be a success in the eyes of her family meant little now that she was struggling to stay alive.

The path narrowed and they were forced to walk in single file. She realized they must look like a multicolored army tromping along. She cleared the silly idea from her mind. It was time to focus. The wind picked up again as they neared the cliff, blowing upward from the water. The moment she got to the top of the stairs, the frigid gusts replaced the air in her lungs. At the head of the pack, Estelle wasn't deterred. She moved fast. Her solid gait assured Penelope that she too could make it down without plummeting to the hard-packed sand below. Since the journey up, she had dreaded the return to these stairs. She certainly hadn't imagined walking down with legs tightened by terror.

After one step, it was clear that the rain had made the rock as treacherous as ice. Each time the sole of her foot slid on the wet stone, her stomach lurched like she was already falling over the steep edge, but she kept going. What other choice did she have? Fran followed, then Liam, and finally Philip. The sense of their bodies behind her made her almost as nervous as the lack of purchase beneath her feet. If one of them fell, they would take her along with them. Or worse, if one of them was pushed.

The wind was much fiercer on the exposed stairs than it had been by the firepit. It forced tears from her eyes and took away her ability to see anything beyond the descending steps. The farther down she went, the more vulnerable she felt. Pieces of sand scoured her face. Her eyes and nose were raw by the time she finally reached the beach. Estelle was already moving steadily along the rock wall to the patch of beach that faced the open ocean—the misleading finger of land the captain had been so wary about. Penelope laid her hand flat on the craggy surface of the rock wall as she followed. It undulated slightly, carved into curves by centuries of wind and water. In front of her, Estelle stopped just before an outcropping, tucking herself into the scant shelter offered by the slight jutting out of the cliff.

"The wind isn't as bad here," she said. "From this angle, the fire would be visible for kilometers."

Penelope didn't have time to respond. Pounding footsteps from behind made her duck in fear before she realized Fran was running toward the water, sprinting as if being chased. Penelope pushed off in the same direction. The thick sand caught at her feet like a sticky treadmill. Her thighs burned in her fight against the ground, but she refused to let up. She could see what Fran was running toward now. There was something on the sand. Something that looked like a body.

She was out of breath by the time she reached her friend who was already kneeling. Penelope struggled for a full inhalation. It felt as though she were choking on her own throat. The body was facedown and spread out like a sea star that had been washed ashore. The thick head of dirty-blond hair was crusted with sand that was almost identical to it in color, as if the body was becoming part of the beach.

Philip came from behind and flipped the body onto its back. Penelope was overcome with nausea when she saw it was Neil. His eyes were caked with the same sand that coated his hair. He was unseeing, blinded, sightless. His eyes were just like those of Nina, Star, and Hector in the damaged photograph. She stumbled away. Her insides contracted violently as she threw up. She wiped the back of her mouth roughly then returned to the group.

Liam began to shake Neil's shoulders, calling his name as if he could wake the dead young man. The gesture caused Liam's sleeves to fall back from his wrists, revealing deep red scratches that ran up and down his forearms. The kind of marks another person would make if they were fighting for their life.

CHAPTER **TWENTY-EIGHT**

If the walk down to the beach had been a military march, the return to the lodge was the slog of a defeated army betrayed by a hidden spy. Once they reached the building, Penelope could see the others darting looks of fear and suspicion toward each other as they stripped off their outerwear. Her own mind was racing. There was no longer a shadow of doubt. Someone was hunting them. Someone skilled.

The main room was cold, gray, and felt almost as damp as the kitchen had been the night before. Penelope glanced at the fireplace. For an instant, she saw the face of Ruth Stone, staring out with her mouth wide open and poised to consume them all. She blinked hard and the image disappeared. It was replaced by a new version of their group shot. This time, Neil's eyes were gouged out.

She put a hand on Philip's forearm to steady herself. The silence in the room made her sick. It felt as though they were all dead already. She couldn't hold in the question that had filled her head since they had laid Neil's body respectfully on the beach. Estelle had been nearly hysterical as they'd crossed his arms over his chest and dusted the sand from his eyes.

"How did you get those scratches, Liam?" Penelope asked.

She hadn't meant to shout, but her accusing words echoed in the large room. The others turned to stare at the man who was leaning against the back of the couch to support himself. Fran was at the fireplace, while Estelle froze in the center of the room. Liam looked at Penelope with wide eyes, his lips slightly parted. The pause was incriminating, Penelope was certain.

"What kind of scratches?" Philip asked her.

Estelle and Fran also looked at her questioningly. Penelope was stunned that none of them had noticed Liam's injuries, but the discovery of Neil had been so chaotic.

"Deep ones. They looked fresh. How did they happen, Liam? Were you with Neil last night? Did you throw him off the cliff? Is that why you weren't worried about him this morning?"

She thought of the intruder Estelle had heard in her room. Had it been Liam? Had they stopped him from killing Philip's mother?

Fran turned to stare at him in horror.

"Neil would have listened to you if you asked him to come to the cliff," she said. "He would have followed you anywhere."

Liam took a step back.

Did he feel cornered?

"No, no! I swear I never left my room. I didn't even hear Neil's door opening."

"I did. Or at least, I heard something." said Fran, with a glance at Penelope. "I couldn't sleep after all the commotion, so I opened my window for some fresh air. Something walked past the bunkhouses last night around two a.m., just after the rain stopped. It sounded like an animal, so I didn't wake anyone. But maybe I was wrong. Was it you, Liam?"

"Of course not!" he yelled.

"Did you hear it too, Estelle?" Fran asked, but she shook her head. "I took a sleeping pill."

Philip jumped in. "Did you convince him to come outside with you in the dark, Liam? Maybe you told him that you knew a way to get off the bluff. Fran is right. Neil believed anything you said to him."

Don't talk about him in past tense, Penelope wanted to cry.

High spots of red appeared on Liam's cheekbones. "Of course I didn't. Fran must have heard Neil leaving by himself. That explains how he got to the beach."

"Why would he do that?" Philip asked.

"I don't know! Maybe he was going to start a fire like he said earlier! He could have slipped. The stairs were covered in water."

"We can't keep pretending these deaths are all accidents," Fran said. "Neil was too far from the stairs to have fallen."

Liam gaped at her as if she had stabbed him in the back.

"I'm not turning against you," Fran said, "but we can't afford to fool ourselves any longer. Danny didn't suffer because of mislabeling. Star wasn't poisoned by her own foolishness. Hector didn't slip and hit his head by accident. Neil didn't mistakenly die in the middle of the night. I'm even starting to question whether Nina's fall was an accident or something designed to look like one. There were ten of us when we got here and now there are five. We can't keep telling ourselves that everything is okay."

"It's Danny. It's been him the whole time," Liam insisted.

Philip spoke up again.

"Wait, wait. For all we know, Danny's been hurt too. Some psychopath might be camping in the woods beside the lodge, using this place as their own personal hunting ground. We still don't know what happened to the Reddings."

Penelope's scalp crawled. Had she brought them all here to be slaughtered? She met Philip's eyes and saw the same terror that was coursing through her own body.

"So a murderer has been living here for ten years waiting for their next victim?" Estelle asked.

Philip shook his head. "God, I don't know. I don't know anything."

"None of us do," Fran said, before moaning softly. "That poor boy. How are we going to tell his parents? I just can't believe this is happening."

Her sadness made her seem frailer than she had on the steps.

"At this point we can only hope that we get the chance to deliver that news," Estelle said.

Her words spurred Penelope back into action.

"You still haven't told us what happened to you, Liam," she said. "How did you get those marks on your arms?"

"This is bullshit—pin the blame on the black man, hey, Penelope? It's Danny. We all know that!"

"This isn't about race," Penelope cried.

She remembered her father's words from one Sunday when he was nestled in his favorite armchair watching football. The best defense is a good offense. Liam hadn't been so convinced of Danny's guilt the day before when he was accusing Marianne. Had his strange theory about his ex-girlfriend been an attempt at deflecting attention away from himself? And now that they were beyond supernatural explanations, was pinning the blame on Danny another ruse? Before she could demand answers, Philip spoke.

"Can I take a look at your arms?" Philip asked. "Maybe we can put this to rest now. If we turn on each other, we're all at greater risk."

Liam braced himself.

"If you are accusing me of something, you'd better say it outright, Philip. I'd like to hear you tell me that I tried to kill Danny but actually murdered Nina instead. Then I had the balls to carry her dead body into the woodshed like I wasn't responsible. After that, what? I forced Star to eat whatever the hell that shit was? You know me. I didn't do this. These scratches are not from Neil. I ran into a thorn bush yesterday when I went up the trail with you. How could you think this of me?"

His voice broke. When he spoke again, his anger had been replaced by sorrow.

Or something designed to look that way? Penelope thought.

"I could never hurt Neil. Or anyone else. Jesus. This wasn't me. I'm just as scared as the rest of you."

"Isn't that exactly what the killer would say?" Penelope asked.

Liam shook his head. There were lines scored across his forehead. "Fine."

He yanked up his sleeves, then extended his arms to the group for viewing. The marks were as angry as she remembered, but Penelope couldn't be sure upon closer inspection that they were fresh.

"Look at them, Philip. You're a doctor. I swear, it was a bush. I swear. Estelle, did you notice them yesterday during our walk?"

The older woman shook her head. Her silver earrings swung back and forth.

"I'm sorry, Liam. I didn't notice a thing."

Estelle took a step toward him, then stopped as if unsure. Liam looked crushed by her hesitation. For a moment, Penelope felt guilty. If Liam really was innocent, these accusations must be hellish for him to bear. After all, he had been closer to Neil than anyone else in their group. Still, they had to be sure.

Fran, Penelope, and Philip circled Liam to examine his arms more closely, while Estelle hung back. Though he seemed to be doing his best to act calm, beads of sweat dotted his forehead despite the chill in the room. The physical reaction sent a creeping sensation down Penelope's spine. Was it possible that the man standing before them was behind everything that had occurred since they'd arrived? She was overcome with desperation to find the solution to the terrifying events of the past two days. She knew it was awful to accuse him, but if he was the one who had been harming them all, they had to find out.

Philip ran a finger down the long, almost parallel, lines of scratches that ran from Liam's inner elbow to his wrist.

"The scratches have started to scab. They definitely happened in the last twenty-four hours, but I can't tell exactly when."

Philip's reluctance to lay blame on his old friend triggered her fear. She needed an explanation.

"What kind of bush scratches like that, Liam? These marks look like they came from fingernails, not thorns," Penelope said.

"Penelope," Philip warned. "You have no way to be certain what you're saying. Please."

She felt stung. It was he who had revealed how deeply untrustworthy Liam really was. How could Philip not suspect him? Liam pulled his arms from Philip's grip and tugged his sleeves down again.

"I have no idea what kind of bush it was. Fran's the botanist. I got whipped by something on the downhill. It was steep as hell and slippery and my bike was going fast. I didn't even notice that I had a mark on me until I came back here."

A huff of disbelief escaped Penelope before she could contain it. Philip shot her a reproving look.

"We have to stop accusing each other and focus on what needs to happen next. Fran was absolutely correct. One accident could be explained, even two. But five people have been hurt or killed in less than forty-eight hours. One of them has completely disappeared. We're all in danger. Someone is trying to harm us. We have to get off the bluff. I say we prepare a quick breakfast and then head up the trail as far as we can go. I suggest you all pack what you need. Bring warm clothes, headlamps or flashlights if you have them, and your rain gear. We are hiking out. We don't have a choice."

Penelope took a long deep breath to push her emotions aside. Philip was right to put a halt to the bickering between them. They had to use their energy to escape before anything else happened. She cursed herself again for bringing the wrong bag on the trip. It meant she would have to travel lighter than the others. There was no way she was wheeling a carry-on suitcase up the muddy trails.

"What about the signal fire?" Fran asked.

"Do you want to go back down to the beach?" Philip replied.

No one answered.

"So we'll try to walk out through the forest?" Estelle asked. "That seems nearly as dangerous as staying where we are."

"We'll keep trying to find a cell phone signal as we walk. Does anyone still have batteries?" Philip said.

Estelle and Fran nodded. Liam and Penelope shook their heads. She had forgotten to charge hers before they'd lost the generator.

"If we can get a signal, we may be able to call a boat to come for us. But I think we should be prepared for every contingency—including spending a night outside."

Penelope stepped closer to Philip, who put his arm around her shoulder.

"I agree with Philip. We can't stay here another night. It's too dangerous," she said.

"Thank you," he said.

He squeezed her arm gently.

"I'm in as well. Why even bother with breakfast? Let's go now," Liam said.

Fran paled at his suggestion.

"I need to eat before we walk. I feel light-headed already."

"Let me make you something," Penelope said.

"Please, let me come with you. I'm always glad to help."

The offer was polite, but Penelope could sense a plea underscoring Fran's words. It seemed she didn't want to be left alone with the others. Penelope was flattered by the woman's trust in her. She realized that besides Philip, Fran was the person she most wanted to protect from the dangers of Stone Point.

"Of course," she said, taking the woman by the elbow.

Before leading Fran into the kitchen, she looked pointedly at Philip, trying to signal to him to keep an eye on the rest of the group. She still wasn't sure they could believe Liam. Though he sounded sincere, anyone capable of killing so many people would have to be a convincing actor.

The dining room was cold, and Penelope could hear the wind whistling menacingly through the hole in the kitchen roof before they swung open the door. She steeled herself as they entered the wreck of a room, guessing that the initial damage wrought by the tree could only have been amplified by the overnight storm. She was right.

Each of the buckets they had emptied the night before now overflowed with brown-tinged water. The icy liquid had spilled onto the floor, leaving the entire back half of the kitchen, which must have sunken slightly over time, covered in two inches of water. The feet of the potbellied stove had been engulfed, making it look like a bloated cow stuck in a swamp. Already, she could smell the mustiness of water damage in the room. She gathered her strength and walked closer to the tree, which seemed even more precariously positioned in the daylight. The one bright side of the destruction of the generator was that they were able to wade through the standing water without fear of being electrocuted.

She heard a low hum as she approached the fridge. Apprehension prickled her fingers. She grasped the handle and pulled the door open. The buzzing became a high-pitched scream. Black writhing shapes were everywhere. A mass of ugly fat flies flew into her face. Legs, wings, and eyes enveloped her. Grasping appendages tried to burrow into her nostrils, mouth, and hair. She jumped back from the open fridge. The moving cloud fragmented and dispersed to all the available surfaces of the kitchen. Penelope clawed at her hair and ears, trying to shake out the lingering bugs. As the creatures slowed and began to rest on the counter, shelves, and walls of the room, their repulsive vibrations hummed in her ears.

"Good god," Fran whispered with revulsion as she peered around Penelope into the fridge.

"It's all ruined," Penelope said, pressing her hand flat to her belly to calm its seizing.

She could see white lumps writhing on all the items inside the refrigerator. Maggots curled toward her in greeting from the lip of a half-opened package of bacon. She shut the fridge door fast, gagging on the sour bile that burned her throat. Her skin still felt like it was crawling with flies as she imagined Nina's and Star's bodies covered in the same white writhing worms. Panic painted black dots on her line of vision making her swat the space in front of her eyes. She wanted to gasp cold, clean air and not the murky, fly-filled atmosphere around her, but she forced herself not to run from the room.

"Without the food from the fridge, there's so little left to eat," Fran said. She had a greenish tinge around her eyes and mouth. "I'm not even sure we have enough to pack for our hike. The last thing we need is for everyone to start getting hungry. They'll be even more panicked without food. What should we tell them?"

The older woman looked at Penelope as if she had an answer then leaned forward to place a hand on Penelope's arm when it became clear that she didn't. Her touch gave Penelope the strength she needed to speak.

"Let's salvage as much as we can," she said. "Then we'll tell the others."

Fran let out a choking sob.

"This is all such a nightmare. It's so surreal, Penelope. How on earth did we get ourselves into this situation? And how do we get out?"

"I don't know," Penelope said, turning to the shelf where several flies had landed on the cast-iron pan that had burned Star's hand.

She had been so worried that Star's inept cooking was going to sour the whole trip. Now, she was terrified they would all starve. Was this how Ruth had felt in the days before she'd been forced to eat her own husband? Was that how this was going to end for them?

CHAPTER **TWENTY-NINE**

9:22 A.M.

After she and Fran had delivered the news about the failed fridge and deposited the last loaf of bread and a half-empty jar of peanut butter on the dining room table, the group fixed sandwiches in resigned silence. Penelope struggled to shake the image of the writhing insects as she lifted her sandwich to her mouth, but it was impossible to swallow the stale bread, so she set it down. An awful giggle threatened to emerge at the idea that she should save the peanut butter to use as a weapon against Danny. The swallowed laugh became a cough in her dry throat, and Philip rubbed her back as she took a gulp of water.

Once calm, she picked up the sandwich again and forced herself to take a bite. She had to finish it. She needed the energy for the hike, and they couldn't afford to waste a single bite of food. As she chewed, she looked around the dining room table at the others who were moving fast to make the most of the remaining daylight hours. Their faces were set in determination. The grandfather clock beside them was silent. Its frozen hands still read nine twenty-three. No one had bothered to rewind it the night before, Penelope thought. She looked at her watch and registered with disbelief that the stopped clock was displaying the correct time. She hurried to eat her sandwich. Whatever the day might bring, Penelope knew she didn't want to be around when the stopped clock was right again.

On the table between them was the remaining food. One can of baked beans, two heel slices of bread, an unopened box of six granola bars, and a container of dried apples. There was also a handful of teabags and a bag of coffee beans. On meager rations, it was enough to get them through the next twenty-four hours. Penelope had been half expecting Liam to make a joke about the bottles of wine that remained untouched, but the man had done nothing but stare grimly at the table since they sat down.

"Maybe I could swim out," Liam said abruptly. "If we can't get over the ridge. I do laps every morning at the gym. How far is it to shore from here?"

"You won't make it without a dry suit," Philip said. "At this time of year, the water is cold enough to cause hypothermia within five minutes without one."

The room became silent again. Penelope noticed that Liam had barely touched his sandwich. She wondered if his guilty conscience was interfering with his appetite. Penelope jammed the remaining quarter of the sandwich in her mouth, eager to get on the move. The idea of staying another night with Liam made her skin crawl as much as the thought of the rotten food and the strange coincidence with the clock.

"We should pack up our things," she said, once her mouth was clear.

Philip agreed. "Good idea. We'll all have to do this together. To be safe."

"We move from room to room together?" Estelle asked.

"Yes," Philip said. "It seems safest to stick to groups of three or more from here on out."

The full meaning of his words sank in. In a group of two, one person would be vulnerable.

"I'm only doing it if I can choose my group," Estelle said.

"What do you mean?" asked Philip.

"I refuse to go anywhere with Penelope. I'm staying with Liam."

Penelope was shocked. Waves of anger seemed to be coming off Estelle. Fran and Philip both looked toward Penelope with a question in their eyes before turning back to Estelle.

"What are you talking about?" asked Philip.

But Estelle was focused on Penelope.

"You've been accusing Liam. But I don't trust you. It was you who put us all in danger."

Penelope's eyes threatened to fill with angry tears at Estelle's accusations.

"How can you say that, Estelle? I'm in the same danger as you."

And I've been working much harder to get us out of it, she thought as Estelle continued.

"You haven't done a thing right to keep us safe. Our guides have disappeared. We've no way to contact the mainland. There isn't even a canoe, for god's sake. How could you bring us here with no way out?"

"Let's all calm down," Philip said.

But Estelle didn't listen.

"The lack of security here is extremely irresponsible. Since we arrived, I thought you were completely incompetent. Now I wonder if you've only wanted to be perceived that way."

Penelope's blood ran cold. There was a hardness in Estelle's eyes that Penelope had never seen before. Was this the temper that Philip had been talking about? The woman spoke the next phrase as if she were sliding a blade into Penelope's soft stomach.

"Liam showed me your book. A person who wrote something like that is capable of anything."

"What is she talking about, Penelope? What are you talking about?"

Philip's voice grew louder with each word, but Estelle's became quieter. She stared directly at Penelope.

"Penelope knows what I'm talking about. You want us to fixate on Liam's guilt because you don't want anyone to look at you too closely. You planned this whole thing. You assembled this group. I had no idea who would be here until I got to the dock. The only person who knew us all was you—and Marianne. Was this some kind of sick way to make amends with her? Why don't you tell Philip what you did to his sister?"

"What the hell is going on here?" Philip said, reaching out to touch Penelope on the shoulder.

She was grateful for the show of support, though terrified it wouldn't last. She knew what Estelle was about to say, though she had no idea how Marianne's mother had found out that what she had done to Marianne was the worst thing of all.

"Have you read her book, Philip?" Estelle snapped.

He seemed taken aback, though Penelope had never pressured him to do so. "Not yet."

"Then why don't you ask your girlfriend what she wrote about? Or better yet, maybe she can show you. I brought a copy here for that reason."

That was why they'd found it on the bookshelf, thought Penelope with dread.

"Isn't the book about a family?" Philip said.

Estelle snorted.

"Not just any family."

"Why are you accusing Penelope of being behind all this?" Philip said. The volume of his voice was now close to a shout.

"It's the only thing that makes sense, Philip! Think about it," Estelle cried, turning to Liam. "These awful events can't be random. We're here for a reason, even if Penelope is the only one who knows it."

Penelope stiffened as everyone looked at her.

"I didn't do this," she said. "I have never hurt anyone in my life."

She didn't dare meet Philip's eyes as she lied.

CHAPTER **THIRTY**

10:15 A.M.

Estelle rose quickly enough to knock her chair over.

"Let's go, Liam," Estelle said. "I need to show Philip who Penelope really is."

Liam swigged the last of his coffee before setting down his mug and walking out of the room behind Estelle. Fran, Penelope, and Philip sat in shocked silence for a moment before Philip found his voice.

"I'm not sure what just happened," he said.

He seemed as confused as Fran, which made Penelope both thankful and guilty.

She looked at him helplessly. She had no words to explain, but she knew she had to try. "I—"

He held up his hand.

"We can deal with my crazy mother later. In the meantime, we have to get out of here. Let's stick to the plan, okay?"

"I'll go try to calm her down," said Fran. "It's her fear talking, not her logic."

Penelope almost cried at Fran's support. She hadn't been sure if the whole group was going to turn against her.

Fran spoke gently. "If you'd prefer a backpack, Nina left her day bag in the gear room. We need all the water and supplies we can carry, and your suitcase isn't ideal."

"Thanks, Fran," she said.

"Okay, come on. We've got to go," said Philip.

He took the plates to the kitchen, leaving her no opportunity to explain. She followed Fran into the gear room. She wasn't looking forward to telling him the whole story later, but hopefully her confession would be tempered by their elation from escaping Stone Point.

"It's that one," Fran said, pointing at a worn-looking pack. "I'm going to head down and see if I can talk some sense into Estelle."

Penelope nodded. Nina's bag was hanging on the hook beside where Danny had placed his coat two nights before. She hastily stuffed food into it, trying not to think about how morbid it was to use a dead woman's bag. Philip joined her and wordlessly put on his rain gear. With him by her side, she stepped out again into the misty morning, welcoming the rush of cold air on her face. The wind had stopped howling and the temperature had risen a couple degrees since they'd found Neil at the beach.

As they approached Bunkhouse B, Liam came out looking solemn. Estelle was already on the porch with Fran, who was speaking to the other woman. She didn't stop when Philip and Penelope came into earshot.

"You're right to be worried," Fran said. "In the last two days, I've borne witness to the deaths or disappearance of five innocent human beings because they agreed to come on a research trip. Like you, I'm at the point where I'm frightened of my own shadow. But we're all in this together. I don't know what Penelope wrote in her book, but I trust her. She's not the one to blame."

"Maybe you're in on all this with her," Liam said. "You're awfully quick to defend someone you barely know."

Penelope couldn't bear to hear Fran derided.

"Of course she's not," Penelope shouted back. "That's ridiculous. Look at her. Fran is the last person we should suspect."

The others glanced over at Fran as Penelope spoke. She was so thin and pale in the gray light that Penelope was becoming concerned. She and Philip joined the others. The deck was too narrow for a group of their size, so they had to crowd together beside Philip, who took Fran's wrist in his hand and laid a finger across it.

"Your pulse is a bit weak."

Fran smiled. "Low blood pressure. Drives my doctor crazy."

Penelope put her hand on Fran's shoulder.

"Don't touch her," hissed Estelle.

"Do you honestly believe I'm going to murder Fran in broad daylight?" asked Penelope.

"Frankly, I don't know what to believe anymore," Estelle responded.

"You can believe that I've learned who to trust in my fifty-two years," Fran said. "Penelope is a good person. We all make mistakes."

Penelope was gratified by the strength in the older woman's voice in spite of how she looked. Estelle blinked hard and seemed temporarily at a loss for words.

Liam took a swig from a water bottle. "Want some?"

"Actually, yes," Fran said, lifting the bottle to her lips.

Penelope bit back a warning.

"Are you going to be okay, Fran?" she asked.

"I just need a brief rest before we head up the hill."

"Thank you for what you said about me," Penelope said. "I appreciate your trust."

"I meant every word," Fran replied. "Whatever is in that book, you're not the only one who's done something wrong in her life, Penelope. Don't be too hard on yourself."

Fran shivered. Penelope rummaged through her bag for a knit cap.

Estelle and Liam locked eyes on her movements, which she tried to ignore.

"Here, Fran, take this."

"Don't trust her," Estelle warned, reaching out an arm to block Penelope from handing the toque to Fran and inadvertently jostling Fran in the process.

"Ouch," said Fran.

Estelle ignored her and rounded on Penelope once again.

"What you did was unforgivable. Have you told Philip yet?"

The silver-haired woman tossed her head angrily toward her son. Philip looked at Penelope, who burned with shame. The rest of the group turned to her as well, but all she could see was the question in Philip's eyes. This was not how she had pictured her confession.

"I didn't mean to—"

Her explanation was cut short by Estelle, who was now looking at Fran.

"Fran? FRAN?" Estelle cried.

Fran's head slumped forward. Her skin was drained of color.

"Fran?!" Penelope said as she grabbed the woman's shoulders.

Philip pressed his fingers against Fran's neck as Penelope lifted the woman's head by cradling her cheeks.

"Fran!" she sobbed.

"Is she okay?" Estelle cried.

"I can't find a pulse," he said through gritted teeth.

Fran's lifeless brown eyes stared at them, the tall green cedars reflected in her empty gaze.

CHAPTER **THIRTY-ONE**

11:07 A.M.

Penelope followed Liam and Philip with tears streaming down her face. They carried Fran into the bedroom where she and Estelle had slept the night before. She knew it wasn't logical, that they had to get off this cursed piece of land where the Stones and the Reddings had died before them, but she couldn't bear the idea of leaving Fran's body on the porch for animals to find and feed upon. It wasn't right that the woman was dead. Penelope couldn't save her, but she could make sure she didn't become food for something awful. They laid her on the crisply made bed. Seeing the hospital corners that Fran must have turned before heading to the firepit that morning made Penelope feel as if her heart had swollen so large that it now rested in the base of her throat, preventing her from taking a proper breath.

"Do you want to say a few words?" Philip asked.

Before she could, she heard someone coming. Philip's gaze darted toward the door. She turned to look behind her and saw Estelle standing there seeming as stricken as Liam. Penelope couldn't help but wonder if one of them was feigning grief. What had been in that water bottle? She forced herself to continue.

"I only knew Fran Brant for a short time, but I am grateful that I had the chance before . . ." Penelope's voice cracked as she struggled to find the words to honor her friend. No other death on the bluff had affected her like this.

"Her presence brought me hope," she said. Her throat felt too tight to keep going. She looked at Philip plaintively and he picked up where she had left off.

"May she rest in peace," he said.

"May they all," said Liam, his eyes fixed on the window where fingers of cedar beckoned them outside.

The wind had picked up again. Penelope wondered if he was thinking of Neil or if he was considering how to kill the rest of them.

"May we all carry on to mourn them properly," said Estelle.

Her jaw was set so firmly that Penelope could see the sharp, clean line of bone beneath the skin. Instinctively, the group bowed their heads for a moment. Penelope focused on Fran's body in an attempt to ignore the insistent repeating voice in her head. *Go, go, go.*

Philip was the first to speak. "It's time," he said. "We need to leave."

"Let's head out," said Liam.

"I'm ready," said Estelle.

After the others left, Philip spoke in an urgent whisper too quiet for them to hear.

"I can't be certain, but it looks like poisoning," Philip said. "Fran must have eaten something toxic."

Or drank, thought Penelope. "How long would poison take to work?"

"Depends on what it was, but usually ingesting is quick. It had to have happened during breakfast. One of them did it."

"Could it be faster than that?"

Philip nodded bleakly. She wondered if he was thinking of Liam's water bottle as well. Her blood froze. Someone had slipped something to Fran that morning. No imaginary stranger lurking in the woods could have had the opportunity. It must have been Liam or Estelle. Penelope swallowed hard.

Or Philip.

She tried to force her mind away from suspecting him. Yes, Philip had coordinated the logistics of the trip, which gave him opportunities not afforded to the others, but that meant little. After all, Marianne had been the one to select the team, and she'd been all too willing to go along with it. Philip had only hired Captain Tedders, worked through meal planning with Star and Neil, and designed the itinerary with Danny and Nina. Besides, what possible motive could he have? Any of the others could have realized that Stone Point's isolation made it the perfect place for a cruel and horrific game. Philip wasn't a game player. She trusted him, and not just because she didn't have another choice. This trip was about completing her book. Everything he had done had been by her request. He moved toward Penelope with an understanding expression on his face as if he knew exactly what she was thinking.

"We'll get through this," he said.

"Oh god, I hope so."

Out in the weather-beaten landscape, they paused to pick up the packs they had dropped, and then Liam led them up the spongy trail that climbed the hill to the left of the lodge. Estelle walked behind him as he skirted around the upended roots of the tree which had fallen into the kitchen. Philip and Penelope followed. It was so like the trail she had hiked with Fran on the other side of the bluff that it was almost like walking through a distorted mirror.

She was wiping away another tear when a sharp noise ricocheted through the woods. Penelope jumped and stared at the three people in front of her, expecting one to fall over dead from a gunshot. She felt a rush of sick relief that it was all over, that the attacker had finally revealed themselves, even if finding out the truth meant a bullet was heading her way. But no one fell. Then the rattling began again.

"It's only a woodpecker," Philip said, frozen in front of her.

Misplaced fear rippled through her body as she reconciled the reality of a bird with the guess of a gun. There was no shooter in the trees. They were still alive. For now. Philip didn't move. Estelle and Liam were still walking up the trail, seemingly oblivious to the noise. Philip whispered to her.

"That was a false alarm but a good reminder to stay alert. Keep a little distance between us and the others as we walk, in case all hell breaks loose. The numbers are dwindling now and whoever is behind all this might be getting nervous. I'll protect you as much as I can, but you need to keep your eyes on those two. If you see anything strange, we'll break off from the group and take our own path," he said. He paused to look at her searchingly. "If we don't stick together, neither of us are going to get out of this alive."

"I'm with you," she said.

He nodded briskly before his eyes filled with emotion. She became overwhelmed by her own. It was a bizarre time to say it, but this might be the only chance she had to admit her true feelings.

"Philip," she said. "I love you."

A shadow flickered through his eyes. She had surprised him as much as herself, she realized.

"I love you, too, Penny." He kissed her hard. "Now go. We can't let them think we're planning anything."

She nodded. The lump in her throat felt solid, but her heart was lighter. If she was going to die, at least she wouldn't die unloved. The path of dirt and needles beneath her feet gave softly as the weight of her body pressed onward. She kept her eyes down and her breath held as she walked by the decrepit woodshed where Nina lay and shuddered. The path steepened and her thighs ached again with the pull and push of her steps. *At least I'm getting the exercise I'd hoped for on this trip*, she thought stupidly. *If only I can survive long enough to enjoy its benefits.*

The trees tightened around them as the path veered farther to the left. After what felt like an hour or so of silent hiking, the forest thinned again, and she found herself looking down the side of a cliff. Forty meters below them was a rocky beach.

By now her legs were shaking, and she stumbled on a jagged rock. Philip's hand was warm on her back as he steadied her.

"You okay?" he asked.

"Fine," she said, though it took all her strength not to scream.

"Let's take a break here."

She nodded.

"Up ahead where the path gets steep, there's a waterfall. It's really pretty, though the drop is intense. It's the farthest I got before I turned around. It was hard to tell if the trail continued past there, but I'm sure we'll find a way."

Gets steep? Penelope thought. Her legs were already protesting enough to make her feel nervous on the narrow path with sharp rocks so far below. She gulped gratefully from the water bottle Philip offered her.

"How far are we from that?"

Philip tilted his head as he tried to gauge the distance. There was no sign of Liam or Estelle, which suggested they were still trudging along, unaware that Philip and Penelope had stopped for a break.

"It took me about fifteen minutes to bike it, so maybe half an hour to walk? I'm hoping that once we get above the waterfall, we'll be able to see a way out. I told Liam to meet us there so we can figure out the next step. This is a tough climb, so take your time. You don't have to keep up with anyone. I'll be right behind you."

"I'm fine," Penelope said in what she hoped was a confident way, pretending to wipe water from her hands, while she pressed hard on her cramping muscles. "Let's go."

She focused on the mechanical motion of pushing her heels down then lifting them up. As promised, the path soon grew steep enough to hunch her back. Her body seemed to sense that crawling on her hands and knees would be a safer and faster form of movement on the scrabbly surface.

Memories darted through her mind as her lungs struggled to keep up with her growing demands for oxygen. Neil's smiling face at the boat launch when they'd docked. The toast with Liam's red wine before their first dinner. Estelle's pale face in last night's darkness. Fran's warm brown eyes. She focused on putting one foot in front of the other, not daring to look up to see where—or how far—the ridge might be. The straps of Nina's backpack dug uncomfortably into her shoulders, and she felt the skin rubbing raw through her layers of rain gear and long underwear. At least she wasn't wearing lingerie today.

As the whisper of the water grew slowly into a roar, her next step felt as if it had landed on level ground. She raised her head. The trail was still distressingly close to the edge of the cliff. About six inches to her left, the land fell away in a staggering drop. Directly in front of her was a river flowing right off the cliff with a solid wall of granite looming up behind it. She dared to edge closer to the place where the water fell. Between the tall pines clinging to the bank, she saw plumes of thick, white water spewing over the rocks. It fell with such force that the water seemed not to be moving at all but hovering in midair, an endless loop stilled by the power of its own momentum. On the horizon beyond the falls, mountains rose like guardians. The bright emerald of the tree line darkened to a shadowy bottle green before changing hue entirely to a deep blue in the far distance. The mountains seemed to go on forever, spiking their way across every bit of the horizon she could see. She heard a slight hiss. Rain had begun to fall again. She craned her neck to see the bottom of the waterfall when Philip stopped her.

"Don't get too close to the edge," he called from behind. "Erosion beats up the earth here pretty bad. Better to stay as far away as possible."

Penelope turned to answer when a low, deep boom louder than thunder filled the air. The ground shook beneath her feet. The air was vibrating. Small rocks began to rain down on them from the granite face. Bigger boulders rolled and crashed onto the path, blocking out the sight of Philip. It was a rockslide, she realized, terrified. They were in the middle of it.

A rock the size of a large dog crushed the ground in front of her, knocking against the trunk of a tree so hard that she heard it crack. The dirt below her feet thudded like the walls of a stadium during a rock concert. Sliding rock and tumbling granite were everywhere. Gray, black, and brown flashes piled up around her. She ducked and rolled away from the collisions. There was nowhere to go but up the trail.

They ran. Rocks fell like rain. Her heartbeats shook her chest, loud enough to collapse her eardrums, louder than the thumps of rock hitting earth and dirt and trees. Philip reached for her arm. She turned to grab his hand. A sickening wallop pounded against the back of her head, just above her spine. Her brain came untethered, hitting the inside of her skull, front and back like a trapped Ping-Pong ball. Her eyes spun upward. The world went black.

CHAPTER **THIRTY-TWO**

6:36 P.M.

Violent sickness jolted Penelope awake before her eyes had time to open. She turned to her side instinctively, coughing and heaving. As she retched, her head lolled like in the dreams she'd had as a child when it grew too big for her body. A bucket was pressed into her hands. When she opened her lids a sliver, light cut across her eyes like a knife. She squeezed them shut again.

"Philip?" she choked out.

Then, the pain arrived. The force of her heaving made her brain slosh inside her head. Hard waves of agony hit her as she struggled to lift the bucket. The only time she had ever been surfing, on a vacation to Mexico in her twenties, she had fallen off the board on her first wave. Each time she tried to escape the water, she had been pummeled by another wall of it. It had felt like this.

The memory of the rockslide came rushing back. She forced her eyes open all the way. The brightness drove in. She fought the urge to close them again. That day in Mexico, another surfer had dived in to save her. Who would save her now?

"Philip?" she cried again.

"Penelope, it's okay. You're safe," said a woman's voice. Estelle.

Penelope blinked to bring her into focus. The eye movement made her dizzy and she had to shut them to contain it. When she slowly opened them once more, the shapes in front of her molded into recognizable forms. She was back in the lodge, lying on the couch. Estelle was seated across from her, though she was barely recognizable. There was a lump on her forehead the size and color of a bruised peach, and a bandage wrapped around her hand. Her face was so filthy that only the creases around her eyes showed white.

"Where is Philip?"

The fire in the grate crackled before the other woman spoke again. Her voice was full of sorrow.

"You're safe here," she repeated.

The unfamiliar comfort from Estelle made Penelope raise her head too fast. Her vision burst into agonizing flares, but not before she saw that she was alone on the couch.

"Take a breath, take it slow. You've got a helluva concussion," said Liam, from her left.

She turned her head, slowly this time, trying to understand why he sounded so far away. He was facing the window, staring into the forest. Light rain beaded onto the panes, reminding Penelope of braille. She wondered desperately what it said.

"What happened to Philip?" Penelope said. "Is he okay?"

The vile smell of the bucket in her hands wafted up to her nose, making her stomach pitch. Estelle seemed to sense her discomfort. She took it from Penelope and set it on the floor. Penelope shifted herself up to a fully seated position to put distance between her face and what had recently been inside her.

Instead of answering her, Estelle lifted a tumbler to her own lips and took a deep drink of amber-color liquid. Something in the fire snapped. Liam turned to her, his face in shadow as the gray light from the window backlit his body. His voice was shaking.

"There was a rockslide. I heard the first crash coming from up above us, and I tried to shout, to warn you, but it was too late. It happened so fast, there were rocks everywhere, it was like the whole mountain was falling on our heads. There wasn't anything we could do but run."

He shook his head and the outline of his body fuzzed in Penelope's vision. She blinked. Estelle stood up and lifted her fingers delicately to the goose egg on her forehead as she spoke.

"I was hit as soon as it began, enough to knock me to the ground, but not knock me out."

She walked past Penelope to the bar to refill her glass.

"What happened to Philip?" Penelope asked again.

Liam picked up the story, his words coming out so quickly it was difficult for Penelope to follow.

"When the rocks stopped falling, I lifted my head. Estelle was gone. I looked all over but couldn't see any sign of her. I was panicking, thinking she might have been crushed, buried by the slide. It looked like a precipice had fallen, maybe a ton of gravel, sand, and rock. The whole pile was huge and unstable. It didn't look like I could get through, but I climbed it anyway and I saw her lying on the ground, bleeding."

Estelle winced.

"We didn't know where you and Philip were, if you had been hurt, if we could reach you," she said. "I called your names, we both did, screaming, and heard nothing. We didn't know what else to do, so we came down the trail as fast as we could."

"We weren't thinking clearly. No one in their right minds would have dared climb over those rocks, shit was falling down as we stepped on it, but we didn't know what else to do," Liam said.

"That's when we found you," said Estelle. "I thought I was hurt badly until I saw you. Your head was so bloody. I thought you were dead, but you were still breathing, moaning, so we got you back here as fast as we could."

"You carried me down the trail?" Penelope asked incredulously.

"I thought that was going to be enough to kill me," Estelle said, raising her glass toward Penelope before taking another swig.

The looseness of the woman's joke and gesture suggested the alcohol was having an effect. Liquid slopped over the side of her glass. Estelle didn't seem to care. Something in her eyes scared Penelope. She remembered Estelle's earlier accusations. If Estelle really didn't trust her, why had she gone to so much trouble to save her? Penelope blinked again and forced herself to focus.

"We built a stretcher out of a couple of branches and a jacket. Turns out I learned something in that outdoor first aid class I took in high school after all," Liam said.

"You carried Philip down with that as well?" Penelope asked.

Her thoughts were sluggish as she tried to comprehend how they'd managed that and where they'd put him.

"No," Estelle said before draining the rest of her glass. "Philip was too far gone for us to get to."

"Too . . . far?" Penelope asked.

"We couldn't see him at first because he'd gone over the edge. The rocks must have pushed him."

"What do you mean?"

"Philip fell off the cliff," Estelle said. Her tone was emotionless.

"Fell?"

"He was knocked over the ridge, Penelope," Liam said. "Estelle spotted his body at the bottom of the cliff. That lime-green coat was hard to miss."

Penelope had never heard the man sound so miserable. He ground the heels of his hands into his eyes as though he was trying to get rid of the memory.

"We couldn't climb down to him, but it didn't matter. Nobody could survive that fall," Estelle said.

"Did you check?" Penelope asked. Her voice was shrill.

"We didn't need to," Liam said. "From what we could see, he was . . . pretty messed up."

The image of Philip's strong body broken into pieces made her gag again. She reached for the bucket, and then threw up, swiping at her mouth with the back of her hand when she was done. Liam and Estelle both averted their eyes but looked back when she began to speak. Her voice rose with every syllable.

"No, no, no, no. Philip was right behind me. He might have fallen but he isn't dead. We have to go back and help him. We have to bring him here."

Estelle looked away again. Penelope's anger rose at the sight of his own mother's resignation. She knew the woman hadn't cared about her children while they were alive, but surely she could find some love for them now that they were dead.

"We can't just leave him there!" Penelope cried.

Liam looked at her with a tenderness in his eyes that she had never seen.

"First we have to get out of here, Penelope. Then we'll come back for him. For all of them. When we're safe."

The words were almost impossible to accept, but it was his expression that undid her. She couldn't bear him looking at her like she had lost everything. Because he was right. First, Marianne. Then Fran. Now Philip. She had been left all alone again. No one had her back.

She didn't trust Liam and felt something close to hatred for Estelle. Both of them had abandoned the people she loved the most, but now they were all she had. She was vulnerable—a sheep among the wolves. The stabbing pain in her head increased like it was warning her not to be rash. The act of piecing together thoughts was painful. She raised her gaze to the fireplace. The group photograph was still there. No, it had changed again. Estelle's eyes followed her own.

"It was here when we came in," she said. Her voice was still dull.

Liam nodded.

"Someone is messing with us. This is why we have to focus. Get the hell out of here while we still can."

Despite the gathering darkness, she could make out Fran's empty eyes. Philip's gaze had also been rendered unrecognizable. But there was something else.

Her own eyes were scratched out just the same as the others. The assailant had intended for her to die too. But she was still alive. Whoever was doing this had made a mistake. She had survived. She looked to the photograph of Ruth instead of her own damaged face. A burst of flame from the fire made the young girl's eyes sparkle. If the killer had erred once, they could do it again. She still had a chance.

"So how do we get out of here?" she asked.

"The ridge route was a bust. If we want to escape, it will be by boat. About a hundred meters from the rockslide, the trail ended."

"Ended?" Penelope asked.

Other questions swam away from her before she could ask them. It wasn't just the photograph. Something else was wrong too. Liam didn't seem to notice her struggle.

"Yeah, the trail just doesn't go any farther," he said. "Dead end right at a rock face. Steep as hell, way higher than anything we saw as we were walking up. It could take days to figure out a route, and even an experienced climber would need hours to climb the rock face safely."

"Is Danny an experienced climber?" Penelope said.

Estelle walked slowly back to her place on the chair. "Liam and I were just discussing that."

He crossed the room and settled beside Estelle. For a moment, the three of them seemed almost comfortable. Sharing an enemy made it easier to feel united.

"He is. He has the skills to attempt it at least. But as far as I know, he had no gear. Free climbing something like that? It's almost suicide," Liam said.

"I didn't see any ropes when he boarded the boat . . ." said Penelope before trailing off as another thought darted through her mind.

Was it possible that Danny had sent additional items when they shipped his bike across early? His climbing gear? A gun? Her memory faltered as she tried to remember if Philip had created a list of things that would be sent over. Philip. Her heart ached.

"I think Danny's still here," said Estelle. Her voice was no longer flat. Instead, it was inflected by a strange combination of softened consonants and sharpened fury. "Maybe he even caused the slide."

"Caused the slide?" Penelope asked.

Liam jumped in.

"A small detonation could have done it on an unstable slope like that. I had to hire a crew to do some rock scaling at the vineyard once. It's pretty simple. Danny mentioned to me that he used to work ski patrol. If he knew how to bomb an avalanche, he could have figured out how to do the same thing to rocks."

"So he tried to kill us all at once this time?" Penelope asked.

"Yes. Maybe he got tired of the game. Wanted to take everyone out at the same time to make sure the job was done before the boat arrives tomorrow morning," said Estelle.

"Oh my god," Penelope said.

"For what it's worth, I think the slide was another of his weird tricks. I don't think he climbed up the bluff. I think he's still out there waiting to pick the rest of us off one by one."

Estelle downed the last half inch of liquor in her glass. In the short time Penelope had been conscious, the room had grown darker. She could no longer make out the fine lines in Liam's face or the discoloration on Estelle's forehead. There were candles laid out on the table between them. How long had she been asleep?

"What time is it?" she blurted.

"Almost seven," Liam said softly. "The sun is setting. We're all staying in here tonight. I've grabbed us some blankets."

Penelope noticed crumpled linens flung across the back of the chair Hector had favored. Liam spoke again.

"There's still a little food. You should eat."

Penelope turned her head carefully in his direction. "Thank you."

"We need to look out for each other now," he said. "If we can make it through tonight, we'll be safe. The boat will come in the morning, and we can forget this ever happened. When we make it out, we can send the police in to get Danny. Hopefully he's not as goddamn resourceful as Ruth Stone."

Estelle's laugh was bitter.

Penelope didn't respond to either of them. Instead, she let her gaze drift back to the mantel. The blank marks across her own eyes didn't fill her with horror as she would have expected. Instead, she felt oddly resigned. As the darkness relentlessly gathered around them, she realized why. It was better to be dead on Stone Point than alive. After all, you didn't have to worry about what was coming if the worst had already arrived.

THE LAST DAY

CHAPTER **THIRTY-THREE**

4:13 A.M.

Answer the phone, she thought, as the mechanical tone roused her unpleasantly from sleep. She opened her dry and crusted eyes with diffi- culty, annoyed that Philip had forgotten to silence his ringtone before he went to sleep. As she came to full awareness, her annoyance shifted to sor- row, and then fear. Philip wasn't beside her. She wasn't in her bedroom. He was dead, and she was being hunted.

But the sound didn't stop.

She bolted upright before a jolt of pain knocked her back down to the couch. The pillow wasn't enough to soften the blow. Her head pounded. She cautiously touched the wound, jerking her hand back at the feeling of a bandage caked in blood. She patted her chest, trying to figure out why she felt so weighed down. A quilt had been laid on top of her body. Who had put it there? Someone had been taking care of her. Was it Liam? Or Estelle? She wasn't sure which was more surprising. She must have fallen asleep while they spoke.

She looked around the dark room, lit only by a dying red glow in the fireplace, trying to find the source of the irritating noise. A prone body, legs curled up to fit the length of the chair, was across from her. Estelle. To her right, the other chairs had been pushed against the wall to make enough space on the floor for Liam to sleep. She tried to connect the disparate thoughts in her head into a clear understanding of what was happening. Images bounced against each other jarringly. Estelle's sloshing drink. Liam throwing wood on the fire. Rocks falling. Danny disappearing. Philip . . . dying. Her head pulsed along with the incessant repetitive signal before she realized it was the sound of hope.

A phone! A way out. Somehow, somewhere, a cell phone had connected to a network of people that could save them. She needed to find it.

She slid her legs off the couch. The cold wooden floor chilled her bare soles. Either Estelle or Liam had slid off her boots so she could rest. She wasn't sure which as each seemed unlikely to spare her such kindness. Halos of white pain appeared around the objects in the room, but she set her jaw and stood up. With care, she placed one foot in front of the other. *Toe, heel, toe, heel*, she thought as she padded by the still forms of Estelle and Liam, past the fireplace to the reading area. It felt like a walking meditation. She moved as if in a trance. The hair on her arms prickled as the phone chirped on and on.

As she passed the reading area, she noticed something odd. There on the table where Hector had placed his books, her novel had been laid out. It was open to page 280, the start of the last scene in the book. The chapter that had caused Estelle to call her a murderer. The pages splayed to each side, barely contained by the broken binding of the spine. A passage was underlined in dark red. *That is important but not the most important*, Penelope told herself before continuing onward through the dining room door. Once through, Penelope turned to stare at the face of the grandfather clock. Nine twenty-three. *That matters*, she thought.

She paused at the long table where they had eaten their first meal together, before swinging open the door to the kitchen. The wind whistled through the hole in the roof. Cold water from the kitchen floor sucked at her bare feet, but she walked on. First it was painful. Then she was numb. The phone wasn't in this room. It was outside. She opened the back door and walked onto the rocky path that led to the woodshed. The signal was louder now. She was going in the right direction. It was inside the shed where Nina's body had been laid to rest.

This matters the most, she told herself, as she waited for the next sound. It came from a spot near her feet. She was getting close. She took another step and kicked something soft. A scavenging animal? She jerked back in fear before realizing the object was still stationary. Not an animal. Nina's backpack. Penelope stared at the bag lying outside the woodshed door. How had it got there? Hadn't she carried it up the hill? She picked it up, then slid her hand into the pack. Inside the largest compartment, a small zipper ran horizontally across the back of the bag to secure a concealed pocket. Penelope opened it and pulled out a crumpled piece of paper. She heard another trill. It was coming from a side pocket. She unzipped it and pulled out the phone. No, not a phone.

It was one of the windup flashlights Fran had found. Poor Fran. Why was it emitting a sound? As Penelope held it, the noise began to fade. The charge was nearly gone.

Her damaged brain sought clarity in confusion. She had found something important, but she couldn't hold on to it. She blinked. The answers began to slip away. Something had been solved but now was disappearing again. The backpack, the book, the clock, and the woodshed. They all mattered. But why? The chilled air bit at her cheeks, and she slowly came to realize that there was a more immediate problem to tackle—she had to get back into the lodge without a single speck of light to show the way. In her strange half-awake state, she had navigated through a world as black as a mine shaft, had walked to the door of the woodshed in darkness, with nothing but her mind to guide her.

Even the moon seemed to have disappeared from the sky. Panic rose in her throat at the idea of returning on the same dark path until she remembered the flashlight in her hand. She turned it over and wound a crank on top. The light that it emitted was weak but better than nothing. Taking several careful steps back to the lodge, she found the cold handle of the kitchen door and turned it slowly, letting herself into a room that smelled even more of damp and rot than it had earlier in the evening. She reached out a flat palm to the wall, letting it anchor her as she traced her way back to the swinging door. The pallid beam from the small flashlight shook along with her trembling hand.

She pushed the kitchen door inward and used the dining room wall in the same way as a line to the door leading into the main room. It came quicker than she anticipated, and she stubbed her toe on the unyielding wood. Swallowing a swear word, she pushed that door open gently. A light shone in her face. For a brief instant, she rejoiced before realizing there was also a gun pointed directly between her eyes.

Click.

CHAPTER **THIRTY-FOUR**

5:06 A.M.

Penelope stared at the empty barrel inches away from her nose. Estelle had just tried to kill her with Fran's gun.

The other woman gasped in horror when she realized what she had almost done. Penelope felt weak. Philip had saved her life by removing the bullets. Even in death, he was protecting her.

Estelle dropped the gun and her flashlight to the floor, sinking to her knees beside them.

"I thought you were Danny," Estelle whispered, her head in her hands. "I heard a noise. I thought you had come to kill us all. Oh god. I thought it was loaded. I nearly killed you. What if I had killed you?"

Without thinking, Penelope knelt beside the crying woman, wrapping her arms around her shaking shoulders, ignoring the rush of dizziness that accompanied her sudden movements.

"Shhh. It's okay, it's okay."

The light shining up from the flashlight on the floor shadowed Estelle's tear-stained face as she pulled herself out of Penelope's arms. Penelope could see the bones under her skin like a skeleton wearing a human mask.

"What were you doing? Are you crazy? I could have shot you," she whispered angrily. "There's a murderer loose. Why would you be running around the lodge by yourself in the dark?"

Penelope shook her head. "Estelle, I need to talk to you."

She helped the older woman to a seat in the reading nook. Her book was still open on the reading table. She didn't need to pick it up. She knew what was written on page 280 though she wasn't sure exactly what it meant.

Yet.

"I found something," she said.

She held out the hand holding the flashlight.

"What is that?" said Estelle.

"It's one of the windup flashlights the Reddings kept here, but I think it has some kind of alarm on it. The sound woke me up. I found it outside the door to the woodshed. And that's not all."

As Estelle held her own flashlight steady, Penelope smoothed the crumpled paper out on the table beside her book. Too late, she realized that her haste to see what was on it had led her to ally with a woman she still wasn't sure she could trust, but she couldn't turn back now. Estelle looked over her shoulder as they read the ten names scrawled on its surface.

DANNY

STAR

HECTOR

NEIL

FRAN

PENELOPE

PHILIP

~~NINA~~
LIAM
ESTELLE

"Did you write this?" Estelle asked in a voice that was nearly too strained to be heard.

Penelope didn't recognize the printing. The block letters were neat and tidy—almost without personality.

She spoke in a low tone. "No. I found it in Nina's backpack. It was dropped on the path."

Estelle stared at her.

"It's not in the right order," Estelle said.

Her voice was more confident now.

"What do you mean?"

Estelle held up the flashlight. The yellow beam shook as she read the names out loud. "It's a schedule of the attacks. This is exactly how it happened. Except for Nina."

"And me."

Estelle nodded. "But that was because we saved you. You would have died without us."

Penelope didn't know how to respond. She scanned the list again.

"Nina's crossed out," she said, running a finger over the thick line.

"It looks like someone wasn't happy that their plan had to change," said Estelle.

"Liam is next."

Estelle shone her light on the sleeping figure. As if on cue, the man snorted and turned, the purple sleeping bag rustling as he struggled to find a comfortable position on the hardwood floor. It was too dark to see the photographs on the mantel, but Penelope sensed the dark eyes of Ruth Stone on her. The gaze no longer scared her. Instead, it reminded her of what she had to do. There was only one direction they could go in now. She had figured out what they needed to do.

"We have to look in the shed," she said.

CHAPTER **THIRTY-FIVE**

5:25 A.M.

The older woman's voice was tight.

"That's ridiculous. We have to get to the beach not the shed. When does the boat arrive?" Estelle asked.

Penelope remembered Philip reassuring them the day before. Her heart felt as heavy as a stone.

"Nine a.m."

Three and half hours from now, she thought as she wiped her bruised eyes tenderly. There would be time to grieve later. So long as she was still alive.

"Is there any food left?" Liam asked, rising up halfway from the floor.

His eyes were heavy lidded, and he rubbed them roughly. Penelope felt uncomfortable seeing him so close to sleep. It was too intimate, too casual. Estelle didn't seem to feel the same hesitation. She carried the backpack over to him along with the note and the windup flashlight.

"We haven't touched any of the food. I think there are a few dried apples left," Estelle said. "But we can deal with that in a moment. First, you should know that Penelope found all this."

Liam gave a shout of joy.

"That's a windup flashlight," Liam said excitedly. "I should have remembered we had these. Some of them can pick up radio signals."

He wound it up, slid a dial on the side, then frowned at the hum of static. He slowly rotated it through the channels. Nothing could be heard but a frustrating hiss.

"It was making a sound before," Penelope said.

Liam responded. "There's an alarm function on this model—kind of like a small siren. It's to scare off animals or whatever."

"So we can send a message?"

Liam tossed it aside.

"No. I thought we might hear something from the mainland, but these can't transmit—only receive. Where did you say you found this?"

Penelope explained about the pack's position outside the shed as Liam unfolded the paper and squinted at it. The room was freezing. Penelope began to build up the fire. After a moment, Liam shrugged off the sleeping bag and stood up to join them. The three of them formed a half circle in front of the fireplace, which was now bursting with orange and yellow flames. Penelope looked at her watch. It was ninety minutes before dawn.

"Why the crossed line through Nina?"

"Isn't it obvious?" Estelle said, her voice cracking with tension. "The killer had to change their plan."

"So, I'm next?" Liam said.

He began to pace, then stopped to stare at the note in his hand again. Penelope's forehead ached. She had been trying to assemble all her ideas, but they still refused to knit together. The snapping of the fire was almost too loud to bear as she began to speak.

"Danny and Nina almost killed Marianne a few years ago then tried to cover it up," Penelope said.

"What?" Estelle responded. "Why would you hire them if you knew that was true?"

"I had no idea when I asked them to guide the trip. On the first day, Fran overheard Nina screaming at Danny. Since then, I've been wondering if what happened to her wasn't an accident at all."

"It seems far-fetched to imagine that her fall could have been deliberately planned," said Estelle.

"And that doesn't explain Danny's disappearance," Liam said. "Do you think he wrote the list?"

Though she couldn't answer his question, Penelope was glad to hear no note of distrust in his voice.

"When I asked them to come on this trip, maybe Danny realized a remote location was the perfect place to get rid of the people who could implicate him."

But that doesn't make sense either, Penelope thought in frustration. *Only Nina knew about the accident before they arrived.*

"So why the list? Who knew about the thing with Marianne?" Liam said. "I certainly didn't. Did you?"

Estelle shook her head. Penelope knew she was missing key pieces. Somewhere in her mind they existed. She willed herself to bring them to the surface. Her headache pulsed in time to her heartbeat. A clear thought wended its way through the pain.

"Philip knew."

His name was like a weight on her chest.

"Which explains why Danny would have wanted to kill him," Liam said. "But why everyone else?"

She was so close to the answer. Her thoughts fragmented into isolated moments. Marianne wearing a ski jacket. Hector and the probation hearing. Nina's cold stare on the dock.

"You were the one who said it. We were all tied to Marianne somehow," she said. "It has to do with her. I'm sure of it now."

"Marianne." The name seemed to stop Liam in his tracks.

"Yes," replied Penelope. "You were right. These deaths all have something to do with Marianne."

Estelle and Liam stared at her.

"Penelope, no offense, but you've had a bad head injury," Liam said. "I'm just as freaked out about the way we're all connected to Marianne, but she's dead. The killer is very much alive."

"Somebody put Nina's bag outside the woodshed. They set off the signal so I would find it."

The two of them looked at her like she was babbling, but she couldn't escape the feeling that the shed was important. That it mattered. She persisted.

"We need to check the shed," Penelope repeated.

"What? Why?" Liam asked.

"Maybe it's crazy. But it will only take a minute. We know this list means something. It's evidence. Maybe there's more inside."

"Nina's body is in the shed. I know because I put it there." Liam scratched his scalp vigorously. "I need a cup of coffee before I can think about going back in there."

"Why are you trying to lure us into the woodshed?" Estelle said. "I think we should go to the beach and light a fire. It's open enough that we'll be able to see anyone coming."

Penelope could see she was back to being a suspect in the older woman's eyes, but she didn't care.

"Estelle, Philip was your son," Penelope said. "We need to find out what happened to him. You left him and Marianne once. Please don't do it again."

Estelle's eyes widened in indignation. "How dare you? What good will it do either of them if I get killed?"

"Please. We need to know."

"You have a head injury, Penelope. We have to leave all this for the police to sort out," Liam insisted. "I'm not sure what you're saying is real."

"The backpack is real and so is the list. Whoever did this left them for us to find. We'll be sitting ducks on the beach if I'm right and Danny's still out there waiting to pick us off. I'm going to the shed with or without you. We have to find out the truth."

Liam swore under his breath.

"Fine, you can see Nina's dead body for yourself," he said. "Then we're heading to the beach."

Estelle huffed, but Penelope ignored it. Maybe this was all nonsense but if Danny was not to blame, it was one of the two people in front of her. She shivered as Estelle turned and grabbed her backpack, unzipping it to take out a small box.

"Penelope, if this is a trap, you better let your partner know that I've got a gun."

She loaded it smoothly enough to make Penelope wonder where she had learned to do it.

"What on earth are you doing?" Liam asked. "Where did you get a gun?"

"Fran brought it," Penelope said.

"And she showed me how to use it," said Estelle.

Liam looked at her as if she was a stranger, and then back to Penelope.

"You'll be thanking me for carrying this weapon if Penelope tries anything," Estelle said sharply.

"Penelope has a serious concussion. If I were you, I'd be worrying about Danny. Do you remember if he knew the time of pickup? Is he going to be waiting for us at the beach?"

Penelope struggled to recall the moment when the boat pulled away. Philip had called goodbye to the captain. Had they confirmed the time?

"I don't remember," she said.

Liam shook his head. Penelope forced herself not to touch her pounding forehead and give him the satisfaction of seeing how the injury was affecting her.

"Look, I don't want that gun anywhere near me, Estelle. Isn't there a moment when everybody starts to panic in situations like this? Leave it in the safe." Liam spoke sternly. "It's too dark to even know what you're shooting at right now."

"No," Estelle said.

Her voice was calmer than Liam's, but it sounded far more dangerous, given the loaded gun in her hand.

"Estelle, there's a safe behind the bar. Keep the gun in there until the sun rises. There's a dead body in that shed. It's dark as hell in there, and you won't be able to see a thing even if you are all Annie Oakley. I trust you, but we can't guarantee that calm heads are going to prevail. Listen, if you put the gun away, I'll leave my knife."

"You don't have a knife," Estelle said.

"Want to bet?" Liam knelt and reached into his boot, brandishing a hunter's knife. "I carry this when I'm riding, in case I need to cut any branches out of my way. I kept it with me all night. Just in case."

Liam's voice was tight with emotion. The tension between the two of them made the room feel small. Penelope's lungs began to burn. She had been holding her breath. She had to end this standoff.

"Maybe none of us can trust each other, but we can't fight amongst ourselves. We're a group of three—the safest number, like Philip said. Please, we only have to last a few more hours. Put both weapons in the safe and set the code to something we'll all remember," she said. "We can open it again after we check the shed. We stick together or we die."

Estelle scowled but clicked on the safety of the gun. Liam nodded, then began to walk toward the bar in the far corner of the room. Estelle and Penelope followed. Liam pulled open the door of the safe and slid the knife in point first, holding it open so Estelle could do the same with the gun. Penelope wondered if Estelle could see the way his hands trembled. *Maybe he wasn't angry? Maybe he really was scared?*

He punched in four numbers to set the code, then recited them aloud.

"Seven-seven-eighty-nine," he said.

"Marianne's birthday," Estelle murmured.

"Thank you," said Penelope, though his choice of code unnerved her.

Without another word, they gathered their jackets and a pair of shoes for Penelope from the gear room, then walked toward the dining room. Penelope had to move slowly to keep the room from spinning; she could barely keep pace with the others. As Liam held open the door, her knees nearly buckled.

"You've got a bad head injury," Liam said. "You should be resting at the beach not stomping around in the dark."

Penelope couldn't risk shaking her head no as another wave of nausea threatened to overcome her. She wondered fleetingly which of the two of them had cleaned out the bucket she had used the night before. Once through the door, Liam walked behind her, matching her speed as they moved into the kitchen where Estelle was staring at the destruction.

"What a mess," she said. "It smells awful in here."

"That tree almost pulled the whole side of the lodge down," Liam said. "This entire place could fall over soon."

Penelope realized that neither of them had stepped foot in the kitchen since the storm. She, Fran, and Philip had taken care of everything for them. Now she was the only one of the helpers left. She had to see it through. Liam slid past her and opened the door to the path outside. It creaked loudly.

Estelle quick stepped through the door and Penelope did her best to follow suit. The three of them moved up the path to the woodshed. The small building hulked before them in the thinning darkness of pre-dawn.

"Keep an eye out for anything else on the path," Penelope said. It was possible she'd missed something that had been left for them in the darkness of her earlier search.

Liam beamed his flashlight down and then onto the shed's stacked log walls.

"I can't see anything but puddles," he said.

"Okay, let's keep going."

Estelle was on her heels. As Liam opened the door to the shed, Penelope could see nothing but blackness enveloping the cone of light shining from his hands. Air gusted out. It smelled like wet dirt and rot. She gagged.

"Where did you put Nina?" Penelope asked, her voice thick with apprehension.

"Goddamn it. It was dark. And I was drunk. I need to look around."

Her mind spun with the horror of what Nina would look like now and she tried to prepare herself for the shock. But instead he faced the light toward them. Penelope winced at the assaulting beam.

"Look, I don't want to be an asshole, but can you put your hands on my shoulders, Estelle? Penelope, do the same to Estelle. I'll keep the light on so you can see my hands. That way, no one gets any surprises," he said. "I'm not gonna lie, this is freaking me the hell out. I never wanted to come back in here."

Penelope could hear fear in his voice. Either he was genuinely scared or incredibly good at faking it. She wasn't sure which.

"I'd feel a whole lot better about going into the creepiest woodshed in the world if I had a gun in my hand," Estelle said in a hostile tone.

Penelope hadn't wanted anyone to be armed, but now she knew how Estelle felt. Could an animal have found its way in here as Fran had worried? She wished again that she hadn't left the bear mace back in Vancouver. Liam spoke.

"And I feel a lot better knowing that you don't," he said. "Nobody would choose this place as a hideout. Trust me."

The terror in his voice seemed to convince Estelle. She laid her hands on his shoulders, and Penelope did the same to Estelle. As their human chain entered the space, Penelope immediately understood what he'd meant about no one wanting to stay for longer than necessary. The dirt floor was moist beneath her feet and a strong acrid smell of animal seared her nostrils. She longed to remove one hand from Estelle's shoulder to put over her nose, but she kept it in place. As her eyes adjusted to the inky edges at the periphery of Liam's light, the group shuffled awkwardly forward into the small space. Penelope had to bite her cheek to keep from hyperventilating as the darkness surrounded her.

Liam circled the shaking light around the interior of the rickety shack. A skunk had clearly been making the woodshed its home for some time. Penelope coughed. Gray cobwebs thick as unspun wool hung from the corners, long enough to cover half the wall in places. The logs were pocked with the entry and exit holes of small rodents and animals. Scattered around the dirt floor were rounds of cut wood, the same kind of pieces she had been pulling from the stack left beside the fire. Likely, they had been cut by Ethan or Simone Redding. She clenched her jaw to distract herself from the fate of the couple. *What's left inside this shed won't even last us a week if the boat can't get here*, she thought.

Liam kept sweeping the wavering beam around the space. Something skittered into a pile of discarded bottles and garbage in the corner before scratching its way back between the meager stacks of wood. Penelope jerked, half expecting the bony hands of William Stone to come reaching for her. Or worse, the bloated corpse of Nina Withers. Her throat was sore from her swallowed scream. Liam continued to work the light, tilting it up and down the garishly orange pieces of wood, stacked together like an ill-fitting jigsaw puzzle, then across the back of the shed. In the farthest corner was a crushed oil jug—another contributor to the stench in the tight quarters. Finally he lit up the last wall on the right. As the flashlight found nothing but dirt floor and decaying logs, she could feel tension building in her neck.

The shed was empty.

CHAPTER **THIRTY-SIX**

6:45 A.M.

The group hurried back to the lodge. Estelle shouldered past Penelope in a near sprint to the safe. She swung the door open. It was empty.

"No!" Estelle cried.

Penelope stopped in the center of the room. Before she could register what was happening, Estelle stalked forward to grab Penelope by the upper arms. She shook her hard enough to transform the dim sparks from the fire into sickening bursts of light.

"Stop it, stop it! Let go of me!"

But Estelle didn't stop.

"Did you do this? Are you working with Danny? Or Nina?" Her voice rose in panic. "Someone else knew how to get into this safe. Did you tell them to take our weapons?"

Estelle let go and raised her right hand. Penelope braced for the jolt of flesh on flesh when Liam grabbed Estelle's wrist. Philip had been right. His mother's temper was terrifying.

"Estelle, stop! Look at this!" he yelled, gesturing toward the floor.

The faint orange of the fire was reflected in a series of wet footprints. Liam used his flashlight to trace the route from the hearth to the safe then back out the door to the gear room.

"Someone else was here. The tracks lead outside. This isn't Penelope's fault."

Penelope shot him a grateful look before returning her gaze to the floor. She remembered the wet spots she had found in her room the first night. Her headache became a hammer. Her lungs tightened like they were being squeezed. She couldn't get a breath.

"Penelope didn't do this, Estelle," Liam repeated. His voice was louder now and he seemed out of breath. "How could she have tipped off Nina and Danny when she didn't know about our weapons until we showed them to her? She was with us the whole time during the search. Nina and Danny have been working together all along. Philip was right when he told us Danny was the most likely suspect—he just didn't realize that Nina was alive too. I knew there was something off about her. She gave me the creeps from the beginning. This is a damn nightmare."

He paused. His eyes darted around the room before he spoke again in a frantic rush of words. Penelope was having a hard time doubting his fear. The man seemed terrified.

"We have to grab as much food and water as we can and go now. We have to make it to the beach without them finding us."

Penelope touched the bandage on the back of her head as pain flared again. The tenderness there felt as spongy as her thoughts. How could Nina have been behind the killings? They'd all seen her die. And how could they evade the killer or killers on the way to the beach? Everyone on the trip had known that the boat was scheduled to arrive soon. Hadn't they? Her legs turned to jelly as she tried to remember who had known what and when about the plan.

"I'm not sure I can walk," she said.

Estelle glared at her, but Penelope's skull was pounding too hard for her to care about anything but staying alive.

Estelle and Liam hurried to gather food as Penelope returned to the reading table for the list. It was evidence. She didn't want to leave it behind.

When they were done, Liam said, "Let's go."

Estelle carried the remainder of their food and two bottles of water in Nina's backpack. Liam had a bag of blankets. The sack of wood, matches, and newspaper that Estelle had prepared for the signal fire was still down at the beach, left behind after their horrific discovery of Neil. Penelope was empty-handed. When they opened the door to the lodge, she saw that dawn had tentatively arrived on Stone Point. The wan morning light was filtered by gray clouds, which made the sunrise seem as hopeless as she felt. The rain had returned.

She wished she could clutch someone for support when they descended the stairs of the bunkhouse, but the idea seemed more dangerous than going alone. She didn't want to hold the arm of her own murderer.

There was too much information to process. She didn't know who to trust. Each footfall on the wooden boards made her head bounce sickeningly. The patter of the rain sounded like footprints of tiny animals. Penelope looked at the path that would take them to the beach. It was still wet with mud and looked so much longer than she remembered it. The temperature had dropped significantly, and she shuddered. The triangle of hypothermia from the outdoor recreation course that she had taken to impress Philip when they first started dating came to her mind: cold, wind, and rain equals death.

She lifted her hood over her head, flinching as the stiff fabric brushed against her wound.

"What time is it?" she asked after several steps.

Estelle glanced at her watch. "Seven thirty."

"Ninety minutes to go," Liam said, his jaw tight.

A branch cracked. Estelle jumped and Penelope jerked in surprise, then regretted the movement immediately. Her heart thumped. All three of them froze as the ferns to their right moved like they were being blown by a violent wind before a black crow emerged.

"It's just a bird," Penelope said, as if Estelle and Liam needed help to identify the flying creature speeding through the air.

"I thought it was Nina. She has the gun. One shot could kill any one of us," Estelle said.

Now her voice was full of fear instead of anger. They began to move again in watchful silence. Each step thudded in Penelope's temples. The trail sloped downward and the ground became uneven. They reached the firepit. Liam raked his head as he scanned the trail in front of them before they continued past the cleared area between the bunkhouses to the point where the forest enclosed the path. The trees swayed and creaked beside them. Up ahead, large patches of leafy brush loomed ominously. Anyone could be hiding in there, but it was their only way to safety.

Liam stopped short. Penelope and Estelle halted as well. The abrupt change in motion jarred her head again. She watched him carefully, wary of his intentions. It was a strain to keep her eyes focused.

"Did you hear that?" Liam looked from side to side. She was close enough to see thin red veins snaking around his pupils. "Something is there."

"What do you mean?"

"Someone is watching us." His eyes flicked to the trees, and then back to Estelle. "I can feel it."

"We have to keep going," Penelope whispered hoarsely.

Neither of them looked in her direction. She couldn't remember ever feeling so scared.

"We need to get to the beach. We need to light a fire," Penelope urged.

She took a step, but Liam didn't follow. He seemed paralyzed by fear.

"Back when we were dating, bad things used to happen to me when Marianne was angry," he blurted. "One time we got into a fight and I left her apartment to cool down. She didn't want me to leave; she was screaming. The moment I stepped out of her place, a window washer's bucket fell onto the sidewalk beside me. It was so close. Any nearer and I would have been killed. It felt like a warning. Nina was her best friend. I should have known she was just like Marianne."

"Liam, can we talk about this later?" Penelope asked, but he wouldn't stop. Or couldn't. He was acting like he was in a trance.

She looked to Estelle for assistance. The other woman leaned forward to embrace Liam. Penelope watched them in a panic. What was Estelle whispering to him? *Is she telling him how to kill me?*

"Come on, we can't wait any longer," Penelope insisted.

Liam pulled away from Estelle. Her touch hadn't dissuaded him from talking and he resumed immediately.

"I was a coward. That's why I left her the way I did. I mean, I wanted to have children and she did too, but she was so furious when she lost the baby. She told me it was my fault, that I wasn't capable. I realize now that she was devastated. I shouldn't have let her push me away. I should have stayed. I treated her badly after that. She called me one night in tears. She said she had forgiven me. That she understood everything. But I hung up. I couldn't handle it. We never spoke again." Liam was shaking. "I left her when she needed me the most. I've been angry at myself for years for not believing that she had forgiven me. I didn't think it was possible. Marianne was never good at forgiveness. Now it turns out I was right all along. Somehow Nina is getting the revenge Marianne never could."

Penelope reached out to him. "Liam, you have to—"

"Did you hear that?" he cried.

His eyes were wild as he looked from her to the trees. She craned her ears.

"I can't hear anything."

He rocked on the balls of his feet.

"It's a baby. I can hear a baby crying. No, it's a woman screaming. Can't you hear it?"

Penelope was frightened. Liam seemed to be having a breakdown.

"Liam, listen to me," Estelle said, moving closer, but it was too late.

Before they could stop him, Liam bolted into the forest.

CHAPTER **THIRTY-SEVEN**

8:11 A.M.

Estelle and Penelope shouted Liam's name again and again but it didn't slow his frenzied sprint. He tore through the trees so fast that he was out of sight in seconds.

"What do we do now?" Penelope asked.

"We wait," Estelle said. "He'll come back to his senses. It's this place. It gets to everyone eventually."

Penelope stared at the other woman in horror as she realized the two of them were now alone. What was she talking about? Had she tricked Liam into running away so she could finish off her attack on Penelope? Maybe the gun hadn't been stolen at all. Maybe it was still in Estelle's backpack. She watched the woman's hands, searching for the slightest threat of violence. But Estelle seemed lost in her own world.

"At least he can wonder if what my daughter said was true. I know Marianne never forgave me. She hated me from the moment I left her and Philip. Obviously, Philip felt the same way. Otherwise, why would he have brought me back to this horrible place?"

"What do you mean? I was the one who asked you to come here. I needed a photographer, and you were available," Penelope said before Marianne's trip plan flashed before her eyes.

None of this had actually been Penelope's idea. Her skin crawled as Estelle kept talking.

"Philip begged me to do it. He knew I would say no if he didn't convince me. He of all people knew that I would never have wanted to come back here. I did it for him. Now I wish I hadn't. Maybe he'd still be alive if I'd said no."

Penelope had more questions than she could hope to have answered, but she tried anyway.

"Philip called you? To come back? You've been here before?"

"I could never forget this place. Never."

Penelope's jaw dropped. Estelle didn't seem to notice. Her dull monologue was more like a confession than an explanation.

"Ten years ago, I read everything I could about the Reddings. There were so many theories, but no one could explain why a happy couple about to start a new phase of their lives would just disappear."

"What does that have to do with—"

"I was obsessed with the story. By all accounts, he was mild-mannered and utterly devoted to his gentle wife. I kept thinking that if I could understand what had happened to them, I would understand what had happened to me. What I had done. I thought that maybe there was something about this place that made it all happen. Something evil."

"Made what happen?"

Estelle turned to Penelope with an expression that seemed both imploring and hateful.

"Don't condescend to me. You know this already. Marianne told you before she died. Isn't that what made you think it was okay to write all about it in your book?"

Penelope reeled. The final chapter.

Estelle kept talking.

"I never wanted to get married. I wanted to be a photographer, to travel the world, but my parents thought that was ludicrous. They married me off just like Ruth's father did to her. Then my husband pressured me into having children. I wasn't a good mother. I can see that now. I was forced into raising them alone. He worked so much. When he was home, he would get drunk and angry at me. So angry. He used to grab whatever he could find—hairbrushes, wooden spoons. He hit me on the back so no one would see the bruises."

So that was why Estelle had hurt her kids, Penelope thought. It was a cycle of abuse. Her heart ached for Philip and Marianne.

"But it got worse when we got here."

"What happened?" Penelope asked, dreading the answer. The last scene in the book was terrifying and violent.

"It was my husband's idea to come. He wanted to take a family camping trip, but he wasn't the type of person who would let us just set up a tent in a campground. It had to be remote, rugged, something he could brag about to his friends," Estelle said, her mouth twisting.

"When he brought us to Stone Point, I hated it right away. It took us nearly five hours to get here because the waves were so choppy, and my husband wasn't much of a boater, though he'd never admit it. There was no lodge here then, no buildings, just the clearing, the old house, and the shed. Everything was falling apart. I didn't want the kids anywhere near the buildings; they looked like they could collapse at any moment. I was exhausted, but he still expected me to prepare a proper meal with nothing but a campfire. I tried. I couldn't get the fire lit, and Marianne and Philip both started screaming. They were nine years old, old enough to know better, but they were both hungry and tired. I can see that now."

"What do you mean they were both nine years old?" Penelope interrupted. "Philip was older than his sister."

Estelle looked at her as if she was stupid.

"They are—were—fraternal twins."

Penelope was shocked. How had she not known that? Estelle was far away again.

"I don't know if all twins do this, but they would feed off each other's emotions. They had this game they would play. Like hide-and-seek but worse. One of them would hide for hours until I found them. The other one wouldn't say a thing to help me. I would get frantic with worry, terrified that they were actually missing. It got so bad that I had to sit them down and tell them only cruel people act like that. Cruelty is for the cruel."

Penelope felt sick. Marianne and Philip had both explained the phrase so differently.

"But what happened here?" she asked, certain that she already knew, but needing confirmation of the awful truth.

"They ran by me and knocked a bucket of water into the fire, soaking all the kindling and paper I had laid out. I screamed at them. Something came over me, I still can't explain it."

"What did you do?" Penelope asked again.

Estelle's answer took Penelope by surprise.

"My husband raised his hand to hit me, but I dodged him. I ran away, down this path, down the steps, down to the dock. I couldn't bear to be beaten again. I think I wanted to draw him away from the kids in case he turned on them. When I got to the boat, something snapped. I thought I was doing the right thing. It felt like being here . . . finally gave me the strength to get away. I took the boat back to the mainland. I left my kids alone," Estelle said.

A desire to know and an urgency to leave collided in Penelope's confused thoughts. She knew they shouldn't stay, but she was desperate to hear the rest of the story. "We should go to the beach now, Estelle."

Estelle didn't acknowledge her.

"By the time I arrived back in Squamish, my anger was gone; I felt nothing but shame and fear about what I had done. I came back to collect the children, but my husband was furious. I knew he would never forgive me, but I thought Philip and Marianne would understand. Instead they wouldn't even look at me. My husband told me to leave and never come back. So that's what I did. I tried for years to convince the twins to come live with me, but they refused to take my calls or answer my letters. I could only hope their father never treated them the way he treated me."

Penelope was torn between reacting to the devastating truth and facing the horrifying reality. She knew she should drag the older woman to the beach, but the knowledge that the book she had stolen from Marianne was based on a true story eradicated her survival instinct. It was why her friend had been so afraid to publish it. Marianne had handwritten nearly everything that Estelle had just described in her notebook. Penelope had claimed it as her own. But there was still something missing. Penelope had to know the answer, despite the pressure they were facing to get somewhere safe. The last scene in the book ended with a child scarred in a fire after the mother beat her in a fit of rage.

"What happened to Marianne's wrist? The burn?"

Estelle breathed in sharply.

"The scar on her wrist? That happened years before. When the two of them were little, almost four years old. Philip wanted to help with dinner. He convinced Marianne to bring a chair to the stove when I went to the bathroom. I heard her screaming while I was on the toilet. He had pulled a pot of water onto her arm. It was awful. Her wrist looked like raw meat. I lied about it to their father and took the blame. I was always so scared he would turn on them."

Estelle stopped speaking. Emotions pummeled Penelope. Guilt at misjudging Estelle. Shame at stealing Marianne's story. Bewilderment at the assumptions she'd made when Philip had described his childhood.

Penelope looked at Estelle. All the color had drained from her face. Her expression had changed from detachment to fear. The forest seemed to be closing in around them. *The boat, the boat, the boat*, Penelope told herself. It was their only hope. They had to get to the beach. She could no longer separate fact from fiction, but she knew that if Marianne was trying to exact revenge from beyond, she would certainly want Penelope dead for taking her story.

"Estelle, we've got to go," she insisted.

The other woman nodded mutely. They crept down the path together. They were almost there. Suddenly she saw a smear of blue between the tight trunks of the trees.

"What is that?" she cried.

The color blurred in the watery air, then became indistinguishable before disappearing completely. Her gaze wavered. Had she imagined it? She opened her eyes so wide it hurt. Danny's coat was red. What color had Nina's coat been?

Her voice shook as she called out, "Who's there? Danny? Nina?"

Estelle stiffened beside her.

"There!" she cried. "By the gazebo pad!"

They both took a step back.

"Danny?" Penelope yelled.

"Nina?" Estelle screamed.

For several long seconds, Penelope trained her eye on the color. It didn't change. They stood stiff and still like mice in the shadow of an owl. Penelope tried to take a deep, calming breath but she couldn't seem to inflate her lungs all the way as she stared at the spot of bright blue. What the hell was it?

"It's not moving," said Penelope.

Estelle took a tentative step down the path, standing tall to try to make out the shape. Whatever it was seemed to be lying in wait.

"Come on," Estelle said. "There's no other way to the beach. We have to keep going or we'll never make it out of here."

She bent to grab a craggy rock and Penelope did the same. The blood rushed in and out of her head. She stood still for a moment to control her light-headedness before following Estelle, never letting her eyes waver from the blue patch.

"It's almost time for the boat," said Estelle. "We have to move faster."

As they closed the distance, Penelope gasped. Nina was waiting for them, stiff and unmoving. One step closer. She was looking straight at them, her face blank, her eyes unblinking. Penelope edged nearer. What had Star said about this place? That there was real power here? Was this a trick? But as Estelle approached the woman, Nina didn't move an inch. Penelope could see that her body was propped against a pile of rocks to keep it upright. She stopped about six meters away. Estelle boldly continued to the edge of the pad while Nina stared out lifelessly.

"She's dead," Penelope said.

"Should I check her pulse?" Estelle asked in a shaking voice.

It won't do any good, Penelope thought. Before she could say the words out loud, Estelle leaned over. Penelope didn't have time to shout a warning as a hooded figure in red dashed toward the other woman from the trees, rearing back before planting hands hard on Estelle's back. Estelle didn't have a chance. Before Penelope's eyes, she fell onto a spike of rebar left exposed by the Reddings' unfinished construction. Her pinned body looked monstrous in the morning light.

There was only one thing to do.

Penelope threw the rock.

CHAPTER **THIRTY-EIGHT**

The rock's weight wrenched Penelope's arm. She hoped it was heavy enough to hurt. The stone hit the hooded figure on the shoulder with no more than a glancing blow, but it was enough to knock them back from the path. Penelope sprinted toward the rocky stairs. She could hear someone shouting behind her but she couldn't make out the words.

Her head felt as if nails were being driven into it. Her feet slid down the wet granite of the slippery stairs. *Keep going, keep going, keep going.* Her sole hit the edge of a step. She lost her footing and righted herself just in time. Conflicting facts needled her like the cold spikes of rain. Liam was gone. Estelle was dead. Marianne was behind it all. How could Marianne have anything to do with it? Who was chasing her?

Her foot missed a step, and she stumbled, fighting to keep her balance, throwing herself backward to avoid pitching forward onto the same hard sand where Neil and the agents before him had died. Her vertebrae smashed against the corner of the step. She scrambled onto all fours like a panicked animal. A rock came tumbling down the cliff like the one that had fallen when they'd first arrived. This time, it was caused by a real threat. A scream plummeted from the top of the bluff.

"Penelope! PENELOPE!"

She scrambled to her feet. Her elbows were raw. Her back was seizing. She had to keep running or she was going to die. Gulls squawked and circled above. Or were they vultures?

"Penelope!" the man shouted again.

She could almost recognize the voice. Was it Danny? Or Liam?

She heard a shot and looked up, expecting to see someone aiming at her, expecting to feel the searing burn of a bullet in her body. Instead, there was no one at the top. The figure in red was already a third of the way down the stairs.

She had no choice.

She ran.

Clumps of sand flew up from her heels, pelting her back. The wind from the frothing ocean whipped its way across her face. Tears streamed from her eyes. She forced her aching legs to keep digging in and pushing off as they fought to find traction on the changing surface.

She needed to hide. The boat was coming soon.

Her toe caught on a rock, and she tipped headfirst into the wet sand and landed palms flat, hard enough to send daggers of pain shooting up her wrists and arms. A film of black descended over her eyes. Her head throbbed. She dug her fingers into the ground. Grit wedged its way into the tender flesh under her nails.

Don't stop. She pushed up, wobbling onto her feet as dizziness threatened to take them out from under her. She peered behind her. The figure in red was nearly down the stairs, moving fast. The beach stretched in front of her, curving around the rocky face of the bluff toward the forest. The trees.

She swallowed hard to force vomit down, pushed her toes into the crumbling earth and ran again. Her thighs ached and burned, her breath ripped at her throat, but the ground finally changed from sand to roots beneath her feet. Branches whipped her face. She dug her sand-filled nails into her palms, feeling the sting as they cut her skin. Her back crawled with the idea of a hand reaching out to yank her down. The trees grew thicker. Their green leaves jerked back and forth as the icy wind screamed. Every part of her hurt. She dove down, feeling something tear from her shoulder as she rolled into the underbrush.

She froze, ears cocked like prey, to hear how close the killer was before creeping forward, but all she could make out was the wind raging and the waves roaring and crashing. She had to hide. To her right was an indent in the granite cliff. Her hands and legs shook with heightened adrenaline and ratcheting fear. The pounding in her head threatened to drown out all other sounds.

She wedged into the rock, trying to make herself as small as possible. Something from her back pocket rustled against the rough wall. The list. She slipped it out, her body heaving with panicked breath as she uncrumpled the paper. Maybe there was something here she had missed. She stared at it in shock. There was something written on the other side of the page. It was a letter composed in handwriting more precise than that which had been used to write the list. She could never forget the person who had written this way. It was Marianne.

Before she could read it, the forest erupted in front of her. Something burst through the bushes like a monster. It only took a moment to find her. She had been a fool to think she could hide. He grabbed her arm and pulled her toward him. His face was battered and bruised. He was almost unrecognizable as the man she loved. Almost.

"I lied," Philip said. "The boat isn't coming until this afternoon."

Penelope bowed her head and waited for the end.

CHAPTER **THIRTY-NINE**

9:01 A.M.

A seagull screamed in the distance. The waves pulled the rocks in and out in a chattering dance. She wailed as he dragged her to her feet. Her head caught on something. She felt a chunk of hair ripping away before an agonizing blanket of stars flickered in her eyes. She stumbled, trying to keep up with him, as he dragged her back to the beach. Her knees buckled and she fell onto sharp rocks. She looked up and saw the barrel of a gun pointed at her head.

Philip is the killer.

It was impossible to comprehend. Penelope wondered if she would hear the sound of the gun before she died. She hoped not. Then Philip began to speak. She didn't lift her eyes immediately. The malice in his voice had changed to something that sounded mournful. For a moment, his words washed over her as if he could still be a source of comfort.

"When I read the letter, I felt like they had killed me, along with her," he said. "You must have felt the same way, right, Penny? When you read it?"

The plea in his voice made her remember him as he used to be. The man who could solve her problems. The one she loved. She had been so proud to be by his side. She had been so lonely before Philip came along. Maybe that was why she had done what she had to Marianne, her writing partner and best friend, a woman who had trusted her with her life's work. She had convinced herself that Marianne chose her to execute her will in order to give her the manuscript they'd worked on together. To give her a chance at the life she had always wanted but didn't have the talent to earn. She had nearly convinced herself it was true.

Philip was still talking.

"You're not like the others. You survived." He sounded incredulous.

Penelope dared to look at him. He had lowered the gun to his side.

"The letter?"

"It was on the back of the list I left for you. Didn't you read it? I hoped you would be the one to find it. I thought it was only right to reward you for getting away by giving you all the answers you needed in Nina's bag. She died too early and you're dying too late. But it doesn't matter. The plan is still the same."

Estelle had been right. The list was the order they were supposed to die in, and Philip was still intent on seeing it through. But she had escaped once. She could do it again.

"I haven't read the letter yet," she said, showing him the wrinkly paper still clutched in her hand. "I didn't know what it was."

"Read it. Then you'll understand."

His eyes filled with the emotion she had previously read as terror. Now she could see it was something different. Like excitement, but uglier.

Penelope's hands were numb as she lifted the page to her eyes. The letter was dated a few days before Marianne had died.

Dear Philip,

I wanted to call but I knew I couldn't. It's still so hard to speak to you without falling back into my old ways, but I've changed, and I know you can too. I'm writing you instead because we've spent our lives being angry, but I'm not mad anymore.

After Liam left me, I was so furious. I wrote our story the way we always believed it. The way Dad told us it happened. The way we told each other. It took a year to finish it. It was hard. But when I completed the last page, I realized something was wrong.

It was Ruth's story that didn't make sense to me anymore. Do you remember what we used to tell each other about the Stone Witch from when we were kids? It came up in a conversation I had with a neighbor years ago. She had a different theory about what happened to Ruth. Since then, I hadn't been able to get it out of my head. I believe Ruth Stone was accused of a murder she did not commit, and then was forced to kill to protect herself. It all seemed connected to our story because of what happened to us at Stone Point. Ruth Stone was found guilty before she could tell her truth. I started to wonder if everything we'd been told about our mother had been wrong as well.

I visited Stone Point to find answers about what happened to us and to Ruth. There's another inscription on the rock that I'm not sure anyone else has ever seen. It's by the stairs, a little way away from the one she must have made to warn people off who were tracking her. The words made me realize we had it all wrong. I looked harder. I found a child's grave. When you come and read it for yourself, you will see that she was not who people thought she was. Accusations, assumptions, and lies change lives. Sometimes, they end them. So I kept asking questions. The most important thing I learned wasn't about Ruth Stone. It was about Mom.

We were nine years old when Mom left. Dad told us she burned my wrist on purpose. He said she dumped boiling water on me from the stove in the kitchen at Stone Point, remember? That she was heating it on a burner when she lost her temper. I believed that for my whole life. But the boat captain told me there was no power or lodge at Stone Point until Ethan and Simone Redding came. Dad's story was a lie—one of many.

We were wrong about our mother. I think everyone's been wrong about Ruth. And we've been wrong to carry all this hate in our hearts, too. I want to see our mother again. I want you to come here to see if you feel the same way. I've planned a trip for you and me and others as well. There are people who have wronged me in my life. I want them to gather with us so I can hear their side of the story. I want to forgive them.

Danny Mason forgot to charge the satellite phones, then lied because he was scared.

Star Winter was desperate enough to get good grades that she cheated and lied.

Neil Hawthorne bore false witness for Star because he loved her.

Hector Anderson fired a teaching assistant to protect me.

Fran Brant took the blame for Pete's disappearance.

Nina Withers protected her business partner so he wouldn't lose his license.

Liam Connors broke my heart, but I broke his too.

Estelle Walsh wasn't a good mother, but she tried.

We have to forgive others, Philip. It's the only way for us to forgive ourselves. I have enclosed instructions for the three-day journey.

Yours always,
Marianne

"I got it in the mail two days after she died," Philip said. "The day after you called. She must have written it right before her aneurysm burst."

"She wanted to forgive them," Penelope whispered.

This had been about Marianne the whole time. Liam had guessed it and so had she, though neither of them had been completely correct.

"How could I forgive them?" Philip said fiercely. "Look at this. They were the reasons Marianne died. The stress, the hurt, the pain they caused her. Death by a thousand cuts to a person with a life-threatening aneurysm inside their brain. Their actions were fatal. People hurt her. I had to protect her. I always protected her."

Penelope remembered Estelle's story of what had really happened to Marianne's wrist. Fear gurgled deep inside her as Philip kept talking.

"I did try to follow her advice at first. I wanted to honor the wishes of the dead, you know. It had been a sudden break—this change in her. After I got the letter, I finally understood why she had pulled away from me. Right after she and Liam broke up, after she lost the baby, she moved out of the place we shared. She stopped telling me things. She said she had to heal on her own. I had no idea she was even working on a manuscript until I read this letter."

The mention of the manuscript gave Penelope chills. Had Philip ever wondered where the book had gone? She shook it off in pursuit of the real answer.

"But why do all this? It's the opposite of what she wanted."

Philip exhaled heavily. "I was shocked after I read that letter, just shaken to the core. I wanted to hurt them all. Marianne was my life. She was everything to me. Losing her almost killed me. Then you came along. Being with you was wonderful. I need you to know that. I thought you would change me."

Despite his words, he raised the gun, and Penelope breathed in hard, but instead of pointing it toward her, he held the grip flat against his forehead, as if it helped him think. *This is important*, she thought. *He really does love you. Use it. Keep him talking.*

"Thank you," she said, letting her eyes fill up with the fearful tears that had been threatening to fall since Estelle had been pinioned on the rebar. "That means so much."

Philip cleared his throat and lowered the gun again. Penelope wasn't sure if she was imagining it, but his eyes seemed misted as well.

"Everything changed though when I found Marianne's battered notebook in her car last Christmas when I went to visit Liam. It was shoved under the seat—looked like it had been there for years. It had a draft of her book in it. I'd brought the early copy of *The Myth of Vultures* with me on that trip. I wanted to surprise you by having read it when I got back. That's how I realized they were the same. You stole my sister's book."

Penelope hung her head as Philip continued.

"Liam and I talked a lot about Marianne when I was there, and I heard how cruel he'd been to her in between the lines of his sob story. He doesn't hold back when he's drunk—which is often now. What kind of man leaves a woman for not being able to have babies? He told me about Star and Neil and Hector and how much Marianne had despised them all. We even talked about that stupid cat she loved so much and what she believed Fran had done to it. Learning all that on top of discovering how you had betrayed her with the book? I was a wreck. I had to wait for a few weeks before I could see you again because I was so furious. I wasn't sure if I could act normally, but it turned out not to matter. When we finally met for dinner, you were so preoccupied about the deadline that you didn't even notice I hadn't been making plans with you.

"I took Danny out and got him drunk too, to learn what had happened on their ski trip. By the time we saw each other again, I'd come up with a plan. I knew the story of the Stone Witch would be too tempting for you to resist. And it was—turned out you'd already found the idea on your own. It seemed like fate. After that, everything came together so easily, which made me think it really was the right thing to do. My mother, well, that was a harder phone call. I had to pretend that this was a way for us to heal. I knew it's what she'd always wanted: forgiveness."

She could sense Philip was becoming enthralled with the retelling. Her mind raced as she tried to come up with an escape from the beach. She had to keep him talking.

"But why did you kill them all?" Penelope chose her words carefully, making sure to separate herself and Philip from the rest of the group. "Marianne wanted to forgive them."

"Marianne wanted to change the past by putting on rose-colored glasses. She told me once that her new friend Penny was such an optimist that she wanted to be like her. She wanted to forgive Estelle? What a joke," said Philip.

Disappointment in herself cut through the terror of her situation. Marianne had wanted to emulate the trait in her that was the most forced. Pretending to be something she wasn't had made her friend love a part of her that wasn't real at all.

"Our mother abandoned us," he said, before laughing in a terrible way. "My father was strict, but he wasn't a liar. Besides, there were things Marianne didn't know. Like the fact that you betrayed her. I couldn't let you get away with that. But you survived the rockslide. It showed you were worth more than the others. So I wanted to tell you the truth."

Penelope swallowed hard before she spoke again.

"That's why you left Nina's backpack by the shed? With the list?"

"It was a risk. Estelle or Liam could have found it, but Stone Point has a way of making things right."

The words were deeply unsettling. It triggered another question that had been bothering her all along.

"Did you lie about Neil calling you the night before we arrived? Have the radios been defective the whole time?"

Philip laughed, and she had to force herself not to run from the terrible sound, knowing he would shoot her if she made a sudden move.

"No, he called me that night. I knew he would freak out if he couldn't get through to the mainland. After we arrived, I set up a navigation jammer when you thought I was napping."

A navigation jammer?

"So Danny is dead?"

"Danny was easy. I've known about his peanut allergy ever since we took a hiking trip together years ago. I told him I'd contacted a boat and that he had to go get the phones from Neil, then guide it in. I warned him not to tell Neil about the boat because the guy was such a blabbermouth and I wanted to keep the circle small. There's a trail on the beach that leads to the base of the waterfall—it takes five minutes to get there from here. Danny was so out of it that he didn't question it when I led him there. It was easy to hit him over the head at that point. I'd already lent him my coat so you would think it was me at the bottom of the cliff after the rockslide later on," he said. "It was tight, but you didn't suspect a thing."

She should have realized that Philip hadn't been wearing his lime-green coat on the hike out with Estelle and Liam—he had chosen his rain gear instead.

"Nina wasn't supposed to be next, but I had to roll with the punches. She was asking too many questions and making people suspicious that something was wrong by arguing with Danny. I slipped a sedative in her drink after I popped the balloons with a laser pointer, but she must not have liked Liam's wine. I saw her pouring it into your birthday flowers when she thought no one was looking."

Penelope made a small noise. She knew it had been odd that the flowers had wilted so fast.

"Still, must have been enough to slow her reflexes when Danny knocked into her. Better safe than sorry, though. When I checked her pulse, I injected her with a shot of fentanyl I scored on one of my shifts downtown, to be sure. Neither of them suffered—I'm not a monster. For anyone unaccustomed to an opioid, it's almost instantaneous heart failure. No pain."

"Oh, Philip," she said. "I can't believe you did all this. It's so elaborate."

He seemed to think she was encouraging him.

"Yeah, it was. Like a puzzle that kept getting more difficult the more I played. Star was a little tougher than Danny. I was hoping to inject her with the fentanyl right before she went to bed, but then she stayed up late with Liam. I had to hide outside the cabin in the morning while you were in the lodge, waiting for Neil to go to the outhouse. My mom saw me coming back from their cabin, but luckily she was too distracted to notice."

"I thought Star ate poisonous plants," Penelope said.

Philip shook his head as if amazed at his own luck.

"That was all Fran. I mean, maybe Star harvested something noxious to eat, but the cause of her death was fentanyl, plain and simple. I tried to nudge you toward telling the group that Star was a drug user, but when Fran picked up another ball and started running with it, I went along. Everyone seemed so convinced of Star's mistake that there was no point in me continuing with an alternate theory."

"What about . . . the others?" Penelope asked.

Philip looked to the horizon and Penelope shifted her legs from a kneeling position to a crouch. He turned toward her again and she held her breath in terror that he would notice her readying to flee, but his voice didn't change.

"I biked down fast when I was up on the ridge with Liam looking for Danny. Liam had no idea that I'd come back into the camp so fast. I knocked on Hector's door after I saw him going into the bunkhouse with Fran and Estelle. I was betting he'd be up for another history lesson before the storm hit, and I was right."

Hearing that Hector's bravado had been his undoing almost broke her heart. Her legs trembled. She had to make a move somehow.

"Later that night, Neil was just as easy to lure away from the group when you and Fran were cleaning up dinner, though by that point, I thought I'd have my work cut out for me. I told him I'd heard a boat and that we had to get to the beach as fast as we could. We walked to the edge of the gazebo pad to look at the water. Then I pushed him off the cliff. It was raining so hard he didn't hear me getting close. When we found the body, Fran was so certain that Neil couldn't have fallen, but she was wrong. A body can really get some distance from the top of that cliff. Fran was the hardest. Everyone had become so suspicious at that point that I had to take the risk of injecting her on the porch at the same time everyone was fawning over her."

Poor, poor Fran, thought Penelope. *I could have saved you.*

"Then the rockslide," Penelope said.

"That was simpler. I set up the explosives on the first day, right after I got the navigation jammer working. I had to ride hard to avoid the others, but luck was on my side."

Penelope was disgusted by the proud tone in his voice.

"When we got up there, I just had to get you all to the right spot, then press the remote. It was fairly straightforward," he admitted.

Because we trusted you, she thought. His boasting made her want to scream. She dared to look down at the ground for a stone to throw in his face, but there was nothing in her reach.

"When the rocks came down, I hit you on the back of the head to be sure you'd die in the slide. But you're tougher than I thought, Penny." He smiled. "It's nice to have a chance to explain it all to you. I really do love you, though obviously I can't forgive what you did to my sister."

"I love you too," she lied.

Philip nodded vaguely. Penelope's throat tightened. His story was almost over, and she hated to think of the way it was going to end.

"Once you were unconscious, I set off the larger slide to buy some time, then I scrambled down the cliff to find a hiding spot. I laid there for hours, until I heard Liam and Estelle spot Danny down below. He was wearing my coat, so they were certain it was me."

He sighed.

"This was all supposed to be over yesterday, but I had to get the gun first. Thanks for that, by the way. I thought I might have to wrestle it away from my mother, but you and Liam made it a lot easier for me with the whole safe thing. I was watching you through the window and came in to grab the weapons as soon as you three left. The property managers sent me an override code as a safety precaution when they confirmed the reservation. I circumvented your combination as soon as you left the room."

He smiled at her again, and she found herself returning the easy expression.

"And the photos? Why bother with that?"

"Marianne loved a dramatic touch," he said. "I thought she would appreciate that. I printed a dozen of those shots after my mom uploaded it onto the computer. It felt important to set the mood for you all."

"But why take Danny's jacket?" she said, gesturing toward the red coat he now wore.

"I had to. I'm leaving here, after . . . I finish," he said. His voice shook slightly as they both processed what the rest of his job entailed. It made Penelope think she had a chance. She had to keep him talking.

"Why take Nina's body out of the shed?"

Philip exhaled hard. "That was an ugly part of the plan, but I had to make sure Estelle got close to the rebar. Hard work, but it paid off."

He rubbed his jaw. The familiar gesture had a disturbing air of finality. Penelope rocked onto the balls of her feet, ready to run as soon as he broke eye contact again.

"How will you get out of here?" she asked.

"There's a trail that heads up the ridge where I set off the slide. It's hard climbing and it will take me a while, but I'll get out long before the captain shows up this afternoon. I called him to change our pickup time before we left Vancouver. By the time the search party gets here, I'll be long gone."

They looked at each other in silence. She had run out of questions. He had explained it all. There was only one thing left to do. She had never wished harder for that stupid can of bear mace.

"Philip," she said. "It doesn't have to be this way. We can blame it all on someone else!"

He raised the gun, leveling it at her chest.

"I'll tell everyone it was Danny! Or better yet, Estelle!" she screamed.

His finger shifted on the trigger.

BANG.

The sound was a physical force. Her eardrums spasmed. Her jaw ached. Her head throbbed. The waves sucked and churned at the shore as the echo of the bullet wobbled through the air.

Was this how it felt to die?

She was stunned when Philip crumpled to the sand face-first.

"Philip?"

Her breath was ragged as she gripped his broad shoulders, heaving him over so she could stare into his face. His eyes were open but unseeing, just like in the photos he had distorted. Somehow, he had drawn his death with his own hand, tempting the forces of Stone Point.

She looked up the beach, and for an instant, saw a young girl with burning dark eyes staring into her own. Penelope blinked, and the girl was gone. In her place was Fran Brant.

"Turns out Danny did bring a gun," the woman said.

AFTER

The room went dark. Penelope stiffened. Blood pooled to her feet. She was terrified. An orange light appeared. The perfect circle of its beam trained on the figure standing before her.

"Everyone, we have come together today to hear the words of a fascinating woman who has captured the attention of so many," said the announcer.

Penelope smoothed down the front of her dress. Despite appearing at dozens of events like this over the past year, she had butterflies every time. Speaking truth might never come naturally for her. She had been trained to always highlight the positive, though she'd known in her heart that life was more complicated than that. She'd been taught to be perfect, so she had become fearful of failure, though she knew deep down that nothing good can be made without something going wrong along the way. She had lied about who she really was for so long that she had almost convinced herself she was someone else. As a result, she'd betrayed her closest friend, then fallen in love with a murderer. Stealing Marianne's words had seemed like the only way to be the hero in her own story. But it had made her the villain. One of them at least.

Three months after Stone Point, she had sent a draft of her second book to Vivian, who called her the next day.

"Hon? It's Vivian," the voice said.

My editor, Penelope reminded herself. Trauma had made it difficult to retrieve simple memories. She knew Fran, Estelle, and Liam felt the same. Once Fran had compared it to the fuzzy thinking she'd experienced while taking a low-level dose of opioids to manage the pain from her botched hip surgery. Then again, Fran had noted wryly, the tolerance she'd developed as a result of the drug had saved her life. Liam used repetition to help him remember. He had told Penelope the story of Estelle urging him to run and hide in the broom closet of the bunkhouse after she realized his sanity was fraying so many times that Penelope could recite it by heart along with him.

"Estelle was like a mother to me," he always said at the conclusion. "She saved my life."

Estelle, on the other hand, preferred not to relive the moment her shoulder and chest muscles had torn when her son tried to kill her. Penelope couldn't really blame her for that, though she was grateful that the horror they had been through had given her three close friends who understood why she cried sometimes for no reason at all.

"Hello, Vivian," Penelope said into the phone.

"How are you doing?"

"I'm fine."

Vivian waited a beat. "Are you working?"

"No."

Another pause. "Okay. You sure you're fine? You sound tired."

"I am tired. Some days are hard. It all comes back in a rush."

Vivian breathed audibly.

"Yeah, I wanted to talk to you about that. This manuscript you sent us? It's . . . different. We were expecting a novel similar to your first one. This is nonfiction, a memoir."

"That's right," Penelope said.

Silence. When Vivian spoke again, her tone was harsher.

"So you're admitting to plagiarism?"

"Yes."

"What happened to the stuff you were going to write about the Stone Witch? I've got some writing prompts for you. They've had investigators on the site since you left. Guess who they found trapped in an underground tunnel in William Stone's old still?"

Penelope's mouth dried as Vivian kept talking.

"Simone and Ethan Redding. They were buried under the ground the whole time."

"That's awful," Penelope said.

"Awful, sure, but it could make your next novel even stickier. It's like a book waiting to be written, right?"

"I'd rather go with the memoir."

Vivian's voice became cold.

"We can't use this. It implicates us too. It means we published a story you stole. It would be a scandal."

Penelope sighed. "It's the truth."

"According to you, Penny."

"That's all I have," she said. "And please don't call me that."

Vivian hung up.

Penelope had never heard from her again, so she self-published the memoir. For a short time she had been inundated on social media with people asking for an interview, a quote, or a photograph. She had ignored them all. Instead, she organized a small speaking tour. Her venues were always schools, youth groups, and places where children and teenagers would be. She wanted to speak to people who needed to hear what she had to say before it was too late. People like her, who didn't know how to be true to themselves. People like Liam who used substances to build walls around their pain. People like Ruth Stone, who were misunderstood in their life and their death. People like Marianne Solanger, who had hated so much, she'd only had a short window to love. People like Philip, who didn't understand how to love at all. People like Estelle, who had been silenced so long she didn't know how to speak.

She, Liam, Fran, and Estelle met for dinner once a month since returning from Stone Point. The injuries Estelle had received that day might have been fatal without Penelope and Fran's help. Liam had been shell-shocked when they'd found him in his hiding spot. It had taken hours to coax a single word from him. Their conversations were sometimes difficult, but Penelope never regretted having them. She knew it was hard for someone like Estelle to heal. She'd been broken for so long.

Sometimes, she thought about the hours the four of them had spent on the beach waiting for Captain Rod. It had been almost nine thirty when Philip had died, a fact that alternately disturbed and comforted Penelope, depending on her mood. The light from the fire she and Fran had lit to keep the unconscious Estelle and the traumatized Liam warm had revealed another secret of Stone Point.

On the first day they'd arrived, in their rush to get to the lodge, no one had noticed the second message carved by Ruth that Marianne had written about in her letter. Star had been right. It took all five elements for them to be able to understand the truth of Stone Point and the tragedy of Ruth Stone and Marianne Solanger. After she and Fran read it, they'd added fuel to the fire, making the smoke almost thick enough to obscure the shape of the boat when it finally approached, but there was no mistaking the whine of the motor as it pulled up to the dock. Before calling out to the captain, Penelope had read the words that had been etched into the stone one last time so she would always remember.

I thought I had found my own true home
I loved them so much now I'm left all alone
Joy and sorrow were bred in my bone
When I gained then lost the ones of my own
I found him in death then she failed to thrive
Now here I am the last one alive

A round of applause called her to the microphone of the high school theater, where a group of adolescents sat in the audience. She rubbed her lips together. They were painted with a new shade she had picked out the week before. She liked it. She smiled at Fran, who was sitting in the front row. The microphone puffed as she began. Her first lines were always the same.

"The only thing that will hurt you more than not believing the truth of someone else is hiding your own."

Penelope took a deep breath before she continued. Despite all odds, she had survived the Stone Point killings. All her life, she had believed she was not good enough, but it turned out she was exactly what she needed to be. Returning from Stone Point had taught her to accept herself for who she was. She wasn't a novelist or an optimist, but she was a survivor. Escaping a multiple homicide was a strange way to find self-worth, but now she knew that whatever she was, it was enough.

ACKNOWLEDGMENTS

Writing a novel during a global pandemic as a working mom was . . . interesting. The requirements of social distancing and the scarcity of my time made these months seem like one thousand years of solitude. My past three novels have had pages of people to thank for helping with the creation of a story, but these acknowledgments go to a deeply treasured skeleton crew. As the world heals and the wrongs of the past are reckoned with, I hope my next book will contain my usual overly effusive pages of gratitude. For now, however, I must honor everyone who played a part in this one.

Laurie Grassi, your reputation as an incredible editor preceded you, and every conversation, email, and note I received from you upheld every bit of praise I'd heard. You are so talented, kind, and insightful. This book would not be the same without your astonishing gifts. Thank you.

Karen Silva, your intuition, attention to detail, and delightful comments made me laugh and gasp every single time I reviewed a new draft. I am deeply impressed and honored by the level of care and love you took with this book, and I am so grateful.

Gordon Warnock, you are my consiglierie, backroom strategist, and, at times, therapist. I am in awe of you and in debt to you. I'm so glad I found you. Your emails have talked me off a cliff and made me believe in myself more times than I can count.

Ben, Thompson, Eve, and Clover. I love you each with all my heart. This one's for you, kids (when you are old enough to be okay with your mom writing these kind of books).

Morgan, Marc, Jasper, and Emmerich, you are incredible and wonderful and treasured by me.

Jeff and Joanne, thank you for giving me a place to plug in my computer and create. You saved us when all seemed lost.

Kim Slater, Nate Nash, and Miss Olivia; Kate Rose, John Bennett, Abigail, and George, I can't imagine life without my chosen ones.

Teena, Neva, Bria, and Graham, you are rad. Those afternoon movies really saved me.

Christina McDonald, Megan Collins, Samantha Bailey, Roz Nay, Marissa Stapley, Catherine McKenzie, Andrea Bartz, and May Cobb, thank you for reading an early draft and pulling me out of the sea of doubt with the lifeline of your words.

And to the enormous number of people I wish I could have seen over the course of writing this book: Ava Perraton, Deryl Cowie, Darlene Cowie, Joan Jacobsen, Chris Cowie, Donna Cowie, Auntie Carla, Helen and Myron Smith, Auntie Linda, Uncle Dale, Cousin Sherri, Natasha, Siryn, Phoenix and Griffin, Linda and Ulrich, Lee Carney, Karen Dodd, Mahtab Narsimhan, Sonia Garrett, and Caroline (Rae Knightley), Deborah Wade, Tatiana Lee, Tasha, Julie and James, Danielle, Chris, Anne-Marie and Teo, Kelly and Carlo, Christine, Shauna and Ian, Charlene and Steve, Mel (never give up!) and Jamie, Celia and Dave, Zoe, Grant and Alison, Daniel, Nancy and Georgia Stubbe, Andy and Rocio and Mel and Brent, Charlotte Morganti and Alison Dasho.

ABOUT THE AUTHOR

Photograph @ Ben Greenberg

AMBER COWIE is a novelist living in a small town on the west coast of British Columbia. Her work has appeared in the *New York Times*, *Salon*, the *Globe and Mail*, *Crime Reads*, and *Scary Mommy*. Her first novel, *Rapid Falls*, was a Whistler Book Awards nominee. She is a member of several writing groups and holds an undergraduate degree from the University of Victoria. She is a mother of two and reader of many books. She likes skiing, running, and writing stories that make her internet search history unnerving. Visit her at **ambercowie.com** or on Twitter and Instagram **@ambercowie.**